The
TRYST

Center Point
Large Print

Also by Grace Livingston Hill and available from Center Point Large Print:

Dawn of the Morning
Miranda

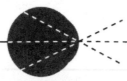

**This Large Print Book carries the
Seal of Approval of N.A.V.H.**

The TRYST

Grace Livingston Hill

CENTER POINT LARGE PRINT
THORNDIKE, MAINE

This Center Point Large Print edition
is published in the year 2014.

Originally published by
J. B. Lippincott Company in 1921.

All rights reserved.

The text of this Large Print edition is unabridged.
In other aspects, this book may vary
from the original edition.
Printed in the United States of America
on permanent paper.
Set in 16-point Times New Roman type.

ISBN: 978-1-62899-351-6

Library of Congress Cataloging-in-Publication Data

Hill, Grace Livingston, 1865–1947.
The tryst / Grace Livingston Hill. — Large print edition.
pages ; cm
Summary: "After overhearing a terrible conversation between her
mother and sister concerning her, Patricia Merrill flees to New York
City, assumes a fake identity and finds a job. When her childhood
sweetheart shows up, she is torn between maintaining her secret or
confiding in him"—Provided by publisher.
ISBN 978-1-62899-351-6 (library binding : alk. paper)
1. Large type books. I. Title.
PS3515.I486T79 2014
813'.52—dc23
                                                    2014028579

The
TRYST

1

Patricia Merrill, richly clad in gray duvetyne with moleskin trimmings, soft shod in gray suede boots, came slowly down the stairs from the third story, fastening her glove as she went. The top button was refractory and she paused in the middle of the stairs to give it her undivided attention. The light from the great ground-glass skylight overhead sifted down in a pool of brightness about her, and gave a vivid touch to the knot of coral velvet in her little moleskin toque. She was a pretty picture as she stood there with that drifting light about her like silver rain, and a wistful look in her eyes and about her lips.

A voice sailed out like a dart from the half-open door at the foot of the stairs and stabbed her heart: "Has Patricia gone?"

Why would her mother always call her "Patricia" in that formal, distant way, as if she were not intimate with her at all? And she always pronounced it so unlovingly, as if it were somehow her fault that she had such a long-stilted name. If they only would call her Patty as the girls used to do at school. How different it all was from what she had imagined it the last two or three years, this home-coming, with father far away in South America on business. He would have been at the station to meet her and called her his "little Pat!" A sudden mist grew in her eyes. Were mother and Evelyn always so much bound up in each other, and so distant? Their letters were that way, of course, but she had expected to find them different. It was all wrong keeping two sisters apart so long. If Evelyn hadn't been strong enough for school and college they should have kept them both at home, and let them grow up together as sisters should.

The pucker on Patty's forehead deepened as the button grew more troublesome while these thoughts went through her mind like a flash, and then Evelyn's voice rasped out:

"Yes, she's gone at last, and I wish she'd never come back!"

Patty stopped trying to button her glove and stood as if turned to ice, staring down the rich Persian carpeting of the stair to the half-open door of her mother's room, one hand fluttering convulsively to her throat, her eyes growing wide with horror and amazement.

"Hush!" said the mother's voice sharply. "Are you perfectly certain she's gone?"

"Yes, I am. I heard the door slam after her five minutes ago. She asked me to go with her. She fairly begged me. I suppose she thought she'd score a few more points against me! Oh, how I hate her! It isn't enough that she should turn the head of every man that comes to the house, but she had to set her cap for Hal Barron. She knew he belonged to me and that we were as good as engaged, yet she spends all her smiles on him every time he comes to the house, and this morning a great big box of American beauties comes with his card for 'Miss *Patty* Merrill,' if you please. Bah! I hate her little playful ways and her pussycat smile, and her calling herself 'Patty.' What right has *he* got to call her Patty, I'd like to know. She asked him to, of course! How else would he know? I think it is cruel to have her come home this winter just as things were going so nicely for me. I thought you promised to get father to send her away somewhere? I don't see why she has to live here with us anyway! Didn't you ask him at all?"

"Yes, I broached the matter, but he was very severe, as usual, said it wasn't possible, of course, talked a lot about her being young and needing the protection of being here, reminded me of the conditions on which we occupy this house—it really was most unfortunate that I mentioned it, for it put him in such a mood that I didn't dare say anything about your trousseau—and the time was so short, you know—only a few minutes really in all!"

Then Evelyn raged in:

"It's simply unendurable, and I can't see why you couldn't have done something about it before it was too late!"

"If I had known he was going to sail so soon—" The mother's voice was almost pleading.

"It doesn't make any difference. You should have done something long ago. It's simply not to be thought of that I shall sit quietly and be cut out by that little pink-cheeked, baby-eyed kid. You can at least see that she doesn't get all that money to dress with, anyway. It ought to be mine. It takes a lot to dress me right, and you know it. I simply *have* to have things that become me. I can't put on *any*thing the way she can and look perfectly stunning. I wonder where she got the knack, anyway. They don't teach that at college. The sly little cat, she just intends to show me that she can get any man she wants, but she shan't take away the only one I ever really loved, not if I have to *kill* her! Oh, you needn't look so shocked. It won't be necessary. I'll find a way to get rid of her!—Mother—Did she ever suspect that she wasn't—!"

"HUSH!" hissed the mother. "Shut that door, *QUICK!* Mercy! I didn't know it was open! If a servant should happen to hear! How many times have I warned you—!"

The slamming door shut off further words and left Patricia standing stricken in the pool of skylight on the stairs. Her delicate face white as carven marble seemed to have suddenly turned to stone. Her small gloved hands were pressed against her breast and her breath was suspended in the horror of the moment. The power of motion seemed to be gone, and her impulse was to sink down right there on the stairs and give way to the numbness that was creeping over her. Her strength had left her like water falling through sudden apertures. Her eyes were fixed in a blank stare of unbelief on the closed door just below her, and she seemed to have lost the power to think, to analyze, to take in what she had heard. It was as if unexpectedly a great rock had struck her in the face and stunned her.

Then below on the first floor a door opened and steps came up the first flight, steps and a broom trailing over the hard wood. The blood returned violently to its function and Patty's feet were given wings. She turned and sped up the few stairs and into her room as softly as a bird might have gone, locked the door and dropped limply to the edge of her bed, staring around her room with its familiar objects as if to assure herself that she was really alive and the world was going on as usual.

She tried to rehearse to herself the dialogue she had heard on the stairs and to make out what it could possibly mean. Always had she known there was a barrier between herself and her mother, and of late she had suspected it extended to her sister also, but never had she thought it anything serious like this. Once when she was a little girl she remembered asking her father why her mother was not more "mothery," and he had smiled—

smiled with a sigh she remembered now—and said that it was just her undemonstrative nature, that she must not think because the mother did not kiss and fondle her that she was not loved; and she had always treasured that and tried to be satisfied with the cold formalities that had passed between them. But now—*this*—and Evelyn, too! It was beyond grasping! The only thing that seemed clear to her bewildered, hurt soul was that she must get away. Evelyn hated her and thought her trying to get away her lover. The only way to prove to her sister that this was not true was to go away and show them that she did not want any such thing. And she must go at once, quickly, before anyone saw her. Afterwards she could think what to do. Perhaps she could write to them and explain. She would have to think it out. But now she must get away.

She arose cautiously and gave a wild glance around the room. Her pretty patent leather suitcase lay open on the window-seat half packed for a week-end house party to which she and Evelyn had been invited. They were to have gone that afternoon. Now with a pang she realized that all the pleasant anticipations were impossible. She could never go and meet the friendly faces and know all the time that her own life was broken, degraded, unloved.

She caught up a few things that lay scattered about the room, tiptoeing about with no lighter tread than a butterfly would have made, and giving about as little heed to her packing. Anything that came in her way went in, and without much ceremony of folding. When it was full she shut it and hurried to the door. Her handsome silk umbrella lolled across a chair and she snatched that and went softly down the hall toward the back stairs, cautiously working her way to the second, and then the first floor, pausing to listen when she heard a servant coming, lest anyone should see her. She let herself out of the servants' side entrance and walked swiftly down the side street, turned the corner for a block and then took another side street, putting herself as quickly as possible out of her own familiar neighborhood, and reflecting that it was fortunate that she had been home so short a time that she would not be recognized by many, nor her absence seem noticeably startling. She could just slip away and leave the home and the whole field to Evelyn and they could say she was away and nobody would think anything about it. There would be no shame or disgrace for her father to face when he returned. She felt like a little mouse that had suddenly been dropped from a great height, so hurt and stunned that all she could do was to scuttle away and hide under a dark wall. That was what she wanted now, a dark place to hide, where she might close her eyes and sob out the hurt and perhaps by and by think out the meaning of this terrible thing that had come to her.

Her own frank nature would have prompted her to go straight to her mother and sister and have a thorough explanation, perhaps be able to convince them that she had no such sinister designs as they were attributing to her, and that all she wanted was their love and a closer understanding. But there had been something so final, so irrevocable in the shock she had received that it seemed that there could be no mending, no possible explanation. There was nothing to do but get away as quietly and quickly as possible.

The crisp, clear air brought back a faint color into Patricia's cheeks, and took away a little of the bewilderment. She was able to summon a passing taxi and give directions to the station but during the short drive she sat as one stunned, and could not seem to think her way ahead of her.

At the station she paid her fare and allowed a porter to carry her suitcase.

"N'York train, Miss?" he asked quite casually in the manner of his knowing kind.

"Why—yes," said Patricia with a sudden decision, New York, of course. The idea was good. That was far enough away, and no one would ever think of looking for her there. She had never been to New York, but what did that matter? She could think all the better in a strange place.

"Got your tickets, Miss?" asked the porter as they neared the train gate.

"Oh! No!" gasped Patricia still looking bewildered. She was just wondering why Evelyn had thought she wanted Hal Barron for her own exclusive property, and the matter of tickets seemed so trivial.

"Better step to the window and get them, Miss. There ain't so much time. Right this way."

"Oh!" gasped Patricia, following him blindly through the crowd and bringing up at the window where three were already in line ahead of her.

"Got your 'commodations, Miss?" asked the porter eyeing her paternally, and deciding she needed protection.

"Why—no—not yet!" She drew her breath in a little quick flutter. There were so many things to be thought of, and she was going away into strange scenes with no one who cared—oh, her father! He had always protected her so carefully! What could he think? But her *father!* What—how could it all be reconciled anyway?

"Pretty late, Miss! 'Fraid you won't fare very well. Like me to see if there's anything left?"

"Oh, yes, please!" she answered gratefully, and moved up to the window as the last of the line moved on.

The porter put down the suitcase and went away for a moment. "Nothing left but the drawing room, Miss. Care to have that?" he asked anxiously returning a moment later.

"Oh, yes!" sighed Patricia gratefully, handing

him a bill from the roll in her bag. She had no idea how much she had, as much as was left of her allowance that had been paid her a few days before. She had not bought much since but chocolates, a magazine or two, and some flowers for a little sick girl. She had paid for her ticket and there seemed to be a lot left. She did not count it. It was not likely she would have been able to bring her mind to take in whether it was much or little. Money meant nothing to her just then save a miserable bone of contention between herself and her sister. Money, what did she care about it, if she could have only had love and a home! She would gladly have given up the pretty clothes. They had not meant much to her in themselves. She had always enjoyed picking them out, and wearing things that harmonized and were becoming, but that was such a minor matter compared to the great things of life!

The porter took her ticket, and managed the whole affair for her, and she followed him relievedly to the gate and out to the train.

It all seemed so strange, this journey, following a porter with her suitcase, out of a train gate to a pleasant compartment. She had always enjoyed journeys so much before, and this one was like hurling herself into space, knowing not where she was going nor what she was going to do when she got there. It must be that condemned men felt this way as they walked to their doom! And what had she done? Why had it all come upon her? Was she right in going away till she found out?

This last question beat upon her brain as she felt the train begin to move. A wild impulse to run back and think it out came upon her, and she half rose from her seat and looked about her frantically, then sank back into her seat again as she realized that it was too late. The train had started. Besides, she could always return after she had thought about it and found out what was the right thing to do. With a faint idea of looking her last upon familiar things she glanced out of the window and was comforted by the porter's respectful salute accompanied by a smile of most unporterful solicitude. He had just dropped from the front end of the car to the platform, and had been watching for his lady as the drawing room window passed. Patricia sank back on the cushion with a passing wonder at his care. She did not know that her sweet face had taken on a look like a lost Babe in the Wood, and that any man with a scrap of humanity left in his breast would be aroused by her wistful, hurt eyes to protect her. But it comforted her nevertheless and helped to relieve the tension. She put her head back and closed her eyes wearily. A soothing tear crept over the smart in her eyes that had been so intolerable. Somehow with it came a complete relaxation, so new to her vigorous alert youth that it was fairly prostrating. She longed inexpressibly to lie down and sleep, yet knew she must not until the conductor had been his rounds. But she put her head wearily against the window glass and watched the passing scene with unseeing eyes, as the city of her home traveled fast across her vision, and the train threaded its way gradually from crowded city streets to suburbs, and then out into the wide open country. And yet she could not think. Could not even bear to face the words she had heard such a little time before that had turned all her bright world into ashes, and clouded the face of the universe.

The conductor came his rounds, and then the Pullman conductor, and she was left at last in peace. Her head dropped back on the cushions and she sank into a deep sleep of exhaustion from the shock she had received. The miles whirled by, the sun rose high to noon, afternoon came gaily over the western plains, and still she slept.

2

The sun was casting long, low shadows over the valleys and plains when Patricia awoke, her cheek crumpled and pink where it had rested against the cushion. She sat up suddenly and looked about her startled, trying to realize where she was. For an instant she remembered the house party and thought she was on her way; but Evelyn was to have gone to that, and Evelyn was not in the compartment. Then all in a rush came the memory of Evelyn's sharp voice rasping on her quivering heart, and she remembered. She was on her way to New York and she must have been traveling a long time!

She glanced at her wrist-watch and saw it was half-past five. She had not eaten anything since morning, and in spite of her trouble a healthy young appetite began to assert itself. She resolved not to think about anything until she had been to the dining-car. At least she would be better able to bear the pain of it all, and think clearly after she had eaten. She arose and straightened her hat at the long mirror, opened her bag, got out a diminutive comb and fluffed her pretty hair, shook out her rumpled garments and wended her way to the diner.

But somehow thoughts would come, and after she had made her selection from the menu and sat back drearily she found that just across the aisle from her sat a mother and two daughters, and their whole atmosphere of happy comradeship brought back the sickening memory of her own unhappy state. She glanced out of the window to turn aside her gloomy thoughts and tried to interest herself in the wonderful landscape, but somehow the whole face of nature seemed desolate. Rock and tree and sweep of plain that would have enraptured her eyes a day or two before were nothing more than a map now, a space over which she had to travel, and a light little laugh from one of the girls across the aisle followed by the loving protest, "Oh, Mother, dear!" pierced her like a knife. The tears suddenly sprang into her eyes and she had to turn her head and pretend to be watching the view to hide her emotion.

And then the errant thoughts rushed in and almost overwhelmed her. Why did her mother and sister feel so unloving toward her? Why had she ever been born into a world where she was not wanted? No—that wouldn't do exactly, for her father was always loving and kind, always understanding of her, always anticipating her longings and trying to supply their need. Perhaps he had realized how the other two felt, and had purposely kept her at school so long that she might not feel it, knowing that she was sensitive, like himself. Was it possible that he had missed something in them himself? Perhaps she was like her father and Evelyn was like the mother. That was it, of course. She recalled how often her father had repeated the phrase: "You mustn't mind them; it's their way, little girl. They are all right at heart, you know."

For the first time the words seemed like a revelation. He, too, had felt the sting of the proud looks and haughty words, and yet he was loyal. How he must have loved her mother! And of course he understood her—or *had* he? Could anybody be lovable who had such an unnatural feeling toward her own child as had been shown this morning? *Stay*—was she perhaps *not an own child!*

Her eyes grew wide with horror and she stared at the waiter blankly as he brought her order and set it in array before her. The thought seemed to rear itself up before her eyes like a great wall over which she could never climb, and for a moment she seemed to be sinking down into a horrible place from which there was no possible exit. For, like a convincing climax, came the words she had heard from Evelyn just before the door closed: "Did she never suspect that she wasn't—!"

Wasn't what? What could it possibly mean but "wasn't an own child"?

All the pent-up loneliness of the years came down upon her like a flood to overwhelm her then, and she sat staring blankly before her, forgetting where she was or that there were people looking at her.

"Will you have your coffee now or latah, lady?" the hovering waiter broke in upon her unhappy reverie. He felt that something was wrong and could not quite make out why she sat and stared ahead with her dinner all nicely before her.

She roused herself then and summoned an answer, scarcely knowing or caring what it was, but the floodtide of her thoughts surged back into more natural channels. How ridiculous for her to think of such a thing! She was just a girl in a story, imagining a thing like that. Of course that was not true; for she could remember her father telling her about the night she was born and how he sat alone and thought about the little new soul that was coming to his home and for which he would be responsible; and how a surge of great love came over him at the thought. He had told her that one night when he bade her good-bye at the boarding school, and she had been more than usually dreading the parting. He had seemed to understand her so well and to anticipate her dreads and to know just what she needed to make her own soul strong. Oh, why did he have to be sent to South America just now when she was coming home? If only he could have been here for a day so that she might have had a few minutes' talk with him! If only he were somewhere in this country now that she might fly to him and ask him the meaning of all this that had come upon her!

She turned to her plate and her healthy appetite reasserted itself and made everything taste good. It was comforting to think over her father's little note, left on her dressing table under the linen cover just where he used to leave bits of surprises for her sometimes when she was at home for brief vacations, or in her little girl days before she had gone away at all. The note was precious. He had not forgotten her even in his hurry. She knew every word of it, every line of every letter was graven in her heart:

Dear little Pat: *it ran,*

This isn't the kind of homecoming I had planned for you at all. A cable has called me to South America to look after my business interests there, and I have only an hour to catch a train that will get me to the boat just in time. I'm overwhelmed with sorrow not to be at your commencement, little Pard, as I told you in my telegram. If I had twenty-four hours leeway I would wire you to go with me, but there isn't an hour to spare, I must make this boat or lose out. But never mind little Pat, you're my own brave little daughter, and we'll make it up when I get home, so be of good cheer, and don't mind the bumps on the road till I get home.

Your disappointed old Dad,
who loves you more than tongue can tell.

As she went over the letter in her mind her face brightened. Surely, surely, how had she forgotten! He called her "his own brave little daughter." What a silly she had been to imagine she was a stray child he had picked up on the street, or taken from some hospital.

And what would he think of her running off in this frantic way at the very first "bump on the

23

road"? Would he blame her and say she should have stayed behind and borne it? Oh! No! Surely not that! But would he have said she ought to have asked for an explanation before going away? Perhaps—but if she had they would have been obliged to keep her whether they wanted her or not, because it was their duty. This way they were relieved of her without any act of their own—and she was relieved of them! Yes, that was the truth, she just couldn't have faced them and kept an unmoved countenance after what she had heard. She would always be thinking how Evelyn had said she hated her, and the dreadful tone their mother had used in reply, quite as if she agreed with Evelyn, only it was not wise to say so. Patty gave a little shiver as she remembered the hard, cold tone. Somehow each time she thought of it the hurt was just as keen and new. She drew a deep breath and tried to get away from it all for a few minutes, forcing herself to watch the people around her.

Back in her compartment she faced the now darkened window and frowned into the night face to face with her problem again.

Oh, if she could have gone with her father! And yet even that might have made trouble, for it had often seemed to cause jealousy when she was alone with him for long, and sometimes when he had stopped at school to visit her he had apologized for bringing no message from them, saying that they did not know he was coming that way or they would have sent one, and she had often suspected that he had a reason for not telling them, so that there grew up between her father and herself a quiet understanding like a secret pact. Somehow in the light of what had happened things in the past seemed to take on a new significance. It was like the time when she went to call across the way on a neighbor never visited before, and looked over at her home in astonishment that it seemed so different from what she had thought, so now she seemed to be standing outside of her own life and finding out what it really had been.

The thoughts whirled on an endless chain in her mind, and she was no nearer to a decision about things. Her mind simply seemed to refuse to act farther, except to throw back upon her the word she had heard that morning. Lying at last upon her berth she fell into a troubled sleep in which she seemed to toss in an endless round of puzzle and bewilderment.

The second morning of her journey the train rolled into the Pennsylvania Station in New York and Patricia Merrill, no nearer a decision about what she ought to do, but neatly groomed and with shining eyes sat up and watched the approach eagerly. Somehow during the night the mists had rolled away from her mind and she was at peace again. Whatever had been the cause of the trouble, whatever was to be the outcome, she was here in the great city of her heart's desire, and was all a-quiver to see the glories which she had read and dreamed about for many years.

Plans, she had none. She grasped her shiny suit-case and fell into line with her fellow-travelers, for a little moment forgetful of the terrible thing which had driven her forth from her home.

An attentive porter speedily relieved her of her baggage, and it seemed quite natural that she should give him a generous tip, unmindful of her rapidly diminishing resources. The porter herded her with a chosen few around a sheltered way to an elevator, and so, still in the state of luxury to which she had been born, she rose to the station floor to face an unfriendly world single-handed and alone.

It was not until the porter enquired where she would go that it suddenly occured to her that she had made no plans whatever, and in a small panic she dismissed him and sat down in the waiting room. With a gasp of dismay she realized that in her unchaperoned condition she must be exceedingly careful. Her years of school and college had been unusually sheltered ones, and certain laws of social life and etiquette had been drilled into her very nature. Not in an instant could she face the new and strange complexity of her situation and solve her problem.

There were acquaintances and friends in New York, of course, whom she might look up and be at once sheltered and welcomed. But that was out of the question under the circumstances. She must do nothing to bring disgrace or scandal on her father's honored name. No one must know she was there!

She knew the names of hotels of wide repute, of course, but shrank from going alone to one. Besides, in such a place she was likely to be recognized by some one sooner or later, for she had many school friends who lived in the East, and had met many people traveling in the West.

She was glad that she had written her father just the night before leaving home, and would not have to write him again for a few days. Somehow perhaps she could plan an explanation which would make the Eastern postmark seem perfectly consistent with the kind of life he expected her to live during his absence. Perhaps he would think she was visiting a school friend, or gone East for a course of study—or—But that did not matter now. She must know what she was going to do immediately, *to-day!*

Her eyes wandered to a company of gypsies in soiled and gaudy garments and many jewels who had swarmed into the seat across from her and she watched their absorbed chatter. There was a poise about the swarthy old grandmother in her tiers of flowing scarlet and purple calico skirts that would have set well upon some platinum-set bejeweled woman of society. With entire unconsciousness of the staring throngs she ordered her flock of sons and daughters and grandchildren, and Patty, fascinated, watched; saw the goodwill, and kindliness between the whole little company, and felt a sudden choking aloneness in her throat.

All at once the gypsies picked up their babies and their belongings and walked majestically away, as unobservant of any but themselves as if they had been passing by an ant hill, and suddenly Patricia, roused to the fact that she was hungry, that it was twelve o'clock, and she had not thought what she ought to do.

She arose with determination and went to check her suitcase. Then she started out into the great unknown city to find a place to eat. While she was eating she could think perhaps.

She wandered across Seventh Avenue, across the tangled tracks where Broadway intersects Sixth Avenue, stopped timidly to glance up at the elevated, then walked on uncertainly up Thirty-third Street and turned into Fifth Avenue. Ah! She had read and heard of Fifth Avenue, and here she was at last!

Presently she came to an inviting tea-room and dropped into it as naturally and happily as a flower blossoms on its native heath. Without thought she ordered what she would as was her wont, and ate with relish, watching the people about her, and thinking still about the gypsies, contrasting them with this and that one she saw about her, wondering what their lives might be, and if any had a trouble like her own. In the midst of her thoughts they brought her the check marked with the costly sum of her dinner, and when she went to pay it and put beside it the usual tip for the waitress, she had nothing left in her pocketbook but one gleaming silver quarter, and fifteen cents of that she would have to use to redeem her suitcase!

3

For two midnight black minutes the gay little throng at Mary Elizabeth's popular tea-room vanished into a medley of color and sound without meaning to Patricia Merrill's startled ears and eyes, while the chrysanthemums in the many paned windows swam like motes in the color of the room. Her head began to reel, and a queer faintness and fright possessed her, as one who finds herself suddenly upon the brink of a bottomless abyss, with more momentum on than can be instantly controlled. It was as if she swayed there uncertainly for long fractions of time anticipating a fatal plunge, which was inevitable, no matter how hard she tried to save herself. Then, gropingly, her fingers found the glass of ice water just replenished by an observing attendant who was a judge of duvetyne and moleskin and had an eye for high finance.

The cold touch of the glass to her lips, the frosty trickle of the water down her newly parched throat, brought her back to her senses once to ask herself what had brought her to this startled brink of fear. Then over her wearied senses rolled the answer almost stalely. Why! It was only that she was alone in a great and strange city without funds! Ten cents between her and starvation! A paltry dime between her and the street! It seemed somehow trifling beside the great sorrow that had brought her on this sudden pilgrimage. After all, what was money? Just a thing with which you bartered for more things! One could get along without *things*. At least without many of them! Hadn't she always managed without pocket money when her allowance ran out before the month was up, and without borrowing, too! Her father had hated borrowing and had succeeded in making her hate it also. Of course she had her board at the school, but surely there must be a way for an able-bodied girl to earn her bread in a great city. Of course there would be! She had once helped another girl with her lessons at school and earned enough to get through till allowance time without asking her father for any in advance. There would surely be some way. Of course there were friends to whom she might apply, but they were out of the question because her hiding might be revealed, and father wouldn't like it to have anyone know she had come away so peculiarly.

No, she must meet the emergency herself, and she would!

She set her firm young lips and straightened up self-reliantly the warm blood rushing back into its normal course once more as her fears vanished into the sunshine of the day, and the chrysanthemums and pretty ladies resolved themselves sanely into their proper relations. She was able to look about her calmly, and face the situation. She had been a fool, of course, to be so absentminded as to let her money all get away from her so swiftly. She just hadn't been thinking of money. Of course if she had counted it at the start and set out to save, she might have eaten toast and tea on the train, and have even traveled in the common car. That was probably what people did who earned their own living. She would have had enough to carry her through the first day or two comfortably if she had done that. But there was no use crying over spilled milk. The money was gone and she must get out and find a way to earn her living. She had not an idea in the world what she could do, for she had not been educated with such an end in view. She had fluttered about in her studies from science to literature, and arts, about as a butterfly in a garden goes from flower to flower, looking at them all as curious amusements, not at all connected with her daily living. She had never really taken an hour of her schooling seriously, although she had been a bright student as students go. But as for any practical knowledge that she could turn to now as a help in her need, it was as alien to her as a strange tongue. She tried to think what she could do—what other girls did who had to earn their living. Anne Battell had been a statistician, and was now in a fine position, getting a fabulous salary. But Anne had been training all her school life with this object in view. Norah Vance was doing interior decorating with a big department store in Chicago. Elinore had gone to China to teach music in a college. Theodora and Emilie Whiting were in some social work, and that plain little Mary Semple, who worked in the college office for her board, was a stenographer somewhere. But they all had got ready for some life work, while she, Patty Merrill, had only been getting ready to go home and have a good time. It seemed she had for years just been existing till she could get home and enjoy being with her people, and now that she had got there, there wasn't any home nor any love nor any people for her. Even her father was away off in almost another world, and there was no telling whether they, any of them, even really belonged to her at all more than in name. It was all dreadful and suffocating and she must not think about it. There were tears swelling up her throat and bursting into her eyes, and that good-looking young man at the second table to the right was looking curiously at her. In a moment he would see those tears—he half-suspected them now—he had no right to look at her so curiously! She must brace up and stop the tears! It was all nonsense anyway! There was work somewhere for her and she would just go out and find it! She would scare up something just as she used to scare up a costume out of nothing in a sudden emergency for a play sometimes only three minutes before the curtain rose. She would go out and try the first thing she came to. Maybe she would go up some front steps and ring a door-bell and ask for something! Why not! Anyhow she must get out of here into the cool air and conquer those foolish tears!

With a little motion of proud self-reliance she gathered up her gloves smilingly, paid her check with a curious glance of awe at the lonely silver piece sliding about in the otherwise empty purse and calmly made her way out of the crowded room, head held high, followed by the admiring glance of the aforesaid young man. There was not a sign about her from the tip of her coral and fur toque to the tip of her suede-shod feet that she was going out to seek her fortune, else I'm sure from his eyes he might have followed her. Coolly she turned up the avenue when she reached the door, and made her way as if she had had it all planned out beforehand, and walked on up among the gay shoppers.

The way seemed interesting and beautiful, and

she was not unduly impressed by her situation, now that she was out in the sunshine again with the clear, bright autumn air tingling her cheeks. There would be a way, and this was an adventure. Since home was not what she had hoped and she needs must have come away alone, why not make a game of it? There would be a way out somehow. There always had been, although, truth to tell there had never been anything really terrible to face before. Somehow that very fact made it hard to believe that this was a truly serious occasion. She felt as though perhaps it might be just a long dream after all and she might wake up soon and find Evelyn calling her to get ready for that house party. Things were queer anyway. Here she was away off here, and but for her own act of going away—but for her having come downstairs at that very minute when Evelyn thought she was gone and began to speak—she would have been at that house party at this very minute, smiling and talking and having a good time with a lot of nice people and never thinking of such a thing as that some people in the world had to earn their living. It was queer, too, that she had to be bothered just now with finding some work to do when she needed all her time and faculties to think about what had happened to her. Queer that she couldn't have time to feel bad when a terrible thing had happened just because she had to find things to put in her mouth, and a place to sleep nights. The whole world was a queer place. It had often struck her so before, at odd times, when things hadn't gone just right and when that ache for home had come in and spoiled things; but now it seemed that *everything* was queer, and hard, and always had been.

On up the avenue the shops grew less fascinating, and churches lifted frequent spires with fretwork of marble, and gothic arch. And now great piles of marble, ornate and stately, cluttered up a whole block here and there, intruding on the busy life, like selfish canines who have squatted in the way of traffic, and are too indifferent to care that they are impeding progress. Indifferently she recognized that these were mansions where her kind condescended to spend a few days or weeks now and then when business or pleasure caused them to alight briefly from their flitting pursuit of pleasure. What if she should walk up to one of them and demand employment? Well, why not? The next one she came to perhaps—but the next one was still with closed shutters and an air of not having waked up for winter yet, and her feet strayed farther. Another stone mansion loomed ahead, with carved gateways in a high and ornate stone fencing about a velvet patch of grass and flaunting autumn flowers. The big plate-glass doors in their heavy iron grills had just been closed with that subdued thud of perfect mechanism, and a luxurious electric car was rolling out the gateway as Patty came to its crossing. She glanced up and saw a lady sitting within, rich furs about her shoulders, and a painted haggard look upon her face that reminded her of her mother; the look of a woman who was frantically trying to have a good time and being bored to death by it. Patty knew it well and it did not interest her. She would not have looked again, and would have passed on, but just then the glass doors shivered themselves open with a little gasp of haste and a liveried person hurried out and made some sign that attracted the attention of the chauffeur, who stopped the car on the sidewalk directly before her, so that she had to pause and wait until it was out of the way.

The liveried person came breathlessly to the car and spoke to the lady who looked annoyed:

"Mrs. Horliss-Cole, Miss Marjorie says some one has just telephoned from a hospital that Miss Morris has met with an accident on the way here, and has broken her leg. She says you'll have to get some one else to take her place."

The lady in the limousine rumpled her thin forehead peevishly and uttered an exclamation of dismay:

"How tiresome! Well, Rogers, why didn't you tell Banely to telephone and arrange for some one else?"

"Beg pardon, ma'am, but Banely went out for the afternoon an hour ago. She said you told her you would not need her."

"Oh, yes, of course! Well, I suppose I must come back and 'phone, Miss Sylvia is so particular—! Well, Parke, you'll have to back in again. Rogers, you might call up the agency on the library 'phone. I'll come right in."

The car rolled noiselessly back again to the great doors and the lady got out and went into the house. Patty walked on, but her mind was full of what she had just heard. Suddenly she stopped short in the way, almost upsetting a little man who was racing breathlessly down town and hadn't counted on her being there when he got there.

Patty's cheeks were rosy with embarrassment, and she felt as if he could see the guilty thought that had stopped her written all over her face as he lifted his hat with a hasty apology and hurried on. She made a beeline for the tall granite fence that separated a strip of velvet green in front of another stately mansion from the sidewalk, and leaning against it tried to steady herself. Should she do it? Ought she? Why not? Perhaps it was the very opportunity for which she was looking! It seemed that way. Was there a chance in the world she would get it, she a stranger without recommendations? And what should she call herself? It would not do to use the family name, both for the sake of her father and also because it might lead to her family finding out where she was. Assumed names were not nice things, however, and it troubled her even to entertain the thought of one. But she turned swiftly now that the impulse had become a resolve, and walked back the block and a half she had come since passing the lady. The last half block she almost ran, for the terrible thought came to her that perhaps the lady was already through with her phoning and she might miss the only opportunity New York had for her.

But a glance through the handsome iron grill work showed the car still standing under the ample porte cochere, and she turned in with a wildly beating heart and cheeks that resembled lovely roses. She was so afraid that her courage would fail her now before she got in; and she *must* see that woman and try to get the position. Oh, she hoped it was something she could do! Yet how did she know it was a position? Perhaps it was a dressmaker, or an entertainer, or even a dinner guest. Well, what of it? She had heard of hired dinner guests. At least it could do no harm to try. And the lady had mentioned an agency. Perhaps it was a cook she wanted. No! Nobody would call their cook "Miss Morris." Nor even a waitress! And how wonderful that she should have overheard the woman's name! It was so much easier to ask for a person at the door by her name. Without it she would probably have been unable to gain audience.

With hasty feet she mounted the broad stone steps and stood within the shadow of the arching pillars with her hand on the bell. She could catch the reflection of the bright coral knot of velvet in her hat and suddenly she felt so strange and queer and out of place, she who had been accustomed to enter such homes as an honored guest; begging entrance to ask for a chance to earn her living! Almost it seemed as if she must go back in a panic to the street and be lost in the throng again. Only—what should she do to-night if she failed to get anything anywhere? Panic stayed her feet while panic also drove her away, and between the two emotions she wavered, setting her firm little lips and trying to keep from trembling as she saw the liveried person coming down some inner white marble steps with stately tread. Oh, crazy, crazy thought! Why had she followed it? What excuse could she find now to get gracefully away, she the daughter of an honored family, sneaking her way into the front door of a Fifth Avenue mansion to get a job to earn her living! Appalling thought! And she had actually planned it and come back to carry it off! How could she possibly face this gravefaced servant?

Then the plate-glass door opened with a stately sweep and the cold-eyed servant stood surveying her critically from the knot of coral on her hat to the tip of her gray suede boot. He evidently recognized that her attire was altogether correct, and with a second glance at her exquisitely fitting suede gloves, he opened the door an inch further and looked at her enquiringly. Then she opened her cold little lips and heard her own voice from very far away, saying over the charmed words like a lesson she had learned:

"I want to see Mrs. Horliss-Cole for just a moment on very important business."

The man noticed the shade of anxiety in her tone and glanced at her shoes and her gloves once more to reassure himself before he replied hesitatingly:

"Mrs. Horliss-Cole is very busy this morning. She was just going out and was called to the telephone—!"

"Yes, I know," broke in Patty breathlessly, "but I won't keep her a minute. I think perhaps she'll want to see me—!"

The man hesitated, and looked her over once more for a fraction of a second, appraising her garments doubtfully:

"Not from the agency, are you? Beg pardon, ma'am, but Miss Morris didn't send you, did she?"

Patty nodded engagingly.

"It's about that," she admitted eagerly.

"One moment, Miss," he said, his dubious deference changing almost imperceptibly, "I'll speak to Mrs. Horliss-Cole."

He departed and Patty found that suddenly she had all that she could do to control a violent trembling which had seized her whole body, and was absurdly manifest in her upper lip. Now, *what* should she say if she got a chance to speak to this grand lady?

4

Somehow Patty's heart seemed all at once to have gone up in her throat, and a frightened mist was getting before her vision. Why had she come to this awful house anyway, and what should she do when that woman appeared—if she really did appear, which seemed doubtful? If she could only get out without passing that servant again! She cast a wild look toward the door, and measured the distance. Then she saw a maid cross the hall and look toward her appraisingly, and disappear again. Presently the man-servant appeared and walked toward her more deferentially:

"Sit down, Miss. Madam will see you in a moment." He drew a chair and Patty sank into it. Then she really had gained an audience! The sparkle came into her eyes once more. At least it was an interesting adventure. She must stop that trembling!

She gripped her hands together and tried to smile. Her singing teacher had once told her that that helped to control stage fright. Well, this surely was a good time to put it to a test. So she stared determinedly at an ugly jade idol on a pedestal and smiled her sweetest smile, albeit there was a bit of a tremble to it at the corners. Then she set her brains to work, just as she used to do in class when she knew a hard question was coming to her to answer; so that when the maid finally came back and summoned her into the august presence of the lady she was quite her reliant little self again and ready with what she had to say.

The lady must have been impressed with her presence, for she put by the phone to which she had been giving an annoyed attention when Patty entered, and looked at her surprisedly, a puzzled enquiry growing in her eyes. However, Patty gave her no time to voice her question. She came straight to the point:

"I have come to ask if there is any position in your household that I could fill? I belong to a good family who live at a distance from New York; I've had a good education, and circumstances have suddenly thrown me on my own resources. I am willing to do almost anything, and if I don't know how I can learn."

She lifted her sunny eyes to the cold world-weary ones before her, and smiled a confiding bit of a smile that frankly put the whole matter in the lady's hands.

"Did you come from the Agency?" asked Mrs. Horliss-Cole. "I don't quite understand." Then to the telephone: "Yes, yes, Central, I'm waiting, of course."

"No, I didn't come from the Agency," answered Patty coolly. "I was passing as they called you in and heard the servant say that there had been an accident and some one had failed you. I don't understand what kind of a person it is that you need, and maybe I won't do, but I need to get something dreadfully right away, and I thought I'd try."

Mrs. Cole put up her lorgnette and eyed Patricia over thoroughly:

"How ex-troid'nry!" she said icily. "And haven't you any references?"

"References!" Patty's face grew suddenly blank with disappointment. "Of course! I forgot you would need them. No, I suppose I haven't any. You see, I've never supported myself before, and I didn't realize I would need them."

She grew thoughtful.

"Of course there are people here in New York I could get to say I was all right, but I don't think it would be wise. It might hurt my family very much if it was known that I was doing this. I guess then I will have to try and find something else—" She sighed and turned toward the door just as a voice from the telephone receiver broke in: "No, Mrs. Horliss-Cole, I'm afraid I can't send you anybody before tomorrow. I've been talking with that woman and she says she couldn't arrange to leave New York on account of an invalid child that she has to get into a home first. I'm sorry—!"

Patty had turned and was walking slowly into the hall when Mrs. Horliss-Cole snapped out:

"Tell her to wait!" and went on talking on the telephone.

The maid rushed out and brought her back as Mrs. Cole hung up the receiver. As Patty returned she noticed for the first time another girl, about her own age, dressed in a dark, handsome, tailored suit and hat, with a big skin of brown fox thrown carelessly across her shoulders. She was sitting in the window-seat with the air of waiting to speak to her mother before going out, and her dark eyes fixed themselves on Patricia's face with a stare that was half-insolent in its open curiosity.

"How soon could you come if I decided to take you?" asked the lady in a fretful tone as if somehow it was Patty's fault that she could get nobody else.

"Why, right away," answered Patty, interest returning to her eyes.

"Have you any objection to traveling and being away from New York for several weeks perhaps?"

"Not at all."

"Mother," put in the girl in the window impatiently, "why don't you 'phone to Zambri's? You know they *always* have somebody."

"Be still, Marjorie," said her mother. "Zambri was very impudent the last time I 'phoned him when I got that woman to help Hester, and besides I haven't any time this morning. What did you say your name was?" She turned back to Patricia.

Patricia hesitated.

"Would you mind very much if I didn't use my own name?" she asked with a troubled look. "I'm not ashamed of working, you know, but I would rather not have my family find out about it for a while. Could you call me by the name of Fisher, Edith Fisher? It was—my grandmother's name."

"It makes no difference to me what name you choose to go by, I suppose," said the lady coldly. "You seem to have good manners, and if you have a good temper and a little common sense that's about all that's necessary. I suppose I might as well try you. References don't amount to much nowadays anyway. People give references to servants just to get rid of them sometimes, although of course the Agency people usually find out about them, but if I decide to try you, how long will you likely stick to your job? Provided you prove satisfactory, of course?"

Patty wrinkled up the dimples of her nose and mouth quaintly, "Why, I don't know what you want me to do, but if it is anything that I can reasonably do I should think I might promise to stay all winter. That would be my intention. I'm not a quitter!" There was just a suggestion of rippling laughter in Patty's tone.

In spite of herself, the lady softened. Somehow one couldn't talk to this pretty, well-dressed child as if she were an ordinary servant.

"Well, your duties won't be arduous," she said looking at Patty doubtfully. "My husband's sister,

Miss Sylvia Cole, goes South to-night for a short stay and needs a companion. She's not an invalid exactly, but she's elderly and she's a little peculiar. She won't have a maid, she's old-fashioned, you know. She likes to do things for herself; but she has to have some one with her who can do them for her when she is not feeling able, and she gets lonesome, too; doesn't like to go around alone. But it takes a lot of patience to wait on her. Do you think you could keep your temper? She won't stand anyone who is impudent."

"Oh, I'm sure I wouldn't be impudent!" said Patty, suddenly realizing that it was not going to be all fun to go to work, and quaking in the depths of her heart at the thought of the elderly ogress whom she was to serve. Ought she perhaps to say no, and run away quickly while the going was good, before she bound herself for a winter to this peculiar old person? But where could she go? No, she must take this job if she got it, for she had a sudden terror at the thought of night coming on and finding her alone and penniless in the great city.

"I believe I shall try you," said Mrs. Horliss-Cole thoughtfully.

"I should say you better consult your sister-in-law, Mother, dear," interrupted Marjorie pertly from her window-sill. "You know Aunt Sylvia. If she doesn't like her, nothing doing!"

"Don't interrupt, Marjorie. Your aunt has

already given her consent to having Miss Morris and she doesn't need to know the difference. I really can't be bothered to go over the whole long argument again. She wanted Hester, you know, and I simply cannot spare her with all the fall sewing to be done. That's all right, Miss Fisher, I think I'll engage you. Is your trunk packed? You'll need to be here ready to begin your service by four o'clock, I should say. Can you get your trunk ready by that time?"

"I have only a suitcase with me," said Patty, suddenly feeling very small and alone, "and that's checked at the station. It won't take me long to get it."

"Oh, very well. You can have your trunk sent after. And if you like, you can ride down to the station now and we can arrange about salary and hours and so on, by the way. Then the chauffeur can bring you back while I'm at a committee meeting. Unless you have shopping to do. If so, he can wait for you."

"Thank you, no," said Patty. "I'd rather take a little walk if you don't mind, unless there is something you want me to do. I've never been in New York before."

Mrs. Horliss-Cole turned and stared at her curiously:

"How strange!" she said, as if she were an article in a museum. "You really don't look it. You have quite a sophisticated manner. But I don't think I shall trust you for a walk. It would be too easy to get lost in New York and the time is too short to risk it. The chauffeur can take you about awhile in the car and tell you the points of interest. Miss Cole will be getting uneasy if you are not back here by half-past four. Come, we'll consider that settled."

Patricia, as she followed her employer through the luxurious period-rooms out to the car, felt suddenly depressed. She was glad, of course, that the matter was settled and that she had found something so altogether respectable as being companion to an old lady, and that she had found it so soon. But somehow there was that in the curt tone of Mrs. Horliss-Cole which put her into another class entirely. Nothing unkind. Oh, no! But a certain careless condescension in her manner as she swept along her wide halls, giving a last direction to the maid, calling the man-servant to order for allowing a chair to stand at a certain forbidden angle. It seemed that when she moved everything else had to move also, and now they were all following her, the man, the maid, and even her daughter, hurrying with long annoyed strides:

"I should like to know, Mamma, where I come in? I've been waiting all the time while you did that tiresome telephoning, and I told you I *had* to see you—!"

They drifted into the car and Patricia perceived that she was expected to get in also.

It seemed strange to ride out through those stern grilled gateways where a few moments before she had stood, a young, frightened stranger, watching this same car and this same unknown lady. And now she was in her employ and practically pledged to remain for the winter. She felt somehow like a caged thing. Why had she not waited to see the great new city first, the city which she had always longed to see and be a part of? It would have been so delightful to go about as she pleased and search out all the places of which she had read and heard. But of course she must not think of that now. She ought just to be glad she had the position.

Marjorie and her mother were talking earnestly. They paid no more attention to her presence then if she had been the tassel on the silk curtain of the car. It was something about a young man of whom Mrs. Horliss-Cole did not approve. She told her daughter that the thing must stop right where it was; there must be no more correspondence, nor even a farewell meeting. Marjorie must arrange the matter herself, and not make it necessary for her parents to get into it, or there would be no coming out for her that winter. She would simply be sent away to school for another year, where she could be watched most carefully. The young man appeared to be something connected with professional athletics, a prize-fighter even perhaps, and Marjorie had met him during her past year at school. He had come as coach for her basketball team. The mother had bitter blame for the teachers who allowed her daughter an opportunity for intimacy with one so low down in the social scale, and nothing but contempt for the girl who had so lowered herself as to want to make a friend of one whom her family despised. Patricia, watching Mrs. Horliss-Cole's lips, was reminded of her own mother's mouth when she was disapproving of her, so cold and haughty. Sitting there in a stranger's car, driving swiftly toward a life of service for a whimsical old lady whom she had never seen, Patty wondered if all mothers had mouths like that. If she ever married and had a daughter, would her mouth look like that when she talked to her? Could she possibly imagine herself getting so far away from a dear daughter of her own as to talk in that cold, hard tone to her?

She eyed the other girl furtively, the girl with the big, bold, handsome eyes and the sullen mouth, and felt sorry for her. After all, perhaps all girls were misunderstood by their mothers, and perhaps the mothers were misunderstood, too. She could see that it might not be very pleasant for Mrs. Horliss-Cole to have her daughter corresponding with an embryo prize-fighter; but then, perhaps the mother had never made a friend of her daughter and therefore the girl was thrown on her own resources. She almost thought she would like to be friends with this queer, haughty girl. She reminded her much of a former roommate at college. But of course this Marjorie wouldn't consider making a friend of her aunt's companion. She almost giggled a little to herself then as she thought of it. Companion! Companion with a capital C! How odd it was. And if she hadn't happened to have her little world upset back there a couple of days ago she would at this minute probably have been playing tennis or eating lunch on the terrace, or driving in somebody's wonderful racing car, or doing some one of a number of other delightful things at that house party. Evelyn would have been there, and they would have been going about together, apparently loving sisters, and she would have been accepting Hal Barron's attentions in a perfectly good sisterly innocence and never have suspected the hate in Evelyn's heart.

Patty awoke with a start to the fact that Marjorie and her mother had ceased their conversation and the girl was staring at her with open intent. Suddenly, without meaning to in the least, Patty smiled at her, a ravishing smile of perfect equality and good fellowship, and after a second's surprise and haughty hesitation Miss Marjorie Horliss-Cole allowed a flicker of an answering smile to light up her own big melancholy eyes so that they were really beautiful.

But Mrs. Horliss-Cole was speaking now, as if she had just remembered the existence of her new dependent. She was not altogether sure, but this pretty young upstart needed a little setting down and showing of her place. And so in a very cool tone she began to talk about wages and duties, and to lay down the law pretty thoroughly about what Miss Sylvia liked and disliked until Patty was wholly indignant and a trifle frightened and wished she might get out and run away—only there was the great city, and night coming on with no money—and the impossibility of going back to her home.

Nevertheless there was something sweet and innately dignified about Patty, childish as she looked and sometimes seemed, that made it impossible to quite snub her. She had a way of opening her eyes wide and looking straightly and innocently through one that somehow froze the would-be freezer, and left herself untouched like a flower that did not understand it was being looked down upon.

At the station Patty was not allowed to go for her suitcase herself, but had to surrender her check and sit under a long lecture to Marjorie from her mother, while the chauffeur went after it. Somehow it made her feel like a prisoner, and she was glad indeed when Mrs. Horliss-Cole and her daughter were left in front of a large club building, and at last she was whirled away through a maze of city streets and out upon Riverside Drive.

The chauffeur pointed out Grant's Tomb and a

number of other points of interest, at first condescendingly, but finally with a touch of respect in his voice as he saw that Patty held herself aloof, and presently she was taken back to the great house on Fifth Avenue and taken in charge by the maid she had seen before who took her to a pleasant bedroom and told her to make herself comfortable and rest awhile until Miss Cole was ready to see her.

Patty took off her coat and hat, readjusted the soft embroidered crepe overblouse, washed her face and hands, and rearranged her hair. Then she sat down with a fresh magazine to await her summons, but the maid presently returned to say that Miss Cole did not care to see her until it was necessary. Patty waited until the door was shut and the maid's footsteps could no longer be heard down the polished hall, then she said out loud, quite viciously, "She's just an old crab, I know, and I wish I was back"—she caught her breath and her lip trembled—"back in college!" she finished bravely, and then throwing herself down on the pleasant-looking bed she buried her face in the pillow and had a good cry, after which she fell asleep and dreamed she had caught the last ship for South America and was sailing to meet her father.

She awoke with a start to find the maid bending over her with a tray in her hand:

"Madam says you're to have your dinner up

here, and you will be ready to start in half an hour."

She set the tray down on a little table, drew up a chair, adjusted a shaded electric lamp, and left the room.

Patty sat up and watched dazedly, and then as the door closed after her felt that she must rush out and bring her back and beg her to help her out of this awful situation. But she didn't. She was a good sport, was Patricia. She remembered just in time how her father used to call her his "little Pat" with that tender proud accent that meant he knew she would always have courage to "carry on," and instead she got up, washed her face again just to get the sleep out of her eyes, smoothed her hair, adjusted her pretty toque, and sat down to the inviting tray. Being very hungry she ate with appreciation and realized that she felt better. After all it was as good as a play what she was doing. And she could always get out of it of course if it became unbearable. She wouldn't be any worse off than she was before she saw Mrs. Horliss-Cole. Why not make a good joke of it, and see what would happen? Perhaps the old lady wouldn't be such an ogress after all.

She was entirely ready when the summons came and followed the maid down through the long halls, this time to another door where the car stood waiting with the old lady already inside. There was a gentleman standing by the door talking to

Mrs. Horliss-Cole, and from the few words she overheard she decided it must be Mr. Horliss-Cole, and it became evident that he was going with them to the station. Miss Cole's face was in the shadow and she did not speak to Patty, save to make an inarticulate motion of acknowledgment when her sister-in-law told her that here was the new Companion.

The girl was put into the front seat with the chauffeur, Mr. Horliss-Cole got in with his sister, and they whirled through the brilliant lights of the city. Patty caught her breath with delight as they turned into Broadway, her first sight of the fairyland of lights, and the chauffeur half-turned and asked her if she spoke. So Patty sat very straight and tried not to look as if she saw anything, until they rolled smoothly into the station.

There was a little stir as a porter rushed up with a wheeled chair, and Mr. Horliss-Cole gave Patty some bags to hold while he helped his sister out. In a moment more they were down the elevator and in the drawing-room compartment of the Pullman; Mr. Horliss-Cole had kissed his sister and departed.

Then, and not till then, did Patty get a full view of the face of Miss Sylvia Cole, and Miss Sylvia looked full into Patty's face and took stock of her.

"Well," said Miss Sylvia curtly at last, "you're quite a child, aren't you? I thought they told me you had gray hair. I knew they were lying, somehow, they always do. Pretty, too! I'll be bound! Some combination for a companion. A pretty child!"

Patty laughed a silvery little bit of a laugh that rang out like a bell.

"I'm eighteen!" she declared brightly, "and as for my looks, I can't help them. Would you like the hot water-bag on your feet? They told me you would want a hot water-bag as soon as you got in."

"They told you that, did they? Well, then I *don't*. If they said I did, I don't. I don't want anything that that crew put upon me, and you can put that down and remember it. I just want to be let alone awhile. When I want anything I'll tell you. Now, sit down there where I can look at you."

Patty sat down laughing and faced the old lady, and thus their journey together was begun.

5

An old man with eyes like a hawk and an arrogant beak sat shriveled into an invalid's chair in the sunniest window of the best suite in the hotel, querulously watching the driveway that wound up among the trees, glimpsable here and there at open points, until it curved in with a wide sweep at the elaborate gateway and rolled up under the porte cochere.

"You're sure the telegram said he would come on that train, Hespur? You haven't made a mistake about it? Where's the telegram? You've thrown it away, I suppose. You ought never to throw away a thing like that until the time for it is over. I've told you that a thousand times—"

"Telegram right here, sir." He laid the yellow paper in the trembling hand of the invalid. "It says he'll be on the afternoon train."

"Well, isn't there more than one train in the afternoon?" queried the old man excitedly, his voice rising portentously. "What right did you have to jump to that conclusion? I've told you more than once—"

"It's the only train from the North, Mr. Treeves."

"Well, what right had you to think he was coming from the North, you rascal? You're always so cocksure of yourself!"

"You said he came over on a transport, sir! The telegram was sent from New York—!"

"Well, there, there, *THERE!* Don't say any more about it. He hasn't come, has he? You were wrong, weren't you? The hack has come up from the station, hasn't it, and he hasn't come? And you knew the doctor said I mustn't be excited!"

"He might've walked, sir; they sometimes do, you know."

"What nonsense! Walked! The nephew of Calvin Treeves *walk* up from the station when he could just as well ride? He knew he could ride! I

57

tell you, you are a fool!" The old man's face was purple with rage.

"There's some one turned in at the drive just now, sir. He's carrying a suitcase, sir."

"What bosh! As if my nephew would carry a suitcase! Walk and carry a suitcase up to this hotel with all those hens and cats down there on the veranda knitting and clacking their tongues. He would have more respect for me than to do a thing like that. If he didn't, I'm sorry I sent for him! I'll teach him to disgrace—!"

The trembling old claw-like hands gripped the arms of the chair, and the selfish old voice trembled dangerously. There were sparks of fire from the dim, disappointed old eyes, and the puffy veins on the withered face swelled purple and congested.

"Just keep calm a minute, sir, there's some one at the door. You know the doctor said you mustn't get excited, Mr. Treeves—!"

"Keep calm! Keep calm!" muttered the angry old man, trying to lift himself to his feet, and then dropping back helplessly with a groan.

The man returned with a card.

"He has come, Mr. Treeves."

"How could he? That fellow walking wasn't my nephew. He would have been in uniform. That man wore civilian clothes. He ought to have been in officer's uniform. It was outrageous—! An insult to the name! My nephew a private! But he won enough honors to make a good showing even in private's uniform, and give those *cats* something to talk about at last!"

His eyes glittered with a gleam of triumph.

"Well, tell him to come up. Better late than never, I suppose—"

The old man settled back against his pillows and closed his eyes, drawing a deep breath, as if gathering strength for the interview. Then he sat up with a tense alertness and a feverish quiver of his lips that betokened his deep feeling, and looked toward the door as a tall, well-built young man, dressed in a business suit of brown, entered and looked at him. The young man had crisp brown curly hair cut close, and pleasant brown eyes, but there was a look of aloofness about him as if he were holding any friendliness he might have in abeyance for the present. Even the attendant felt it, and if the truth were known perhaps honored him the more for it. It was a trait of the Treeveses, this independence, this being able to stand alone and demand respect. A look of admiration dawned in old Hespur's face as he stood watching the young man advance into the room.

John Treeves walked over toward the withered little figure of a man in the chair and stood, as a soldier might stand, at attention, although there was that in his attitude that said he reserved the right to his own thoughts and would give inward respect only to whom respect was due.

"You have sent for me, Mr. Treeves?"

"Why don't you call me Uncle?" whimpered the old man irascibly.

"I understood that you did not wish to own me as a nephew. You disowned my father as a brother, for marrying my mother, and you refused to acknowledge me as your nephew some years ago. Why should I presume to call you Uncle?"

"I sent for you, isn't that enough? No need to have a nasty temper about it," replied the old man testily.

"You have sent for me, Uncle Calvin."

The old man's face softened just a shade.

"There that sounds better," he gloated like one who has conquered as usual. "Now sit down and let me see what you're made of."

A swift flicker of anger went over the young man's face and left it hard and cold:

"Thank you. I prefer to stand until I know why you sent for me."

The old man straightened up and looked at his nephew, half in admiration, half in fury:

"You prefer to stand, you young rascal!" he fairly snorted. "You do, do you? Well, I prefer that you sit! Do you HEAR! Hespur! Here! *Make* that young man sit down! MAKE him sit down, I say!" he screamed, thrashing the air vigorously with a frail claw of a hand. "Is this the way that paragon of a mother taught you to behave to your elders, you young rascal? Hespur! HERE!"

Hespur, the obedient, advanced coolly like a

well-trained animal that was set to do the impossible, but was swept aside like a toy by the strong arm of the young giant, who wheeled and strode toward the door:

"That will be about all!" he said as he paused with the knob of the door in his hand. I never allow my mother to be spoken of in that tone. I will bid you good afternoon and good-bye, MISTER TREEVES."

The old man sat agape in wonder. Not in years had anyone dared to oppose him like this! Nay, even to reprove him. He was too angry and astonished for articulation. Old Hespur stood in line with him watching with admiration the retreat of the young visitor, looking down at his arm that had been gripped in the giant vise, as if an honor had been conferred upon him. This surely was a young gentleman to be proud of, a true chip off the old block!

Then while Calvin Treeves still stared and spluttered for words, the door opened, and the young man went out and down the hall.

The old man was stunned for a second, then turned to his faithful servitor:

"Hespur! Go! Bring him back!" he pleaded like a child who has been punished and is suddenly repentant.

The young man pausing before the elevator door was suddenly confronted by the old servant, bowing before him with distress in his face.

"Oh, sir! He is sorry! He didn't mean it! Come back, sir, quick! The doctor said he must not be excited, sir. He might have a stroke. He's a mighty sick old man, is Mr. Treeves, and he don't rightly know how disagreeable he gets."

"Did he *say* he was sorry?" asked the young man, looking at the servant keenly.

"No, sir, he didn't *say* he was sorry. But he *meant* it, sir. He wouldn't rightly know how to say he was sorry. He never made a practice of saying he was sorry, sir!"

"I should say not!" said the nephew with flashing eyes and quivering upper lip, the kind of quiver that denotes a hurt soul; but he followed the serving man back albeit with his head held high and a haughty, stern chin. He came into the room once more and stood at attention.

Again that gleam of triumph in the old eye:

"You young rapscallion!" breathed the old man with a chuckle. "You certainly are hot-headed enough!"

"Sir, no one may speak so of my mother without having to account for it. If you called me here to insult her holy memory, it is time that I went. You gave her a lifetime of insult and if it had not been for her forgiving spirit I would not have been here to-day."

"Oh!" chortled the old man. "She had an eye to my sending for you some day, did she? Rather long-headed wasn't she?"

The old servitor started anxiously and looked toward the young man whose set jaw grew more and more stern and manly with every word, and who was looking straight into the wicked old eyes with an unflinching gaze:

"Sir," said the clear young voice, "it was when I was a child, and I had told her I hated you and would never forgive you for the way you had treated her, and she said that no soul ought to go into eternity unforgiven and I must not refuse you that if you ever asked."

The old man blanched as if he had been struck by the words, and then a wave of purple rage rolled up over his withered face:

"Well, wait till I ask then!" he roared it. "I want no old woman's talk about eternity! I sent for you to-day because I wanted *YOU,* not because I wanted forgiveness. Sit down, young man, and let's get to business! I tell you I won't be annoyed this way. You've got to do as I want you to do. I'm an old man, and I can't stand this excitement!"

He fumbled around for his handkerchief and mopped his congested forehead, panting for breath, as the wave of rage passed away and left him weak and feeble.

"Sir, you've got to apologize for the way you spoke of my mother or I'll never sit down. I know of no business I want to talk over with you, and if your business is not worth an apology I would better be going."

The old man stopped mopping his face and stared at his nephew.

"Apologize!" he muttered. "Ha! Ha! Apologize! Why, son, I never apologized to anyone in my life. You don't expect me to begin now—!"

"Very well! I will bid you good afternoon—"

"Stop!" spluttered Calvin Treeves. "STOP! I apologize! Now, sit DOWN!" He fairly shouted it.

The young man sat down sternly erect on the edge of the chair, but the effect was the same as when standing. Calvin Treeves realized this, and fairly whimpered his disappointment:

"Take this other chair and be comfortable!" There was almost a pleading note in the dictatorial old voice. "What is your business, Mr. Treeves?"

"Call me Uncle—," crooned the old man.

"What is your business, Uncle Calvin?"

The old gleam of triumph came back:

"That's better, nephew, that's better. Now we can talk. Well, my business is this. You see I'm all alone in the world. I'm getting to be an old man, and I'm sick. I want some one to belong to me, in whom I can live my life over again. In short, I want to get acquainted with you and feel that there is some one in the world to whom I can turn."

The old man stopped and eyed the younger keenly, anxiously.

The young man looked up with the stern look still about his mouth and eyes:

"I'm afraid that is impossible!"

"Why?" cringed the old man as if he had been struck.

"Because of the way in which you treated my mother. You let her struggle on all those years when I was a child, and never offered to even help her to find something to do to earn her living and mine till I was old enough to help. You even refused to help pay the funeral expenses of your own brother, and when mother asked you to lend her enough to pay the interest on the mortgage of our house for one year until she could earn enough to pay you back, you told her she was an interloper and had cheated my father out of a fair start in life. Afterward, when my mother lay sick in the hospital for weeks and I was cared for by strangers, you never lifted your finger. Do you think that I could care to live on intimate terms with one who did all that?"

The old man seemed to wither and shrink before the scathing tone of the young man. His thin hands like yellow parchment clung claw-like to each other, and he cringed before the young eyes that condemned him.

"You are very harsh in your judgment of me!" he put in plaintively. "Your father was engaged to a woman both beautiful and rich who would have made his life a different thing—"

"Knowing my mother, I can only rejoice for my father's sake that he married my mother instead of this woman!"

Young voices are so cold and clear in condemnation. The old man shivered.

"I never saw your mother!" he whimpered placatingly.

"That was your fault," scathed the son.

"I'll say this much for her, she did well in bringing you up."

The young man lifted scornful eyes.

"You know nothing about me; how can you say that?"

The cunning gleamed in the old eyes again:

"I know all about you. I've followed your career ever since you entered the army. I know you and am proud of you, and I want you for my own."

There was a curious pathetic hunger in the old voice that the young man could not ignore. Because he was the son of such a mother, he knew he must not pass it by.

"Why did you do that?" he asked at last after a long pause of troubled thought.

"Because when I happened to see your name in the paper I was proud that there was one of my name to go over. I had no son myself, and was too old to have any part myself, but—you were there—and I followed the war through you. I had a man over there finding out everything you did. I knew every turn you took. I know all the honors you won. I'm proud of you and the way you have honored the name of Treeves."

There was still that plaintive appeal for love in

the old voice, the wistful look mingling with the cunning in the spoiled old eyes. John Treeves looked up and pondered and then spoke:

"I could not give you my"—he carefully considered the words—"affection, nor my"—he considered again—"confidence, sir, so long as you feel as you do about my mother. I think, sir, there would be always a wall between us."

A look of cunning twinkled into the little, old eyes:

"Perhaps by knowing you I should learn to know her better and think better of her. I have thought better of her since following your career. Anyhow"—in a fretful tone—"that was a long time ago. Let us put it all by and begin again. If I made a mistake then I can't right it now, can I? Suppose you begin and tell me all about yourself. I shall doubtless get glimpses of your mother through that. Go ahead! I want to know all!"

The young man's lips looked stubborn at first. Even the old servant could see that the order was distasteful, that to talk of himself was never a favorite employment, and to talk about his sacred life with his beloved mother seemed a sacrilege in this presence. The fine brows drew down lower, and the whole face looked ominous. The little old man sat huddled in his pillows and watched fearfully. He wanted to conquer, more than he had ever wanted anything in his life before. This strong vital young man with his beauty and his independence, his audacity and his impudence had in these few minutes become of immense value to his lonely frightened old life. For he was frightened. He had even begun to admit it to himself in the still watches of the night when reality clutched him and made him face the future. He knew he had been a bad old man and a bad young man. He had had his own way all his life, had got himself riches and made others poor, had torn a tempestuous supremacy through his family and his neighborhood and his whole world and made everybody who did not fear him hate him— everybody save old Hespur, whom he had abused more than all. He knew, and wanted to buy back a little of his spent happiness by grafting to himself a young, strong, beautiful life; wanted to buy a whole Heaven for himself by making a late reparation to the child of the woman he had ignored in her trouble and given nothing but contempt. He wanted to do it in his own lordly way and not to enter Heaven by the lowly door of repentance as he knew the rest of the world must do. And so he sat and quavered and hung upon the words of the young man, his nephew, frightened lest here too he should fail, yet determined that he should not.

At last the nephew looked up:

"What do you want to know?" he asked reluctantly.

"Anything, everything that you can remember," cackled the uncle joyously.

The young brows drew down and the young voice was cold:

"That would be impossible!" he said in that tone of haughty withdrawal. "There is very little that you have a right to know. You forfeited all that long ago."

The old man crouched as if he were hit and shivered in his padded silken robe.

"I will tell you a few things," went on the nephew.

"My mother and I lived in two rooms over a bakery for a long time and mother had to sell bread to get bread for herself and me! But she kept me in school as soon as I was old enough and every evening she went over my studies with me. Sundays we went to church, and in between services we took long walks in the woods when the weather was good and she talked to me of life. I shall never expect to hear greater wisdom from any lips than the things she said to me. And she was but a girl when she began to teach me! It was so that when I went to college my teachers wondered where I had got my advanced ideas, and how I came to be so well trained in concentration, and it was all my mother's doings!"

He looked up, and the old man was still huddled silently in his pillows, with his bright wild eyes peering out piercingly, watching, listening, being condemned!

"She slaved at fine sewing and embroidery half the night to keep me in school and prepare me for college, and she went without everything she could without my finding out, to spend the money on me. I even caught her going without the necessary plain food herself in order to have me well fed. She did all that, and denied herself everything possible, and do you think I could easily sit down and make friends with a relative who *let* her do all that for his own brother's son, and was amply able to have helped her? Not that she would have accepted charity. What she needed was a friend and a little kindly advice just to feel there was somebody back of her ready to lift the burden if she should fall under it. She would have paid with interest anything that had been loaned to her. But instead she was compelled to borrow from her own vitality, and you, YOU were to blame! You are a bad old man!"

The cool young voice pounded out each word like blows of a hammer driving in a spike. The old man seemed to shrink and shrivel before each one.

"You shan't say that!" he snarled. "I never did anything wrong."

"It's not what you did, it's what you refused to do!"

The old eyes quailed:

"Well, perhaps, I can make it up now!" he whimpered.

70

"No. It's too late. You can never make up what you missed doing."

The old man sighed and lifted a trembling claw aimlessly to his lips as if to steady them:

"Well, well go on with your story—!" he evaded.

"There isn't much more. I went to work vacations and nights and mornings as soon as I was old enough and lifted as much burden as I could, and then she would have me go to college. I worked my way through that—and Seminary—"

"What were you preparing for? Anything special?" There was deep interest in the old eyes. He wanted to avoid getting back to the discussion of his own faults.

The young man hesitated and spoke the words as if they were something sacred:

"I was preparing for the ministry."

"What?" said the old man suddenly erect. "You mean a diplomatic service?"

"Oh, no," said the nephew, "theology!"

"You don't mean you were going to be a preacher! Oh, the devil!" and he finished with a cackle from the tombs.

The young man fixed him with a stern eye.

"Oh, well, go on with your story! The war came along and spoiled you for any such milk-and-water woman's job as that! I know the rest. Enough for the present. We'll talk about the war after dinner. Hespur, take the young gentleman to his room. He'll want to prepare for dinner, and I'm going down to the dining-room myself to-night to do him honor. Hear that, Hespur? You can hunt out my evening clothes when you come back. That's all, nephew! Go and get ready for dinner!"

Then quite naturally John Treeves found himself following the old servant to a suite of rooms directly across the hall from his uncle's.

"I hope you'll be entirely comfortable," said old Hespur adoringly. "You'll find plenty of hot water for your bath, and you've only to ring and I'll come. Would you like me to unpack your suitcase, sir, and lay out your things?"

"No," said John Treeves with a weary smile, "I haven't much and I'm used to doing for myself. A bath will feel good, however."

Nevertheless, when he was left to himself he did not immediately proceed to the white-tiled bathroom whose door stood so invitingly open, but strode to the window, thrust his fingers through his hair, with his elbow on the upper window sash and stood staring out into the beauty of the hotel grounds, and off at the purple misty mountains in the distance. But he was not seeing the beauty. He was thinking of what he had just said to his uncle, and his blood was still boiling over the remembrance of his mother and the indignities she had suffered from the old despot. And yet, in spite of it all, there had been an appeal in the old reprobate's eyes that somehow would not be denied. He had not meant to stay all night—not definitely—yet here he was staying, and he wondered if he had done right to yield even so much?

A car was driving up to the veranda below, and its Klaxon attracted his gaze idly. Two travelers were getting out, one an old lady, quite crippled with rheumatism apparently, and one a lithe young girl who sprang from the car nimbly and turned a charming face up to the front of the building with an appraising glance, then dropped her eyes with a quick motion and put out her hands to assist her companion.

John Treeves started and said aloud to himself:

"That looks like Patty Merrill! I believe it is! I'm going down to see!"

6

Miss Sylvia Cole was generally regarded by her friends and family as an old crab who was too important to be put in her place and punished for her biting sarcasm. Her keen insight into shams and a peculiar sense of humor were not generally understood nor appreciated by her victims. When she sat facing Patricia in the sleeper that night regarding her future companion much in the same light that a cat regards a mouse with whom it intends to enjoy a playful hour before devouring, she suddenly came face to face with her own sense of humor, and burst out laughing in a dry cackle or two at the thought of being attended in her invalidism by this handsome infant.

"Marjorie would have been far more suitable in appearance!" she declared, thinking her thoughts aloud as was her custom.

"Yes, but Marjorie wouldn't have done as you told her to and I shall," declared Patty brightly.

"You're no more used to doing as you are told than Marjorie, I can see that with half an eye!" said the old lady, scrutinizing the girl.

"Oh, yes, rather," reflected the girl pleasantly. "I'm not long out of school, you know. Besides I am earning my living now and I *have* to do as I'm told. Will you have that hot water-bag?"

"No, I don't want that hot water-bag now or ever. Such bosh lugging a drug store along just because I'm going a few miles from home! Well, if you're going to do as you're told you better understand that I don't want to be nagged and bothered. When I want anything I'll tell you, and I don't hire you to know more about my wants than I do. Understand? Now all I want to-night is a drink of water and to be let alone."

"That sounds easy," said Patty smiling; "I'll get the water. I'd hate to be nagged myself. It makes one feel all riffley inside."

"Exactly," said the old lady grimly. "I think we shall get on very well. And you needn't tell me any more about yourself than you want to. I shan't ask you."

"Thank you," said Patty pleasantly, "I appreciate that. Perhaps I shan't. Now, which bed is mine, or do I sit up?"

"I'll take the lower berth and you may have the couch. And I like the light turned out and a screen in the window at the foot. I believe that's all. Good night."

So they slept. And in the morning they were in Washington and drove straight to the New Willard, took a room and rested—at least the old lady rested. The girl sat by the window and silently studied out the city trying to locate the different points of interest and wished she might go out and take a walk. But she was a working woman now and must do as her employer wished, and her business was to stick by the old lady. So far that had not been difficult, but she could see that Miss Cole was used to having her own way and might not be pleasant to live with if by any chance that way was crossed.

They took the afternoon train soon after lunch and arrived at the Pine Crest Inn as the sun was beginning to slip behind the blue hills and send long slant shadows among the autumn foliage.

"Isn't it perfectly gorgeous here?" said Patty joyously as she got out of the hack and looked up at the face of the great hotel sitting majestically above the grandeur in its frame of autumn color.

The sunset rays touched her face into vivid beauty, and Miss Sylvia reflected with grim satisfaction that perhaps people would think she was bringing a lovely daughter to the Springs for a bit of rest before the winter's season should begin. She resolved to have some pleasure out of the idea and tucked it away in her mind for further consideration.

The hall porter glided out of the door to meet them and attached himself to their baggage and Patty helped Miss Cole up the steps.

It was just inside the door that Patty saw John Treeves, hurrying down the wide staircase at the opposite end of the long hotel lobby, and her heart stood still within her for one brief second. Not since five long years ago had she seen that face, yet she knew it instantly, and with a bound of joy for the comrade of a blessed summer when she had been left behind in a little New York village while her family went abroad. Then came the instant realization that she must not be recognized and she turned her face away and looked coolly toward the office desk. She was trembling all over, and trying with all her might to look natural and unconcerned, telling herself that of course he would not recognize her. She was only a little girl with short skirts and her hair down in two long plaits when he knew her.

She managed to write in the register with a tolerably firm hand, but as she turned away toward the elevator she came almost face to face with Treeves. This time, however, she was prepared, and managed a blank unseeing stare straight past him, although he had stepped up and was just about to speak to her. In sudden panic she turned abruptly toward Miss Cole and began to speak to her, and in a second more they were shut into the elevator and gliding upward, while the disappointed young man stood below hesitating, dismayed, but in nowise uncertain as to her identity, or daunted as to the final issue. She didn't know him. That was natural after five years, and she not expecting to meet him. He was changed, of course, but not so much. He passed his hand over his smoothly shaven face, and looked down at his trim new suit and shining footgear, glad that he was in proper civilian garb to meet her. Then he strode to the register to get the number of her room and send up his card. She would know that anyway, if she did not recognize his grown-up face.

But he stood before the register page with a startled, unbelieving look, for there before him right on the page, where he had seen her writing there glared out at him two strange names: "Miss Sylvia Cole, New York; Miss Edith Fisher, New York."

Her name was not there! What could it mean? Had his eyes deceived him? He had been mistaken, of course, but how strange that there could be two people in the world with that look in their eyes. Well, it had shown him one thing and that was that he wanted to look up Patricia Merrill right away and have a talk with her. He had felt a desire for something to comfort his homesick soul ever since he landed, and now he knew what it was. He needed the soothing, uplifting presence of a woman who understood him. His mother was gone, but there was one girl who had seemed to understand him once and who was closely associated with his mother's sweet memory. He would like to see that girl! This stranger, Edith Fisher, or Sylvia Cole, whichever she might be, had looked enough like Patricia to be her sister. He was glad he had seen her. He would watch for her in the dining-room. It would be good to look again and recall the sweet lines of the face of his little pal, Patty. And then, just as soon as he could get free from his old rascal of an uncle, and get a few other things fixed up, he would take a trip out West and see if he could find her. Perhaps he might manage to satisfy his antique relative's curiosity and get away in the morning, in which case he could take the western trip at once. He turned with a sigh and made his way back to his room, where he found his impatient uncle's servitor already demanding his presence again. He hastened through a brief toilet and presented himself before his uncle.

The old man sat in his wheeled chair in full

evening garb looking more ghoulish than ever in the dead black and white of dinner coat and stiff collar. The bright, restless eyes fixed themselves in a kind of gloating satisfaction on the young man. It was a possessive, selfish look such as he had worn all his life with regard to anything he desired, and reached after, and acquired and hoarded, almost the strongest element in it being to keep it from others. Before he had seen this young man, even when he was still following his honorable career in the army, he had not been quite sure whether he would seize this prize or fling it aside as unworthy; but now the old eyes snapped with pleasure, and the jaw set firmly with determination. This young man was *his;* no one, not even the fellow himself, should say him nay. What a wonderful set of shoulders he had! What line of limb and curve of feature! Heavens! How handsome he was! He must have got that from that poor little country upstart of a mother. Sometimes country girls were that way, healthy and handsome, and a strain of such stock wasn't a bad thing in blood that had been blue for centuries. Now it was over, and she out of the way he could afford to let bygones be bygones. For the boy certainly was stunning! What a sensation he would make in New York society!

Already he was planning his life for him—travel and polish and clubs! The right women! Gad! What a hit he would make with the women! But he would take good care to fix things so that he couldn't make his father's mistake. The hoarded millions would come in there all right. He would tie them up in such a way that the boy could only marry a desirable girl. He must learn to keep the other kind of girl in the background where other respectable young men of wealth and reputation kept their amours. But he would learn. There was keen intelligence behind those eyes. And he knew just where to get the right tutors. He rubbed his hands together in glee. Already he could see the flaring headlines bearing the name of the young and talented nephew of Calvin Treeves, the multimillionaire! Ah! What a future! He could bear, now, to sit back in a wheeled chair and know that his hour was over, for now he could live again through the career of this young man. It almost seemed as if Calvin Treeves must be a corpse dressed up, save for the weird twitching of lips and brow. The keen little eyes focused eagerly and with satisfaction on the broad shoulders and well-set head of his nephew. He noticed with pride the easy grace of his walk, and his look of being at home anywhere, but his only remark was an impatient: "Well, ready? Let's move!" and the little procession went forward to the elevator.

Treeves marked the obsequiousness of the servants as the old man's chair rolled through the hall and into the lift like a chariot of state. He saw a look pass into the faces of all who served from the least bellboy to the highest in the house, that look of deference to riches, and his soul rebelled within him as he noted the slight reflection of glory that fell even to his own share because of being in the company of this little old selfish dried-up soul of a man in a withered shell of a body. Again the old wrath boiled within him, and he was almost at the point of turning away from the situation and bolting in disgust. Yet after all there was something pathetic in the smirk of satisfaction that sat upon the waxen lips. This was all the man had, this human adulation. And not for himself, either; the deference was for his riches! What a life to have lived so long, and to have nothing but this at the end! Self incarcerated in that withered old body, shortly to be driven forth into an unknown country where riches of earth count not and deference for such reasons in unknown!

Down in the bright world of the hotel dining-room such thoughts quickly fled. Treeves was searching everywhere for a face. He paid little heed to the gaiety about him, and acknowledged the introductions his uncle gave with indifference. He did not expect to meet these people again. They were out of his sphere. They were interesting merely as specimens from another world. His eyes idly appraised a florid mother, her well-groomed head set off by a black velvet band with jeweled slides above her broad expanse of pink enameled chest. Her pallid daughter, with limpid eyes and an anaemic droop, stood beside her. He wondered why she cared to show so much of a long skinny back, and then his eyes hurried through the group of faces just beyond and Adele Quatrain realized that she had not made a hit with the stunning young nephew of the millionaire.

"He's got the Treeves manner all right!" said the uncle to himself as he watched the young man with satisfaction. "He won't fall for the first little fool that angles for him, that's certain. He takes the first entrance into his own as if he had been here always. It's not going to be difficult at all to train him. That distant air suits him well. No one would guess he was not to the manner born. His mother couldn't have been so bad after all, and I suppose I shall have to say so to him, for he seems to be quite set on her. After all, she's dead and can't make us any more trouble, so what's the difference. And blood will tell. His father was Treeves all through, if he did marry a poor country parson's daughter. It isn't as if she hadn't had some education of course. This certainly is going to be a good move. I shall enjoy myself! But what is the young cuss looking at? He hasn't taken his eyes off the main entrance! I swear it's almost as if he was watching for some one. He can't have found any friends here surely! I must keep my eye on him. I won't have him making any undesirable acquaintances!"

But although John Treeves watched the main entrance to the great dining-room most carefully, and searched with eager eyes the faces of those seated about the tables, he could not find Patty Merrill nor her double.

The dining-room was long and built of glass, opening on three sides to the mountain scenery. The sun, like a great red ball of fire-opal, slid down in the majestic display behind pines and juniper and fir, sending long purple and gold bars through the interstices and left a gorgeous sky behind to linger and glow and die slowly into the deep purples and blues of night. The brilliant lights of the dining-hall began to be felt with the dessert and coffee.

"Doggone his fool hide! He isn't impressed at all!" mused his uncle, gulping his black coffee and eying his nephew savagely. "Where in thunder did he get that cool manner? One would think he had been a millionaire all his life! If he wasn't my nephew I'd call him an upstart! And he is! Of course he is! An *upstart!* But I like him and I'm going to keep him! That manner will go all right, only he must work it on *me!* I won't have it! I'll teach him he can't go that way with me! He's got to knuckle down and do as I say or I won't have anything to do with him! I'll teach him!"

Meantime, Patty Merrill, in a pleasant suite of rooms on the third floor of the hotel, stood at a window watching the sunset and trying to calm her excited heart and think what had really happened.

She had unpacked Miss Cole's bags, hung up her belongings, and spread out her toilet articles with unaccustomed but intelligent fingers, and a kind of childish pleasure. It was like playing dolls or taking a part in a bit of comedy, this posing as a lady's maid and companion. It really amused her. Miss Cole did not seem a hard woman to please, and so far their relations had been entirely amicable. Now and then during the journey she had lifted her eyes to find those of the older woman upon her in a frank questioning stare. A stare that would have seemed almost impertinent if it had not been kindly. She felt too much alone in this great experiment she had launched herself upon, to resent a pleasant look, so she had answered it by a flush and a smile which somehow seemed always to turn the look, and once or twice had brought an answering smile.

Miss Cole was lying on the couch in the sitting-room of the apartment, a steamer rug over her feet, and her head upon a linen pillow that always accompanied her on her journeys. She had closed her eyes and said she would rest until dinner was brought up; and Patty, feeling herself dismissed for the time being, drifted over to the window and dropped down upon the broad window-seat. Looking into the heart of the valley where the shadows among the pines were deepest and smokiest, she began to feel sad and full of vague fears and uneasiness. Was that really John Treeves that she had seen downstairs, or was it only her imagination? How would he be here? And if it were really her old comrade, what ought she to do about it?

Since leaving New York her situation had been so entirely novel and amusing that she had had very little leisure to think it over or become depressed. Now, however, the full force of her exile came upon her. She was a fugitive, and must remain unknown. It would not do to be recognized by this young man who knew her family, whose mother had been a dear intimate of her mother in their childhood days, and who would undoubtedly think it his duty to persuade her to return home if he knew she was here under an assumed name; would very likely consider it his duty to let her family know of her whereabouts. Not that he would be disloyal to her wishes if he knew all, she was sure, for he had been a wonderful friend, but how could she possibly explain the unloving attitude of her mother and sister that had made it impossible for her to remain at home? No, for the sake of her father, and the honor of the family she must remain hidden, much as she might desire to renew the acquaintance of the beautiful summer which seemed now so long ago. She drew a deep sigh and her eyes grew dreamy over memories of walks and rides and picnics, and John Treeves's home, the little white cottage at the end of the village street, which would always seem to her the personification of the word Home; the strong, sweet, womanly, merry mother who had taken her into her arms and kissed her for the sake of her own mother. That kiss and the gentle loving tones that had told her of Mrs. Treeves's childish friendship for Patricia's girl-mother, had served to soften many a harsh word and cold action during the years, because she could always remember little beautiful loving things that Mrs. Treeves had told her about her mother as a child, and somehow she had succeeded in putting the halo of that childhood about the haughty head of the mother who had never shown her the deep love she had always craved.

The sun had slipped out of sight now into the deep blue heart of the pines, and the crimson streak was fading from the ether above. Patty drew another soft little sobbing sigh, scarcely audible, and a tear unbidden slipped out of the fringes and dashed silently down her cheek. Then startlingly grim from the shadows of the room where she had supposed her patient to be peacefully sleeping, came a voice, very much awake indeed:

"How long have you known that young man?"

7

Patty, with a gasp, emerged hastily from her retrospection and dashed away the tears from her hot cheeks.

"I—I beg your pardon?" she tried to say briskly, trying not to seem in a panic, "I thought you were asleep, Miss Cole—*Madam!*"

"Don't *MADAM* me!" was the sharp retort. "I asked you how long you had known that young man. I know you thought I was asleep. You thought I didn't see down there in the office, too, but I'm not blind if I am rheumatic, and I've been young once if I am an old maid. I want to know how long you have known him."

"Why—I—" began Patty with her heart going like a trip-hammer playing trills, "I'm not sure that I know him at all. He looked a little like some one I met five years ago when I was visiting friends in New York state, but I wasn't sure." She was breathing more freely now. This sounded perfectly reasonable, and was entirely true.

"Well, he's the same one, and you know him, and he knows you, all right. I tell you I'm not blind. But what I want to know is how long and how well you know him!"

There was a touch of dictatorial sharpness in the voice that put Patricia a bit on her dignity.

"His mother and my mother were school friends. We played around together one summer when we were growing up. That is all," said Patty, coolly.

"There, there! Now child, don't you go to getting uppish about it. You think it's none of my business, but you must remember that you were an utter stranger to me until yesterday, and that you're young and pretty; and whether you think I have the right or not, it's my moral responsibility to keep an eye on you, and you mustn't resent it."

"I know, Miss Cole," said Patty quietly yet with a tiny bit of aloofness in her tone, "but you saw that I turned away without recognizing that young man. Wasn't that sufficient?"

"H'm! That was just the trouble. He looked to me like a perfectly good young man, and why didn't you recognize him?"

Patty stiffened and was glad that it was dark in the room. There was something in the arrogant old woman's voice that made her want to both laugh and cry.

"I am not in a position to recognize anybody at present," said Patty.

"Position fiddlesticks!" said the old lady. "That young man would only honor you the more if he thought you were earning your living! I can't be mistaken in a face like that!"

Patty laughed outright.

"Oh, indeed, you misunderstand me," she said,

"I wasn't worried about my position as earning my own living. But I told you in the beginning that there were reasons why it had become necessary for me, and none of my friends know the circumstances. It is very necessary for the comfort of those I love most that nobody should know anything about it at present. I do not wish to be recognized nor to have any of my friends find out where I am."

"H'm!" said the old lady speculatively. "You didn't run away, did you? Not that I care, but I'd like to know. It might make matters simpler."

"Why, yes, I think I did," said Patty thoughtfully, "but I had a perfectly good reason for doing so, and I'm not going back even if you try to make me, for I'm sure I did right."

"Well, I'm reasonably sure you did, too, if you say so," responded the astonishing old lady, "and I'm not going to try. But there's something I want distinctly understood. You're not here in any menial position. I never travel with a maid, and I won't have a companion. I hate 'em! You are a distant relative of mine taking a trip with me. Understand?"

"But, Miss Cole, I couldn't put myself in a false position—"

"Nothing false about it. It's perfectly true. You are a distant relative of mine. Dates back to Adam. You can like it or not, but you can't deny it. And that's what I hired you for, to be a young relative taking a trip with me. See? You can call me Aunt or Cousin, or whatever you like, but I'm a relative, and as long as you stay with me that's what you are to be! I like the fun of taking a pretty young girl around and playing with her. I'd take Marjorie if she'd let me, but she's too much of a high-flyer to be tied to an old woman's apron strings, and besides, she's a too-near relation. So, if you're agreeable I'll be Aunt Sylvia or Cousin Sylvia, after this, or just plain Miss Sylvia, if you like that better."

"You're very kind—Miss—Miss Sylvia—" said Patty slowly, "and I'll do my best to be the nicest relative I know how and play around with you. But only, you'll please not expect me to hunt up any of my former acquaintances. I want to be— just Edith Fisher now. I must, you know. It's necessary!"

Her cool young voice was quite determined and there was an extended silence in the room while the older woman thought it over. Then came her voice like an electric spark:

"Be what you like!" she said snappily. "Only don't be a fool! Some people aren't worth sacrifices!"

"Mine is," said Patty firmly.

There was an impatient stir from the bed:

"Don't tell me you've fallen in love with some *other* young man when *this* one was around!"

Patty laughed out happily.

"Oh, dear no! Nothing like that! It's only a very dear relative. I haven't thought about falling in love yet!"

"H'm!" said Miss Cole unbelievingly. "Well, ring for dinner—unless you'd like to go down. I'm feeling perfectly rested."

"Oh, no, please!" said Patty hurrying to the bell. "I'd much rather stay up here to-night; it's so cosy!"

So they had their dinner served upstairs, and Patty, with rosy cheeks and eyes that shone like stars, exerted herself to be as bright and entertaining as possible, while the old lady watched her grimly and with a kind of satisfaction that the girl would not have understood. After all, Miss Cole found great joy in a girl who could be entertaining to an old woman when there was a perfectly good and perfectly willing young man downstairs with whom she might have companied if she had tried.

Patty, as she lay in her bed in the little room just off from Miss Cole's bedroom after the evening was over, thought about it all, and her cheeks grew warm in the darkness once more over the questions her inquisitor had put. How was she to conduct herself the next day, and the next, and all the days, supposing John Treeves were to remain in the hotel? It was not at all thinkable that she could entirely escape meeting him, although she meant to try her very best to do so. And she could not bring herself to tell him her trouble and expose her mother to criticism. Father would not like that. Father would expect her to keep the honor of the family. Only so could she explain her action to him on his return.

She fell asleep in the midst of her troubled thoughts at last, but drifted into a dream of that summer long ago and a long sweet day's walk with John Treeves and his mother, through a wood where they had often gone together. It was a vivid dream, in which even the leaves on the beeches were picked out in clear relief against the sky, and the rocks were as real as life with the pretty lichens and moss. She seemed in her sleep to notice every lovely detail of the woods. Even the smell of the pines was there, though perhaps the pines outside her window might have had something to do with that. They spread their lunch on a giant rock that jutted among the pine needles and she remembered the little cakes and the tiny pies in round tin pans—blackberry and cherry— how good they tasted again! And then the day was over, and Mrs. Treeves put a loving hand on her arm and said: "Don't worry, dear. You are doing right, and your father will soon understand it all perfectly, and so will your mother. Don't be afraid. Just go straight ahead." Then she kissed her lovingly on the forehead and the dream melted into the wonderful morning with the warm rays of the sun shining on her face like a caress, and a wonderful piney smell blowing in at the window.

There were cheerful sounds everywhere, a distant tinkle of china and silver, voices on the piazza below, the honk of a Klaxon, the plunk of a tennis ball on a taut racket, all the sounds of a well-ordered establishment of luxury and ease. Somehow the morning looked good to Patty in spite of her perplexities, and the new day held a quiver of all sorts of beautiful possibilities. The gentle face and voice of Mrs. Treeves, her kiss and her words lingered like a benediction in her heart as she arose and went about her dressing with alacrity, and a song in her heart; although she checked it on her lips lest she waken her employer. She need not have worried, however, for Miss Cole had been wide-awake for some time, and full of ideas. Now she suddenly voiced one of them; in a question:

"Have you got any evening dresses?"

Patty stopped in the act of putting in a hairpin and whirled around to the door of Miss Cole's bedroom:

"Oh, good morning! I didn't know you were awake! I hope I didn't disturb you."

"Have you got any evening dresses?" asked the alert voice once more. Patty laughed amusedly. This woman was always asking such odd questions:

"Why, I believe so. I'll look. I hardly know what was in my suitcase. I didn't pay much attention to my packing."

Patty emerged in a moment from her room with a billow of rose-colored chiffon over one arm, a soft shining turquoise silk and a puff of cream-colored embroidered tulle over the other.

"There seem to be three!" she giggled. "I'm sure I don't know what use they will be to me."

"It is a rather odd collection for a girl to bring along when she runs away to be a lady's companion," said Miss Cole grimly, her eye kindling with interest. "And only one suitcase to carry everything, too!"

"Well, you see, I was going to a week-end house party when I decided to leave, and my suitcase was half-packed. I didn't really stop to consider what I was bringing along."

"H'm!" said Miss Cole eying her sharply. "That doesn't sound very hopeful for my comfort this winter. You're not very likely to stay here if you come from things like that—! You'll get another impulse and run back again, I suppose, just as I begin to get used to you!"

"No!" said Patty decidedly. "You needn't worry about that. I'm not a quitter, and I haven't got a yellow streak in me. My father always told me that. Besides, there are reasons why I couldn't possibly go back, not for some time anyway."

"Oh!" said Miss Cole. "You've got a father, have you? What will he think of your escapade?"

Patty suddenly sobered:

"My father is—in South America at present. I

couldn't consult him of course because I had to act quickly, but I think he will feel I did right."

"H'm! Well, I hope so. Now spread out those dresses. They're very pretty. I guess you may wear the blue one to-night. We're going down to dinner to-night and stay awhile in the evening."

"Oh—but!" said Patty aghast. "These will be far too giddy for a—a lady's companion to wear. I have a little dark silk—a dinner dress, you know. I'll wear that!"

"You'll wear the blue!" said Miss Cole decisively. "Didn't I tell you I wasn't to be crossed? I guess I know what will be suitable. And you're not a 'companion,' remember! Don't mention that again! We're near relatives—through the Adamses, you know—!"

There was a grim humor in her tone, and Patty, eying her thoughtfully, broke into smiles once more and said:

"Oh, very well, Miss Cole, just as you say—"

"I've decided you're to call me Cousin Sylvia!" said the grim voice insistently.

Patty laughed merrily:

"All right, Cousin Sylvia. Will you have your breakfast sent up now? And what will you have?"

"No," said the old lady, "I'm going down. You may pull down my window and turn on that radiator. I'll be dressed as soon as you will."

"Oh, but—!" pleaded Patty aghast. "Don't you

think it would be better for you to rest this morning after the long journey?"

"No, I don't! And I told you once I didn't want to be advised what to do. I feel like going down to breakfast and I'm going down."

And so in spite of all the girl could do they went down to the dining-room. But Patty need not have worried for John Treeves had been summoned to breakfast in his uncle's room, and was not visible to the inhabitants of the hotel until late in the afternoon.

Patty was relieved to find that there were but few people in the dining-room at that hour, and quite enjoyed the ceremony at breakfast. After the meal was concluded the old lady insisted on having wraps brought down and sitting in one of the many rocking chairs on the wide front piazza. Patty established her with many furtive glances, and many attempts to slip away unobservedly. But the old lady had no mind to lose sight of her pretty young companion. She watched her like a cat playing with a mouse, and she kept a sharp eye out for any guests of the house who came that way, particularly any of the younger men. She sent Patty upstairs numberless times for magazines, pen and writing case, a book she was reading, and finally her knitting bag; and eyed her keenly each time on her return to see if there were signs of an encounter with her former friend. If she had known that Patty, slipping through a window into the writing room, had searched out an obscure and circuitous route to the staircase, and avoiding the elevator had run like a ray of sunlight up the stairs and down again, she certainly would have been vexed. The morning slipped quietly and uneventfully along, with Patty established in a big chair beside her charge, reading a magazine, and Miss Cole writing letters and watching the office door. Sounds of merriment drifted back from the tennis courts, "Love fifteen." Miss Cole watched Patty out of the side of her eye, noted the soft pink color on her round cheek, the lovely lines of lip and brow, the shining brown of her hair, the dainty grace of her lithe young figure, and wondered what slip of nature had set this child for a servant's part in the play of living. She had the look of one who had always been carefully guarded, the starry trustfulness in her eyes that belongs to those who are beloved in their circle of life. Miss Cole resolved that the child should be put back in her place if it was in her power to do so. She should not sit in a corner while others whirled by in the wild joy of life. She must get into things right away and have a good time here. Her face softened as she watched the girl, and took in her charm. Something that would have been motherhood if it had ever had a chance, stirred in her crabbed old heart, and reached out to this sweet, young thing.

"Edith, you go get your hat and coat and take

my letters down to the village post office. There's no dependence to be placed on these hotel mail boys. I've been in this place before!" She spoke suddenly, looking up from addressing an envelope, and Patty looked up with a start.

"Oh!" she laughed. "I—I forgot!"

"Well, it's no kind of a name for you to be using, but it's as good as any for the present, I suppose. Here, take my purse and get a special delivery stamp put on that one. Now go, and don't hurry! I'm going to take a nap right here in the sunshine and I shan't want to be disturbed for an hour at least, so you can take your time."

Patty thus dismissed, went off on her walk, but the old lady would have been disappointed if she could have watched her taking a bypath into the woods and keeping entirely away from the regular walk, where all the hotel guests promenaded. Patty, on the other hand, would have been astonished if she could have seen the alert old lady who rose from her chair as soon as the girl had disappeared around the turn of the walk. She steered straight for the office and consulted the hotel register, gleaning a few names for further consideration. She asked an abrupt question or two of the hotel clerk, and then giving a comprehensive glance around the circle of rocking chairs ranged about the big open fireplace, she selected one which commanded a good view of the front door, the wide staircase, the descending elevators, and had the added advantage of being next to a woman whom she recognized as an old habitué of the hotel. Not that she cared for the woman, or had ever given her even scant courtesy in the years gone by, but just now she felt she might make use of her. So she dropped down in the vacant rocker and fell upon her knitting grimly:

"Well, I see you're back again early. Who's here now? Any of the last year's people?"

The woman in lavender looked up surprised at the friendly tone and prepared for a good hour's work. Here was one whom she had longed to question and had always lacked the opportunity.

"Oh, how *de*lightful, dear Miss Cole. Are the Horliss-Coles down this season? I thought I saw your niece with you last night."

"No, that wasn't my niece, that's a young cousin named Fisher, Edith Fisher."

"A cousin?" asked the lavender one, pricking up her ears, and *not* a Horliss-Cole? "You didn't have other brothers or sisters, did you? Excuse me for asking, but we were discussing that matter here on the porch the other day, and I said I thought there was another brother—or was it a sister?"

"Oh, no, nothing like that," declared Miss Cole with a grim set of amusement to her thin lips. "There were only two of us, Jim and I. This girl's related farther back. We both had the same great-grandfather several times removed. Adams, the name. You wouldn't probably know."

"Now you speak of it, I do remember hearing of the Adams-Fishers. There was a Fisher-Adams down here last week. Probably he was related."

"Probably," said Miss Cole, dryly.

"What a pity he isn't here now! It is so interesting to trace relationships, don't you think, Miss Cole?"

"I presume there are plenty of young men left, aren't there? Who is here anyway?"

"Oh, there's the most interesting man, just back from France, Dunham Treeves! You ought to see him. He's handsome as a picture, and abso*lutely* indifferent, they say. He's a nephew of old Calvin Treeves, you know, the multimillionaire, son of his only brother, who died a number of years ago. They say it's quite romantic, his being here. It seems there's been an estrangement in the family or something, and Calvin wouldn't recognize his brother's wife. But she's dead now and this younger man has appeared on the scene. Mrs. Burleson says that he is to be Calvin Treeves's heir. She ought to know, for Burleson has been old Treeves's lawyer for the last twenty years—"

"H'm! Calvin Treeves's nephew! How old is he?"

"Well, I should say twenty-five or maybe twenty-six—nobody seems to know exactly. But he's stunningly handsome and has no end of honors on his head. Though the queer thing about it is he won't wear any of his medals nor his uniform nor anything. They say his uncle's peeved about that, and of course it is trying, but then I understand the best young fellows are pursuing that indifferent method, and it really gives a kind of éclat, you know. But it makes it hard for the relatives. I really don't see why they won't wear their uniforms, though, they do look so fascinating in them, especially if a man has legs! Legs, you know, are really a thing to be proud of, there are so few. I should have adored to live in the time when gentlemen wore short breeches and knee buckles; they must have given such an air of refinement, and thread lace ruffles—!"

"I think we have fools enough now without putting ruffles on them!" snorted Miss Cole, forgetting her affable role for the moment.

"Oh, well, this Dunham Treeves is no fool, I can tell you. They say he was head of his class in college!"

"They say! *They say!*" grumbled Miss Cole. "Who are *they,* I'd like to know? Or is that what Calvin Treeves wishes to have believed about his beloved nephew?"

"Oh, now dear Miss Cole, you are so funny!" chirped the lavender lady. "But really this young man is a very superior fellow, indeed. And independent! Why he doesn't look twice at a girl! And the girls are just crazy about him!"

"Poor fools! Well, how does he look?"

In the course of half an hour Miss Sylvia Cole

gathered sufficient data to be sure of the identity of the young man, and excusing herself with scant ceremony she took another look at the registry book. Yes, there it was "J. D. Treeves, Maple Brook, N. Y." She shut the book and her lips together with a snap of satisfaction and went back to her sheltered corner of the piazza in time to settle herself into the semblance of a profound nap before the return of the girl.

Late that afternoon they were sitting, Patty, and her employer, in a sheltered nook of pines down one of the winding paths that led from the hotel into the resinous grove. There were comfortable rustic seats in plenty scattered here and there in quiet corners, and paths of pine-needle paving threaded the whole hillside, in such cunningly devised pattern that no one intruded upon another, though often they were close enough for a voice to carry from one to another. Miss Cole had settled herself with a book and promptly gone to sleep among a multitude of cushions. It was quite obvious that she was asleep. Patty, with a book in her lap lay back on other cushions and let her eyes follow dreamily the hazy mountain line in the distance, just visible through a carefully trimmed opening in the plumy green curtains about their harbor. Down the mountainside she could hear gay voices calling, and childish laughter, and up above in other paths subdued chatter floated now and again in fragments, and it all made the world seem very far away, and herself a lonely little soul stranded here with a queer old stranger. Almost her heart began to fail her again, and a tear stole out beneath her lashes. She flashed it away with a furtive glance at Miss Cole, and straightened up with a firm little upper lip, setting herself to study the beauty about her. It really was a wonderful place for a girl without a home to have dropped down into, and she ought to be very glad. She was. She even managed a watery little smile at the gentle snores that issued from Miss Cole's direction.

Suddenly a voice broke the whispering silence of the pines, a voice that she could never mistake:

"Patty Merrill! Is that you down there on the next path? I've been looking for you everywhere. Won't you come down to the first patch of sunlight below you and wait for me? I've something to tell you."

8

Patty half started to her feet and lifted her eyes to the plumy wall of green above her, her lips parted to answer, a wonderful light in her eyes and a wonderful color in her cheeks. Then she suddenly remembered, and sank noiselessly back into her seat, turning fearful eyes in Miss Cole's direction, every muscle tense, her very breath bated. But a reassuring snore lurched suddenly and abruptly into line, and Patty relaxed a fraction, with another furtive glance upward, very, very cautiously. It seemed to her that the simple lifting of her eyelashes made a noise like thunder and her heart was beating so wildly it almost choked her. She felt so frightened and so deceptive, and so disappointed. How good it was to hear his voice again! If only she might answer! If only she could go down to him and they might have pleasant converse and wander about this lovely mountain as they used to walk in those good days so long ago! Was there any possible way she could explain her situation without involving the honor of her family? Her heart clamored wildly for permission to lead her willing feet down that sunlit piney way, but Duty, writ large, stood in her way. If what she was doing was questionable in any way, at least no one should ever find it out until her father knew it all and told her what to do. She could not explain and therefore she must remain unknown.

The minutes beat themselves away, and she heard a strong quick step on the path above. She had to put her hand on her lips with one finger against her throat to keep from crying out, so eager was she to answer that call. And now it came again and made her heart leap up once more to answer:

"Patty! Patty Merrill! I say, you are coming down, aren't you?" And then his voice dropped away as voices did in that quiet nook, and it might have been anybody, calling to anybody else, and gone on by to meet them. If she sat quite still and went on with her reading, Miss Cole would never suspect that she had been called, not even if she had been awake. Patty settled back laboriously in her chair and tried to look relaxed and natural with her magazine open to an advertisement of brick houses upside down, but she was holding her breath and with every heart-beat something was crying out within her that she was letting the opportunity of meeting her old-time friend go by. She might never have it again on this earth. He had drifted out of her ken these five years. She did not even know where he was living now, for her old aunt had died the winter after her visit, and there were no other ties. For some strange reason the correspondence which they had promised each other had been broken up, partly by her mother, who had discouraged her writing to boys while she was so young, especially to that boy whom she styled as "back country," and partly because of the lack of an answer to her own first letter. She had buried deep in her heart the hurt that had come after all the weeks and months of waiting for it, and tried to make pride hide her disappointment, but something in his voice, as he called, had obliterated all her resolves to be cool if she ever met him again. Somehow his voice had commenced just where they left off when they were children and in her lonely wandering state the appeal of it was very great.

Nevertheless, she held herself quiet, and waited till she heard the steps no more. Waited longer till she knew he must have decided he had made a mistake and gone on, waited with white face and sad drooping lashes on her cheeks.

Miss Cole awoke abruptly with a sort of snort, and looked at Patty keenly with a frown, as if she would read her through and through, but Patty arose and tried to cover her confusion by a bustling attention to shawls and pillows and a magazine that had fallen.

Miss Cole wanted to go in at once. It was growing cold. She had stayed out altogether too long now. Yet she would go by the lower path, which was much longer, and when Patty with glowing cheeks and downcast eyes finally acquiesced and followed her bearing pillows and shawls and other paraphernalia, they arrived at the patch of sunlight below to find it uninhabited and lonely and Miss Cole puffed and scolded all the way back up the incline as if it had been Patty's fault that they went down.

When they got back to the hotel Miss Cole said she would write some letters, and she sent Patty down to the office three times to see if the afternoon mail had come yet. Patty found it trying, but managed a roundabout way and used her eyes instead of her tongue, returning undiscovered. In fact, the young man who was the innocent cause of all this disturbance was walking several miles down the mountain very rapidly and trying to make up his mind what he would do next. He had made the experiment of calling out from the sheltered path after he had seen the girl who looked like his old friend go down in that direction, because it seemed a very good way to test out whether it was really his friend or only some one who resembled her, without making an embarrassing situation. She had not answered, and of course he had made a mistake, but somehow he felt more disappointed than the circumstances merited. After all, he had been very well content these three years he had been away in a foreign land. Why should he have such an ungovernable desire to see a girl who had not chosen to answer his many insistent letters, and who had so promptly forgotten him after their pleasant summer together? Of course she had been his beloved mother's admiration, and that probably was the psychology of the thing. He wanted his mother, missed her more every minute he stayed in this land of his birth, and his soul cried out for anything that had been dear to her or associated with her. He was foolish to think any girl could help fill his mother's place in his need! Perhaps after all it would be a wild goose chase to run away out West to find her. Why should he? Not now, anyway, not until after his tryst had been kept. Then he would know what he was going to do. That was only a week off anyway. Scarcely time for a western trip. He would get away tomorrow, if possible, or the next day at the latest. He had no relish for the sort of life his uncle was leading, and no love for the selfish old man who seemed to desire to own him body and soul probably to satisfy more selfish fancies. It disgusted him to be flaunted around like a hero, and stood up before the hotel ladies as a kind of tame pet. If it were not for the pitifulness in the old man's eyes sometimes he would go without hesitation, but something seemed to say to him that he must wait a little longer and fulfill whatever exaggerated duty had brought him here. Then he might go freely and without compunction.

He walked far down the mountain that afternoon, until the long shadows fell into the deep pool of silence in the valley, and the fragrant darkness warned him that he must go back if he did not wish to be lost on the mountainside.

He emerged from the quiet blackness of the trail at the top with a feeling of deep sadness upon him, and went straight to his room, where he found an anxious summons from the old servant. Hespur had been vibrating between his master's room and the nephew's for the last two hours, and his haggard face showed how hard his task had been. Treeves hurried to answer the call to his uncle's presence and found the old man writhing on his bed in a fit brought on by excessive anger:

"You had no right, you young rapscallion—!" he blustered furiously, his face growing purpler as he saw the young man at last. "You had no right to go off without letting anybody know—!"

"There! There, Marster! Mister Treeves, Marster!" soothed old Hespur laboriously. "The young marster he didn't realize how set you was on havin' him—!"

Treeves, furious at the injustice of the old man, yet alarmed by the condition into which he had worked himself, set himself to explain and soothe even as the servant was doing. He had wandered farther than he realized and dark caught him suddenly. The paths were obscure, and he had gone out of his way in returning. Unconsciously, as he went on talking in a gentle tone as one talks to babies and very sick people, something of the spirit of the serving man came upon him and he was able to understand how Hespur had stood all the abuse and toil during the years, and how the master had become an old child, his charge to love and protect even against himself.

There was no going down to dinner that night. A doctor was summoned and the room settled into the quiet of a sick room until at last the old tyrant slept and his nephew and servant were free to go to their rest.

After that experience Treeves decided to humor his uncle until he had recovered his former poise, and for three days he made himself as agreeable to the cranky old invalid as it was in his power to be. On the morning of the fourth day, however, matters came to a crisis. The old man announced that he felt better and that they were going down to the ballroom that night. There was to be a dance and he wanted his nephew to attend and make himself agreeable to his friends. His desire was to sit on the sidelines and watch his nephew dance with the girls he should pick out for him.

Young Treeves, after listening with growing disgust to the program marked out for him, decided that the time had come to make a stand, and with as pleasant a manner as he could summon in his present state of mind, he endeavored to explain that he had already lingered longer than he had expected, and must leave that afternoon. He had an engagement to meet of long standing, and if he went at once he would barely have time to stop for a few hours in New York and give messages to the families of two of his associates abroad. He was sorry of course to disappoint his uncle, but it really was impossible for him to remain any longer.

The old man raged and swore and raved, and then fell to begging in such a piteous wail, begging that the nephew would at least stay for that evening, the scant old tears actually coursing down his ghastly cheeks and the old servant lifted tortured eyes of appeal to his face. Here was the whole thing to go over again with the old tyrant. John Treeves's anger rose against it all. It was the same spirit that had bullied his sweet young mother. Somebody ought to have spanked the old uncle years and years ago and taken it out of him. He half turned away in disgust, and then wheeled back:

"Stop!" he commanded in the voice that during the war had always been obeyed, although he was not a commissioned officer. "Stop! You are an old coward! You have no control over yourself and no reason in your actions. You have just come out of three days' illness which you know might have been your last, brought on wholly by your own will, and kept up by your will. You are trying to bully me now into obeying your will just because you are too much of a coward to face the slightest opposition to your will. You have bullied people all your life, and I don't wonder that you are not very happy now. But didn't it ever occur to you that you never really get your way that way? You never can bully people into giving you real obedience. They may do a few things you make them do, but they hate you. You never have their love, or their real obedience, and that's what you want, isn't it? You can't ever get anything going at it that way. You've bullied a great many people in your time, but you're coming to an end, and there's God. You can't bully Him, you know!"

His voice had grown quiet and steady now and

he was looking straight and unflinchingly into the wild old eyes, holding them, controlling them, forcing them to keep quiet and listen.

The old servitor with trembling hands was holding to the footboard of the bed, and watching his master's face with sharp anxiety. This young man was standing out against the old tyrant, and the old tyrant was keeping still and listening, but what would happen next? This would kill the master, the poor—old—bad—old—master!

From the first word Calvin Treeves had fixed his bright, bad, little eyes on his nephew's face as if fascinated. It was a new thing for anyone to stand out against him. A few had opposed him, but none had stayed to reproach him—none had dared! And this young whiffet! This handsome, smart, courageous son of his own brother! This keen tongue that sounded not unlike his own in the cutting way it had of choosing words and hurling facts, whether true or false, straight into the soul of a man! Ah! This was something new. He gasped—and listened!

"And now," finished John Treeves, his tone growing steadier and quieter, like the passes of a mesmerist when he has gotten the subject under control:

"Now you're going to rest a few minutes before you have your glass of milk, and then we are going to wheel you down the pine trail under the trees awhile in the sunshine and let you see how wonderful it is outdoors to-day. We'll have a pleasant walk and then we'll have lunch together, either up here or down in the dining-room, whichever you feel able for, and after that I'm going away. I'm sorry to disappoint you, but I have got to go. It is something important in my life—"

"Is it a girl?" The little old ferret eyes fairly stuck into him like pins in their eagerness.

"No. It is not a girl!" said John Treeves emphatically.

"Will you come back again?" The voice was almost a whimper now. The old man was cowed. Hespur relaxed his hold upon the bedpost and drew a deep breath, murmuring half aloud:

"He's comin' through. My great fathers! He's comin' through! The young mister has got him an' he's comin' through!"

"Possibly," said the cool, casual, young voice. "It may depend a good deal on you. If you treat me to any more of these baby acts of yours, I'll never come within a thousand miles of you again, if I can help it. If you want to be an uncle of mine you've got to act like a MAN!"

"Now just listen to that!" murmured Hespur as he turned away weakly and looked out of the window. "Oh, my old marster! He's got you."

And it was so that Patty saw them, watching the trail from her window, where she was reading aloud to Miss Cole, who acquired a severe cold and had been obliged to spend the last three days

113

in her room much to her disgust. The old man muffled in robes and furs, peering meekly out on the splendor of the mountain, Hespur pushing the wheeled chair, and the tall, straight, young giant stalking by the side. Her heart gave a little spring of mingled gladness and worry. She had thought him gone away. There had been no sign of his presence for three whole days.

And then, that afternoon, he packed his suitcase and went away to the tryst.

"Hespur!" called the old man weakly as the young man's footsteps died away down the hall after his farewell. "Hespur!"

"Here! Sir!"

"Hespur, you've got to follow him, you have! I can't stand it not to know what he's doing."

"Yes, sir," bowed Hespur uncertainly, not unwilling. "But what, sir, will you do?"

The old man groaned:

"I suppose you'll have to leave me with that dog of a foreigner that came up from the kitchen the day you had to go up to Washington for me."

"All right, sir. I'll go, sir! When shall I go?"

"Now! Catch that same train, do you hear? But don't let him know you're on it. Don't let him see you once. Understand? Follow him every step of the way till you get to the bottom of what sent him off in such a hurry. But don't let him lay eyes on you nor suspect! Do you see?"

"I see, sir. I'll try to make it."

"Don't *try!* MAKE IT! You've GOT to make that train!"

"All right, sir!" and Hespur vanished.

Five minutes later a heavy-footed, thick-faced, stolid man-servant presented himself for orders, and Hespur, with no baggage and struggling into his overcoat as he ran, jumped into a cab and was whirled down the mountain side to the station, swinging himself on to the last car of the train as it began to move.

9

Letter from Miss Sylvia Cole to her sister-in-law, Mrs. Horliss-Cole:

Dear Kate:—

You'll find two boxes done up in tissue paper in my top drawer of the bureau. They're for your Horliss twins. I don't suppose you remembered you had any nephews or that they were due a birthday this month, but I promised them some old fashioned mittens and there they are! Don't you forget to give them to them!

I wish you'd have that Banely woman do up my black velvet dinner dress and the gray chiffon evening rag. I'm feeling better down here, and I may go down evenings sometimes. You might send my laces, too. Not that I approve of an ugly old woman in gewgaws, but of course you're so anxious about the honor of the family that I have to humor you.

There's a mob of people down here asking for you. Everybody's gone wild over a handsome young nephew of old Calvin Treeves just back from France. They say he is booked for heir. Tell Marjorie she needn't think she has to run down here and angle for him. I don't want her, she's too much trouble, and besides he has a girl already. You'd better look out for your health and cut out some of those committees. You looked as thin as a shad when I left.

As ever, Sylvia.

P.S. The charming infant you picked up on the street to take care of me is doing very well. She knows her place better than most. You needn't bother sending anybody else, I'll manage to rub along with her.

When Mrs. Horliss-Cole finished the reading of this epistle she handed it over to her daughter, who was lolling over a novel and a box of chocolates on the other side of the open fire:

"I don't know but you better run down and see what Aunt Sylvia is up to now. Something queer, I'm sure, or she never would have sent for those dresses. I begged her to take them with her, and even had Banely smuggle them into her trunk, but she fished them out and said she didn't want any fool things like that. She was only an old woman and she was going to have a good time and be comfortable. There's certainly something that needs looking into, Marjorie, and I can't leave home now. You'll just *have* to go. There are evidently young folks enough to make it lively, and you do nothing here but mope anyway. Your Aunt Sylvia will make the best of it when she finds you're there. Get ready and go down to-morrow night and I'll send Banely down with you. It'll do her good to have the trip. She can come back the next day."

Letter from Miss Sylvia Cole to her cousin, a prominent lawyer in the West:

Dear Harter:—

You did quite right about the mortgage, and I will leave the settlement of the other business to your discretion. It's better than mine any day in the week. I'm down here in the old mountain house. When Kate wants to have any big doings or put across some unusual extravagance she ships me here for rheumatism or some other fancied ill. I did have a pain in my back for a day or two caused by the damp sheets the chambermaid insists on putting on the beds, but nothing that wouldn't have got well in New York just as well. So off I was sent. However, it's just as well, for when Kate gets a notion it has to go through no matter who stands in the way, and I'm getting too old to stand between Jim and his annoyances always. If Jim can stand her let him have his fill. I enjoy getting away once in a while. If it wasn't for Jim's making such a fuss I'd have taken one of those little apartments I own in your city and kept house by myself. I'd be much happier that way, and I'm not sure I shan't do it yet sometime.

By the way, do you know any people out your way by the name of Merrill? Pretty prominent people I should imagine. There's a daughter named Patricia, or Patsy or something like that. If you happen on them tell me who they are. One meets all sorts of people at a place like this.

Speaking of Jim, he's well, but he has his hands full. Man is born to trouble as the sparks fly upward, and I guess we all get our share. But he seems to like it, so why should I worry? Remember me to Mary.

I'm glad she doesn't paint her face. Somehow the world never got what it promised to be when you and I were children. I'm sick of it.

Yours as ever, Sylvia.

When Harter Briskett read this he polished his glasses and said with a reminiscent smile, "Dear old Silver! She's the same old girl, no matter how much money she gets. I wonder if she could possibly mean the Daniel Merrills. The West is a big place. I must tell her that New York doesn't quite cover the globe! Has Dan got a girl named that, I wonder?"

Letter from Patricia Merrill to the postmaster in her western home city:

Postmaster . . .

Dear Sir: I am sending with this a package of addressed and stamped envelopes, also extra stamps with which please forward to Miss Edith Fisher all mail belonging to me until further notice. I am uncertain about my address for a time, but all mail sent to Miss Fisher will be promptly forwarded to me.

Sincerely, Patricia Merrill.

Letter from Patricia Merrill to her father, evolved after three sleepless nights and a good cry:

Dear Daddy: You will be surprised to see I am not at home, and maybe you will be afraid something is the matter. But it is perfectly explainable and I am pretty sure you will agree with me when you come home that I did right in coming with Miss Cole. You don't know her, I know, but she's a peach, and you'd like her a lot. She has a kind of grim humor that makes some people call her a grouch, but she isn't, especially when she likes you, and I'm quite sure she likes me. We are having an awfully good time together at the most beautiful spot in the South right among the pines. It is wonderful here. Mountains everywhere, and such sunsets. I don't believe they have any finer in South America, and although Daddy dear, you know how much rather I would be there with you than anywhere else on earth. But as that wasn't to be I feel that I am pretty well fixed, and if you could see me you would quite approve. You see I had to decide in a great hurry. It was one of those times you used to tell me about when one has to use the best judgment one has accumulated from all the teaching of the years. I tried to, indeed I did, Daddy, and I haven't felt self-compuncted a bit about it since, so it must have been right. I would rather not explain any further until you come back, if you don't mind, for things like that are so unsatisfactory to tell, and besides letters sometimes turn traitor and tell some one else you don't want to have know, so if you will trust me, and I know you will, dear Daddy, I'll just wait for the wherefore till you get back.

You can't tell how I am missing you, but I'm really being brave and doing just as nearly as possible what I think you would like to have me do under the circumstances. Now don't go and imagine I'm needing pity, for I'm in the most beautiful spot ever. You should see the wonderful view from my window, the plumy pines, with a hazy smoke blending them in the distance, the winding trails and the lovely smelly depths where I love to walk. Miss Cole is a peach if she is getting old. She has a grim humor that you would love, Daddy, and she likes me. She really does, I'm sure, for she sits and looks at me through her eyelashes when she thinks I'm not looking, and she has a sort of 'mother' look on her lips when I look up suddenly.

You know what I mean, Daddy dear. She tries to plan things to please me too, and we're having a beautiful time together. I read aloud to her and she likes my voice she says. I play I'm reading to you sometimes, and it makes it a lot happier time, because often I can think how you would look and what you would say to some of the things I read. I've always counted so much on getting home and reading to you because you told me once you loved it. So hurry home, Daddy dear, and I'll save up lots of nice things I think you'd like to hear. We'll read aloud every night for half an hour or so after the other folks have gone to bed or gone out somewhere times when you and I don't need to go.

So Daddy, have a beautiful time, and store up all the wonderful stories about South America for me. Remember I'm interested in every tiny thing you see and do, and hurry home to your loving daughter.

Pat.

P.S. You better just address the letters as usual, for no telling how long we'll stay here, and of course they'll be forwarded if I should stay as long as an answer to this.

Comfort yourself about me, precious father, I'm having the very best time I could have without you.

Letter from Mrs. Daniel P. Merrill to her husband's lawyer, Norris Mason, Esq.:

Dear Mr. Mason:—

I am so sorry to have to apologize for Patricia. She is such a child yet in spite of her coming of age. Last evening a friend of her school days swooped down upon her and simply carried her off for an extended trip. I hesitated very much to let her go in her father's absence, but the girls simply would not take no for an answer, and after all there was no real reason why I should interfere with her pleasure.

It never occured to me that she was due to come down to the office on her birthday and see you. Mr. Merrill reminded me just before he left that it was so arranged, but I suppose it slipped her mind as it did mine until the last minute. Then of course as everything was arranged it was too late to delay. I suppose, however, it will make no real difference to delay the conference until her return, which is a little indefinite at present, as her friends have not made all their plans. She asked me to let you know why she did not respond to the summons you sent her, and to ask if you would kindly send her usual allowance to me to forward to her, as her address was somewhat uncertain.

I hope it will in no way annoy or inconvenience you that the appointment was not kept, and suppose with Patricia that it was some mere detail of her coming of age which can as well be arranged later.

Regretting that my daughter was unable to come to the office I am very sincerely,

Anna G. Merrill.

The lawyer handed the letter over to his partner with a troubled sigh:

"I wonder what that woman is up to now!" he said.

Letter from John Treeves, addressed to Patricia Merrill, in her western home, with "To be forwarded" written across the corner:

Dear old friend:

Not that you are old, of course, only as a friend, I remember distinctly that you were just two years lacking two months younger

124

than myself. I hope you haven't forgotten.

I've been through the war, and lost my precious mother, and now I've come home and I'm lonesome and want to see some one that used to belong. I saw your double the other day, or what I suppose might be a double of what you might look like now, and it made me want to see you. I'm going back to Maple Brook to-morrow and shall be rather busy for some days, after which I expect to take a western trip—perhaps. If you are at home and care to see an old comrade write me at Maple Brook within the next week.

Here's hoping for both.

Sincerely,
John D. Treeves.

This letter was written the day before John Treeves left his uncle.

Letter from Tenbroek, Mason & Co., lawyers, to Daniel P. Merrill:

Dear Dan:—

That little girl of yours appears to have gone off on a picnic with a school friend, so I haven't been able to have the little talk with Pat I promised you on her twenty-first birthday. Your wife has written that Pat left word I should send her allowance to Mrs. Merrill and she would forward it, as the address was uncertain. I haven't done it yet. Perhaps I won't. I think I'll wait till Pat gets back. It depends on how things turn out. If I were you I'd come home as soon as you get those papers signed. Let 'prospects' go to the dogs. You are more needed here. Don't worry, of course. I just wanted to put myself on record as having broken my promise, but I guess she'll soon be home and I can keep it. If I knew where to get her I'd take a little trip and settle up, but Mrs. Merrill seemed mighty uncertain about her whereabouts when I called her up, so I'll wait a few days.

I hope you are taking it easy and getting the real rest you needed. Don't worry about business. Everything is turning out all right. The Mattison contracts came in O.K. right on the date, and everything is moving just as it ought. Here's hoping you come back soon.

As ever, Mason.

Letter from Marjorie Cole to Larcia Getchel, a school friend of the past winter and spring:

Dear Larch:

The fates are against me and I can't come to your house party! You can't think how furious I am, but mother has put her foot down hard and there doesn't seem any way to make her take it up again. I'm being hounded down to the Mountains with Aunt Sylvia under the pretext of looking after her. There's a perfectly stunning nephew of an old miser down there, and mother has heard of it. She thinks of course that he will take my mind off of Al, but she'll find she's missed her guess. I'm going to mope and mope until I get back again and have my own way. Not too much though, for mother has promised me a new fur evening coat if I go without making a fuss, so I'll wait till I get it before I mope too decidedly. Tell Al I'm no end sorry not to see him, but he understands how it is, and this is just one of the things that will balk all my plans if I don't keep my maternal parent soothed. It was perfectly ducky of you to plan it all and ask me up there, and I thought for a while I could pull it off, but it didn't work right, so I concluded I better bide my time till mother gets immersed in winter affairs, and then it will be easy to slip off for a week end real often. If that old weasel of a butler hadn't poked his nose into it I would be with you now but he thought he had to blab about my meeting Al, and of course Mother was all up in the air. But I'll be as docile as possible down in that dull old hole, and she'll forget, and let me do as I please again.

Do write me while I'm down at that tiresome old dump, and don't forget to give Al the enclosed letter, that's a darling.

Yours for keeps, Marjorie.

Telegram from Mrs. Horliss-Cole to her sister-in-law at the Mountain House:

Have room reserved for Marjorie, who will arrive to-morrow night. See that she meets the right people and don't let her get interested in any more queer people. If that Al turns up or annoys in any way telegraph or phone immediately. Marjorie will bring things. Keep me posted as to her behaviour. I'm sending Banely along.

(Signed)
Katherine Von Houghten Horliss-Cole.

Telegram from Miss Sylvia Cole to her sister-in-law, Mrs. Horliss-Cole:

128

The man's gone. He left this morning. It won't be necessary. Besides, I don't want her. I'm here resting and can't be bothered. Send things by parcel post.

(Signed)
S. Cole.

Telegram from Mr. Horliss-Cole to his sister:

Marjorie and Banely leave on to-night's train. Have room reserved. It will please me greatly if you can distract her attention for a week or so till I can get to take her on a trip somewhere.

(Signed)
Jim.

Telegram from Miss Sylvia Cole to her brother, James Horliss-Cole:

All right, only don't hold me responsible if she runs away.

(Signed)
S. Cole.

10

As John Treeves sank back in his seat in the train it was as if a great burden had rolled away, a relief come upon him. He cast off the thought of the ghoulish old man as one casts away a disagreeable duty done, and he felt free to give himself to the thought of the life that lay before him. His conscience was entirely satisfied with the forgiveness he had given to the old unrepentant soul who was his uncle, and even the pang of pity that had occasionally stirred his wrathful young heart had been amply compensated, he considered. That he should remain longer in that atmosphere of worldliness and superficial show for the sake of satisfying an abnormal pride in a man who was on the brink of the grave did not appeal to him as either a necessity or a virtue. He had done his duty, more than done it, by answering the old man's summons and by giving a tentative promise that he might return later.

Now as he sat back and looked out of the window on the rapidly passing landscape, he felt somewhat like a person who has entered a vast amphitheatre and taken a seat before the great curtain about to rise on the most important scene of his life. He felt a breathless attention and wonder as to what his eyes should see when the first act should begin. This wavering beautiful landscape of mountain and valley and soft fringe of pine with a glimmer of silver lake in the distance was like the beautiful painted curtain before the stage, and of interest because it made a fitting frontispiece for that which was to follow. In spite of his reason he found himself wondering what was behind the beauty for him in the days that were to come, as one wonders what is being arranged to be seen when the curtain rises, and what the players are doing behind the scenes in the minutes of waiting before the hour has struck.

For the next few days were to decide his future. Of that he was as certain as if a great court had so decreed it.

And now his thoughts must needs go backward, back behind those terrible days of France, of horror and uncertainty and blackness of night and pain and loss; back to a time five years ago—five years in a few days now. His birthday! And he, at his mother's request, had come home to spend it with her.

How frail she had looked and sweet and young as she stood to receive him with open arms and a smile so wonderful upon her lips, and about her eyes. Eyes which even then must have known the secret of the brief space that was to be hers yet here upon the earth. There had been something unusual about her. He had felt it even as he took her in his arms and laid his face against hers. He felt she had changed in the brief few weeks since he had left home for the fall term. She did not look sick, and her old vitality seemed to be as great as ever, no failing of breath, nor pallor; only a lovely fragility, a light in her eyes as if she had seen further into mysteries than others see, a something that made him glad he had come home, even though it had at first seemed an unnecessary extravagance after such a short absence; a great trembling in his heart for the future—the future that was now his to walk alone in a world without her.

But that day she had not let him feel sad. She had blessed him continually with her smile, and the look in her eyes, and she had been ready to make the most of every minute, for she had known he must return by the midnight train in order not to miss important classes. She had drawn him into the little cosy living room, with its table set for the evening meal they would have together that night when they should return from the day she had planned. There were the dishes he had always loved, with a bit of a flower in a clear glass vase with a slender stem. He knew the flower was the single product of the plant in the sunny window, tended and fostered for this occasion. How every little petal stood out now in clear relief, the details of that dear day. There had been other days after that, many and beautiful, but that day stood out as a notable landmark, a kind of turning point in his career.

On the table stood the willow basket already packed, the basket they had taken so many times before on little pleasant excursions together, sometimes alone, sometimes with one or two other choice friends, or again with some one who needed a rest and a bit of cheering. It was all tender and beautiful, his memory of her. He had always known it, of course, but as he reviewed it now he took in the lovely fact as he had never taken it before, and a wave of indignation went over him against the worthless old millionaire who had presumed to trample upon her. Not that he had ever been able really to hurt her, only it hurt him to think he had tried; to know that the old man could never be made to understand what exquisite holiness he had blasphemed.

There was a rug and a book, and his old cap and sweater ready also, and his mother was wearing her tramping boots and a dark blue skirt and blouse that made her look so young and girlish, with the little soft gray felt hat on her shining hair that would escape in little soft rings about her face and neck.

It had been a wonderful day, a day like this one, with sparkling air and a sky of softest blue that warmed and mellowed the red glow and the golden shimmer of autumn and parried the very thought of death that their radiant beauty foretold. They had walked to "the mountain" as they, the villagers, called it, a favorite walk with them since his childhood, and one where they had spent many a glad day together. It had seemed so natural to turn their steps that way that neither had even questioned where they were going. They just walked along together, conscious that all things troublesome were for the moment pushed back—or forward, and they were here, just they two, together for the day. There would be separations, and sorrow and disappointment perhaps, but they were not for this hour. Here was to be only peace.

It was up this mountain she had taken him when he was a little fellow, the day before he went to school, and had read to him, and played with him, and finally talked with him about the deeper things of life which he would meet out in that world to which school was to be the opening door. It was here they had come the day she told him about his father who had left them before he could remember, about his great love for his mother, and the wonderful days they had had together before he was taken away. Here they had come when he was about to unite with the church, the little old brick church in the village where his grandfather had preached, and she had talked with him earnestly about the great step which he was about to take, and together they had kneeled on the moss at the foot of a sheltering tree while she prayed for him—such a prayer! He could hear the tones of her voice even now in his soul though the words were gone beyond his memory.

Here, too, she had brought him the day her first story was accepted with an accompanying check that would make the nest egg for his college course, and sprung the surprise upon him after the day was almost over. And there were other days—the time when he was about to leave home for college—and again when he was considering whether he should go to the theological seminary and prepare for the ministry.

But this day, this twenty-first birthday of his, that was to mark a turning point in his life, a time when he should come definitely face to face with himself and his own beliefs and opinions as over against what he had been taught, he had felt underneath all the joy a sense of uneasiness back in his mind; a knowledge that there was that in his heart that would pain his mother if she knew it, and a wonder whether he would be able to keep it from her clear searching gaze. Her eyes had always been able to read his face, and his eyes had always given back glad answer to her question when he had been absent for a time. Now, however, he was conscious for the first time that he was keeping something back, something which as yet he had not given a name, and it had made him restless and ill at ease, even in his joy of seeing her.

Their walk had been much like other walks in its quiet converse; just items of the way; about a bird that flitted across the sky with a touch of silver darting across its wings in the sunlight; about the mass of color against the foot of the hill, and the tall pine that was their trysting place, far and quiet above the town, with a convenient rock for shelter from wind or sun or rain; about the braided center of the brook they paused to watch crossing the bridge, where a clutter of little golden beech leaves had patterned themselves gently in with the dimples of the stream.

The day had been much like other days, quiet and peaceful and dear. They had climbed to the top. He had noticed that his mother's step did not lag, and that the color in her face was clear, and her eyes were bright as if her interest in the day was vital, and as young as his, if not even more so, for indeed he had felt old that day, coming twenty-one, and with the burden of dawning individuality and doubt in the back of his mind.

They had eaten their delectable lunch like nectar and ambrosia after the university eating club. She had made angel cake as light as down, a great treat, because he knew it took eleven eggs, and eggs were dear. They were part of the price of his education—the eggs she raised and sold. And there was a little cup of fruit salad, oranges and grapes and other fair fruits. He could recall the delicious flavor of it all, and little chicken sandwiches cut in rounds. He smiled with a sigh as he remembered she had excused the extravagance by saying she had made a bread pudding of the edges. How they had had to think of every little trifle like that in order to get through and make both ends meet!

And there was that little good-for-nothing old man, rolling in luxury, sitting idly in his chair and cursing everything that foiled him, sending down on his tray every meal more than would have kept the two of them for a whole day, having his clawlike old fingernails manicured and his withered old countenance massaged; and his mother, his exquisite little mother, sweetly starving herself to death that she might make angel cake for her son's twenty-first birthday!

Not that he wanted any of that money, even though half of it rightly belonged to his father, who had been cheated out of his inheritance by the scheming old brother! No, he was proud that he and his mother had gotten along and held their own without assistance, but he could not forget that the uncle had refused to help in the first terrible need.

It had not been until after the napkins were folded and the basket repacked that she had settled back against the tree trunk and looked down into his eyes, as he stretched below her on the grass and said with that gentle voice of hers that somehow drew confession from the most reluctant lips,

"Now, son, what is it?"

Slowly, hesitatingly, feeling his way for the

words because he had not allowed the thoughts to take definite form before, he told her of the change that was creeping over him. He apologized for it on the ground that he supposed it was because he was beginning to be a man. He tried to belittle the significance of it, to make light of it, to treat it as if it were a mere passing fantasy, but her clear eyes saw through all his subterfuges, and he knew they did, and finally it was out in faulty hesitating sentences. He did not feel as he used to feel. He was not so sure of things. The old faith had been shaken. The things they had read and talked about together were losing their force with him, the arguments of learned men were presenting a strong and unbroken front before his faltering protest. The Bible no longer stood the matchless and perfect book of God. There were portions of it that his reason could no longer accept, although his heart was eager, anxious, for her sake, if for no other, to cling to it as long as he lived. There were glaring errors of chronology, contradictory statements, impossibilities of action, absurd dogmas—!

Little by little she drew it all from him with her strong true eyes that would not be deceived, yet seemed to hurt so as they listened. As he thought of it now at the distance of the years he could seem to see her eyes quiver and cringe as before a blow at each new revelation of his change of heart, yet she had not flinched. Those eyes had looked him bravely back with even a quiver of a smile on the lips that had grown white. She summoned strength to probe him further. Had he lost the sense of Christ? Did he mean that he no longer believed in the Deity of Christ? No, he hadn't quite gone so far yet, he owned, but she saw beyond his doubt and knew that he was wavering in that direction.

Her lashes had drooped low on her white cheeks and she had been silent awhile struggling with her own emotions. He knew she felt she must not let him see the shock it had been to her. Perhaps he had not known it so surely then as now that it was a terrible shock. It was nearly five years ago, and he was young then—ages younger, it seemed, than now.

How she had swept those long lashes up at him suddenly with a piercing look of deep indignation in her eyes, and a tremble of wrath in her voice as she asked:

"And those teachers of yours that are so wise, have they given up God, too?"

"Oh, no," he hastened to tell her. "No, they were sure of a Supreme Power"—and he hastened on with the rigmarole that had worn its way into the wall of faith she had wrought so hard to build about her son.

They had talked until sunset, quietly on the whole, yet underneath each knew that the soul of the other was writing in torture. He did not want to hurt her, and she knew it, but yet neither could he deceive her, for so she had ingrained the truth in his soul. In his young arrogance he had not seen the depth of her anguish then. He knew it now. The sorrow of the years had taught him what she had suffered, she whose faith was supreme and whose love for him was unalterable. The agony of having dealt that blow to her had been growing in him all the way home, was almost unbearable now, as he neared the old home and the trysting place, he felt as if he could not go there where she had been and know that his last talks with her had all been of alienation. For though she had struggled against it, and sought with all her strength of will and winning love to hold him to the old ways, she had seen him drifting away more and more each time, and he had felt a sort of fatality in it.

He marveled as he thought of her own faith. That in itself ought to have held him to something. What was that verse he used to read with her, "But continue thou in the things which thou has learned and hast been assured of, knowing of whom thou hast learned them; and that from a child thou hast known the Holy Scriptures which are able to make thee wise unto salvation through faith which is in Christ Jesus."

Were they? Was that true? Had he made a mistake to leave faith for reason? Well, he would know. If there was such a thing as finding out he would do it now. He had promised her and he would do it. Nothing should be left undone that he could do to bring back the old faith, the old assurance that these things she had taught him were true.

She had not attempted argument that day. It was as if she had seen the whole thing coming and had been praying about it, as one accepts a terrible illness laid upon a loved one. So quietly, so pitifully she had taken her stand, as if he were under some kind of hallucination. She was so sure, and so uplifted by her faith. She had not advised him to drop his theological studies. She wanted him to go on a little further. She hoped, he could see, that the way would clear again, and his faith shine out the brighter because of the momentary dimming. She had asked him to promise to read his Bible and to pray more than he had ever done before, and she had reiterated the promise that whosoever would do His will should know. And he was willing enough until they came to the question of what was "doing His will." Right there they had split. She said always first, "And this is His will that they might believe on His name," and this phrase had become a meaningless chant on his ear. His interpretation had been to love his neighbor and do good to those in need. He felt that in service should that "doing" be found. He had given himself to social service, spending all his time not actually needed for his studies in a large city settlement, toiling earnestly in the slums to uplift fallen humanity. He learned many useful things, but he did not learn assurance of his faith in Christ. His mother said he was not "doing the will" and therefore could not claim the promise. He continued to recite to her his sacrifices, and she only looked at him with deep, sorrowful eyes, and that faraway smile that haunted him always after he had gone back to the University and his theology, and once when he had spoken of a life of sacrifice as the supreme offering that a man may render his Maker, she murmured sadly: "Behold, to *obey* is better than sacrifice. His orders are to *believe*."

But he had turned away impatient and found fault with her for being narrow and old-fashioned. He had told her the times were changed since his grandfather's day, that this was the age of progress. Science had made great strides, men must not be tied by the superstitions of the past— and then he had turned and found her weeping quietly, as if she would not be comforted, and then he had been obliged to go to his train while she still wept uncomforted. Indeed, what comfort was there for him to give, since he must be honest?

John Treeves had long ago settled down in his seat in a hunch with his hat drawn over his eyes. There were tears in his eyes now as he sat there with the rumbling of the train jolting his aching head, and pounding in rhythm with his aching heart. For all at once it came to him that old Calvin Treeves had not been half as cruel to this gentle mother of his as he, her loving son, had been, for he indeed had broken her heart.

It was only a week and a day after that sorrowful leavetaking that they sent him word that she had taken pneumonia and was very sick. He had hastened to her bedside and sat with her night and day, but had known from the start that she was steadily slipping from him. And hour after hour, as he sat staring blankly before him, longing with all his heart to do something to comfort her, knowing there was but one thing he could do, yet helpless to do it it seemed, because the air seemed leaden and dark about him and the sky was black above. Then most unexpectedly she had opened her eyes with the old sweet smile and looked into his very soul:

"Son, you will promise me something—," her voice was the faintest whisper:

He bowed his head and sobbed upon her hand, "Anything, anything, mother darling!" then waited breathlessly to hear her words:

"You will not preach—*against*—him!"

"Never, Mother. Never!" he raised his head vehemently.

She smiled and seemed relieved. For a time, she held his hand and later she slept. Most miraculously from that hour she grew better. The last afternoon before he went back to his studies they sat together. She was able to talk a little now, but the main subject of their thoughts had not been broached between them. As the shadows grew dusky in the room, and the flame of the open fire flickered softly on the hearth, she put out her hand to his.

"Dear, I've been thinking. There is something else I'd like you to promise me."

The pressure of his hand told her she had her wish:

"I have read somewhere about the Indians, that when an Indian boy comes to the age of manhood there is a certain rite which he must perform before he can cast aside the garments and the name of his childhood, and become a man. He goes apart into a lonely place in the wood or desert where he can commune with himself and the Great Spirit and there he meditates, and chooses his new name, the name of some animal whose skin he is henceforth to wear like an amulet, a name which shall be significant of the life he means to lead. When I read it I thought it would be good if all young men went apart to meditate with God before they took upon them the sacred responsibility of manhood. And I would like my son to do that. When you have finished your studies I have a fancy that you should go to the old rock on the mountain where you and I have gone together so often and stay there until you have found yourself and your new name, and know what you ought to do in life. I want you to get away from the world long enough with God and the Bible and search for Him, honestly, with your whole heart. He has promised that you shall find Him when you shall search for Him *with all your heart,* and I feel sure that He will keep that promise to you and to me. And so I have written you a letter, see, it is sealed, and I will put it in the little secret drawer of my desk where you used to love to go and find your father's picture and the little Bible I carried to church when I was small. No, son, don't open it now. It is for that day, when you shall go alone into the open and stay till you find God. Take my Bible with you, and my letter, and stay until you have found Him and He has told you if you are to preach for Him, and what you are to say. If you find Him not you will not have searched with all your heart, and YOU MUST NOT PREACH. But—YOU WILL FIND HIM. He never fails.

"See, I have thought it all out. You will be twenty-four, almost when you are through your studies. Take a little rest during the summer, just to get away from all you have been thinking and studying, get out and be glad in the out of doors, and then on your twenty-fourth birthday, or later if anything hinders your graduation, take the letter, and the Bible and go apart to fast and find your soul and your God. Will you do this for me? Will you keep this tryst with God?"

And he had bowed his head and promised.

The war had come and whirled him away into a purgatory of time just as he was through his studies, and now, two years later, he was back and his twenty-sixth birthday was approaching, was but three days off, and he was on his way to keep the tryst. But the mother who had sent him had slipped away to God while he was in France, and the news of her going had come to him like a shock after the war was over, when he was almost on his way back to her, and he had only her letter, the unread letter, and her precious marked Bible to take with him into the wilderness to the trysting place.

11

The little white bungalow at the extreme end of the village street, in Maple Brook, had not been opened since the neighbors straightened everything with mathematical precision on the afternoon after the funeral, and when John Treeves, weary and heart sick, put the key in the latch and threw the door open, a dusty, unfamiliar atmosphere flung out to greet him. The little home where his mother and he had spent so many happy hours seemed an alien place in that first breath. But when he had stepped in and closed the door, and lighted a lamp that still had some oil left in it, the old sweet home look rushed around him and stung the tears into his eyes. There on the mantel was the clock he had saved up his pennies to buy for her on Christmas, staring at him with silent face, a kind of epitome of all the loneliness since the dear mother who was the heart of the home had gone away. The stone about the rugged little fireplace had been scrubbed clean of all suggestive cosy smoke, and the fireplace was empty, swept and garnished with only a laurel leaf and a spray of dead asparagus fern as a reminder of funeral flowers. He strode over and brushed them down the ash damper out of sight with a sigh that was almost a groan, and dropped into her little cushioned chair beside the hearth, his head upon his hands:

"Oh, Mother! Mother! Mother!" he moaned, and the agony reached to the curtained window sash where a man stood outside with his ear strained, and his eyes vainly trying to see what was going on inside. Something in the voice brought a choking feeling into old Hespur's throat, and made him rub his eyes hastily.

By and by John Treeves summoned courage to go the rounds of the little house, and look into every dear corner. It seemed almost as if he must find her somewhere if he only searched long enough. It was worst when he came to his mother's bedroom, with the closet door just a bit ajar and a corner of her pretty blue and white bathrobe glimpsing out so naturally, as if she had just cast it aside.

He did not feel like eating, though he had bought some things in the city before coming out and had intended to cook himself some supper. Instead he snatched the little faded bathrobe from its hook, and wrapping it in his arms flung himself down upon her bed, with his face in her dusty pillow, and there he fell asleep.

Old Hespur, outside in the starlight, waited long and anxiously, but at last concluded the young man was asleep, and crept away to find a scanty lodging for himself. It was hard on a man who was getting old and had been used to ease and luxury to knock around like this and not know from hour to hour what was to be his portion, but Hespur would go through fire for his crabbed old master. Some might have thought it was for hope of gain, but it was in reality for love of his pitiful old charge. Besides, Hespur found a warm spot in his heart for this spirited youth who was so like, and yet who had so little toleration for his old uncle. It was only a haymow, nesting warm in the hay that old Hespur found for a lodging that night, for the village were all asleep. But he stole forth at daybreak and found food and water and a place to make a hasty toilet, and then hastened back to watch the little white cottage at the end of the street.

It was high noon when John Treeves, wearied

with his journey and the sorrow of his home-coming, awoke to life again and remembered that it was his birthday, and what he had to do that day. A strange reluctance was upon him as he thought of it, an apathy about life in general, and this day in particular. Somehow he shrank as he was face to face with his promise. He turned his face to the pillow and closed his eyes, wishing with an inexpressible longing that he might just lie here and breathe away his life in sleep, and be put beside the mother who loved him. What was the use in going out into the wilderness in search of a God who had not chosen to come to him?

But when he arose and dashed cold water in his face, and began to go about and think of the day, a kind of excitement began to fill him. A fine enthusiasm for the duty, or should he call it a privilege that was before him? It was the only thing left that he might do for his mother and it was a sacred promise. Then, too, there lay beneath it all a hope that after all he might find his mother's God. It was vague and faint, for he had been through too much to have many illusions left, but still it was there. And if he should find him—Ah! He would follow all his life. It was the utmost he could do to atone for the sorrow his loss of faith had caused her. What a fool he had been not to have known her agony in the full measure of its meaning. Somehow he might have ended it sooner, perhaps by the sooner seeking. By sticking to the old ways and attending church and doing Christian work, the work she loved. How arrogant he had been in his pride that he had cared more to speak out the truth of his doubts than to try to find a way to keep his faith. It puzzled him now to think that he had not tried to stop the flow of doubts, to have kept at least a semblance of the old ways for her sake. What a fool he had been not to know he was walking over her heart every moment! Would that pain in her eyes haunt him the rest of his life?

And it was of her he was thinking as he took his way, with only his mother's Bible and the letter, and went forth into the wilderness on his search.

The day was bright and clear with a warmth in the air that was unusual for that climate and that time of year; and the sky was blue and misty with that highness that comes on days when the mystery of Heaven seems to be about the earth. But his feet dragged as he walked, for it seemed that every step that took him to the old trysting place made him more conscious of the absence of the one who had made those trips so wonderful, and been the heart and life of the day.

And behind him, at a great distance, so that he would not be noticed, walked old Hespur, dodging behind trees at any turn of the road where his quarry might turn and look back, but always keeping him in view.

The road wound across a stream, and gradually

up, up the "mountain." John Treeves walked on with head down, observing nothing as he mounted to the crest above him. Worn out, absorbed with his own thoughts, he dropped upon the hard earth underneath the old tree and buried his face in his hands.

Half an hour later old Hespur, puffing and panting, halting, and all but exhausted, toppled to the crest of the hill, gave one swift glance about, sighted the huddled figure under the bare tree, and slid down out of sight. Stealthily he circuited the great rock, and climbed again until he reached a position where he could see and not be seen, and there he sat him down to wait and try to understand.

Was this lad bent upon some evil deed, and was his conscience repenting him? Or had he come here for some mysterious secret meeting? Perhaps he was a spy! Or again, it might be a girl! Some girl that his friends did not approve. But no! He had no friends from all accounts, save a few villagers in the hamlet below the hill, and perhaps some far-away soldiers in France. And it was plain as the nose on your face that he did not care a whit what Calvin Treeves thought or wished. Old Hespur decided that here must be some deep-laid plot, perhaps for a nationwide reformation of some sort. He had faith enough in the fine brow and the strong Treeves chin to know it was nothing evil. And so old Hespur waited, and from time to time peered forth from his hiding place to see if his companion was still there.

Once he heard the rattle of a paper, and strained his neck to try and see what like it was, for he knew of old that his master was interested in all possible details, and had often been put to it to invent enough to satisfy him.

The letter that John Treeves finally opened tenderly and read with blurring eyes and choking breath was such a letter as could only be written by a consecrated mother who had agonized over her beloved child, and had pleaded with God for his salvation from the infidelity of the world. There was no ranting nor pleading, no attempt at learned argument, nor quotation from theologians. She did not attempt to refute the so-called science wherewith he had bolstered his new freedom from the faith of his fathers. She simply set them all aside and told him that reasoning of man was vain. That religion was a spiritual thing and must be tested spiritually. God was a spirit and those that reached Him must reach out their spirits, not their intellects, to grasp Him. The Bible and its claims either were true or else they were not, and it was quite easy for anyone who cared to put them to the test. Wisdom and knowledge were vain without that spiritual outreaching. Wisdom and knowledge would fall into place and be found all harmonious when the approach was made first by the spirit. Science and knowledge changed from year to year, but there had not been wanting those in every age who had found God by searching for Him with all their hearts, and by taking Him at His Word. That was what she asked of her son, to "search with all his heart," and to make it possible for God to show him the truth, by complying with the conditions of the promises in the Bible.

She recalled to his mind how Abraham had belonged to a heathen nation and had heard God's call and had enough faith in the promise to take his family to a foreign land and become a new nation. She had marked the main great promises, beginning back when God first led His people, and she asked him to read them aloud to himself there on the hill, and then to talk with God about them until he should know. That was the main emphasis, that he should stay there until he should know one way or the other whether he was to be a child of God or not.

There was no pleading with him to get ready to come home to her as some mothers would have written; there was throughout the whole epistle a tender confidence as of one giving directions of a well-known oft-trod way, to another in the dark, with the surety that he would follow and find the way home.

When he opened the little Bible there were no blisters of tears on its thin, worn pages. The print was as clear as when it was new, though the edges of the leaves were frayed and crumpled with much use. He could almost see his mother's confident smile as she bent over the beloved pages. Her faith reached through the years of separation even though a grave was between, and seemed to be drawing him on. He began to wonder how with such a mother and such teaching he had ever got away from it all.

A fine shame and contempt of himself burned within him, while yet he felt that it had been the natural outcome of his own development. And yet, as he held that beautifully worn Bible in his hand, he felt how audacious it had been for him to have the temerity to draw away. He seemed to see his mother's face as it used to look when she read to him on Sunday afternoon; and then the strong yet tender face of his grandfather, her minister-father, whom he dimly remembered, whose powerful and convincing sermons had been only excelled by his devoted self-forgetfulness for others. And yet, on the other hand, stood a goodly company of wise and learned professors, with scholarly countenances, with dignified and cold demeanor, and a bit of a sneer on their lips; he knew like a well-read book the reasoning by which they would try to sweep away his mother's faith with such adjectives as "emotional" and "sentimental" and the like. And he in between the two must act independent of either scholars or mother, and must go out alone to meet God, even as the Wise Men had searched, and studied and fared forth, led by some inner call, to find the light. He had come here to do this, and here he would stay until it was done, although his soul shrank inexpressibly from the ordeal.

Something seemed drawing him back, away from the things he had thought and believed as a little child, something seemed crying out to him that it was foolish and ridiculous for him, a grown man, to take a group of legends and treat them seriously, putting in claims on their strength before he had assurance. And yet—that was what faith was, a taking things on trust—a swinging off and acting as if things were so! That was what his mother had done, and it had stayed by her through the struggle of life clear to the end and kept her sweet and strong—yes, and happy, even through sorrow and toil and disappointment. He recalled the messages she had left for him, and knew that even on her death-bed she was happy in her faith; that with her last breath she spoke the name of Jesus, with a happy smile, as if her faith had been justified. There was absolutely nothing that could stand as an argument against that, though he was fully aware that some cold stranger might urge the whole thing a bit of imagination supplemented by sentiment. But he knew his mother too well to accept any such theory. And there he was, in a strait betwixt two kinds of reasoning when his eyes came to the very verse she had quoted in her letter as an initial promise: "And ye shall seek me and find me, when ye shall search for me *with all your heart!*"

Well, how did one search? He would begin. He would put the full strength of his purpose into it, and dispose of this question one way or the other, now and forever. It was queer though, this searching for a thing in which one did not believe. He read the verse over again, "Ye shall find me when ye shall search." It suddenly came over him that this believing after all was a voluntary act of the will. He could decide to act on a certain hypothesis and go ahead, whether he was really assured of it or not. It was the first time that the idea had presented itself to him in that way. When his mother had asked him to "only believe," he had responded, "I would gladly, if I could." He had always supposed that he must wait for assurance or until the power to believe was given him. Now he suddenly saw that if he willed to believe he could act upon that with as much success as if he knew that the hypothesis were true. It was like getting into a car, or a boat; one might not believe that it was seaworthy, or able to travel, but one could put one's self in its seat and wait for the car to give the assurance. He would try that. He would put himself into God's hands, and see if He would "be found of him."

"Well, then, I will do it now!" he said aloud with decision, and the words echoed back to him from an opposite hill with startling distinctness.

He arose and stood for a moment looking up uncertainly to the brilliant autumn sky, as one approaching gazes up at the house of a stranger upon whom one is about to call. Then with great reverence he knelt beneath the tree with bared head, and as he did so, as clearly and distinctly as if a voice had spoken them came the words he had learned so long ago sitting beside his mother on Sabbath afternoons: "Then shall ye call upon me and ye shall go and pray unto me, and I will hearken unto you. And ye shall seek me and find me, when ye shall search for me with all your heart."

Instantly as if it had been a rope thrown out to him in the midst of an overwhelming tide he seized it with his heart and began to cry aloud to God, "Oh, Lord, I take Thee at Thy word! A God cannot lie! I have come with my whole heart to search for Thee! Oh, be found of me, be found of me, for my soul is in great distress!"

Old Hespur, trained to respect royalty above all else in the universe, at the word "Lord" scrambled to his feet and peered out from his hiding in wonder, but seeing the young man upon his knees, and perceiving no other presence, he got quickly into the attitude of respect and attention, and thus stood behind the great rock for a long time stilled with awe and delight, scarcely daring to breathe lest he should break the mysterious audience, standing as any well-trained servant would stand immovable in the presence of a great and kingly guest.

But no sound of rattling stone or crunching gravel reached the ear of the young man upon his knees. His soul was in the presence of his God and his spirit was holding communion with Him. Every longing that had ever been unsatisfied, every doubt that had clouded his faith, every rebellion that had hindered his growth, these were poured forth from the very depth of his being and laid before the God whom he had come to find. Then like troops of bright angels for everything he had to say, came the promises of God, both from the Old and New Testaments, especially promises concerning Jesus Christ. They were verses he had learned long ago, and thought he had forgotten, perhaps, at least they had not been in his mind for years, though if anyone had asked how they ran he could always have repeated them. But now they came as though fresh and new and spoken like a voice ringing through his soul with a thrill of truth that was amazing, and with a preciousness that was unspeakable and almost incredible; and they seemed not so much to fall into his mind, but into his heart to be put within the voluntary powers of his mind. All the old doubts, the old fallacies, the old impossibilities, were as if shut behind locked doors, rubbish that had nothing to do with the case. What were they after all but the product of men's minds? This was real, this spiritual communion, more real than anything that had ever come into his life, only approached in part by the love of his mother and his life with her. This was something that took hold of his spirit and made him live as he had never dreamed life could be; it was inexplicable, exalting, glorious beyond expression, something for which he would willingly exchange all the worldly knowledge and wisdom he had ever gained. How trivial they seemed to him now. How easily he had been fooled into unbelief by them. Why, why had he not known! How could he have been so deceived?

Then, as if in a revealing light, he saw himself as a sinner. He had never felt condemned before, for he knew that as men went he had lived on the whole a most exemplary life so far, clean and wholesome and kindly. That had been the result of his mother's training and rather an inheritance than a voluntary or virtuous act however; this he now plainly saw. But he saw also that the great sin, the sin of which he had been guilty, had been the neglect of God, the leaving of Christ out of his life, and at once it became clear to him that all sin was comprehended in that one sin, the turning away from Salvation, rejecting Christ and His atonement. His indifference of the past seemed an active ugly thing hurled at the Christ, and he bowed his head at the thought of it, and as if in answer came the words "Come now and let us reason together, saith the Lord, though your sins be as scarlet, they shall be as white as snow; and though they be red like crimson, they shall be as wool." He found himself repeating the words with the Voice, in a note of triumph, and the sense of sin rolled away so completely that he was troubled.

"But I am a sinner!" he kept saying over to himself; "and I should feel condemned! Can I have grieved away His spirit?"

Again came promises, words from the old prophets: "In that day there shall be a fountain open . . . for sin and for uncleanness." "I, even I, am he that blotteth out thy transgressions for mine own sake, and will not remember thy sins." "I have blotted out as a thick cloud thy transgressions, and, as a cloud, thy sins: return unto me; for I have redeemed thee."

His mother's Bible lay on the ground beside him, but he hardly needed to take it up, and turn its pages, so rapidly did the promises come, even before his eyes caught the words with his mother's markings here and there underlining words; and with them came a new clear meaning that he seemed always to have known, but never before apprehended. He talked aloud to God about them until the high, clear day became more glorious it seemed to him than any day that had ever dawned before.

The little quiet village lay like a painted thing

set in its autumn foliage with the little jeweled stream winding through the valley, and in the distance darted a train of cars with its stream of trifling smoke, threaded its way among the trees, paused a brief space, and hurried on to busy cities beyond the hills; but the quiet trysting place was undisturbed as Heaven, and had become a holy place.

12

The man Hespur stood at attention for so long that his old bones ached, and he trembled with the cold, for the air was keen in that high place, and Hespur had not come prepared for camping out as had the man he was watching, and at last during an interval when Treeves had risen with the book in his hand and his eyes thoughtfully fixed on the far hills, the old man silently unbent, and dropped stealthily to the dry moss at his feet, worn out with exhaustion.

For a long time the young man continued to walk up and down on the bluff at the top of the hill, reading—sometimes aloud, sometimes dropping upon his knees and praying. The tired old watcher drowsed a bit and waked to watch uneasily, half-awed, half-impatient, and could not quite make out if it were really prayer or not, this familiar talk with one who seemed not to be there.

More than once he furtively stole a glance around the background to make sure no one else was present, and then he settled down once more, for he was still his master's servant and the orders had been to follow and find out. He could not leave till he was certain what was coming, and this impressive uncanny scene filled him with varied emotions that were overwhelming. But when he got a view of the young man's face and saw the light and uplift there, something seemed to quiet his impatience and fill him with a longing to be out there too with God. Some old disquiet stirred within his soul and made him think of life and how near was another world—only a step!

The afternoon wore away and still that quiet figure waited behind the rock, hungry now, and shivering at intervals, for the air had grown keen and still the young man on the point of the hill sat beneath the tree turning the leaves of the Bible, or gazing across the valley into the distance. The sun grew ruby clear and dropped slowly with a cheek on either neighboring hill, and Treeves closed the Bible and knelt again with reverent face uplifted to the sky:

"Oh, Jesus Christ," he prayed aloud, "if you want me, if you can use me, if you will make me fit, I will preach Thy Gospel. I give my life to thee forever more!"

There was a look of profound ecstasy on the young, strong, uplifted face in the light of the setting sun, and the watcher marveled as he looked and bowed his head with a half-murmured "Amen!"

With a light, quick step John Treeves walked down from the mountain top back to the world again after his sojourn in the desert. His feet seemed to have wings and need no guidance from his mind and he went through the shadows like one who had a purpose. Hespur, as he stumbled cautiously on behind, left in shadow because of his slow-going, felt the darkness coming with a kind of dread new to him. He was not a man of fear, but he had seen a sight that afternoon that had made him conscious of another world lying all about him, and he was afraid to be left alone. For the first time in forty years he wished for his mother, and felt a smarting, choking sensation in his throat and eyes as if he were going to cry. As he stumbled through a tangle of prickly blackberry branches into a clearing, he brushed his hand across his eyes to wipe away the blur and murmured: "He's a fine young man, he is, and he's all right. The old man'll be that mad! But the young one's *all right!*"

An hour later Hespur, footsore, cold, weary, and hungry, having seen his charge enter the little bungalow at the end of the village street, sat himself down at the deserted dining-room table of the only lodging house the village boasted and ordered a large meal. And while he waited he consumed quantities of excellent bread and butter with maple syrup from a glass pitcher in the middle of the table. Fasting and prayer might agree with younger men, but if he had it to do over again he would provide himself with a pocketful of sandwiches, or at least some malted milk tablets.

The next morning, having satisfied himself that his charge was well into the work of sorting and packing away his mother's things and likely to be anchored for a day or two more at least, Hespur boarded a train for the South, and within a few hours presented himself before his master, who greeted him with pitiful joy and wrath.

Two old men together, they almost forgot their usual relation in their satisfaction of being together again. Hespur even forgot himself once and sat down on the edge of a chair while he was talking, for indeed the trip had been wearing and he was not so young as once; but he arose almost immediately and stood stiffly before his master, who was squeaking out little querulous questions:

"You say he walked out in the country and climbed a mountain and stayed there all day without any food? I don't understand what he was doing."

"Why, sir," said Hespur searching his mind for the right thing. "Why, sir, sometimes he appeared to be reading."

"Reading! Reading! What nonsense! Why should

he climb to the top of a mountain this time of year to read? What was he reading? Were you near enough to see?"

"Yes, sir. That is, sir, I couldn't but help knowing, because he read it out, sir. I sort of recognized it as it were, you know, sir."

"Well, what was it?" snapped the old man. "Why don't you say?"

"Why, sir, as far as I could rightly hear, sir, I might have been mistaken, of course, sir, but it seemed, sir—"

"Well, why don't you get there? Why don't you speak? Are you afraid to say it, or what is the matter? WHAT was my nephew READING!"

The last words were fairly shouted and the old man was growing apoplectic.

"Why, sir, now, sir, don't get excited, sir! You know what the doctor said the consequences might be, sir!"

"Shut up about the doctor and tell me what I want to hear!"

"There, there, Mister Treeves, I'm getting there fast as I can!" soothed the servant. "I think, sir, he was reading the Bible!"

"The Bible! The *BIBLE!*" fumed the old man. "You old rascal you, do you mean to tell me you would know the Bible if you heard it?"

"I think, sir, I might, sir," said the servant humbly, "but I might have made a mistake, sir, of course, sir. There's many queer modern things written to-day, sir, and I can't pretend to keep up with the new-fangled kinds of religions, but it really sounded to me, sir, like what my old mother in England used to read by the fireside when I was a boy back in the old country."

"Well, get a Bible then and show me what he read. I suppose you'd know it again if you knew it once, wouldn't you?"

"I might, sir, and then again I mightn't. You know, sir, if I remember rightly, that Bible is somewhat of an extended book, and he turned over many pages, sir, and read little pickings, sir, like you take the nice bits from the tray, sir, that comes up for you to eat. But here was one I could mostly remember if I tried, I think. He said it over so many times. It was something like about going to hunt for God and finding Him if you was in earnest about it when you went. And he—"

"Well, what did he do?" shouted the impatient invalid. "You act as if you were afraid to tell!"

"Oh, no, sir, I'm not afraid to tell. It isn't that, but I think, sir, he was in earnest, and he was hunting. It was a queer thing to do, sir, and one that I never heard of a man doing before, sir, in all my experience, which has been many, sir, but I think if you was to ask me, sir—"

"Get away with all that muddle of words, you rascal! Get to your point. What do you think?"

"Well, I think, sir, as he went out to that lonely place on a mountain *to hunt for God!*"

There was an awesome reverence about the old servant's voice that made his words tremendously impressive. The old man looked at him wildly with his little restless eyes, and then glanced fearsomely behind him and shuddered.

"Don't be a FOOL!" he bawled out. "*WHY* do you think such a nonsensical, unreasonable, lunatic thing as that?"

"Because, sir," quite humbly, "he *said* as much, sir."

"Do you mean he talked to you about it, Hespur?"

"Oh, no, sir! He was talking to God, sir, as far as I could make out, sir. He was down on his knees and looking up into the sky, sir, and he said just like this, just like he might be talking to a friend you know, he cried out, 'Lord, you know that I'm hunting for you with all my heart, and I've come here to pray to you because you promised to hear me and let me find you,' or words to that effect, sir. Just like that, sir!"

"Hespur! You don't think he's out of his mind, do you?"

"Oh, no, sir, not at all, sir. On the contrary, after listening to him all day I came to the conclusion, sir—"

"*Well!* Why don't you SAY what conclusion you came to?"

"Well, I thought perhaps, sir, it might be the rest of us, begging your pardon, of course, sir, who was off our minds."

"What do you MEAN, you old rascal you? I'll discharge you some day pretty soon if you don't look out."

"Well, you see, sir, listening to him for some time, sir, it became quite clear that we are all more or less going to die sometime soon, sir—!"

"WH-H-H-A-AT!"

"Well, sir, I wasn't meaning one more than another, you know—"

"Now you're ex-CI-I-T-ing me! And you know what the doctor said—!" The old man was all of a quiver, and fear crouched in the beady old eyes, fear of his enemy, the only enemy his money had not been able to buy out ahead of him as the years had gone by. Always there had lurked ahead that DEATH, peering round at him menacingly from every corner, and always he had known that one day it would get him—

"Well, sir,—I'm sorry to stir you, sir,—but you would have the telling, sir, and if you'll permit me, sir, it wasn't so exciting a thing when you heard what he read, sir. And if you'd have seen his face, his fine young face with the joy on it as he said the words—words about not being afraid, sir, when the time comes and all that, sir—"

"Well, you needn't talk about it. I don't want to have it rubbed in that I'm getting old—"

"Oh, you're holding your own fine, Mister Treeves—!"

"Shut up! You know that's a lie! Go get a Bible!"

"Yes, sir, I'll enquire if there's one about, sir—"

"Of course there's one about. You get it, and get it quick! I want to see what that young rascal's about anyway."

Hespur departed hurriedly, and returned in a few minutes with a deprecating air.

"They don't seem to have any, not so you'd call it handy, down in the office, sir," he apologized, "and I don't really suppose, sir, that they'd have much call for a thing like that in a place like this where everybody's pretty well off and comfortable like. But the head-waiter did say there was a little girl that helps the chambermaid who was sort of religious like and he's sent to see if she's got one. If she has he'll borrow it for you. I'm sorry I didn't think to stop off in Washington and get you one, but it never entered my head like that you'd care to go to that length, sir. I'm sorry you have to depend on a serving maid, sir, for the book you want, but I asked the man down on the golf links they said was some kind of a preacher if he had one by him and he said no, when he came off on a vacation he wanted to get away from all that sort of thing for a little rest, sir, and he never brought one along, and I suppose, too, that would be quite reasonable, one having to do so much reading of the Bible all the year round being a preacher!"

"Shut your chatter!" snapped the old man, "and tell me what my nephew did. How did the thing end, anyway?"

"Why, he told Him he was going to be a preacher!"

"HE told WHO?"

"Why HIM, the Lord."

"What do you mean?"

"I mean he just talked to Him like I'm talking now to you. He lifted up his face, and you could see he was seeing with his spirit something that wasn't there to eyes. He was seeing God with his soul as near as I could make out, and talking to him right then and there. They got it all planned out between them what he was to do, I think, sir, and I guess there's no going back on that!"

"We'll see!" chattered the old man. "WE'LL SEE! We'll see what MONEY will do!" and his eyes gleamed with grasping satisfaction.

"Now, now, sir, if I was you, sir, I just wouldn't set my heart on that. He's a real headstrong young man, and if I'm thinking rightly, he's got a real headstrong God alongside of him to back him up. I don't think it would be much use, sir, really, and you'd only excite yourself, sir, without any results. You see, sir, that young man has got the same blood in his veins you have, and he's pretty determined. It would be like fighting yourself, sir, if you was to try to turn him. And he's already promised, sir. I wouldn't to try if I was you. It might make it more hard for you later, you know, sir, for you can't get away from things like that when you come to the place where things end. Not that it's near at hand at all, of course, sir, but WHEN it does, I say, you'll be sorry, sir, if you try."

"Shut your chatter! I don't need your advice. I'm going to sleep now, and when you get that Bible I want you to look up all the verses you can find that my nephew read and read them to me just as he read them, do you understand? And if you can't find them I want you to go out to those golf links and find that fool preacher and tell him Calvin Treeves wants him to find those verses and mark them. See? And you can give that servant woman a five-dollar note for her Bible and tell her I'll keep it. Now, pull down those blinds and draw up that afghan and get out! I'm going to sleep!"

13

"Well, she's coming!" remarked Miss Cole with grim satisfaction, throwing down a letter on the night stand beside the bed. "I thought that would bring her. Now, Cousin Edith Fisher, I want you to understand that you're Marjorie Horliss-Cole's cousin as well. No, you needn't put on that impossible stone-wall look. I'll fix it all right with Marjorie. She may be a little high-minded at first, but I know how to manage her, and I'm determined she shall have you for a companion— with a little c—for a while. You see, she needs you. I've been watching you for a whole week now and I'm convinced that a course of you will do her a world of good and get some of the notions out of her head."

"Oh, Miss Co—Cousin Sylvia, I mean— really—I—"

"Nothing of the sort! Fiddlesticks! Now don't get up in the air! It won't hurt you a particle. In fact, I believe you'll rather enjoy it, so go ring the bell and have my breakfast sent up. I didn't think the mail would come so soon or I'd have been up before this. Marjorie comes tonight and we've several things to do to get ready for her. No, you needn't bother with that kimono, I'm going to get right up."

"What is there to do?" asked Patty quietly, a tone of dismay in her voice. Things had just simmered down so pleasantly and she and Miss Cole were enjoying themselves together so much, reading aloud and taking walks and drives about the beautiful mountain country.

"Oh, nothing very serious. But it may take time. Just pull out that big hamper that came yesterday from New York, won't you, and open it while I get into my battle array."

Patty went soberly about the work, and for a few moments there was silence while Miss Cole dressed and Patty worked with unaccustomed fingers over the heavily knotted cords that fastened the canvas cover.

"There's the key," said Miss Cole briskly, fumbling among the pile of morning mail on her bed stand and tossing a small tagged key to the girl. "Just unlock it and take things out. Spread things around on the chairs anywhere. I want to see what's there."

Patty opened the big willow hamper, threw back the tissue-paper covers and gave a soft exclamation of girlish delight.

"Oh!" she cried. "I suppose they are Miss Horliss-Cole's things! Aren't they lovely! Do you want them hung up for her? And what room is she to have? Why, mine of course, how stupid. And couldn't I have a cot in that little dressing room?"

"No, you couldn't! You're to stay right in the room where you are, and Marjorie can take what she can get. I have an option on the room and bath across the hall for her, and you might just 'phone down to the office that it's all right, I'll keep it. But those things are not Marjorie's. She'll bring her own truck with her, enough to clothe a whole orphan asylum; she always does. Those things are for my Companion to wear when she is doing my work. I ordered them, and I certainly hope they will fit you. You see, I can't have you going around always in the same color, even if it is the prettiest outfit anybody ever had. Edith Adams-Fisher should be suitably dressed at all times or my game's up, you understand. What a pity you hadn't thought to put in that Adams as a middle

173

name. I'll see that it's recognized. It sounds well. Now, what I want you to do is to try on all those things, and if any of them aren't right, we'll have to get a seamstress from somewhere and have them altered. No, no protests. This is my work, you understand, and all this paraphernalia is a part of the scheme. It wouldn't work without it, and if everything doesn't go right now it won't be your fault."

"But Miss Co—"

"There! You're forgetting again!" (sharply). "I shouldn't like that to happen in public."

"But really, dear friend," protested Patty, tears of distress coming into her eyes and a tremble in her voice, "I couldn't be an object of charity, you know. If you would let me pay for these things— But truly, I would rather not have them, for they aren't, any of them, suitable for a person in my position."

"Pay for them all you like," retorted the old lady glibly. "You can have all the time you like to pay for any you want to keep after this is over, but mind you, you don't need to feel that way, for I want these things to use for a purpose, and as for your position, it suits my purpose that you shall be a young society girl on a perfect equality with Marjorie. It's what you really are anyway, so that ought not to trouble you any, and if things come out as I hope, as I confidently expect, I shall be amply repaid. Come, try on that dark blue tricolette. You needed one or two little frocks like that to run around in mornings and that looks very suitable and simple. I just wrote up to a friend of mine, a buyer in one of the big New York stores, and told her a young cousin of mine was visiting me, and staying longer than she expected and wanted to have a few things sent down. I knew she'd do the correct thing. I gave her your size and told her to get such things as she would select for Marjorie."

Patty with much protest arrayed herself in the pretty clothes to the thorough satisfaction of Miss Cole, who fairly gloated over the delicate beauty of the girl, and her sweet unconsciousness of it. And while they tried on and criticized or praised the selections, Miss Cole was all the time giving little hints of her longing that her own niece should learn to know a sweet wholesome girl-hood.

"She's only been to finishing schools," she sighed. "It makes me sick! Kate is all for show! You tell her about your schools, and the college life. I believe Marjorie has it in her to be a real sensible child if she only had half a chance. Aren't there riding things in there? I ordered them. It's one of the great sports here, riding, and Marjorie's crazy about it. I want you two to go around together and have a good time. I'll be all right sitting on the piazza or in my room reading, you know, and I don't want you to try to hang around me. Just follow Marjorie's lead. She never could bear to be alone, and she'll take to you and lead you a life of it, I can see that from the start."

Patty Merrill tried to laugh gaily over the prospect, but inwardly her heart misgave her and she looked forward to no pleasant association with the girl who was coming, for there had been that in the toss of Marjorie Horliss-Cole's haughty head, and the curl of her handsome lip that left no doubt in Patty's mind how the young woman would be likely to regard her aunt's Companion as considered in the light of a social equal. The situation looked quite impossible to Patty Merrill, and as she hung in her closet the beautiful addition to her own beautiful but meagre wardrobe she sighed quietly and wished with all her heart she might run away again. It seemed that if one once ran away from troubles one had always to be doing it. Perhaps her father had been right in telling her to brave things out, and she should have remained at home and faced the trouble whatever it was. Troubles never seemed to disappear or grow less when one ran away from them, and here she was face to face with another one now. Well, perhaps it would disappear if she just stayed quietly and faced it. John Treeves had been a trouble, too, and she had bided her time quietly a day and he had gone away. Not that she wanted him to go, for it had been most pleasant to know that under the same great roof there was a friend whom she had known and could trust in any time of need; but it had been so hard to feel that she must guard against meeting him. Well, perhaps Marjorie would be bored and leave too. What was the use of worrying, only it had all been so pleasant with Miss Cole, and she had felt so safe and contented, and now to have it spoiled by this intrusion. Well, it could not be helped and she must make the best of it. She was in a queer mix-up, and must stay by it at least until she could get word from her father and be able to ask his advice.

So the day passed on and the evening came and with it Miss Marjorie Horliss-Cole, who opened her large eyes widely and wore on her lips a slight touch of aristocratic contempt as she looked over her aunt's Companion and noticed that she did not look any more like a person in that position than she had when she was hired.

She was shut in her aunt's room for a good two hours before Patty was finally called. Patty never knew just what arguments the aunt used, nor how she explained her whim of cousinship, but quite naturally when she entered the room Miss Cole remarked: "Edith, I want you to take your Cousin Marjorie into her room where I won't hear your chatter, and cheer her up. She's as blue as indigo, and I can't have blue people around me. I'll ship her back to New York to-morrow morning if she can't brighten up."

Marjorie Horliss-Cole turned her great eyes,

filled with a smouldering discontent, upon the fair young girl who stood in the doorway smiling wistfully, and her manner was most stiff and condescending. It was plain she had promised to accept the new cousin outwardly, at least, but that she did not intend to let her in to the inner sanctuary of her being, and that she resented the idea of a servant being a social equal.

Patty, inwardly shrinking but true to her promise to Miss Cole that she would do her best, put out a friendly smile. There was comradeship—not too much—and apology in it. There was also a look of selflessness that astonished and held the world-wearied girl. This seemed a new phase of girl, and interested her in spite of herself.

"Come on," said Patty invitingly, throwing open the door. "Your room has a perfectly luscious view. The moon is just about due behind the mountain. Don't you want to watch it rise?"

There was something about Patty that was wholly disarming. There might also have been something in the fact that she was so new to playing a part that it was much easier to be herself than Edith Fisher. In spite of her prejudices Marjorie Horliss-Cole was drawn to forget that this girl was in the position of a servant and followed her.

Patty drew her within the room across the hall, switched on the light and then stood back, looking up confidingly:

"Please don't blame me about this cousin

business, Miss Horliss-Cole," she said with sweet dignity, and another alluring smile. "I tried my best to persuade Miss Cole that it could not be, but she seemed so determined that I had to give up. And besides, I find she has made the matter rather public here in the house so that it would look queer for her to withdraw; but I assure you I shall not bother you cousining you. I know just how you must feel toward me, and I hate the idea of it myself. So please feel perfectly safe that I shall not bother you at all; and if you wish me to go away entirely I can do that. I don't want to presume, or to masquerade as a relative of the family."

The haughty aristocrat eyed her wonderingly for a moment and then flashed a friendly smile at her:

"You're a queer girl," she said. "I believe I like you. I think you'd better stay. I shall probably be bored to death, and if you weren't here I should be tied down to Aunt Sylvia's side. What in the world are you doing this for anyway? You aren't a spy, are you? You're too young and pretty for that, and besides, what would there be to spy down here, and now that the war is over, too. But anyone can see with a glance that you are not a servant or else you're awfully clever. Perhaps it's both. Come on and sit down and talk to me awhile and we'll watch that moon rise although I'm sure I never cared much for moons."

"Oh, but they have such wonderful ones here,"

said Patty ecstatically. "Here, you sit in the deep chair. That's just at the right angle to watch the crotch of the two mountains where the light begins to grow first. We'll turn out the light so we can see it better. I watched it come last night and it was wonderful."

"You certainly are queer," murmured Marjorie impolitely. "You make me curious."

She dropped listlessly into a chair, already forgetting her spurt of interest in Patty.

Patty curled up in the wide window-seat with a pillow at her back and her head tilted sideways against the window-frame, a pretty picture.

"I suppose you're a country girl," drawled Marjorie, watching her idly, with already a resumption of the patronage in her tone.

"Oh, no," said Patty brightly ignoring it. "My home is in the city, but I've been in the country at school and college all my life."

"College? Did you go to college?" asked Marjorie wonderingly.

"Just graduated this spring," vouchsafed Patty carelessly as if it were a small thing.

"You look awfully young for that," said Marjorie half jealously. "Did you ever play basket-ball?"

"Oh, surely. Love it."

"I was captain of our team at school."

"Grand! I knew you'd done things when I first saw you!" Patty had forgotten that she was a Companion with a capital C, and was just a college girl now, talking as she might have talked to her roommate. Marjorie Horliss-Cole felt flattered by the genuineness of Patty's tone and grew more interested.

"Well, the coach said I was a dandy player," she admitted reminiscently. "We had a simply peachy coach. He treated us just as if we were men—said it was the only way to make a real team out of us, and he certainly did get results. We played away over all the other schools this year. You ought to see him. He's awfully fine looking and has the finest pair of shoulders in New York. Were you ever in love—Miss—Fisher?"

"In love? Oh, dear me, no; I don't think so—at least—I guess not. But couldn't you call me Edith? That will be easier, and it isn't a bit more intimate. It just doesn't sound so stiff."

"Well, then, Edith, do you really mean you were never in love? Don't you know any men?"

"Why, yes, of course, but not any special ones. At least—there was a boy once, and we had awfully good times together one summer, but we were just children, of course. We liked each other, but that was all."

"Well, I'm in love!" sighed Miss Horliss-Cole. "And I'm very unhappy!" she added, and suddenly with a choking sob she flung herself down at Patty's feet and buried her face in Patty's lap, weeping violently.

Patty was not a little disconcerted at this

confidence. She recalled vividly Mrs. Horliss-Cole's tone as she upbraided her daughter and it occured to her that she was occupying a most critical position at present. But her warm little heart was instantly enlisted in sympathy, and her hand went tenderly out and smoothed the beautiful dark head on her lap.

"I'm awfully sorry you're unhappy," she murmured gently. "Would you care to tell me about it?"

Miss Horliss-Cole appeared to be somewhat comforted at the sympathetic tone, and turned her face so that her voice could be heard:

"It's all mamma that's making the trouble," she sighed. "She won't stand for it at all. She won't even let me see him to say good-bye. I don't mind telling you, because you heard mamma talking in the car that first day anyway. You see he's poor and a nobody, and besides, mamma has no use for athletics. She calls them coarse and low down, and she wants me to come out this winter—"

"Aren't you very young yet?" suggested Patty. "Isn't there plenty of time? I should think if you both really cared you could just wait awhile and everything would come out right. I think if it's the real thing those things come out right somehow, don't you?"

"Oh, do you think so?" Miss Horliss-Cole lifted a tearful face hopefully. "If you could just see him. He's the most stunning! And he's perfectly crazy about me!"

"He would be, of course, if he had any sense at all," laughed Patty gently. "You're rather stunning, you know, when you don't look so unhappy. If I were you I'd forget my troubles and be happy. It pays in the end I'm sure, and it will all come out right somehow. Oh, look, look! The moon is coming! There's the light in the sky over there behind the big pine!"

Marjorie Horliss-Cole snuggled closer to Patty and lifted her head curiously to watch.

"You're an awfully darling girl," she said contendedly. "I think we're going to get on together all right. Perhaps you're going to understand me. Nobody understands me but Dad, and he's always too busy to bother. Aunt Sylvia does some crazy things, but I think she landed on her feet this time when she took a notion to you."

She slipped her arm comfortably around Patty's waist and so together in the window-seat the two girls watched the wonder of the moon as it rose over the mountains.

To Marjorie whose acquaintance with the moon was scant, save viewed from the piazza of a seaside hotel, or glimpsed through the glass of a limousine, it was like a miracle, and for a time it drew her out of herself. To Patty it was a long-loved joy that always stirred her to the depths and made her think of those she loved who were far away. They watched in silence for a time, and then as the great silver disk rose majestically and poured a glorifying light upon the plumes of the pines in the valley, flooding the sky with wide brightness, they gradually fell to talking again as any girls in a moonlit window-seat will talk, and forgot that they were in any different relation to one another than just friends.

Matters were looking most hopeful toward the furthering of Miss Sylvia Cole's plans, and she returned with a look of satisfaction from a scouting trip to the door across the hall, where she had stood for some minutes listening to the low confidential tones that rose and fell pleasantly. And then the very next morning something happened that upset the whole thing, although of course Miss Cole hadn't an idea of it and wouldn't have understood if she had. For Patty, standing on a little upper balcony that opened off the end of their hall, taking deep breaths and drinking in the beauty of the morning, suddenly saw a cab arrive from the station, and a single passenger alight. With scarlet cheeks she fled to her room to consider, for that man with the broad shoulders and the fine determined set of head could be no other than John Treeves. And now, what should she do? She was expected to go downstairs as a cousin of the much-admired Miss Horliss-Cole, and as such would of course be introduced to the nephew of old Calvin Treeves; for she had been in the hotel long enough to hear many stories of the fabulous wealth of the old man, and the famous bravery of the young one. And to meet her old friend, John Treeves, in that way was unthinkable. Masquerading as somebody else! He would recognize her surely when she spoke. She would not be able to keep the friendliness out of her voice. She knew she was as transparent as glass when it came to a thing like that. Moreover, it seemed to her truth-loving nature like acting a lie. It might be for a good reason perhaps, but it was a lie all the same, and she could not get the consent of herself to enter into it. It was quite a different thing to go among a lot of strangers by a name that was not hers, because, as a sort of servant it had been nothing to those people by what name she was called. She was not expected to be anything to them. And the people with whom she had to do all knew that Edith Fisher was not her name, and it was with their full knowledge and consent that it was used. But here she was given an opportunity to have her old friend back again, only she would have to be another person from the one he had known, and she did not care for that. If she could not meet him frankly as herself she would rather keep him as a friend of the past and not meet him at all. So she decided that somehow she would keep utterly out of his way.

Watching her opportunity, for it was still early in the morning and Miss Cole was not yet awake, she sped by a circuitous route to the village store, where she purchased the most ornate veil that she could find. It was not at all beautiful, but it was the best there was for purposes of disguise. Behind this she retired quickly as soon as she had reached a sheltering tree where she could adjust it to her hat and then walked on more comfortably, feeling that not even her own family would recognize her quickly with that flaunting butterfly over one eye and the sunflower scrawling its petals across her lips. This veil would help during the daytime in case Marjorie Horliss-Cole insisted on a walk or a drive. But what should she do for evening when she would be expected to don an evening gown and go down to dinner, remaining afterward for whatever festivities the place afforded. Well, she would have to think a way out of that, and perhaps John Treeves would not stay long. He had gone away before, and he might go again. But even as she thought it, a little choke came in her throat, for she longed inexpressibly to have a good talk with her old-time friend, and sometimes the temptation to just tell him all her trouble as if he were her brother almost overcame her. Still, she knew she must not, for that would be a breach of loyalty to the family. No, she must endure it alone. Perhaps sometime, somewhere, when life had cleared up for her, she would meet him again and really know him as a friend. But that could never be if she met him now under a disguise, for he would have good cause to think her untrue, and that must not be. So Patty set herself to plan a day in which the two women under her care should be entirely satisfied, and yet she should be allowed to remain utterly in the background.

14

John Treeves had dropped all his plans in response to a cunningly worded telegram and had come to what he supposed was his uncle's death-bed. But it was a very lively corpse that greeted him, poking out a withered claw from among a mountain of pillows and cackling like an old crow in his glee over seeing him again.

"Well, well, so you did have a little feeling in your heart for your old uncle, didn't you?"

There was a chirrup to the voice that suggested anything but nearing the other world, and John Treeves's sympathy was slightly dashed as he noted the wicked twinkle in the bad old man's eyes, but he tried to be duly solicitous and succeeded in making the old man feel so well that he declared he must get up at once; and the nephew began to realize slowly that the telegram had been a ruse to get him back. He was annoyed for he had deeper things to think of than being the toy of an old child, and life in a fashionable winter resort had little attraction for him. So, while Patty was studying hard how to avoid him, he was spending much thought in how he might avoid meeting any of the people of the hotel, and above all how he might get away from this most uncongenial atmosphere and give himself to the new plans that were forming in his mind. He agreed quite readily to a drive in his uncle's car, thinking that would be a more pleasing way of passing the morning than housed in the hotel rooms, and might also be more conducive to agreeable conversation, for the old man would be less likely to burst forth into a rage out in the open.

Calvin Treeves was pleased as a child while they prepared him for his drive, and was really quite pleasant and agreeable most of the way. Fortunately for Patty's peace of mind they chose a different drive from the one which she and Marjorie had taken on horseback, and returned to the hotel half an hour ahead of the riders so that they did not come into contact. The old man chose to have lunch in his apartment and kept his nephew close at his side, as though he were afraid to trust him out of his sight.

But after lunch Calvin Treeves had himself established on the wide couch for a nap, announcing to his nephew:

"Now, you go off and do what you please this afternoon; rest or read or ride, if you like. They have good horses here, and Hespur will give the order for you whenever you are ready to go. This evening I'm going down to dinner and we'll meet some of the best people. There are some stunning women I want you to know, and some worth while men. There's Wentforth Gaines, and Archie Van Helden and Bertie Schuyler. They are all good sports, in for polo and golf and the like and they'll be glad to introduce you to our set. You will be accepted, you know, and anything you want goes. I want you to understand that you are to be a leader. There won't be any disposition to question it, you know. I have more money than anyone else here—though they are all pretty well fixed as far as that goes—so you just go ahead and cut all the figure you like. I can see you don't need to be taught how. You've got poise and assurance and all that and I've fixed it up so they will receive you with open arms. The women, poor fools, are all ready to fall on your neck—!"

But his garrulity was interrupted by a sudden wheeling of the victim and a sharp set of his jaw that Hespur could easily see betokened opposition. He hovered behind the young man and murmured apologetically:

"I wouldn't cross him, sir, if I was you. He's that hard to control—!"

A wave of something else swept over John Treeves's face. Was it gentleness, or more like self-control at a reminder? He gave the old servant a gleam of recognition as he turned to his uncle, and began to speak firmly:

"Uncle Calvin, I think perhaps we'd better understand each other right at the start. I really cannot stay here more than another day, and it would not be worth while getting acquainted with a lot of new people whom I shall probably never see again. I came on to see you, and I would rather just stay and visit with you when you are rested. I'll do very well while you are sleeping, for I have a good many things to think about and plans to make."

The old man's eyes gleamed with satisfaction:

"That's just it," he said with a grim smile. "You don't need to make any plans, Dunham. I've decided to take you over and keep you with me. I like you and I need you, and I'm going to put you into the best society and give you all opportunities just as if you were my son. I'm not sure, but I'll adopt you."

John Treeves had been sitting across the room, but now he rose quietly and took a step nearer, and there was in his tone a quiet dignity and firmness that penetrated even the smug self-satisfaction of the rich old beggar, as he said:

"Uncle Calvin, that is quite impossible. I do not belong in your world and never did. I have my work to do and I have fully decided what it shall be. It is as far as possible from the kind of life you are outlining for me. I could not ever consent to be a parasite, even though your offer had come long ago. My mother did not bring me up to be that sort of thing."

The old man's eyes twinkled with satisfaction as he eyed the strong young fellow and recognized the manly ring in his voice. Not for an instant did he doubt that he would be the final winner in this argument, but he rather admired his nephew for making this protest. He seemed all the more worth winning.

"Of course I suppose you are feeling peeved yet about the way I treated your mother, and I'm sorry I couldn't have seen things this way sooner"— there was not the slightest trace of sorrow in the dry old selfish voice—"but if she was as good as you say she was she never would have been one to hold a grudge nor to stand in your way, and very likely she considered some such outcome as this in the future when she told you to be sure and forgive me—" There was a suaveness in his tone that was fairly infuriating to the loyal son's soul, but he controlled himself well.

"Uncle Calvin, I have forgiven you," he said, turning away and looking out the window at the calm mountains in the distance, "but you will give me fresh cause to be righteously angry if you make any more such insinuations about my mother. You seem to think she had great cunning and worldly wisdom, and as you did not know her sweet life and high-minded standards you are perhaps not able to comprehend how utterly distasteful it would have been to her to have her son live such a life as you propose."

"That's all very pretty talk, young man," sneered the old reprobate, "but when it comes right down to living almost everybody likes a good birth. But don't get on your high horse. Wait till you've had a little taste of it. Then we'll see what you say."

"Uncle Calvin, I must leave here on the afternoon train to-morrow at the very latest."

"Tut! Tut! Go and rest awhile and we'll talk about it again," said the old man crossly. "I warn you my temper is getting up, and I won't stand everything. It doesn't do to trifle with me."

"I'm not trifling, Uncle, and I'm sorry to oppose your plans because you are sick, but there is no use talking about the matter any longer. My plans for life are made and I must get away and go to work. I cannot remain longer than to-morrow!"

"What have you got in your mind?" snarled the old man. "Out with it! Perhaps I can help it on."

"Hardly, Uncle Calvin," said the young man, his face softening. "It is something I must work out for myself. I've decided to go with the ministry in some form or other. I may go as a missionary, or do mission work in the city or out West. I'm not just decided about details yet."

The old man suddenly jerked himself into a sitting posture with his eyes snapping and a sneer on his rank old lips:

"Going to be a molly-coddle after all? Well, I

rather guess not. My brother's child is never going to disgrace the family that way. I'll put a stop to that. Of course it's only a fool whim and you'd soon get over it after you tried it awhile, but I don't care to have you waste that time. I'm getting near the end and I want you with me and want to train you up to take my place—!"

"NEVER!" exclaimed John Treeves involuntarily with a visible shrinking from the thought.

"W-WHAT?" shrieked the old man.

"I said, never!" repeated the young man more gently, but still with that firm set of jaw.

"Well, well,—now I'll tell you what I was going to do, young man. I was going to make you my HEIR! Do you understand that? *Now* haven't you any obligation toward me?"

"No," said John Treeves, steadily looking him in the eye. "No, because some one else got ahead of you and made me heir to a far greater estate than you could possibly leave!"

"That's a L-I-E!" yelled the enraged old aristocrat. "I guess you don't know how many millions I have! I guess you don't know that I can buy anything I want. I guess you don't know—I—I—you—you—young r-r-r-r-r-RASCAL! Who is it that has dared to make my nephew his heir and try to get him away from me? Who *is* it I say, *ANSWER* me!"

John Treeves looked at him calmly and said in a low reverent tone, "God!"

The old man looked at him with an expression of frightened awe and shivered. Then he laughed out an unholy cackle.

"High strikes, young man! High strikes! You seem mighty glib in your acquaintance with God. How did you find that out?"

"I have His Word for it," was the quiet answer, and a strange, beautiful light grew in John Treeves's eyes as he looked away to the distant hills, and the Bible verses that had surrounded him all his life from his mother's knee, like bright protecting angels, hovered near and handed him the sword of the spirit.

"How—what—how's that?" asked the old man, a frightened note in his voice again.

"As many as are led by the Spirit of God, they are the sons of God. The Spirit itself beareth witness with our spirits that we are the children of God: and if children, then heirs, heirs of God and joint heirs with Jesus Christ."

"Poppycock!" shouted the old man. "Go and take a walk or a ride. I don't want to talk with such a fool. You'll come out of that soon enough when you've had a little taste of life. Meantime, keep your high strikes to yourself where all well-ordered young men keep their extravagances and excesses. It isn't good form to gabble like that before folks. You must have some conceit to think your God has time to spend leading you round. Get out of here, I say, and let me rest!"

John Treeves went out and walked among the pines, his hands clasped behind him, his eyes upon the ground. He wondered if he had said the right thing, wondered how he came to say what he had said. He marveled at the Bible verses that flocked around him continually since he had met the Christ in the lonely trysting place and given himself over bodily to His service. But most of all, he marveled that in his heart he found a strange yearning desire for the poor old rich man lying so helpless upon his bed upstairs, cursing and fretting and trying to rule, and fighting against God. The feeling was so strong upon him that when he had climbed to the top of the hill and wandered away from the trail to a lonely spot where the ground was matted under his feet with ground pine and wintergreen and laurel, where the pines grew close and dark about him, he dropped upon the mossy carpet and cried out to God: "Oh, Christ, come to that old man and make him see how much he needs Thee. If there is anything I can do to help him find Thee, show me how."

Patty in her room, supposedly resting from the horseback ride, looked down upon the trail and saw John Treeves disappear among the trees, climbing higher, and by and by reappearing farther up. She watched until he came back at dusk, and then she went to Miss Cole and begged to be allowed to stay in her room that evening, pleading a headache which was the honest result of a good cry she had had that afternoon. Miss Cole, studying the sweet sad face with the dark circles under the eyes, gave a grudging consent, and agreed to look after Marjorie herself that evening. Patty went back to her room thankfully and wondered how long she would be able to dodge her old friend, and how it was that Fate had arranged such an unhappy part for her who would have so loved to meet John Treeves and have a good time with him once more.

John Treeves, duly arrayed in fine garments, provided by a thoughtful and cunning uncle and spread upon his bed by Hespur with an apologetic plea:

"He doesn't rightly enjoy himself without the clothes be all right, sir, you know. You won't mind an old man's whim, sir," went down to the dining-room once more with his uncle that night, the cynosure of all eyes.

During the afternoon that bad old man had not been idle nor had he rested:

"Hespur, you go get the list of the guests at the house, and look me out a nice girl, especially nice girl, see, Hespur? Nothing like the right kind of girl to make a man forget his idiosyncrasies. We'll try him with a girl."

And surely it was the irony of fate that made old Calvin Treeves pick on Marjorie Horliss-Cole as a fitting companion of the hour for his nephew.

"She'll do, Hespur. We'll manage," he said, and

fell into an uneasy sleep, waking to lead his man a life of it until dinner-time. And so it came about that Marjorie Horliss-Cole, attending upon her aunt at dinner was introduced to young Dunham Treeves and spent a part of the evening talking to him, while a disgusted aunt and an elated uncle snapped epigrams at one another and watched them. And when Miss Sylvia Cole's patience at last gave out, Miss Marjorie was obliged to attend her upstairs.

Marjorie Horliss-Cole, after having carelessly performed a few trifling services for her aunt, fluttered softly into Patty's room, where Patty, with rapidly beating heart was trying her best to get to sleep and forget:

"I've just slipped in to see how you feel," said Marjorie, settling down comfortably on the foot of the bed. "Is your head any better? I suppose it was the glare of the sun this morning. I hope you'll be able to ride again to-morrow. You certainly ought to have been down this evening. I had a dandy time. We met the young paragon, Dunham Treeves. He's simply stunning! Handsome as a picture and awfully fine eyes. I talked to him all the evening till Aunt Syl got restless, of course, and had to come away just when we were having the most interesting discussion about whether life is worth while unless one has some real work in the world to do. Really you ought to hear him talk. He's just your style. You'll laugh, of course, my comparing them, but he's like my athletic man, in a way only of course utterly different. I tried my best to get him to go riding with us in the morning, but he said he was leaving to-morrow and must devote himself to his old uncle. Old crab! I can't see how anybody could ever stand him even for his money, but I suppose he argues that it can't be long before he dies anyway, and there's really no other way to make sure of inheriting."

"Oh, but he wouldn't do that!" cried Patty earnestly. "He's not that kind of—I mean I shouldn't think any man would be kind to an old person"—she stopped in confusion—"I mean just for money. It would seem so sort of sordid—"

"Well, they do it," said the worldly wise Marjorie. "Heaps of them. And when you see the old skeleton, all yellow and leathery and with his head shaking like a leaf—they say he falls into awful rages if anyone crosses him in the least— why you wouldn't wonder if his relatives weren't caring much about his departure from the world. The world is better off without a man like that anyway. He's a selfish, close, crabbed old creature and never gives anything to any public cause, nor entertains, nor does anything worth while with his money, just keeps it all for show and his own comfort. Well, anyhow, his nephew isn't so bad, and I suppose mother'll be hot foot to get me interested in him. I don't mind playing around with him a little, it will keep mother pacified and she won't be watching whether I write to anyone else or not. Dunham Treeves and I are going up to the top of the mountain to see the sun rise. I got that much out of him anyway. He said he had watched it rise when he was here before, and I made him offer to show me the place. I never saw the sun rise, did you? It's going to be frightful to wake up, but then I can sleep all day after it if I want to. Well, good night. I hope your headache is gone in the morning."

Miss Horliss-Cole departed, leaving Patty in a state of mind bordering on tears. She was safe. John Treeves was going to-morrow and she could manage to keep out of his sight that much longer. But somehow she did not feel happy over it. Another girl was going to the top of the mountain with him to watch the miracle of the sunrise. She had watched it once with him and his mother years ago, and every word that had been spoken on that occasion was just as clearly marked in her memory as if it had happened but the day before. This other girl would stand beside him to-morrow and hear him talk, watch his face with the sunlight on it—. But there! It was ridiculous! He was nothing to her but an old friend whom she might never see again. It was not Patty Merrill, anyway, who was here at the same hotel with John Treeves. It was Edith Fisher, a strange girl who had taken a position as Companion to an old lady, and it was "Dunham" Treeves, the nephew of the multimillionaire, who was supposed to be here pursuing his uncle's fortune. That was not her old friend. He would never do that. If he had so degenerated she did not want to know him! And she turned the other way and tried to smother her thoughts in the pillow, but try as she would the night stretched away and sleep came late to her tired heart, leaving dark circles under her eyes, so that Miss Cole quite willingly excused her from going down to lunch next day.

15

It was after lunch that John Treeves had the final words with his uncle, which settled the matter of adoption once and for all.

"I think," said the uncle suavely, "that you owe me some consideration. I'm willing to have the papers made out to-day. I gave my lawyer orders to come at a moment's notice and he's only waiting my call. I'll make over two hundred and fifty thousand dollars to you at once to live on, and I'll fix up the will so that you will inherit the whole estate. I'd arranged to leave it all to public institutions where they were entirely willing to name them after me. There was the Treeves Art Club—and a new college out in Idaho, and seven libraries, and three hospitals, besides a lot of art galleries and scholarships and medals. But I've decided to cut them all out in your favor. Now! What I want of you is to put yourself in my hands and I'll make the biggest man in the world out of you. Why, you know there isn't anything in the world—possessions or power or experience—that money won't buy for you. Not anything! And I've got the money! I've got enough to put you where you like and make you what you like—what I like, if you'll just give yourself up to me awhile. You're mighty good material and have a good start and a good natural ability, but you want teaching, you want travel, you want art and books and society and rubbing up against the great ones. If I'd had it young enough, I could have done it for myself, but I was busy getting the money together for it so long that I got too old for the rest and I suddenly realized that after all I couldn't have it myself, the thing I'd been working for, it had to be for some one else. One lifetime wasn't long enough for getting the money and the power both, so I picked you out. You are my nearest of kin, and the only one who could possibly be me over again. I have to live in you now, and finish what I've begun, and you've got to yield yourself to me now and let me bring all this to you that I've worked for myself. Do you understand?"

There was a pathetic eagerness in the old voice and the claw-like hands worked in each other restlessly as the little sharp eyes watched their prey and put forth an almost mesmeric power against this strangely baffling but altogether desirable young soul.

"You know," he went on hurriedly, as if he had not said enough, "you know there wouldn't be any limit to it—no place that you couldn't occupy. You'd be as great as the greatest king on earth. You could buy the presidency of the United States. There isn't any ambition you couldn't satisfy or joy you could not drink to the dregs."

But the only words that came to the mind of John Treeves were:

"Then the devil taketh him up into an exceeding high mountain, and sheweth him all the kingdoms of the world, and the glory of them; and saith unto him, All these things will I give thee, if you wilt fall down and worship me."

"You understand, don't you, that I've got enough to back you anywhere," the old man went on anxiously again. "There wouldn't be anywhere you wouldn't be received with that behind you, and there's more than anybody knows, too." There was a look of cunning in his old eyes. "No, not anywhere you wouldn't be received—yes, and welcomed eagerly." There was consummate pride now in the tone.

"Except the Kingdom of Heaven," said John Treeves slowly, thoughtfully.

"W-w-w-w-*what* do you *MEAN?*" he roared frightenedly. "Whad'ye m-m-m-*M-E-A-N?*"

His hands were shaking and his eyes were

starting out from their sockets with mingled anger and awe.

"I mean, Uncle Calvin, that your money would not buy my way into the kingdom of God, and that is the only kingdom I care anything about just now. I have pledged my life and my loyalty to seek that kingdom first and nothing, nobody can tempt me now to break that pledge. I have dedicated my life to preach the Gospel of Christ wherever and however He wants me to do it. You can see for yourself how utterly foreign to this is the proposition you have made."

"Preach! You, my nephew, heir of all this princely fortune! You be a common preacher! NEVER! I won't allow it! I'll balk you at every turn! My money shall queer you in any church you try to get! And not a penny of all my fortune shall go to you unless you give up this silly woman's idea! Do you hear that? You shan't have a cent if you keep up this idea of being a whining preacher!"

John Treeves stood leaning against the mantel, his arms folded, a look of half-amused aloofness upon his face. His voice was quiet as he replied:

"But, Uncle Calvin, I never had an idea of getting your money. I don't want it!"

"That's a LIE!" The old man was breathless. "If that was so, what did you come here for, I'd like to know?"

"I came to forgive you because you had sinned

against my mother and I used to hate you for it."

The sound that issued forth from the old leathery lips was as if a container of many curses and hisses had suddenly exploded and fizzled into atoms, and after it was over he lay back upon his pillows panting and exhausted, a wasted shell of what used to be a man.

"I don't want your forgiveness!" he panted at last. "I want you to take my money and live my life after me the way I would have lived if I had lasted long enough. I want to be young again in you and spend my money for pleasure and fame and power and all the best things that the world can give and money can buy."

Steadily, firmly, kindly the younger voice answered:

"That could never be, because three days ago I gave myself to God in just the way that you suggest, and I mean to let Christ live His life over again in me as far as I am able. I am afraid that you and Christ could never live together; and if I had your money I should only use it to help other men to find Christ as I have found Him."

The old man looked at his nephew speechless with rage, his small eyes open wider than John Treeves had ever seen them, his face purple, his lips twisted in a snarl. At last he managed a feeble trembling gesture of helpless disgust and croaked out:

"Well, go, GO, *GO! Do you HEAR?*" mounting to a shriek with the last words.

John Treeves, strangely sore hearted, yet knowing he was doing right, turned and went from the room, and did not see the helpless tears of the baffled old man upon the bed.

With a feeling of finality upon him he went to his apartment, put his few effects together, and walked out of the place, looking neither to right nor left. He was as sure that the incident was closed as if a voice from above had told him. He knew that he had chosen aright, had not even a second thought about it, yet there was upon him a strange sadness as if he had just witnessed the last judgment of an immortal soul, and all day upon the train as he put his head back against the seat and closed his eyes wearily, there was that sense of having passed through an awful ordeal, and seen a terrible sight.

Back in the hotel, at her curtained window, with troubled brow, Patty Merrill watched him out of sight down the road, with an unexpected sense of loss despite her relief. She knew by the set of his shoulders, by the way he carried his rather cheap-looking suitcase, that he was still John Treeves, of Maple Brook, and had not merged into the rich and admired nephew of old Calvin Treeves, the multimillionaire. Somehow that gave her much comfort in the days that followed. She could not quite bring herself to think of John Treeves as

Dunham Treeves, the society leader, that all the hotel gossips said he was to be.

Back in Calvin Treeves's luxurious apartment silence reigned after the young man had left. Old Hespur stood at the front window as still as an image staring out at the point where the road below emerged from the shadow of the porch, listening with senses alert and keen. On his face was deep anxiety, struggling with a light of admiration.

On the bed the old man lay struggling with his tears that rolled weakly down his shriveled cheeks and dropped in a sobby pool upon the pillow. Walls and doors were strong and thick, but could not hide the sound of the closing door across the hall, nor the determined steps outside going toward the elevator. Breath was suspended till the elevator clicked open and shut its door and descended, and then another breathless space of suspense till Hespur sighted the tall figure below on the path. The old servant made no sound, yet something told the man on the bed he had seen him and that the worst was true. Out of sight and long after, Old Hespur gazed after the young man into the blinding sun of the glorious autumn day, a figure that would forever stand in his memory as the type of what the family of Treeves should have been, and old Hespur's face was wet, too, as he watched; wet still as he turned at last and came to the bedside as if he had been called and stood there unashamed without wiping away the tears. The old man opened his smeary eyes and viewed him through a blur. Then his bird-like claws reached out blindly, and he groped his face into his old servant's hands and sobbed like a little child. And Hespur, like an old mother, knelt beside the bed and drew him close, patting his thin old shoulder and wiping away the tears. Both of them seemed to recognize that there had been finality in John Treeves's action. He would never return nor reconsider. Dunham Treeves, the young aristocrat whom old Calvin Treeves had sought to bring into being, was no more. Regret in great waves would roll up over the two as they thought of little things they had planned for him, how he would look and be and do, how he would play golf and ride and be admired, all the prideful things of a prideful life went past their sorrow like a panorama, and at each new thought the tears came anew until every hope had been reviewed and put away forever as hopeless and dead. Then a long silence came between the two while the servant cherished the old man and tried to think of a way of comforting him.

At last the old man's voice, choked and meek, cracked forth:

"Hespur, there's nothing so really *un*-respectable about it. You know the ministry has always been regarded as quite—*respectable!* It's sissy-fied and effeminate, but it's always been RESPECTABLE!"

"Oh, sir; yes, sir!" the servant hastened to

assent. "Quite respectable, sir! Always, sir! In fact, in my country they're very much looked up to, sir! And I'm thinking, sir, as how the young gentleman will never be effeminate, sir, nor yet a sissy, sir; he's a real Treeves, sir, and a chip off the old block, sir. I'm thinking you'll be proud of him yet, sir, whatever he does."

"Oh, proud of him, yes!" said the old voice wearily. "But what good does that do? He won't be mine and he won't be here—!"

"Well, then again, sir, it ain't so bad when you come to think of it, to have one of the family sort of in with God like that you know. It might be right handy sometimes, you know, sir—"

"You mean to bury me, Hespur!" the old voice croaked with a shudder.

"Oh, no sir; far be it, sir—!"

"That's all right, Hespur, old boy, you didn't mean it, I know. But it's coming all right and I've got to get reservations ready somehow. You know, Hespur, you've always stuck to me, no matter how I treated you."

"I've always tried to be faithful, sir—!" The tears were streaming down the ruddy cheeks and over the immaculate chin.

"You old fool, you! Stop that blubbering! You know I can't stand any emotion and yet you dare—you PRESUME to cry in my presence—! You old reprobate!" and the old millionaire sobbed like a baby.

"Oh, sir! Don'tee, sir! I was never crying. It's the warm of this room, sir. It's the radiators getting that hot, sir!" and he mopped his face with a corner of the pillowcase and tried to look unconscious of the fact that other tears promptly took the place of the tears that had been wiped away.

"You was saying, sir, that preaching as a business was always quite respectable. It is, sir. In my country it's that respectable that some titled men's sons choose it in preference to any other business, sir, even not excepting politics, sir! It's really quite well thought of, sir. And of course if one had a bit of money, sir, it would be quite possible to choose one's living in a most respectable parish, sir!"

"That's it, Hespur!" quavered the old man. "Now you're on the right track. I could leave him the money after all if I tied it up good and strong so he couldn't use it for other people."

"I'm thinking that wouldn't quite do, begging pardon, Mister Treeves, sir; the young gentleman's quite determined, sir, being a chip off the old family block, as it were, sir, and you heard yourself what he said, sir, begging your pardon— I think he meant it. He'd use that money for his work."

"Hespur, I BELIEVE YOU think that would be a good thing!"

"Well, sir, being as you can't take it with you and won't need it when you get done with it, sir, there's really nothing like giving it to the Almighty, sir, who would know as well as anyone just what to do with it. I'm not sure but it might be more your own that way nor any other, and mayhap bring you more good out of it yourself, sir, for I've read somewhere, sir, a story about a good man who lost all his money and his friends asked him wasn't he sorry he had made so free with it, giving it to the poor and building a church, and he said no, that the money he had given away, sir, was the only money he had laid up in Heaven, sir: and I'm thinking, sir, that might be quite true of anybody."

The little old eyes sweltering in weak tears looked eagerly up at the serious face of the servant tenderly trying to quiet his charge in the best way he knew:

"That's quite an idea, Hespur. Are you sure there's anything to it? You've been to church; have you ever heard anybody preach that? I'd be quite willing to give some away if I were sure it would be laid up for my use hereafter. Sort of buy me a home up there, you know."

The old servant looked troubled:

"I don't rightly think you put it just that way," he said hesitating, anxious to be true and yet tender. "You can't rightly *buy* from the Almighty, you know, as He had everything before us, sir, and it's best not to think what we're going to get out of it, sir, but it's safer with Him than otherwheres, I should think, sir. Now couldn't you try to rest, sir?"

The old man lay silent, his eyes closed, thinking hard. The servant tiptoed softly about drawing down shades, pulling up a coverlet, moving a screen, and then settled down in a chair at the bedside, motionless, where the coursing tears could not be seen. Somehow his life was so bound with the old life on the bed, and the old millions in the bank, that he, too, had settled his heart on the hope of the new life in the younger man, and he felt the blow of John Treeves's decision almost as the old uncle had felt it.

It was very still in the room, with only the sound of a bit of charred wood falling apart in the hearth fire. It seemed as though the old man was asleep. Suddenly his old voice cracked out on the silence:

"Hespur, you know how to write letters. Get your paper and pen and write me a letter now. No, I don't want to wait till my secretary comes down to-morrow; I want it written now. Quick! Now, have you found the paper in the desk? And the pen? Well, write:

To Mr. Horliss-Cole
Fifth Avenue, New York City.

Dear Sir:

I remember hearing not long ago that the old Avenue church is soon to lose the eminent divine who has so long filled its pulpit. I understand that you are a prominent officer in that church, and I am writing to say that the day your church installs my nephew, Mr. J. Dunham Treeves as pastor, I will give you my check for one hundred thousand dollars to be used in any way the church shall see fit.

Yours very truly,
Calvin Treeves.

The old hand quavered out the signature, when Hespur brought it to him to sign, and the little old eyes gleamed triumphantly as he dropped back among the pillows, like a withered leaf.

"Now, sir, you'll feel better, sir," chirped Hespur happily, as he folded the sheet and cramped his fingers to the pen for the address: "There's nothing like doing a good thing to make one feel better. That'll be fixing things nicely, I'm thinking. You've beat the devil around the stump this time, sir, begging pardon, sir, I'm thinking."

And at last the old man slept.

16

When John Treeves received the letter from Horliss-Cole inviting him to fill the pulpit of the great city church for the next four Sundays in the absence of the pastor, he read it through wonderingly taking in every word of the brief, curt communication which included all directions and the fabulous price that he would be paid for the performance of the same, and then crumpling it into his pocket took his way out the old hill road and up to his trysting place to think and enquire of his Guide what He would have him to do.

It did not seem to John Treeves that his experience had been a miracle, or anything out of the natural order of life. On the contrary, it seemed the most natural thing in the world. He had simply seen the Truth that had heretofore been hidden from him because he had reached out to it only half heartedly. It reminded him somewhat of the time when, in desperation over a difficult problem, he had gone at last to the teacher for explanation, and had been introduced to the system for obtaining the right answer. It had been a revelation in figures to him that had made bright the whole way through mathematics and taken from the study its perplexities. Farther back it reminded him of the time when after repeated trials he had learned to swim. What had seemed an impossibility became a part of himself, a natural action. And so, when he had once found God it seemed the most natural thing in the world that he should have done so. Every doubt had absolutely dissolved before the experience like ice before the morning sun. God was! Christ lived! He KNEW it! There might be arguments to prove that it was not so, but they were only theories reasoned out by man, perfect in their every step perhaps, but after all contradicted utterly by the fact. And the strange thing about it was that he now understood that only those who had truly sought with their hearts could ever see this. The world would probably go on with its elaborate and scientific arguments to prove that it was all utter foolishness, but there were those who had sought and found and nothing could controvert their knowledge. That was why the ignorant and unlearned often found the Light when the wise and great were left in darkness. It needed the humility of the little child to find. It took the whole heart searching to discover the secret. The fine bulwark of words and reason wherewith he had sought to establish his unbelief stood behind him like a toy wall built of blocks before the strong light of knowledge that filled his whole being. He could go back over it word for word and understand with his mind how he had come to certain conclusions and it was every word and phrase true as he had seen things then, true according to modern theories and conclusions; and yet he now knew that it had all been as the prattling of babes before his present experience. He recalled how when great inventions and discoveries had first come out always there had been many to scoff and doubt until the invention or discovery had become a common fact of everyday life. How men used to scoff at the idea of a flying machine, and laugh at the poor fools who were trying to perfect such a thing! And yet what a common factor it had become! So common that even a child scarcely looked up any more to marvel when a mail plane sailed above his head, and thought no more of it than of the trolley car, or a passing bicycle. How marvelous and impossible had been thought the telegraph and telephone, and all the modern electrical appliances until some one had sought with all his heart and found each one and placed it at the service of the world. And it must be so with religion—with finding God. It was all perfectly simple and understandable when one went about it in God's way. Why was it that more people did not take hold of the promises and try them? Why were their eyes blinded and their understandings darkened? How was it that they could not see? But then, he had been that way himself, and he had been honest. The thing lay in the will; one must be willing to search, and give everything else up if need be until one found. And because he had found the promise true, and knew just where the trouble lay for a great many other people who had been ignorant of the truth like himself, he must be one to tell. Was this letter his call? Somehow it did not appeal to him with its business-like commands, as if the work of the Lord were to be run on a basis of pure efficiency and nothing else. And yet it had come and no other way was yet open.

A long time he knelt under the old tree. It seemed to be nearer to God than anywhere else, and his thoughts were less trammeled there to think clearly. In the chill of the evening he came back, drawing the collar of his coat up high around his neck and shivering, for the air was raw with a tang of winter and the meadows looked bleak and frosty. He was keenly conscious of the loss of his mother, yet full of peace, because he knew that wherever she was she knew and was satisfied, for he had found her Saviour and was to be henceforth what she had longed to have him be, a minister of Christ's Gospel. Where or how, did not matter. He was still not sure that this New York church was the place, for of course he read between the lines and knew that a vacant pulpit was always looking out for a man, and doubtless he was to be on trial. He was not New Yorker enough to realize that this church was one of the most prominent and influential in the whole great city, and that it was a most strange and unexpected circumstance that he, an unknown retiring young man from the country, but just returned to his own land after a long absence, should have been asked to preach there at all, even as a supply. If he had known, it would not have entered into his calculation now, for since his finding Christ worldly considerations had not intruded to trouble him. He had given his all, and nothing gave him even a ripple of regret. He accepted the letter merely as one of the leadings of his new Guide, and did not question how wide a field it was to which he was being led.

When he reached the little cottage he sat down and wrote a brief acceptance of the invitation. Then he set about his simple preparations to leave the little home permanently, putting it in the keeping of a dear old lady friend of his mother's who would be quite comfortable there with her grandson, and who otherwise would have had to remain as she had done for years in the home of an unloving niece and her still more unloving husband. John Treeves might have rented that house furnished at a good sum, or even sold it easily, for he had one or two offers, but it pleased him rather to give it to Mrs. Burnside rent free and feel that his mother's home was going on and doing good as it had done often in her lifetime, when it had been a refuge for many a weary soul for a week or a day or a month in time of need.

Also he liked the thought of going back now and then and finding everything just as it had been when his mother was living.

So Mrs. Burnside brought her geraniums and her old wheezy sewing machine and her grandson with his cheap victrola, and they were established around the Treeves dining table and had their first supper the night before John Treeves left for New York.

He spent that last evening, after supper, tramping out to the old trysting place, and standing among the stars talking with God. Down there in the village the cottage lights twinkled and went out one by one as the villagers retired, but the eternal stars shone on and showed him where was the dear little bungalow at the end of the street that he felt he was really leaving forever. At the other extreme end of the street was the church spire, and one blue star glanced down its side with a spike of light as if to pick it out from the trees the better. Over beyond was the schoolhouse, red brick and white, where he had gone for so many years, and beyond, the athletic field where he had distinguished himself in baseball every spring and football every fall, and where sometimes his mother had sat proudly on the side lines watching, never letting him know how fearful it all seemed to her, always glad and relieved and shiny eyed when the game was over, still and white and courageous that time when he got knocked cold for a minute. How all the little incidents flocked up now to stir his heart with sadness!

He turned away to the quiet stars and began to talk with God aloud:

"Oh, God, I had a wonderful mother! I thank you for her! May I be all and more than she wanted and prayed for. May I never be traitor again to the faith. I'm going out into that sick world—it hurts me to think of it—the world that could have had a war like that! And I'm no better than the world—only—I HAVE YOU! That is wonderful! That is EVERYTHING! And I know what I'll meet there, unbelief, scoffing, cunning reasoning, scholarly argument, selfish, fascinating people, temptations of every subtle sort that ever tried a man. And I'm no strong man, I know that now, or I never would have wandered from my mother's teachings and her Bible and the God I used to love when I was a child. I must be weak and easily led or I should never have come to the pass I did to let my mother go across without knowing I had cast that all aside and was true! Oh, God, you have forgiven me, I know, but I can never forgive myself! May I be kept from falling. You can keep me from falling. I remember your own words: 'And now unto Him who is able to keep me from falling, and to present me faultless'—I commit myself, my soul, my life! Give me wisdom that I may if possible win men from the false way of thinking, whatever bypath they have taken in that direction. Especially show me how to help men out of the new and modern blindness that has befallen the earth, which was my own undoing. Oh, my Saviour, show me how to make men see what I have seen—!"

The night went on and the stars kept vigil with him beside the old tree, where he communed with his God and received, as it were, his commission to go forth and preach, a kind of anointing of the spirit without which no man has a right to go into the ministry, no matter how much he has studied, nor how long he has been in preparing.

He had not felt the cold, nor known that it was late as he walked up and down, and occasionally knelt. Once more the Word was his attendant, bringing verse after verse out of the storehouse of his memory where his faithful mother had helped to put them long years before against a time like this, to make him wise unto salvation. And as he watched the stars and the verses began to come, it was as if an open book were spread before him and he read:

"The heavens declare the glory of God, and the firmament showeth His handiwork. Day unto day uttereth speech, and night unto night showeth knowledge." What was that his mother had read him long ago when he was only half comprehending something about God having taught the signs of the zodiac to Adam, or was it Abraham? He could not remember. And that there was sufficient evidence to make it certain that the signs of the zodiac were known in those long ago days, and that to those who rightly read them they foretold many things that were written in the Bible and made plain much that was sealed otherwise. Ah! He wished he could remember it all. If his mother had read it somewhere others must know. He must look it up. His believing heart no longer saw it a matter for amusement, but rather one for deep thought and research. Ah! What a wonderful thing if God had written His wishes in the heavens in letters of stars to be read by those who cared to learn!

The morning star had made its appearance as he came down the mountain at last, and found his way in the deep darkness just before the dawn more by the sense of feeling than by sight. Mrs. Burnside lifted her head anxiously from the pillow and listened as he let himself into the house and wondered what and where and how, and then sank back to puzzle over it again. "If there was any train up from the city at this hour," she said to herself, "I'd uv thought he had been to the theatre. But he must have been over to Clarion to see some girl and had to foot it home. I do hope he isn't got started wrong over in that horrid France, his mother loved him so!" Then she sank back to thankful sleep again. It was enough that he had given her this wonderful haven of refuge. He must be a good boy after all. She summoned courage in the morning before he left to tell him she hoped he'd remember that his mother wanted him to be a good man, and he smiled reassuringly, and stooped and kissed her wrinkled old forehead.

"Thank you for caring," he said; "I'll remember." And then he walked down the street to the station on his way into the ministry. It was not as he had thought he would go long years ago, nor as his mother and he had pictured he would start away to his first preaching, but he felt that somewhere up with God she knew, and he was content.

17

Marjorie Horliss-Cole had come home. Mountain air was too dull for her. Besides, she had received word that "Al" had a good opportunity of making big money by going to the Philippines for six months to superintend the putting up of a large sugar refinery, with brilliant prospects ahead for a fine business career if he made good and he wanted to consult with her before leaving. She came home, spent a blissful, tearful day with him by means of a hired car and dinner at a country inn while she was supposedly doing some shopping for her Aunt Sylvia, and then bade him good-bye. The horizon seemed now to be dull indeed since he had gone and further intrigues seemed not worth while although her friend who had instituted many house parties in the past offered a number of substitutes as consolation. But Marjorie's thoughts were on the high seas and scanning foreign shores. The other youths who passed for her favor seemed flat and uninteresting, and she preferred to mope, and read novels. Not even the near approach of Christmas stirred an answering smile. Her mother was becoming worried and heaping gifts upon her child, and Marjorie was bright enough to make hay while the sun shone, and maintained her attitude of lassitude. So it was Marjorie who arose languidly from a deep chair in the luxurious library, and flinging aside her book, came forward to meet the young minister as he entered, escorted by the magnificent butler.

"I beg your pardon, Miss Marjorie, I wasn't aware you were in here," he said anxiously. "It was Mr. Horliss-Cole's orders, Miss, that Mr. Treeves should be brought in here when he came."

"It's all right, Bryan, Mr. Treeves is a friend of mine," she said brightly, and he withdrew, warmed by her smile. In fact, she was the light of his old eyes, he having been in the employ of the family since her babyhood.

For a moment John Treeves was puzzled to know where he had met the pretty little girl with the big eyes and restless expression, so far were his thoughts from the few minutes he had spent in her company. But Marjorie Horliss-Cole lost no time in putting him at his ease, and connecting the links without a break between their last conversation and the present. She was past master at all that sort of thing. It was what she had been sent to school for, and it was about all the upbringing she had ever had.

And so for a time he sat and let her prattle, or answered her questions about the war and his experience indifferently enough, glad just to be in the company of a woman and feel in touch with home again. Presently he began to ask her questions about the church.

"It's on the avenue, of course," she answered indifferently, "and it's quite stunning. The windows cost millions of dollars and it's been all remodeled. It's an awfully popular place to get married, it's so well-suited for the decorations, you know. But churches are such dull places. I scarcely ever go since I've grown up. Of course we had to in school, unless we could get up a headache or something. But I'm going to-morrow, it will be such fun to see some one in the pulpit that I know. I often wonder why any young man takes it up though. It must be awfully poky. Of course it's tremendously distinguished and all that if one goes in for something to do and doesn't just care for society, but it's so confining; and if you want to go off to Florida or anywhere with a house party it must be such a bore to get somebody to take your place. Of course we have three assistant pastors now and always one of them can be substituted at the last minute. Oh, yes, I believe they are in charge of missions or something of the sort, but then *any*body can take a mission if one of them is needed to preach. And it really isn't so bad. I believe our minister only preaches once a day, although I'm not sure; I haven't been in a long time. Would you like to go down and look at the church? It isn't far and the car is always ready."

Treeves said he would, but couldn't they walk? Marjorie, with a dash of interest, declared it would be "perfectly dandy," and ran up to get her hat and coat. Together they walked down the avenue to the old stately church distinguished through the years for its line of brilliant pastors and its wealthy congregation.

They stepped within the padded doors and were shut in to the soft, rich gloom. High over the arching vault above the altar glowed great golden letters above a priceless window of rich glass like crusted jewels, "THE LORD IS IN HIS HOLY TEMPLE. LET ALL THE EARTH KEEP SILENCE BEFORE HIM."

Treeves had lifted his hat and bowed his head, a glow of comfort coming into his heart. Here was his Guide. It was all right. He could be at home and give the message. Oh, the wonder that he should be allowed! But Marjorie chatted on.

"Religion isn't quite such a bore as it used to be.

People are broader, don't you think? I have some friends who don't believe in anything and they are perfectly lovely and have the best times. But it doesn't seem quite decent not to go to church once in a while. It's sort of a nice thing for sick and old people, I suppose. But it's so dreadfully dreary. If I had my way I would start a new church like the old temples we used to study about in school where they had girls in pretty Greek costumes dancing, and wreaths and big silver platters of fruit for offerings, and young men in togas pitching quoits. People would come to church then and it would be something interesting. For my part I don't see if there is a God why he wouldn't want things a little pleasant and interesting. Times have changed anyway and people won't stand for serious things. The war did away with a lot of tiresome things. Why, in some churches people brought their knitting! I really wouldn't mind going to church if there was something worth while to do. Come now, confess; isn't it a horrible bore to you?"

John Treeves looked down at the pretty young heathen before him and perceived that here was his first congregation, and what should he say? He understood that the Lord meant him to give a message:

"Why, no," he said with a winning smile. "If it was I wouldn't have any business preaching. It's life, it's great! It's the only thing worth while!"

and a light came into his face that almost startled the girl as she watched him, and wholly puzzled her.

"But why? How?" she faltered. "What is it all for anyway? I don't see any sense in churches. We can be good at home if we want to."

"Yes, but this is God's house. Here we can come nearer to Him than anywhere else. It is here he has promised to be. Look!" and he pointed up to the golden letters shimmering in a slant of afternoon sunlight that had somehow managed to steal into a crimson pane in a lofty window.

Marjorie looked up.

"You don't mean you think He is really here?" she asked wonderingly.

"Certainly." There was a quiet assurance in his voice that filled her with awe. She shivered and drew her beautiful furs closer to her throat, casting a half-fearful glance up toward the altar.

"How perfectly dreadful!" she said. "I shall never dare to come in here again when there aren't a lot of people around. You aren't a *spirit*ualist, are you? So many people are taking that up now. It's quite the latest fad."

"Oh, no," said John Treeves with his warming confident smile, "Spiritualism has to do with departed spirits. God is not departed. He is here; always has been. Christ died, but arose from the dead, and is a living presence today that every one may feel and know."

"Oh, how perfectly frightful!" said Marjorie Horliss-Cole shuddering. "Let's get out of here into the sunshine."

"No, please, wait," said the young preacher putting out a detaining hand. "I don't want you to go away with that impression. I shall have failed miserably in my first message if you do. Sit down and let me explain it to you. It is the most beautiful, the most wonderful, the most pleasant and comforting fact in the world. Christ is not here to frighten us, but because He loves us. He says: 'I came that ye might have life, and that ye might have it more abundantly.' The most of us are living in a little tiresome round trying to get away with time, and not realizing that there is more joy in life than we ever dreamed of. Christ came to be our close friend, to help us in our difficulties, to show us a way out of our disappointments, to forgive our sins, and to save us from their consequences. He does not want us to be afraid of Him. He wants us to enjoy Him, to understand Him, to reach out our souls in any need for Him. There isn't anything we cannot talk over with Him as we would talk to a great and influential friend, only more so, because this ONE will always understand our point of view and always be able to help, no matter how impossible it looks."

Marjorie Horliss-Cole had not sat down in the cushioned pew he had indicated; she had drawn away down the aisle toward the door, with a doubtful look of dissent; but now she paused and looked at him earnestly:

"Do you really mean that you think He will do things for people, *any*body, not just for *ministers? That He would change things so that you could have what you wanted?"*

"I really think so," said the young man bowing his head. "If you were His and He was yours. That's the only condition. 'If ye abide in me and my words abide in you ye shall ask what ye will and it shall be done unto you.' That levels up everybody alike. It makes no difference whether one is a minister or a washerwoman. The only condition is living in Christ and letting Him live in you. There might even be some ministers who wouldn't measure up to that."

"Do you mean that," said Marjorie Horliss-Cole wide-eyed and interested. "Do you really think that God looks on all people as equal? That everybody has the same chance to—well, have a good time and have what they want, and just live and be happy? Would a man—say that had been— well—suppose a man had been a prize-fighter or something like that, not because he was coarse or rude, of course, but just because he knew how and could earn his living that way; do you mean that God would think he was all right and could be made as good as a person in society with plenty of money?"

"God doesn't care for money or society or one's

business, or even whether one has been good or bad. He cares whether a man or a woman lets Him into their hearts to live, whether they are willing to believe in Him, to take Him at His word and let Him take their sins on Him and change their lives into Christlike lives. If a man or woman is willing to do that there is nothing that God won't do for them if they ask. Of course when they take Him in and let Him live in their hearts it may change some of the things they ask for, some of their desires, but it makes them see what are the really great things they want, and it gives them more joy than they ever dreamed of."

"You look as though you had really tried it," said Marjorie thoughtfully.

"I have!" he said with a joyous ring in his voice. "I'm not just talking what I have learned out of a book, I've tried it, and it's all true."

"Well, I want something with all my heart, something that I don't see any chance of ever getting," said Marjorie Horliss-Cole with tears suddenly in her big dark eyes. "Do you really mean that if I would do what you say that I could have it?"

"If you take Christ into your heart to live and find that you still want that thing I really mean that I think He would give it to you."

"Well, what would I have to do?" said Marjorie Horliss-Cole dropping into the nearest pew and clasping her hands on the back of the seat in front, looking up at him with an attitude of surrender.

John Treeves stood before her with a light of other worlds in his eyes and began to tell the story of salvation, slowly, plainly, earnestly as to a little child, making sin suddenly stand out as a fact to be reckoned with, making a loving Saviour ready to forgive a reality. He had learned it all at his mother's knee; it was not just the fruit of his recent experience. As he told it he realized that he did not need to search for the right thing to tell her, it was already there. It had been there all the time, only he had laid it away as a worn-out formula. Now he saw that it was the saving truth which had been made to live again through his own turning to search for the Lord, and the Lord's answering presence and forgiveness. He made it very plain that no soul could save himself or forgive himself, that it was the work of Christ on the cross, and that sorrow for sin and belief in the death on the cross was the sinner's part of the matter. Christ did the rest and transformed one into another creature.

She listened intently but he could not tell how she was taking it. Somehow it did not seem to matter so he told the story. It was as if he were preaching his first sermon in the presence of Christ, and an awe had fallen upon him. He was conscious of wishing to get the message across to his audience, but realized that that was not his part to perform. A verse like a voice rang in his ear:

"Ye have not chosen me, but I have chosen you, and ordained you, that ye should go and bring forth fruit, and that your fruit should remain: that whatsoever ye shall ask of the Father in my name, he may give you." So rang the words, and his heart put up the request, "Oh, Christ, bring this soul to know thee, whom to know is life everlasting!"

The girl sat very still as he finished talking, and without looking up, said:

"Well, it sounds very strange. I never heard anybody talk so before, but if I thought He would do what I want Him to I think I would try it."

Was the child coming to Christ for the loaves and a fish? He looked at her earnestly to be sure; he had made it plain.

"You know it would have to be a real giving of yourself to Christ. You could not expect Him to answer your desire unless you had put all that aside and complied with His condition, which says, 'If ye *abide* in me'—that means staying there forever, you know—'and my words abide in you'—that means that you read His book and make it your own, so that you will order your life by it—*then* 'ye shall ask what ye will and it shall be done unto you.'"

"I understand," she said thoughtfully, "it is awfully queer, but it sounds sensible. I'll think about it. But," lifting her eyes to his face, with a keen, searching glance, "aren't you somehow different from other ministers? I never heard one talk like that before."

"I hope not," said Treeves with a somewhat startled memory that he had never been really ordained as a minister in the church, and was perhaps going beyond his right to speak thus with authority. Then he remembered his mother who had taught him, and his grandfather "John" for whom he was named, who had taught her, and had been an honored minister of the Gospel for many years, and his heart was at rest. If he should be called to this pulpit he would doubtless have to go through the forms of ordination and everything would be duly done according to the forms and ceremonies. For himself he felt his true ordination had been out on the old bluff during his tryst with God, but for the next four Sundays he felt satisfied that his mother's religion would do that New York congregation no harm, even if it were not backed by the great body of an old and historic church. He had mentioned the fact to Mr. Horliss-Cole in his letter that he had gone to France before his last year at Seminary was completed, and was therefore as yet unordained, and Mr. Horliss-Cole had made no demur. Upon him be the consequences of an ordainless preacher for the next four Sundays.

They walked home thoughtfully through the gloaming talking of quite other things, and Miss Horliss-Cole handed him over to her father at the door and disappeared to her own room, but John Treeves found himself in spirit praying that she might find the way, and that he might be given words on the morrow to stir other souls to seek for the Christ.

18

No letters had been forwarded to Patricia Merrill in care of Miss Edith Fisher, and Patty was greatly distressed. Miss Cole watched her keenly and invented all sorts of excuses to get her out into the fresh air. She was quite upset that Dunham Treeves should have utterly disappeared from the horizon just as she was getting acquainted with him, and when he did not return and the days went by she was not at all disturbed to have Marjorie hurry back home. For the present Marjorie had acquired all the good she was likely to get from the "Companion," and there was no one among the young people to keep her spirits up. Miss Cole had made one of her points by getting a speaking acquaintance with young Treeves through Marjorie, and if he should return again she would be able to follow it up herself without her niece's assistance. Marjorie had progressed as far in her acquaintance with Edith Fisher as she was likely to get for a time, and her aunt felt that a little separation would not do any harm, so with a good grace she sent her home, telling her she had tried to keep her from coming in the first place. Patty and Miss Cole had settled down into a pleasant routine of days filled with reading, embroidery and walks, varied by an occasional evening down in the parlor, or a canter on horseback over the piney trails for Patty by herself.

It was while she was off on one of those rides that a stranger arrived at the hotel and asked for Miss Edith Fisher. It so happened that Miss Cole had gone down to the office with a letter she wanted to mail immediately, and heard the stranger talking with the clerk. She faced about, studied him a moment with pursed lips, then spoke:

"You asking for Miss Fisher? Well, I can tell you about her. Just come sit down. I'm not able to stand any longer this morning. I have rheumatism."

The hotel clerk waved his hand in assent. "Yes, Miss Cole can tell you," he said.

She puffed in a leisurely way out the length of the office, followed by the stranger who eyed her keenly, through one reception room after another, until she reached a little writing room that was usually deserted at this hour of the day and sat herself down in a big rocker, indicating another for the stranger:

"I am Mr. Sharp," announced the stranger. "I came on business to see Miss Edith Fisher. Can you tell me where to find her?"

Miss Cole looked him up and down keenly, her baffling eyes telling no tales whatever:

"Well, no, I can't. She's away today. I'm not sure just when she will be back. She didn't say when she left. Is there any message I could give her?"

The stranger looked annoyed.

"Has she gone far?"

"Well, now I'm not sure. She seemed uncertain when she left. She has a lot of relatives around here, and over in the next county. The Adamses, you know." When Miss Cole lied she always wished to justify herself. "Were you in a hurry to see her?"

"Yes, I was," confessed Mr. Sharp. "I wanted to catch the afternoon train to Washington. What time did she leave? Did she go by train or car?"

"No, she didn't take the train. She left about an hour ago."

"Ah! Did you see which road she took? I wonder if I could get a fast car and overtake her!"

"Hardly. She likes to go pretty fast herself," said Miss Cole dryly, "and you never can tell around here which way one takes, the roads wind and twist about till it makes you dizzy, but she's well on her way by this time. Isn't there something I could do to help you out?"

"Are you a relative of Miss Fisher?"

"Sort of," said Miss Cole. "I'm all she has just now, and I would be likely to know a good deal about her affairs." She wore an indifferent air that seemed to care little whether the young man gave her his confidence or not, and he studied her perplexedly:

"I wonder now if you happen to know anything about Miss Patricia Merrill?" he hazarded. "A friend of Miss Fisher's, you know."

A flicker of intelligence crossed Miss Cole's face:

"I've heard her mentioned," she answered indifferently.

"It's really about her that I have come," announced the stranger watching her closely. "Her mail was to have been forwarded here to be sent on by Miss Fisher." He drew forth a long envelope addressed neatly to Miss Edith Fisher in Patty's fine hand. It was one of the envelopes she had sent to her home postmaster.

Miss Cole reached out and studied the handwriting closely:

"Yes?" said Miss Cole encouragingly, as though she knew all about it.

"I didn't know but she might be here now—?" The stranger flung the suggestion at the lady with a tone that was insultingly familiar. Miss Cole was proud of the fact that she was not an aristocrat except by birth, but she knew how to assume the character in case of necessity.

"She is not here now!" she asserted stiffly, and half rose as though the interview were terminated.

"Then, could you tell me where I could find her?"

"I suppose you might leave a note for her in that envelope and let Miss Fisher send it on to her on her return. That was the direction she gave, was it not?"

Somehow Miss Cole could always manage to put anybody on the grill if she wanted to badly enough.

"Yes, but I must see her at once! You see I have a business paper for her to sign which requires haste and I have been sent out here by her lawyers to hunt her up and get her signature at once—!"

"By *her* lawyers, did you say?" questioned Miss Cole with an almost imperceptible emphasis on the pronoun.

"By the—ah—family lawyer, yes. It is a matter that will not wait, and Miss Merrill has been so careless as to leave them in ignorance of the details of her journey—!"

"She wasn't sure herself what she would do next," vouch-safed the lady calmly.

"Oh, then you do know her?" The stranger brightened.

"Well, I know something about her," she assented. "Now, this paper, what is its nature? Because"—as she saw he hesitated and looked at her suspiciously—"Miss Fisher had some directions, I believe, if certain papers—was it one relating to her property?" The game old lady hazarded the question at random and then looked up with as smug an expression as a cat that has just swallowed a bird. Patty might arrive home at any minute and spoil the whole thing. She must end it up as quickly as possible and send this brother on his way. He was a detective; she had scented that right at the start, and a rather common one at that. She hated the whole race of them, and resolved to protect her little alias Companion to the best of her very fine abilities. Besides, she did not believe he came from the family lawyer. He did not look cultured enough for the kind her little girl's family lawyer would likely employ. He was rude and familiar and altogether ill-bred. She did not trust him.

"Why—y-yes! It was. About property! Something that had to be settled up at once?"

"Um-m-m! Could I see the paper?"

"Well, not exactly, you know. It was for her privately."

"I see. But she isn't here, and I really couldn't do anything about it without knowing which one it was."

"I don't see how you could do anything if you don't know where she is," he growled belligerently, suspicion bristling from his glance.

"Probably not," said the old lady rocking indifferently, "but again, I might. I might succeed in getting Miss Fisher on the 'phone sometime and get the address from her if the matter was sufficiently important. We people are bothered a lot down here by very insignificant things and we came here to rest, you see."

"I see," said the young man uneasily, looking foiled. "Well, the fact is, the paper is sealed," he lied glibly. "I was barely told what I have told you about it. I was sent here to enquire of Miss Fisher where Miss Merrill was to be found at once, and I was to proceed to her hotel and hand her the paper. I was on no account to give it into other hands."

"Oh, very well!" said Miss Cole, rising calmly. "I guess your best way will be to run down to Hot Sulphur and see if she is there. Of course she might have gone to Washington this morning; she often does. Try the New Willard; that is where she stops, and if you fail there, there is no use trying this side of New York, I'm sure. I will wish you good morning. Sorry I couldn't help you, I'm sure."

"But wait!" said the young man anxiously striding beside her. "You must let me write this down. Do I understand that this is accurate information?"

"I really couldn't answer for your understanding, young man. Your name is Sharp. That ought to help you some. Try Hot Sulphur—all the hotels— she is somewhat erratic, you know—and then try Washington. If you don't find her at the New Willard, 'phone me. I'll be glad to give you any further information I have by that time, of course. You might leave your card also for Miss Fisher when she comes, and I'll tell her about it. Then if you don't find Miss Merrill she can leave a message here for you when you telephone. I wish you good morning, young man!"

Miss Cole swept into the elevator and was carried up out of sight, but she got off at the first floor above and trotted hastily to the upper gallery, where behind a row of palms she could scan the office unobserved. The young man looked after her angrily, and stepped up to the desk.

"Don't *you* know where Miss Edith Fisher is?" he demanded noisily.

The hotel clerk had not much use for a voice like that in the office. He looked the stranger over haughtily and replied:

"You been talking to Miss Cole, haven't you? Well, then, if she doesn't know, nobody else around here does. Miss Fisher's her niece or something. I can't tell you anything more."

"When does your next train go?"

"Right now, the car's at the door. You better beat it quick, she's just starting," advised the clerk jauntily, and slid himself into a little inner office out of sight.

The stranger turned and beat a hasty retreat. Miss Cole grimly smiling at the upper hall window watched him drive out of sight, and a moment later saw a trim little figure on horseback round the curve and flash past the car around to the stables. The day was saved, or Patty was saved, which was what the day had come to mean for Miss Cole.

While they were eating their lunch that noon at a little table that looked out into the plumy pines, Miss Cole made a casual statement:

"There was a man here to see you to-day."

Patty looked up startled, a great fear growing in her eyes and contending with what looked like a great hope.

"At least he came to see Miss Edith Fisher," went on Miss Cole, not seeming to notice the girl's agitation.

"Oh!" said Patty relaxing, and then her eyes growing dark with thought once more. "But I don't know how anyone would know I was here. I've never told anyone that name—but you people!"

"Not anyone?"

"Well, I told the postmaster at home to forward mail to Edith Fisher here."

"That's it! Have you had any?"

"Not a thing."

"H'm!" said Miss Cole, dissecting her fish, while Patty grew white as she tried to realize what this must mean. "The postmaster has given you away."

"What did he want?" faltered Patty.

"Nothing much. Just sent by some lawyers, he said, to get the present whereabouts of some friend of yours that had to sign a paper right away this minute. You needn't worry about him. I sent

242

him packing. I advised him to look in on the hotels at White Sulphur and if he didn't find her there by all means to try the New Willard in Washington. He's to 'phone me from there and see if I have any further information. And now you needn't tell me anything about it unless you have to."

Patty looked at her for a moment with the tears blurring her eyes, and then broke into a comprehending merry little laugh:

"Oh, you perfect DEAR!" she chirruped softly. "If we were only alone, I'd kiss you!"

"Oh, mercy!" exclaimed Miss Cole crossly, but she looked as if she liked it.

The very next afternoon a card was sent up to the room for Miss Fisher, bearing the name of Harold Barron, and Patty went white as death as she looked at it.

"What is it?" asked Miss Cole suddenly arising from a supposed nap. "Is that Sharp fool here again?"

Patty tremblingly handed her the card and put her hand flutteringly to her throat.

"No," she said in a small dry voice. "No!" with a catch and a sob: "but—now—they have found out! And I don't know what I ought to do."

"Do you want to see him?"

"Oh, no!" Patty shrank back as from a dreaded apparition.

"Well, then, you shan't! Here! Where's my purse?"

She arose from her bed, snatched her purse, and all in her afternoon nap disarray, as she was,—boudoir cap on one side, silver hair in curls about her face, sensible gray flannel wrapper trailing crookedly after her—she marched magnificently from the room. Patty was too shaken to stop her.

She had a moment's conversation with the bellboy outside the door, and sailed in again shuffling her gray felt bedroom slippers determinedly and snapping her purse shut.

"There!" she said with satisfaction as she turned the key in the lock with a click. "That's *that!* Now, let's pack! We're going home to-night! I'm not going to have you bothered like this, and there's no telling how many more will be on your trail by morning. If you want them to come you've only to say the word, but if you don't I'm going to take care of you. I've sent for the hotel clerk and I'm going to make it worth his while to say that we spoke of touring Florida for the winter, so I guess he'll know how to keep his mouth shut. No, you needn't say a word. I *want* to go home. I've wanted to all along, only I hadn't any reason to go, for of course Kate has a lot of goings on at Christmas and she would rather have my room than my company, but I've a perfect right to my room in that house, goodness knows, and as long as it isn't convenient for me to stay away any longer I'm going home. If you don't like it there we'll go somewhere else, but we'll go there first anyhow. You're mine as long as you choose to stay—and—MERCY! child!"

For the first time in her life Sylvia Cole knew what it was to have a grown-up girl fling her arms around her neck, cry on her shoulder, and then kiss her fervently again and again. It almost overwhelmed the poor lonely woman, but she bore it grimly and liked it. Presently Patty, with tear-stained face, and a smile twinkling out between the dimples, began to pack.

"You don't know how dear and delicious it is to have somebody care!" said Patty ecstatically, and then stopped suddenly as if she had said something she ought not to have said.

"Why, child! Haven't you any mother?"

The words were out before Miss Cole realized, but she hastened to atone:

"There! I'm an old fool! I ought to have known better. No, don't tell me a word. I know there's something troubling you and you ought not to tell it or you would have explained long ago. It's all right and I respect you for your silence, so let it go at that. Now, where shall we put those fool evening rags? I might as well have left them in New York for all the good they've done me still—*once!* Well, put them back in their box and send them by parcel post. We've no call to overwork packing. Let's take things easy and enjoy the trip."

Patty silent and excited followed all directions

perfectly, and now and then laughed half hysterically at the flow of original conversation with which Miss Cole enlivened the remainder of the afternoon.

But there was one call of farewell that Patty felt she must make before she left, and Miss Cole seemed to be as conscious of it as she was herself, and perhaps had been planning for it.

19

Several days before these happenings she had been walking back to the hotel from one of the trails where she had left Miss Cole to get the afternoon mail, and choosing a path she had not often gone before she came to a little nook among the pines where the trees were arranged almost like a tiny room, sheltered from the passersby, and quite sunny and pleasant. With a soft exclamation of delight she peered in and then perceived that the room was already occupied by a little shriveled old man done up in furs in a wheeled chair, who glared out at her and flung up a hand angrily, thereby displacing his rugs and dropping a pair of shell-rimmed glasses which had been lying in his lap.

"Oh, I beg your pardon!" said Patty in a soft ripple of excuse. "I didn't know that anyone was here, and I was only looking in to see how lovely it was. Let me pick them up!" and she stooped and laid the glasses back in his lap.

"Who are you?" he demanded, glaring at her fiercely out of his little hard eyes.

"Oh, just a girl that is staying at the Inn with Miss Cole. I'm sorry I intruded. I hope you'll excuse me!"

"Miss Cole, eh? Well, you should have known better, but now you are here make yourself useful. Pull that collar up around my left ear. It's nearly frozen off, and go tell that rascal of a man of mine that he's killing me with all this cold air. He went to get my tonic and he's been gone about two hours. He ought to know better! I shall dismiss him when he gets back."

Patty tucked the furs around him as if he had been a baby and gave a final pat to the laprobe.

"Now, are you all comfy? And shall I go hunt the man? What does he look like and what is his name? Or would you rather I should wheel you back to the house?"

"You couldn't. You'd spill me down the mountain," quavered the old man. "But if I let you go you'll stay as long as he does, and I'm c-c-cold!"

"Of course I'll wheel you back!" said Patty taking capable hold of the chair; "and of course I won't spill you. It's as easy to wheel as a baby carriage. See! I've turned it around nicely; now we'll be back before you know it. Which door do you prefer, back or front?"

"Oh, back, of course! There's always some old cat about, no matter how cold the day is."

Old Hespur, blindly dashing down the path, almost ran over them a moment later in his excitement:

"Oh, sir," he crooned breathlessly. "The chambermaid had been cleaning, sir, and dropped the bottle out of the window. Most careless, sir. I was obliged to go to the bottom of the hamper that came last night for another bottle, sir."

"Get out of the way, you old rascal!" growled the master. "We're doing well enough without you. You might as well get back to the hotel and pack up. You're leaving at once!"

Hespur quite used to such treatment said:

"Yessir!" quite meekly and fell behind, taking the weight of the push as the chair wheeled up the hill. Patty, gifted with wise understanding, kept her place as if she were pushing, and talked in a cheery tone to the old reprobate about the beautiful day and the sunshine and mountains and air, never heeding his growling dissent, and when they reached the door she stepped to his side, saying:

"Now, you'll be all right, I'm sure, and I'll just run on and get Miss Cole's mail—!"

"Well, well, well!" blustered the old man, putting out a detaining hand, but before he could stop her Patty with a smile and a bow slipped away.

That evening a beautiful box of roses was brought to Miss Cole's apartment. "For the young lady with the smile, with Calvin Treeves's compliments."

"What shall I do?" asked Patty turning to Miss Cole with the open box of loveliness and a troubled look on her face. "He oughtn't to be sending me flowers. I didn't do anything but the simplest act of courtesy."

"There are none too many of those left in the world, child," said Miss Cole, "and few falling his way that are not baited with silver. Better run around to his apartment and thank him. He may swear at you, but it will do him good, poor old soul. He's been too crusty and too selfish to get many of the good things of life except such as money will buy, and that isn't much, I've found out."

She ended with a half sigh, and Patty with a thoughtful look at her and wearing one of the roses in her hair and another nestled in her gown, slipped down the hall and tapped at Calvin Treeves's door.

She stayed a half hour that first evening, talking and laughing, relating a bit of happening from her school life, singing a scrap of a tender song, and impersonating a funny old woman she had known in her childhood. When she was gone the old man said to his servant in a tone he kept for the seldom and real things of life:

"That's a fine child, Hespur, a fine child! That's the kind I'd have liked my daughter to be if I'd ever had one."

Old Hespur, deeply moved, and pottering round tidying the already tidied room, agreed:

"She's all that, sir, she's *all* that."

Thereafter just at dusk every evening Hespur tapped at Miss Cole's door and preferred the request:

"Would Miss Fisher be pleased to read awhile to my master to-night?" Or, "He's been having a bad day again. Would the young lady be kind enough to come and give him a bit of cheer?"

So Patty would spend a half hour or more with the old rascal, who under her happy ministrations had become as tame as a canary in her presence. Whenever she entered the room it seemed to the two old men that the sun had suddenly arisen. Hespur would set her a chair, and give a poke to the fire to send the flames leaping up joyously, and would tiptoe away to a point of vantage with a sigh of relief, to enjoy the half hour as much as his master. When she had been coming for three days it seemed as though she had belonged to them for years, and they began to count on the hour of dusk as the centre of the whole day.

So when Patty walked into the room in her traveling dress and hat and announced that she had come to say good-bye, it had all the effect of a bomb on the quiet room.

"What! What—what! *WHAT!*" sputtered old Calvin Treeves in a blaze of anger.

"I'm sorry," said Patty gently. "I want to finish reading that story to you, but perhaps if I get at it I can get the most of it done—!"

"Story! Story be *hanged!* It's you I want! *YOU,* I say! YOU and she shan't take you away from me. I say, she *shan't!* You tell her so from me! You tell her so-o-o-o!"

The tears were rolling down the old man's face and he was trembling.

"Oh, I'm so sorry!" said Patty. "But you mustn't feel that way. Nobody is taking me away from you. I'll always be friends, and maybe some day I'll be where I can read to you again."

"No, *no, NO!*" said the old man shaking his head from side to side like a spoiled child. "If you go now I'll never get you again! It's always so. Everything I get that I like leaves me. It's a curse. IT'S A CURSE! She told me long ago I'd be cursed for my money—!"

"There, now, Master. There, there!" soothed Hespur patting his shoulder lovingly. "It's no curse, sir, it's just life, sir! We's all like that! You have to be brave, sir! Don't you see you're distressing the young lady! We don't want for to make the young lady feel bad. There's tears in her bright eyes. The young lady's been very good, she has, and you shouldn't reward her by getting upset, sir, when she didn't go for to make you feel badly."

251

"Oh, no," said Patty brushing away the tear-drops that had sprung into her eyes at the pitiful sight of the poor old child. "No, I wouldn't hurt you for the world, and you mustn't take such a mournful view of things. Sometime very likely I'll be back. If I get a chance I surely will, but it happens just now that things are so I ought to go. Listen! Suppose I write you a letter! Would you like that? It will be almost like talking to you, and then you can write me one back some day. How will that be?"

"You would forget!" mourned the old man. "Young people have their own lives. You are like my nephew. He came, and I *wanted* him, and he went. He wouldn't stay for all the money in the world. And now you are that way, too? You will go away and forget."

"No, I will not forget," said Patty soberly. "I will write you a letter once a week and tell you something interesting that I have seen. But I don't think your nephew has forgotten."

"Do you know my nephew?" the old man sat up and shot a quick glance at her.

The color flew into Patty's cheeks, but she answered coolly enough:

"I've seen him, of course, but what I mean is this: You probably haven't made him understand that you really care. If you had you wouldn't have lost him. Because I'm sure he hasn't forgotten. He's probably not understood, that's all. I have an idea you are one of those people that shut all the lovely part of them up tight in a shell and show only the hard, prickly side, and expect your friends to guess that it wasn't all hard and prickly."

Patty's smile was adorable, the kind that would make the most unkind truth seem flattery. The old man looked at her sharply.

"You know," said Patty dimpling. "You weren't just really your best when you first met me. If I remember rightly, you gave me a very cool welcome, and if I had followed my first impulse I should just have scuttled off out of your sight in a hurry and never have crossed your vision again—"

"You're a very plain-spoken young woman!" he snarled with a half a smile on his old purple lips.

"Well, isn't it true, Mr. Treeves: weren't you very cross indeed to me that first day?"

"Well, I suppose I was," he admitted shamedly, "but I'm an old man and I'm used to having my own way, and people have to make allowances for me."

"But people won't, you know," said Patty sadly, with a cute little tilt of her head. "They'll just think you are a horrid cross old bear and keep away from you, when they ought to know that you are very nice behind the prickers, and a splendid friend to have!"

"There There! THERE! There! *THERE!*" spluttered the old man beginning to weep again. "I'm not! You *know* I'm not, and what's the use saying it? Hespur, you old fool, don't stand there gaping! Go get that leather box of mine! QUICK!"

Hespur was at his side almost immediately with a dark leather-covered box in his hand.

"Get the KEY, you old fool! What good is the box without the key, I'd like to know?"

"Why, that's just what I said," laughed Patty. "What good is it to have a nice heart unless you give the key of it to your friends?"

"But I haven't a nice heart! I have a bad one!" confessed the old sinner looking into her eyes as if she were an angel come to bring him to judgment.

"Oh no," said Patty quite emphatically. "You've shown me that you have a good heart. We've had some very pleasant talks together here."

"You only came because you were sorry for me," grumbled the old man bitterly. "I saw it in your eye every time."

"No," said Patty firmly, "I had another reason, too. I was sorry for you because I saw you put the prickly on the outside, but I really had another reason for coming."

"Well, what was it?"

"Why," said Patty hesitating, "I didn't expect to tell you that, but I will. There's no reason why I shouldn't. It was just that I once loved your sister-in-law very much. She was the sweetest woman I ever knew—and, when you asked me, I came to see you for her sake!"

"WHAT!" exploded the old man. "My, MY S-S-Sister-in-law! Why, I never *had* a sister-in-law, child! *Oh!* You—you—why you must mean—why! did you mean my nephew's *mother?*"

"Yes," said Patty simply, not understanding why there should be anything extraordinary in that. "I spent a few weeks once in the village where she lived. She was very good to me and I loved her. I think she was the most wonderful woman I ever knew."

"Why—I—I think so, *TOO!*" the old man burst out and the tears flowed gallantly down his cheeks in the first really repentant confession he ever made in his wicked old life. "I THINK SO, TOO, *DON'T I,* HESPUR?" The question came out with a bounce at the old servant so that he fairly jumped up in the air as he answered:

"Yessir! Yessir! You *do,* sir! That you do, sir! I've always said to myself you did, sir! Always, sir!"

"I'm so glad you loved her, too!" said Patty softly. "And now, I've got to go, for I've several things yet to do before we leave and it's getting late. But I'll not forget to write."

Then she stooped and did the most extraordinary thing. She *kissed* the leathery, massaged, powdered, perfumed old forehead with a gentle daughterly salute like a rose breath and was gone.

It was safe to say that a kiss like that had never dropped upon his soul from any lips since his mother had kissed him as a child. He sat quiet, petrified, until the door had closed behind her, somewhat prolonged by a bit of farewelling by Hespur on his own account, and then he dropped his old head on his clawlike old hands and burst into wholesome tears.

"Therey! Therey!" patted old Hespur. "She's gone, but wasn't she a thoroughbred? Never did I see two that would have mated so evenlike. Bless 'em, I hope they sometime meets together!"

The old man looked up a cunning twinkle in his streaming eyes:

"You think so, too, Hespur, don't you? I knew you would. I thought of it the first time I laid eyes on her. Do you think, Hespur, it would do to put it in the will?"

"No, sir, I don't, sir! You know he's a chip off the old block, and there's none like them to get a bit bullheaded if you try to drive them. It's like a calling, this marrying is, sir; it's got to come from above or it won't work the right combination, sir. Better trust to Heaven, sir, if it's meant, sir, it's meant, and nothing'll stop it. It's too delicate a matter, sir, for man's hand to meddle with."

"That's right, Hespur. I'm an old fool. I've bungled my own life and now I'm trying to bungle my nephew's. But say, Hespur, you rascal, what's that on the floor? Is that my jewel box? You old reprobate! You never picked it up! And she never saw the jewels! And I wanted to give her one—!"

He began to sob in dry, hopeless gasps:

"It's not too late yet, sir. I could go take it to her, sir. Pick out what you like, sir, and I'll take it to her quick, sir."

The old hands grasped at the box, a great glitter of magnificent stones, picked up in all quarters of the earth, the pride and the boast of his heart, wrangled and grasped after, and collected, and kept in a wonderful safe in his room; no fit companion for a rich and wicked old man, but yet one of his whims that he had insisted upon.

They hung above the precious stones.

"Shall I give her the ring with the blue diamond?" he asked as his fingers hovered above the azure blaze.

"Why not the white, sir? It's very wonderful with a heart like fire, sir!"

"No!" said the old man sharply, then sadly. "No, Hespur, I'll never give that away. That's the ring I bought for the girl I loved. You didn't know I loved a girl once, did you, Hespur?" His voice was almost a whisper. "But I did. Now, *Hespur!* Don't you ever let me know I told you that, or I'll send you to *THUNDER!!!* Do you *HEAR???*"

Hespur caught his breath:

"Yessir! That's all right, sir! I'll remember, sir!"

"I don't want you to REMEMBER! I want you to *FORGET!*"

"That's all right, sir. I mean forget, sir! I was forgetting, sir, then, sir! That was what I was doing, sir! Did you say you was going to send the blue diamond, sir? I'll get the little velvet box, sir, shall I?"

The ring was hastily encased and Hespur hurried away with the gift, but he was scarcely back again in the room and mending the master's fire when light, hurrying feet were heard at the door, and Patty rushed in:

"Oh, Mr. Treeves, dear! I couldn't take this. It is very wonderful and beautiful, but I couldn't take a gift like this."

"Why not, if I want to give it?" The little old man was trembling and crouching, his last pleasure was being taken away from him.

"Why, because it isn't right. I shouldn't feel right, and if anyone ever found it out they would think I had come to see you for what I could GET! How I should hate that! And by and by you might get to thinking that, too, you know."

"But that is just so you won't forget me!" he pleaded. He was beginning to see how his ill-gotten gains would not buy him a thing that he really wanted.

"Oh, there's no danger of that," she smiled. "And here, if you want to give me a keepsake, let me have the little book I read to you from the first evening."

"It was only a library book. It's gone back!" sighed the old man wearily. "It wasn't mine to give. Nothing is, it seems, that's worth while."

"I'm sorry to make you feel this way," said Patty, troubled, "but indeed I couldn't take a valuable thing like that. Haven't you some little trifle?"

"That's only a trifle," he said fretfully. "If you only knew me better you'd think it was a good thing that I wanted to give it away. I'm not much of a giver. But show her the box, Hespur, maybe she'll find something she'd like better."

"Oh!" breathed Patty as the box was opened and the light flashed out from a thousand facets. For a moment she gazed in wonder, and then her glance traveled rapidly through the collection of rings, pendants, pins, bracelets, chains and unset jewels.

"What is this?" she said, pointing to a little slender gold ring, worn almost to a thread, and set with a single tiny pearl so small as to seem almost mean and cheap in the wonder of display. "Is it something you care for very much, or could I take that?"

"It was my mother's ring," he murmured. "Take it. I should like to have you have it, if you will. She never had money to buy anything better. I kept it because it was hers, but I am going soon where I can't keep it any longer. If you will take it I shall be glad. You are the kind of girl she was."

"I shall keep it very sacredly," said Patty gently, "and I feel honored that you want me to have it, though I should not have chosen it if I had known it was precious to you. I hate to take it from you. You should have it always."

"No! No! *NO!*" he fretted. "Take it! It's not precious! Nothing is precious, I tell you, in this whole blamed world! It's all nonsense to live anyway, and worse to die! It's an outrage to have to!"

"Oh, please don't talk like that. You mustn't! It's wrong you know. There's a God somewhere and He likely loves you. I've always heard that God loves and understands everybody. It's often comforted me to believe that. Try it and see."

"God! GOD! What do I want of a *GOD!* All He'd ever want with me would be to damn me—!"

"There! THERE! Mister Treeves, MASTER! Remember, it's a young LADY you're talking to"—broke in Hespur excitedly—"and she'll miss her train, the young lady will."

"Well, there, *go* child!"

The old man snatched her hand and pressed his withered old lips wildly, desperately, reverently on the soft fingers, then flung it from him.

"GO! I said, and forget all that I have said! But don't forget to write to me! *Don't*—forget—!"

When Patty arrived in Miss Cole's room once more her face was so disturbed and troubled that the elder woman questioned her and Patty told all that had occured:

"It was dreadful, Miss Cole! I felt so sorry for him! He seems to be so lonely, and he carried on so—!"

"Well, it'll do him good!" snapped Miss Cole unexpectedly, although Patty could see she was wiping away a tear. "Yes, it'll do him good!" she reiterated as if to reassure herself. "He's had his own way all his life. He's been selfish and grasping and cruel and overbearing and he didn't care for anybody, so he got more and more money, for money was *power*, and that was what he wanted above everything—!"

"You knew him then when he was young?"

Miss Cole was so excited that for once her alertness did not guard her secrets:

"Yes, I knew him!" she answered, turning to look out of the window into the dark pines. "Oh, I knew him!" (A pause.) "He could have had what he wanted if he hadn't cared more for his ambitions and his own way than for his friends. But he chose this way! He made his bed, let him lie on it! Plenty of people have spent their lives on the beds he made for *them!* Come, it's time we got downstairs! Where is that porter?"

In thoughtful silence Patty followed her down to the office and into the cab. It was not until they were established in the sleeper and everything stowed away comfortably that she ventured another question:

"Do you think I was wrong in promising to write to him?"

Miss Cole started as from a reverie and her eyes were sad and soft as she answered:

261

"No, child, I don't! Poor old soul! Give him all the comfort you can now. He hasn't long for it in this world, and if all accounts are true, I don't believe he has much chance for it in the next—if there *is* a next!"

Patty went to sleep that night with a great ache pounding in her heart and smarting in her eyes, and somehow she felt Miss Cole was tangled up in the tragedy. Then she dreamed that she and Miss Cole were trying to pull old Calvin Treeves out of a deep, dark pool, and he clutched at the slimy bank with his claw-like hands and screamed wildly for help, while his old servant stood weeping.

She awoke to a gray December morning with lazy snowflakes whirling through the air and carloads of Christmas trees everywhere along the side tracks.

20

John Dunham did not accept the pressing invitation of Horliss-Cole to spend Christmas day in the Fifth Avenue mansion. Instead he ate a roasted chicken with onions and squash and a rice pudding, with Mrs. Burnside and her grandson in the little home bungalow at the end of the village street in Maple Brook. Not that he desired to do so. It was as far from his wish as the Fifth Avenue mansion. Christmas Day held sad memories for him, and it was only because he saw that Mrs. Burnside considered it her duty and was severely set upon it, that he humored her and stayed. She made a great deal of his being able to have the comforts of his old home on this holiday of holidays; but every reference she made to the old days hurt him like a knife and he was glad that late in the afternoon he might reasonably plead the necessity for wending his way cityward. Even then he did not present himself at the Horliss-Cole house until very late, preferring to wander about the city rather than to come in on Christmas festivities that did not belong to him.

He had said he would be late and he had hoped to be let quietly in by the footman and escorted to his room without the knowledge of the family. But he had failed to reckon by New York standards and he found everything in full blast about a mammoth Christmas tree whose lights made the great entrance hall one blaze of color, and put to shame the big yule log blazing rarely in the immense, carved-stone fireplace that flanked one entire end of the room. A concealed orchestra behind a wall of palms and ferns on the gallery above the wide staircase were sending forth most delicious strains, haunted with tender old Christmas carols and gay with the lilt of Christmas merriment culled from the music of the ages. Young men and maidens, a select company in gala attire, were dancing and frolicking around the Christmas tree, and the place seemed one mad whirl of joy as he entered. For a moment he stood on the edge of the room and looked about him, feeling most tremendously out of place in his present mood, and wishing with all his heart he had remained in the streets for another two hours rather than encounter this just now. Then Marjorie Horliss-Cole, whose gleaming shoulders and back rose startlingly beautiful in contrast to the amazing frock all gauze and sparkle that was neither midnight blue nor yet deep smoky forest green, rushed forward and took possession of him. Her dark eyes were more wonderful than ever set off by the soft dusky hair in which nestled a string of some strange jewels that held all the lights of blue and green in her robe. If he had put his thoughts into words she seemed like the very spirit and essence of the Christmas tree stepped down off its branches to converse with men.

But John Treeves did not feel that he had time to play with the spirit of Christmas trees that night. His heart was full of the message he meant to bring to the church on the morrow. It was also full of sad memories, and the day with Mrs. Burnside had not been particularly helpful, for that good woman seemed to feel it incumbent upon her to refer to his mother's illness and the details of her death with every other breath, until his heart was wrung with pain and every nerve cried out for rest.

Therefore while he smiled pleasantly at the bright apparition of the girl his spirit shrank from mirth and longed for quiet.

"You are just in time to dance this with me!" she cried brightly, balancing on a silver slipper and holding out a shapely hand.

"Thank you," he said. "I'm not a dancer."

"Oh, never mind that, I'll soon teach you, though I'm sure I don't see how you possibly went through the war without learning. I understand there was a great deal of it over there. Come on, we'll slip in the little reception room till you get the step, and then I'll astonish them all with my new partner. I've taught hundreds. You'll soon get it."

"You misunderstand me," he said gently. "I do not ever dance."

She paused and looked up astonished:

"You don't mean that the church won't let you? I didn't think there were any narrow people like that left anywhere in the world. You know that won't matter in New York. You will be expected to dance. The people will like you all the better for it. Nobody will object in the least."

"But I should object myself," he smiled with that winning graciousness that always took the edge from any refusal. "I'm not under any churchly rules as yet so far as that goes, and I do not know what the attitude of the church to-day, as a whole, would be on the subject, but I know that it is one of the things that I decided long ago I wouldn't do, and I haven't seen any reason to change my mind. I'm sorry to seem a sort of grouch, but I really don't belong at a party to-night. I've had a long, hard day, and I want to make a little further preparation for to-morrow. Would you mind if I went to my room?"

"Oh, not at all, if you feel that you must, but you must come over to the dining-room and have something first—!"

He followed her through the wide corridor into the dining-room, with its loaded table, almost deserted now, save for a stray couple or two who had drifted in to quench a thirst.

A waiter brought him a plate of tempting Christmasy things, and asked his preference in wines, and when he quietly declined any of the latter the girl beside him looked up sharply and challenged him again.

"You don't mean that you never take *any*thing? *Never!*"

He bowed assent a trifle coldly. It did not please him to be put through a catechism about his personal opinions.

"But why? You are surely not *afraid?*" There was a touch of contempt in her voice.

He looked at her steadily, quietly:

"Yes, I am afraid, if you please to put it so. But not because I have any more reason to be afraid than any other man or woman living. I don't touch it because I believe it is a bad thing for anybody, and for my sake as well as for others I believe in letting it alone."

In her glittering butterfly garb she had seemed as far as possible from the girl with whom he had talked in the church the week before, but now her eyes suddenly took on a hungry anxious look:

"Do you mean that you have to sacrifice all the things you want to do in order to live the kind of life you were talking about the other day?"

"I mean that sacrifices are not even considered, if you really want to live that life," he said with his brilliant winning smile, "but in my case it happens not to be a sacrifice. My ancestors did that for me, and I have neither the taste nor desire for such things. But couldn't we find some more pleasant subject for conversation than my personal opinions? They surely can't be interesting to you. Have you had a pleasant Christmas?"

"Oh, so-so!" said the girl indifferently. "Of course I got all the things I told them I wanted, but then I'd have gotten them anyway. Dad always gives me all the money I want, and they seldom interfere with what I buy. And, of course, we've had a very gay time, loads of parties—but it's all a beastly bore when it's done. If you can't have the one thing that you want at the time it doesn't matter how much else you have."

His face kindled:

"Do you feel that way, too? Well, we'll just

have to see what we can find to do for some one else then. That helps a lot. I tried it in France the winter my mother died. Christmas didn't seem to be Christmas, no matter how many turkeys they gave us, and so I just cut it all and went out to find some little French child that was worse off than I was. I found her. Little Marie Louise rolled up in a tattered quilt sick and cold and hungry. Her father had been killed in the war and her mother had been carried off by the Germans. Her oldest brother had been made stone blind by a shell, and her youngest brother, only eight years old, was the only one left to care for her. He had been away all the morning and most of the afternoon trying to get her a drop of milk for her Christmas dinner. He had come back without it and the two were sobbing in each other's arms when I found them, so I gathered them up and took them back to the boys. We gave them such a dinner as they hadn't had for months, and then took up a collection and went out and bought them clothes and things they needed and some toys. There was a doll with a pink dress for the little girl, and everything we could get to make a tree pretty. Then when it was ready we took the children in to look at it, and you should have seen their eyes bulge with wonder and joy. Their little, pinched, white faces got pink with happiness and they just sat down at the foot of the tree and gazed and gazed. We adopted those children then and put them with a good woman to be cared for, and fixed it so that they would be looked after when we were gone. But it made a bright spot in that dreary Christmas for me, I can tell you, that wouldn't have been if I had been trying to enjoy myself."

She had listened intently.

"That's awfully interesting," she said. "I've often thought I'd like to go into settlement work, but mother would never stand for it. I'm coming out this winter, of course, but it's not awfully exciting, because—well—I'm not greatly interested in it. I've thought a lot about what you said the other day—but I don't see how I could—! I've been wondering—why couldn't I get some one else to do that 'asking' for me? Some one that already lives that way? Why couldn't *you* do it and get the thing I want for me? Ministers do pray for their congregations. Isn't that what they are there for?"

"Well, not exactly," said Treeves laughing, "but I get your point. You mean why couldn't I do the living for the whole congregation and they get what they want through me? Well, it isn't done, that's all."

"What do you mean?" she asked puzzled.

"Why, I mean that there is no promise of that sort. The promise is only to those who comply with the condition. And it isn't God's fault that that is so; it wouldn't be possible any other way."

"I don't see why not."

"Why, because it is only when you are in accord with God's will that you ask things that are right and fit in with His plans."

"Then perhaps what I want does not fit in with His plans?" She cast a troubled belligerent look up at him.

"Well, possibly. You could not tell that until you had given up yourself and your will to His plans, then you would know, and you would not ask a thing that you knew was not in His plans."

"Yes, I would! I want it *anyway!* I don't *care* what His plans are. That is making Him just like Dad and Mother. What I want doesn't fit with their plans either, but I mustn't even ask any more or I get sent off to a hateful old boarding school for another whole year."

"Well, but don't you see that God couldn't trust people like that with a promise of that sort? It would be like giving a stranger a blank check and letting him fill it in with whatever amount he wanted, before you knew whether he was trustworthy or not. God only gives His blank checks to His own children who love Him so much and are so much in His confidence that He can trust them not to put themselves ahead of the universe."

"But I want what I want, whether God wants it or not!" declared the girl stormily. "He's no right to put me here in a certain station in life and then dangle somebody else out of another station in life right in front of my eyes and expect me to turn my head away and not see how fine they are!"

Her cheeks were crimson, and her eyes were downcast. She hardly realized how much of herself she was revealing. The young man watched her with an illuminated expression. So then this poor child was being lured by some man who was very likely beneath her! Could he save her, help her in any way to her better self? He could see she was worth saving. There was a streak of frankness about her that was most appealing. It stirred all the gallantry in him, and moved him to her protection. His face softened.

"But you would not want to have your wish if you knew it meant a lot of pain and suffering and disappointment when the illusions were past. Suppose God knows that if He gave you your wish it would bring bitterness and no joy."

"Well, then I want it *any*way!"

She lifted dark stormy eyes to him:

"Wouldn't you rather suffer and be disappointed even, with a real person for company, than go all your life alone in the company of the richest fool that ever walked this earth? I would. Of course you think I'm a little silly like all boarding-school girls in stories, and that I am deceived in my judgment, but I'm not. If you understood you would think I am right. I'm just as sure you would. You seem real! You make me think of him a little!"

Treeves looked down at her startled, the child and the woman in her were struggling together, but the child was uppermost, and he felt he could not turn away:

"Look here, little sister," he said gently, "I guess since we've begun this question we better sift it to the bottom. Suppose we go over into some room where we'll be alone for a few minutes and you tell me all about it, that is if you want to, of course—?"

"Oh, I *do!*" said Marjorie with unspeakable pleading in her eyes. "I have no one; no one to help me!"

"I don't know that I can help you," said Treeves as he sat down in the big leather chair in the library by the open fire where she had led him, "but I can at least find out whether you are being fooled by some man that isn't worth walking over."

A smouldering fire leaped into the girl's eyes.

"There! Don't be angry!" he smiled. "I shan't be any harder on him than you would. Let's hear the story, little sister."

There was an elder, brotherly kindness in his voice that reassured her and she began falteringly to tell her story. Five minutes later Mrs. Horliss-Cole, in search of her daughter, paused a second before the open door of the library and saw the two seated before the fire in earnest converse. A flicker of satisfaction passed over her well-preserved smile and she passed on to her guests once more.

Ten minutes later, having carefully noted down all data which Marjorie had given him concerning one Allen Winters, en voyage to the Philippines, John Treeves sat up and looked at his companion thoughtfully.

"You know," he said with a pleasant smile, "if this young man is all you think he is, he's worth waiting for, and a little waiting never hurt a real true love, only proves it, so I've heard. Of course I don't know much about those things myself, but it seems reasonable, doesn't it? And meanwhile, you're in your father's home. He loves you and has cared for you all your life. He has a right to your loyalty. If I were you I wouldn't do a thing that would in any way be disloyal to your father and mother. You won't be worthy of any great happiness that may be coming to you if you do. You'll only spoil it. If the young man is worthy of you he will agree in that, I'm sure. And besides, you're really quite young yet, aren't you? If this is the real thing, time and—God will bring it out right."

"Why, that's almost exactly what Edith Fisher said," exclaimed Marjorie suddenly. "How funny!"

"Fisher! Fisher!" said the young man startled. "Where have I heard that name?" Some vague disappointment lurked in his memory in connection with it.

"Why, Edith Fisher is just Auntie Cole's

companion. I don't suppose you have met her, though you're liable to see her around almost any time. She does some of mamma's secretary work sometimes, too. She's a very pretty, well-bred girl and a nice sort. They used to have money, I guess, but she never seems to complain. She's very good company when you haven't anything to do. Of course she's busy all the time and doesn't go out or anything, but I often talk to her. It isn't like talking to the girls; she's kind of out of my world, you know—!"

Unconsciously Marjorie had put on her society drawl of condescension as she said this about Patty, and Treeves looked at her keenly:

"You know," he said speculatively, "the young man isn't the only one that's got to be proved. You've got to find out whether you are worthy of him. You can't just stick a little money or a name onto him and bring him into your world, the changing has got to be mutual, and it sometimes takes more sterling grit to step down than it does to step up. Often the stepper-down discovers he is really the stepper-up."

"I don't know what you mean!" said Marjorie Horliss-Cole, lifting a haughty chin and staring at him much as her mother might have done.

"I mean," said John Treeves with a squaring of the Treeves chin, and a kindling of his mother's gray eyes, "I mean that you may not be worthy of your man after you find he is worthy of you. I tell you unless you can get out into his world and be at home you can never expect him to get out into yours. This thing has got to be mutual before you can create a world of your own together."

"Oh!" said Marjorie, a trifle angrily, a trifle puzzled.

"You know," said John Treeves with a wistful look in his gray eyes and a persuasive gentleness in his voice, "I wish you could bring yourself to go at this thing in the way I suggested. Jesus Christ is a strong true Friend, and He can see all the way to the end of this. I can only point the way. But I know Him, and I wish you'd try Him."

"Perhaps I will," said Marjorie softly, with a long, deep look at the first. "But one would have to be awfully sure of Him to give up entirely—EVERYthing that way—!"

"He makes you sure as soon as you do it. There is no assurance beforehand. That is the test."

They were still a long time till the big expensive log in the fireplace fell apart with a soft crushing of rosy sparks that brightened and flickered and grew gray.

"I think," said Marjorie Horliss-Cole with a light little laugh that covered a deeper feeling, "I think it is awfully queer that a man like you should belong to Calvin Treeves!"

John Treeves sat up startled:

"What," said he alertly, "do you know about me and my Uncle Calvin?"

"Why, I met you down at the mountain Inn with him. Have you forgotten already?"

"Pardon me," he said with a slight mortification. "Of course you did. Of course that explains it all. You see, I was a bit upset that evening with other matters, and it passed from my mind entirely where I had met you first."

"That's all right," said Marjorie, "I'll forgive you. You've been awfully good to me. But come, we must go back into the other room or mother will never forgive me."

John Treeves thought of it again the next morning as he sat in the stately New York pulpit and looked over the church bulletin for the day which a thoughtful sexton had placed in the open Bible. He read his own name, J. Dunham Treeves, and pondered. Where did they get that name? Not from him, for he always signed his letters John D. Treeves, or more formally J. D. Perhaps that girl had heard it down at the hotel where he met her. Very likely his uncle had had him registered that way. But the wonder over it lingered, till he was obliged to put it forcibly away. What difference anyway about a name? He was here to preach the Gospel. He must keep his mind and heart open for the message from above. So he rose to speak; and there facing him, as if her countenance were the only one in the vast sea of faces, he saw his old friend Patty staring up at him in wonder and amazement!

21

Quite early that same Sunday morning as Patty was coming down the hall from Miss Cole's apartments she had suddenly come face to face with John Treeves, who was going out for an early walk in the quiet of the day, before the world had awakened to its weekly Sabbath-breaking rollick. The delight on both faces for the instant was unmistakable. John Treeves put out his hands eagerly for greeting:

"Patty!" he said joyously. "I have found—"

Just then a door opened behind him and Patty was recalled to her situation by seeing Marjorie Horliss-Cole come blithely forth arrayed as if for a walk.

The smile that had been on Patty's face went out blankly like a thing that was not. It was just like a curtain falling suddenly and completely on a play just about to begin, the impersonal, formal, business-like attitude of one who serves. Her lips had been open to exclaim "John!" as eagerly as he had said "Patty!" but instead they spoke coolly:

"Miss Fisher, sir, Miss Cole's secretary. Can I be of service to you?"

John Treeves stopped puzzled, aghast, stared at her a moment, his face growing pink with embarrassment:

"I beg your pardon," he said. "I took you for an old friend."

She smiled faintly, acknowledging the apology, swept him a downward glance and turned on her way down the hall, continuing beyond her own room to the servants' staircase, which was in an alcove out of sight. She could hear Marjorie's blithe good morning and a question about going walking in the park, and somehow she knew without turning back that he had watched her out of sight; but her knees were trembling and her ankles seemed to be like water as she sank upon the upper step of the servants' stair and buried her white face in her arms. What an awful mess she had made of things now, and how could she ever get out of it or brave it out? It was like the old legend about a tangled web we weave when first we practise to deceive. She hadn't meant to deceive in the first place; it had seemed necessary. But there must have been something wrong somewhere, for look at all this! Whoever had supposed John Treeves would turn up again where she would see him? And, oh, the bitterness of having to deny him welcome in answer to that joyous sound of her own true name "Patty!" How good it had been! And he had been glad to see her! He surely had! No one could doubt that. Her face grew rosy at the thought and then wretchedly white again as she realized how she had compelled her own voice into coldness and

278

put all recognition away. Forever, too, perhaps, for how could she ever, ever explain it all? In fact, was she justified in making a mess like this to save her mother and sister? How far away they seemed and unreal, as she sat on the back stairs that morning and listened to the servants' chatter down in the butler's pantry: One voice came ringing above the rest:

"Yes, and he's old Calvin Treeves's nephew, rich as a king. They say the missus is just throwing Miss Marjorie at his head!"

"Looks to me like she was willing enough herself!" came a laughing answer from a parlor maid. "They just went past the window toward the park. My word! A young lady don't get up this time of a Sunday morning for a walk unless it means something."

Then the door swung to and shut further sound away and Patty arose, her face white and still with misery and her heart beating violently with a new kind of ache. She went to her room, locked the door, and dropped in a little silent heap upon her bed. It was worse than a long fit of weeping, that dry still kind of grief like inward bleeding that saps the life, and it told upon her young face in gray haggard lines. She roused herself after a while and began to get ready for the day, making her plans to keep absolutely out of sight. She was glad that Miss Cole wanted to go to church. Miss Cole did not often go to church, but had sent for her quite early, saying she had decided to try it once more. They would go in the car that was kept always for Miss Cole's special use when she was in the city, and they would not be bothered with the rest of the family, she was sure. Miss Cole liked it that way and so did the family. Moreover none of the family ever bothered the church much excepting Mr. Cole, who always went by himself in the morning, Patty having overheard remarks to the effect that he went officially rather than personally, and that the office he held was one which had more to do with things financial than with things spiritual. So Patty felt safe. Evidently John Treeves was a guest in the house for the week-end. There had been so many guests the night before, and Patty had been so busy with the little details of the Christmas festivities that she had not noticed who they were to be.

For Patty had gradually drifted into a place of general factotum in the household. Miss Cole sometimes complained that the rest of the family kept her so busy that she had no time to give to the one she was supposed to be especially attending. For Patty knew how to do many things. She could paint dinner cards in a trice, and arrange flowers; she could write many graceful notes in no time at all, and answer the telephone sweetly with just the right inflection to convey Mrs. Horliss-Cole's innermost feelings; she could play lady's maid on occasion, and even gracefully take the place of a dinner guest absent at the last moment. Oh, Patty was a handy person to have about the house and Miss Cole was beginning to grimly reflect that she would better take her young companion away to another mountain resort pretty soon if she did not wish to have her absorbed bodily by the whole family and nothing whatever left for herself.

Marjorie Horliss-Cole had, on the whole, been a friendly person to Patty, although on her return to the city she had dropped the intimate on-an-equality tone of her intercourse, and treated Patty more like an upper servant. Never except in case of an absent guest whose place absolutely must be filled was Patty asked among the family, and then on both occasions—for it had happened but twice—she was condescendingly advised to say as little as possible about herself. But Patty was an adept in that for her own sake and got on admirably. So now she thanked her lucky stars that there was no danger of her being asked down to dinner or having to pass through the rooms again where this most unexpected guest would be likely to be. She resolved to plead a headache after church, which she had good cause for feeling was already on its rampant way. Then a tray would be sent to her room and she would be to herself the rest of the day. Very likely John Treeves would go away on the morrow. She had no notion whatever that he was to be the speaker of the day nor even that he was a minister at all. It was quite natural to suppose that he was here in the house as a guest to see Marjorie. She sighed as she turned away from the mirror where she had been adjusting her hat, and began slowly putting on her gloves. It was her own doing John Treeves was out walking in the park with another girl instead of his friend of long ago. It was her own doing that he would go away again in the morning puzzled and perhaps hurt over what had happened. But she could not help it. Not until her father came home and advised her could she explain her strange situation. That was firmly settled in her loyal young heart.

In a few minutes more she was seated beside Miss Cole in the limousine on her way to church. She was thankful because she felt she would not have to be constantly on her guard as if she were at the house. So absorbed was she in her own thoughts that it was not until he stood up to read the morning lesson that she noticed John Treeves in the pulpit, and even then it was his voice and not the sight of him that suddenly startled into her absorption:

"Who hath believed our report, and to whom is the arm of the Lord revealed?"

It was as if a prophet of old stood up and cried out against them as the age-old chapter rang out under the high-carven arches, and broke into the hearts of the people. There was perhaps no person present who had not heard the words before, yet it seemed curiously original to them, like a new revelation. They had been accustomed all their lives to hearing of the sufferings of Christ. It was the proper churchly phrasing conveying vague pictures of the mistakes of a people long ago about One who had done them all honor and whose position had not been fully understood. But now they seemed all at once forced into a listening attitude of heart that scarcely seemed comely for a stately service. Such phrases as "WE hid, as it were, our faces from Him—" No, certainly not. They had never done any such thing! He was despised and *we esteemed* Him not." The arraignment was unjust! It was an absurd rendering. Still the arraigning voice went on. "Surely He hath borne OUR griefs, and carried OUR sorrows: yet WE did esteem Him smitten of God and afflicted!" Why, yes, of course, that was exactly their attitude, but why should that suddenly seem an accusation? Had not God chosen to smite Christ for their sakes? Was not that the blessed truth that all who comforted themselves by churchgoing on a pleasant Sabbath morning had always hugged to their hearts? What was wrong with that? "But HE WAS WOUNDED FOR *OUR* TRANSGRESSIONS, HE WAS BRUISED FOR *OUR* INIQUITIES, the chastisement of OUR peace was upon Him, and with His stripes WE are *healed!*"

There was a curious breathless attention as the tremendous statements went on. It almost seemed as if the young man had got hold of a new kind of version of the Scriptures, so strangely did the old words sound with the new emphasis, or was it the quiet, direct way the reader had of putting a personal note in his voice?

"All we like sheep have GONE ASTRAY!" Why! Could it be possible that anyone considered *them* still responsible for all this? They shifted uneasily, coughed, glanced about, and sat quiet again to the end. The prayer was spoken as to a visible Presence and in a tone so intimate that it seemed to some of the more ceremonious almost unseemly. The choir chirruped in with an intricate anthem like costly, hand-picked angels from the celestial chorus trilling around and playing at hide and seek among the heights and peaks of melody. It was exquisite, but it was usual, and the congregation drew breath and sat back relaxed and endeavored to forget impressions. The hymn, a stately, churchly one on themes of prophets and martyrs of old, goers-before who had done all the strenuous religion for those of this favored age, drowsed down upon their souls, and they settled into comfort and apathy for the sermon.

If the church pews had been secretly wired and the current suddenly turned on, the people could not have been more thoroughly electrified than by the sermon which followed. Not that it was sensational, not in the least. John Treeves did not take off his coat, nor stride about the pulpit, nor thump the Bible, nor use college or army slang to convey his meaning. He spoke in a quiet, direct, personal voice as if he were talking to one person, about a certain particular act of his life. They were all sinners, and there was no getting away from it. Not just the sin of Adam which they had quietly accepted and grown used to long ago; got so they could joke about it at a dinner party or in the office during the process of a crooked deal; but sin, Sin, SIN. Plain, bald, unvarnished SIN. A Personal SIN, differing in no way from the sin of the degraded lower classes. And worse still, not a far-away childish sin, nor a forgotten sin, but a sin of to-day, now, present, and to be reckoned for at once!

They sat in startled indignation with stern eyes fixed unflinchingly upon him, trying to look the hideous thought out of countenance. Before each one like a phantom danced the special act which represented present sin with him or her, and there was that sense upon them of not looking at one another lest consciousness of conviction should be writ large in their own eyes.

There were those whose indignation drove away conviction; whose haunting memories were exorcised by thoughts of sins so much worse they had not done. And then, suddenly those little sins they had picked out and were ashamed of were swept into a great caldron of sin seething and boiling in which they were overwhelmed. It appeared that the greatest sin of all, the sin that was at the bottom of every sin, was that they had "esteemed HIM not." A kind of hopeless terror seemed to be brooding in the still deep-colored light of the old aristocratic church. Not one of its respected, respectable members would have owned to a panicky feeling, yet it was there beside them in a sickening dismay. If this were true, all this the daring young preacher was telling them, what was there of life that was worth while? What but to be undoing the past, to be seeking forgiveness?

"Who hath believed our report!" There were those of the audience who had never had a very definite idea of who Isaiah was, whether he really ever lived, or what his work in life could have been anyhow. It developed that he was a prophet sent of the Lord to give this message which was not only for the people then but for the people of all time who heard or read. The great sin, the sin of the whole world, was that they had not believed the report. Who were those who had believed? The speaker went on rapidly to picture before them the different classes of people down through the ages who had believed. Mary the Mother had believed, even though it laid a burden upon her heart. The humble shepherds, feeding their flocks in the field had believed and started at once to search and find Him; the Wise Men in far distant lands, knowing not even one another, and following only a star had believed, but they were only three out of all the wise men of the earth. Not many wise nor great had believed. The King—he had believed the belief of fear, but only sought Him to kill Him because he loved himself. Not many mighty, not many rich men had believed. Like a procession marched the men and women of the Bible, each answering yes or no to the question, "Who hath believed our report?" And when the last one was passed there was not a man or woman in the church that had not heard himself or herself somehow described. They were facing a fact they would never have owned before; *they* had not believed the report that a Saviour was born. Oh, born to the world, yes! A large comprehensive Saviour for a large comprehensive Sin in which they were willing to take a modest share provided everybody else took equally. But a personal Saviour and a personal SIN, writ large, that they had not believed—did not believe in now!

At this juncture the speaker brought in the remainder of his text, "To whom is the arm of the Lord revealed?"

And now a great fact suddenly became plain. Believing came before revelation. One must believe the report before it was possible to have the truth of it verified. Indeed, unwillingness to believe precluded any possibility for seeing the truth. It was like a closed door, closed by the will.

Believing was an act of the will. Real believing meant acting on that belief. There were those in the world who professed to accept the truth of the report, but it had made no difference in their lives. Such could never have the revelation of the Lord's arm because they had never gone farther than a mere intellectual belief which was no better than a mere intellectual unbelief because it got nowhere. The proof of belief was willingness to go searching for the Lord. The Lord would reveal Himself to those who searched with all their hearts. The speaker made this statement quietly, but with a throb in the words that gave a personal touch to what he was saying, an eager conviction that it was worth seeking. Every tone, every gesture, every inflection of voice said as plainly as words could have done, "I *know* this is true because I have tried it myself." And then he began to give quick and fast the reasons for making such a search. First, because God had urged it and promised great rewards in the way of revelation and blessing; and he poured forth promises, speaking rapidly and quoting them like something that had been lived into his heart. Second, because those who had tried it had testified of the wonder and glory that had come to them through finding Christ, and he instanced some quiet everyday saints who had fought the fight and worn the glory in their faces. Patty knew he was talking about his mother. She did not know that her own face was wet with tears as she listened. She only knew that something had come to her that day which stirred her deeper than anything she had ever heard, which crystallized and put in motion all the latent hunger and desire and ambition she had ever known.

John Treeves was not preaching a sermon he had made up out of his inner consciousness, nor yet one framed upon the system of theology which he had learned in the seminary. He was giving the message that had been given to him as he knelt upon the frozen ground at the old trysting place on the bluff above the little home town. He had strewn it thickly with scripture, not after careful midnight study to find the appropriate text, but with words from his store of Bible learned at his mother's knee; words whose meaning had long ago entered his soul, and whose convincing truths were unanswerable. Without realizing that he was being great he had preached a mighty sermon that day because he had taken God's words instead of his own.

"Yesterday," said he in that quiet, conversational tone that held the attention so steadily, "we celebrated once more the birthday of the Saviour King. He was born again to us as He was born long years ago to those who lived then. What are you going to do with your King, your Saviour? Will you let Him lie in a manger, or will you cradle Him in your heart? You that are shepherds, will you leave your sheep to follow the star and find your Saviour? You that are wise men, will you go on the search, no matter how long or hard it may be and give Him the great gift of yourself? You that are rich, will you go sell all that you have if He asks it and come and follow Him? To-morrow He will be treading the way to Golgotha again, and that heavy cross is the price of *your* punishment, not His. That burden of sins He will bear is not His but yours. He is despised, and you esteem Him not even though He took your sins upon Himself? What are you going to do about it?"

22

There was a sense of sudden letting down as the organ boomed forth a bit of left-over Christmas oratorio, and a drawing of breath in relief. Ah! Here was solid ground and something quite in the line of regular things to be expected. A truly noble work of art combined with religion. Unquestionably great, unquestionably religious, and yet calling for no responsibility on the part of the listener. Composed by a great master, performed by great artists, well paid for, and appreciated by a refined and well-meaning audience, what more could a reasonable God require in the way of worship? Why was not this greater than the praise of those simple, illiterate shepherds, the myrrh and incense of those long-ago sages? Already the keen air from the outer door had stolen into the church and turned the thoughts of the congregation away from the tense and unusual thought of the hour. In a moment more they would be smiling and bowing and asking after friends as they progressed down the aisle in dignified accord with the rolling of the wonderful organ. A few minutes more and they would be walking up Fifth Avenue and their dinners would be waiting. Then would come an afternoon of friendly intercourse and recreation. Already they were drawing up their wraps, and girding up their thoughts for the next act of the day, and the sermon was a thing of the past.

Not everyone, of course. A few simple worshippers "hid all these things in their hearts" and went away to remember. There are always a few.

Down by the door Marjorie Horliss-Cole paused to speak to a girl friend:

"Isn't he perfectly stunning!" said the friend. "Don't you love the way he combs his hair? And wasn't that a darling sermon? If sermons were all like that I wouldn't mind coming to church oftener. I'm crazy about the way he looks straight at you when he's talking. Wouldn't it be dandy to have a young minister with some life in him?"

Back by the altar Maxim Petrol lingered to speak to Horliss-Cole:

"Say, Jim, tell him to cut out that rubbish about Sin. We can't stand for any such antiquated rot as that. Tell him to give us something a little more modern, you know, with some punch to it, social service and that sort of stuff—"

Horliss-Cole nodded understandingly:

"I'll have a talk with him this afternoon," he said. "Of course he's young. It wouldn't do him any harm to take some post-graduate work in one of our broader institutions. I'll suggest that later if it seems wise. Meantime, he's a personable young man, will fit in well socially. I guess he'll get by. What do you think?"

"Oh, yes, he'll do. Get him to preach up to modern thought and he'll be a prince. It's well to take them young and train them. Going to get in a game this afternoon, Jim?"

"Well, yes, I thought I would. See you up at the links."

Patty, seated beside Miss Cole in the limousine, with her thoughts on what she had just heard, suddenly became aware that she had been spoken to.

"I said that young man was no saphead!" stated Miss Cole over again.

"Oh, no!" said Patty rousing to a polite enthusiasm. "That was a fine sermon, wasn't it?"

"H'm! *P'fine!*" sniffed Miss Cole significantly.

Patty laughed:

"I mean—it was the real thing, wasn't it? I never

quite heard anything like it. It set me to thinking."

"I suspect that was what it was meant to do!" said Miss Cole grimly. "I guess it set a good many to thinking!" she chuckled with twinkling mirth. "He didn't know how near the mark he was coming sometimes. It was as good as a play to see all their pet sins brought out. It certainly did make some of them squirm. Didn't you notice Mrs. Peter Pancoast's neck was as red as fire. Her daughter's been divorced three times and is about to marry a fourth."

"Oh," gasped Patty, "I was thinking of myself, I guess."

"You, child! You haven't any sins alongside the rest of us!" said Miss Cole with a sudden wistful look at the soft pink cheek and delicate earnest profile next her.

"But for knowing the human heart that young man certainly is a past master!" she went on. "He must have had a good mother!"

She looked keenly, significantly at Patty, but Patty only smiled sadly, reminiscently, and said "Yes," with an indescribable little shrinking motion as if some old wound had been touched, and Miss Cole said no more. But Patty went back home to search the Horliss-Cole libraries for a Bible.

She found one at last in the back corner of Miss Cole's sitting-room bookcase, behind a row of old novels, a little queer old-fashioned fat one with rusty gild edges and a faded inscription:

"To Sylvia from her Sunday School teacher as a reward for reciting the ten commandments perfectly." She sat by her own room window reading it earnestly when Miss Cole came to the door late in the afternoon to suggest that they go down to the library for tea with the family, but when she caught sight of the little book, and saw the absorption of the girl in its pages she beat a hasty retreat.

As it happened Horliss-Cole chose to take his tea with the young minister alone in his den, where an admonitory talk would be more private, and so Miss Cole's plans would have missed fire in any case.

"We like," said Horliss-Cole settling back in his deep air-cushioned chair and sipping his tea delicately, "we like a conservative style of preaching in our church. Not that we lean *too* far to modern ideas. They are apt to be overdrawn, as all new things are. Now, the Sermon on the Mount is a good pattern. Give us plenty of that and we shall be satisfied!"

Mr. Horliss-Cole was tall and thin, with a tall, smug, gray face and a cold blue eye. He had long delicate fingers, and when he talked, particularly when he was giving a delicate hint which was really intended for a command, he always leaned his elbows on the arms of his deep chair, braced his thumbs together, and then tapped the tips of the three middle long thin fingers of each hand on one another, punctuating his sentences thereby. In this instance he had set down his Sevres cup on the carved teakwood stand and was elaborating his sentences by measured taps as usual.

John Treeves, his own cup still untasted, watched him curiously with a growing understanding and a slow narrowing of his eyes. What was this old hypocrite about anyway? That was the involuntary question that came to his mind immediately. The Sermon on the Mount! That began with the blesseds. What was the old fellow trying to get at? It was evident he had not liked the morning discourse, but thought there was hope. It all amused John Treeves very much, for he wasn't caring a picayune whether the New York church called him or not. He was waiting to be called by God, and until then he preached wherever he was sent.

"Our people are interested in social service—" went on Horliss-Cole in his cool, oily voice after a dignified pause; and then paused again to let that soak in.

Other verses from the Sermon on the Mount were coming to John Treeves now. Ah! "Let your light so shine before men *that they may see your good works!*" Was that the idea John Treeves wondered thoughtfully, nodding to signify to Horliss-Cole that he was listening.

"Many of our most influential members are interested in corporations and large operations that employ thousands of men-laborers—," the long fingers tapped each other emphatically to call attention to the prominence of the people mentioned. "There are sugar, oil, manufacturing interests of many sorts, and all of them have large plants which involve many problems of the poor. There, for instance, is the housing problem, the educational problem, educating the children of these workmen, teaching the workmen and their families to live economically, teaching them sanitary laws and rules of health, helping the young people to get ready to support themselves, all these questions are most vital and interesting, and should demand the keenest attention from the church to-day. It is the one great solution for all the turmoil that the war has left us. It is the one great meaning of Christianity to make better citizens and better workmen. Then, of course, there is the question of proper amusement and uplift. Our women have been most zealous about providing occasional concerts and lectures for the working people during their noon hours. Some of our best women have actually gone down to the plant themselves and sung or played, and endeavored to understand the working girl and bring culture down to her. It has been most praiseworthy and satisfactory—! Perhaps you have seen the accounts in the papers—"

The rest of the verse was coming to John Treeves now—"that they may see your good works AND GLORIFY YOUR FATHER WHICH IS IN HEAVEN."

The attention that John Treeves seemed to be giving to Horliss-Cole was most flattering. He cleared his throat and decided that the task of making over this young pulpit giant was going to be easier than he had anticipated. Next week, if all went well, he would broach the subject of a course of study somewhere—!"

"Give them the Sermon on the Mount! That is the gospel they want—!" he continued.

"I believe you have an interesting plant yourself, Mr. Horliss-Cole. I've heard a good deal about it since I've been in New York. It is located out of the city, is it not?"

The adroitness with which the question was asked would have gained the admiration of any of Mr. Horliss-Cole's acquaintances, for "The Plant" was the one absorbing interest of his life, and when it was mentioned all other subjects faded into complete obscurity. For he *was* the plant. Had he not made it? Was it not the outgrowth of his own industry and cunning, the work of his hand and heart? Not even his wife and children, nor yet his bank account, meant as much to Mr. Horliss-Cole as that plant, for it was at once the epitome of his own industry and his farsightedness, and of what he liked to call generosity. He liked to tell men about it and have them praise him. He told John Treeves about it now and swelled with pride.

Treeves narrowed his eyes in that attractive speculating sort of way he had and said:

"I should like to see it."

Then Mr. Horliss-Cole completely forgot that he had been delivering an adroit reproof to a young and inexperienced minister and had been getting on very well with his suggestions for next Sunday's sermons, and began to talk about himself. He told about the houses he had built for his men, how he insisted on their all keeping the grass cut or turning them out of the house if they neglected it. How the hospital was all white tiled and there was a rest room for the girls and a library. He neglected to say that these were kept in apple-pie order and used exclusively by the guests who drove out by automobile to view the wonders of The Plant, but that was not generally known. Perhaps he had even forgotten the fact himself. The rooms of course were ostensibly for the girls of The Plant, and as such continually in the limelight. They masqueraded as among the very first of such recreation rooms to be established in plants of that sort.

Horliss-Cole did not return to the Sermon on the Mount. He talked a long time about The Plant, finding it more and more necessary because of that steady, narrowing gaze of attention and interest to make known little details of good works that he himself had thrown in here and there. He did not want to stop until he was sure he had made an impression; and that young upstart of a preacher just would not look impressed. Whatever he might think he sat and held his opinion in reserve, only saying again quietly: "I should certainly like to see it!"

And so after all Horliss-Cole did not get back to the Sermon on the Mount at all that evening, but promised to take John Treeves out to see The Plant the next day.

And at last, free to follow his own thoughts at the close of the day, John Treeves sat in his stately bedchamber overlooking Fifth Avenue and pondered over a face, one face he had seen in his audience that morning, the face with the listening eyes that had helped him to preach. The face of the girl who looked so like his friend of long ago. Somehow he must get acquainted with that girl and see if she knew Patty Merrill! Perhaps she was a relative.

23

Monday morning Patty had promised to take some things to the dressmaker for Miss Cole, who was to call for her in the car at eleven. She was glad of the opportunity to get away from the house as well as to get in a bit of shopping, for she wanted to buy a Bible of her own. In spite of her intensive course in Bible for one year at school she found it most difficult to locate anything in Miss Cole's fine print, faded, old book, and besides, she wanted one which she could feel free to mark, that the verses might come to her like old friends whenever she opened the pages. It was difficult enough to find them in the first place without losing them every time. It seemed somehow that this would be coming in touch again with those precious friends of that dear summer long ago. And John Treeves had quoted such wonderful things which he said were promises of God. It did not seem as if they could really be true. She felt as if she must search until she had located each one of them and made them hers personally. It was like finding a hidden treasure put away in the attic in old chests. It was exciting and wonderful!

So she slipped out early from a servants' entrance, before the household were astir, being most wary, for her experience of Saturday had taught her that the guests did not easily fall into the indolent habits of the household, and might be about even earlier than she was.

At half-past ten Horliss-Cole called his sister on her room 'phone:

"Are you going to use your car this morning, Sylvia?"

"Why, yes, I have to go to the dressmaker's. Why, did you want it?"

"Well, both my cars seem to be out of commission this morning. The Sedan is out for repairs, and the other has developed something the matter with its engine, so Phillips says. Katharine wants to use the touring car to take a lot of women to something, and I promised to take that young minister out to The Plant. Besides, Marjorie has got it in her head that she wants to go along, and I thought you might enjoy the ride. It's a nice bright day—!"

That was one nice thing about Horliss-Cole, he had never forgotten the days when they were both little and his sister used to sacrifice all sorts of things for him.

"Why, yes, I'd like to go," answered Sylvia Cole hesitatingly, "but I *have* to go to the dressmaker's, and there's Edith—I sent her up with some material and promised to call for her at eleven—"

If it had been any other of the employees of the Horliss-Cole household the head of the house would have promptly suggested telephoning her to return the way she had gone, but Edith Fisher was such a quiet, comfortable adjunct to the household. He liked Edith. She was never obtrusive, always ready to help, always quiet and well behaved—a pretty little thing. A handy person to have around saving all trouble about wraps and cushions.

"That's all right, take Edith along. There's plenty of room in the car. She can sit with the chauffeur. How soon'll you be ready?"

Miss Cole considered. She didn't relish having

301

her little companion seated with the chauffeur, but of course that was the only way it could be done, and after all, what matter! The child might not like going and she wasn't altogether sure it was exactly square to her to take her unawares in this way, but she had not seemed to mind the church service yesterday; in fact, had looked very happy ever since, so perhaps she was getting over her extreme offishness about that young man, and anyhow she couldn't resist trying the experiment and seeing what it would do to him. It wasn't her arrangement, and there didn't seem any way out of it. Of course, after she had thought it over, if she felt it wasn't being quite loyal to the girl she could still telephone and explain the case. So she told her brother she would be ready in ten minutes, and the matter was settled. Then Miss Cole had all she could do to get ready and there was no time to telephone, so that was settled, too.

She was quite relieved somehow when she went down to the car to find the young minister was not in it, although Marjorie did not seem to be so pleased about it. It appeared that he had gone on to visit a poor family living in a tiny apartment away up town. They were relatives of a comrade of his who fell in the war.

"Very decent of him, of course," commented Horliss-Cole. "I told him we would pick him up. I don't think he at all realizes what sort of a neighborhood he is going into, not at all the kind of people he will care to cultivate, of course, but then a minister is peculiarly situated. Of course he will realize later that he cannot keep up odds and ends of acquaintances that way."

Miss Cole was rather relieved than otherwise, it seemed so much less like a plot against her little girl, and when Patty came out she quite naturally took the seat with the chauffeur, for it had happened a number of times before that Miss Cole and her brother had taken friends out and that had always been her seat. She did not mind it at all, for the chauffeur was perfectly respectful, and it was fun riding in front. She was not a member of the family nor a guest, and this was her business position, why should she care? The day seemed blithe and gay and she was glad she was going to have a long ride. For company she would have her own thoughts and the wonderful sermon of yesterday to ponder upon. Did God really care like that for individuals? Why, it was all that she had hungered for her mother to be!

Patty was not taking much heed as they went on into the narrower streets among the looming new apartments with cheapness written over their very sidewalks, where swarmed flocks of little children already fending for themselves. But when they stopped before the dingiest of the lot the chauffeur, scanning the numbers carefully, and getting out to disappear within, she was a bit surprised. It was not the way of the Horliss-Coles to be getting service from small individuals this way. They usually dealt with large employment places when they needed extra help. Of course it might be some fine embroidery or something of the sort. Mrs. Horliss-Cole had ways that were never foretellable. But when presently the chauffeur returned with John Treeves in his wake, Patty caught her breath and the color stole hastily up behind her ears and over the roundness of her cheeks. Miss Cole saw it and felt condemned, but satisfied. The child hadn't forgotten him yet, anyway. Then she turned her attention to the young man.

John Treeves evidently did not notice Patty until he was seated in the car just behind the chauffeur, where he had an excellent view of her sideface. By that time Patty had full command of her features, however, and the soft, lovely color which suffused her cheek might easily have been caused by the crisp morning air. Miss Cole saw him almost start as he looked at the girl, and pause in his speech to Marjorie; then instantly controlling his expression, he dropped easily into conversation once more, but from her vantage point behind Marjorie she could see that he cast furtive glances quite often at the front seat.

Patty's little gray duvetyne shoulders sat erectly indifferent, and her head was not turned a hair's breadth toward the back seat. She was as apart from the people behind her as if she had been riding in a car of her own. And yet somehow there was always that about her that would not let her seem like a servant even to the casual observer.

Patty was glad; glad that she was not back there with them. She could not have controlled her eyes. They would have wandered and told tales of her identity, she was sure. It was in the eyes where people really lived and looked out, and she was sure he could not have looked into her eyes long at close range without recognizing her, as she could not have looked into his without knowing him; no, not if it had been many more years. She would not have trusted herself to keep herself out of her eyes for long in his presence. But one's back can be a closed door and Patty locked hers and bolted it.

Marjorie Horliss-Cole was chattering away with more than her usual fervor, Patty thought, and John Treeves answered her interestedly. They seemed to have a basis of friendliness that was more intimate than Patty would have ever expected between those two. It hurt her a little until she realized that it had no business to hurt her, and then she resolutely put it out of her thoughts and tried to enjoy the day; but in spite of herself she was keenly conscious of all that was said in the back of the car, and of the eyes that were upon her more than of the beauties of the day.

They turned downward toward the river again and kept it in sight like a silver ribbon tied about the sparkle of the day, until they wound out into the open country and came at length to the knot of buildings feathered with tall plumes of smoking chimneys, set close beside the water and nested about with rows upon rows of small tiny houses, as like as peas in many pods, neat and clean and efficient looking as an incubator, reminding one that the details of life were reduced to the minimum and energy husbanded on a large scale.

Horliss-Cole, suddenly roused from a seeming apathy, began to talk eagerly:

Those were the offices in the wide building in the centre, to the right was the social club and hospital, to the left the factories, beyond the hotel, then the housings and the school. He indicated the aisles of little gray one-story shacks, miles and miles of them, it seemed to Treeves, as he looked down the vistas and tried to fancy living in one with a family of seven or ten. "Bungalows," their perpetrator called them. They had no more resemblance to the little cottage at the end of the home street than a dandelion has to a chrysanthemum. It made him heartsick to think of them in comparison. He glanced around the little company quickly for sympathy in his thought. Horliss-Cole was complacent; his sister wore an inscrutable look, watching him narrowly with a grim, half-mirthful twist of one corner of her mouth; Marjorie was utterly indifferent, not considering the familiar shanties any more than if they had been the grains of sand under her expensive little shoe; the chauffeur sat with eyes ahead, seeing nothing as good chauffeurs should. Instinctively his eyes sought Patty's face, and he caught the echo of his own thought there, compassion and a longing to change it. He had somehow known that face would look like that. She lifted her eyes coolly, unseeingly, and glanced beyond the Hudson, and he turned quickly away. If that was not Patty he had no right to be looking at her, and every evidence seemed to point that way, except his inner consciousness, which cried out to insist that she look at him and be herself.

His eyes went beyond the Hudson to the bluffs and hills shining in the cold sunlight, and then back to the river's edge, which was cluttered and bordered with warehouses and factories. The car, at the owner's bidding, rolled down one of the broader ways between the large buildings till it stood on a small pier. There was a bit of an artificial bay cut into the land just here, surrounded by buildings on the three sides, making a hollow square of water wide enough across for two large vessels to enter and dock without interference. Mr. Horliss-Cole had just given it to be understood that all the buildings on both sides of the little inlet belonged to The Plant and were constantly taxed to their utmost capacity. The great open doorways yawned from floor to ceiling in each story, each with an immense floor space behind, and windows at the back through which the sunshine blared and showed in some hurrying workers going about with large parts of automobiles working like a hive of bees. In the warehouses just opposite the Horliss-Cole car the doors were all open wide, and the floors empty. A block and tackle, swaying idly from the peak of the roof, seemed but just set free from labor, and a steamer plowing away a few rods down the river with a curving silvery wake showed where the machines had gone that had filled the vacant floors. The city in the distance down the river, with its many tall shafts and chimneys belching smoke against a cold bright December sky, typified the world where the machines were going to be snatched up by the eager purchasers and whirled through space for business or for pleasure. John Treeves wondered what it all amounted to anyway? To make more machines for more people to struggle and buy, to catch up with the great mad procession of the world struggling to get all out of life that was in it—Ah! Why would they not see? Why must so many be blind? A great ache came into his soul to cry out a message that would be heard, a message that it was not all of life to do these things, that they were starving their souls and starving their brothers—!"

But into the midst of his cogitations came Horliss-Cole's oily satisfied voice:

"Now, we'll get out here and I will show you the points of interest. Marjorie, do you care to come? Sister, I suppose you would rather sit in the car, you've seen it all so many times."

Edith Fisher was ignored, much to her own content. She sat quietly watching the steamer move down the river like a sloppy old fat woman in a shawl with a basket, kicking her feet out behind as she walked. Then her eyes came back to the warehouses across the stretch of water. The sun was in such a position that every big window was lit up with brightness, and it looked like a house of glass. It was the warehouse next to the river end and built with a view to showing off the finished machines that were ready for transportation. A great electric arch spanned the hollow square of water from warehouse to pier with HORLISS-COLE in immense letters that blazed at night for miles, and were easily readable by day. Everybody knew Horliss-Cole. How strange that she, Patty Merrill, should have happened to drop down into this family and take a temporary root! And yet did anything just happen in this world? How strange that she should also have "happened" here on this old friend whom she had not seen for years and under such circumstances that she must remain a stranger to him!

24

On the ground floor of the warehouse across from her Patty could see the head and shoulders of a young girl about her own age sitting at a typewriter making her fingers fly like lightning. Now and then the pages would come out and a fresh page go in, and the girl's fingers flew on. Patty grew interested, wondering what kind of a girl this was and whether she lived in one of those funny little houses back there, or went back and forth from New York every day when her work was done. She was a slender little thing with delicate shoulders and her hair arranged carefully. It was hard to tell at such a distance, but she seemed to be very pretty. Once she came to the window and pushed up the sash a little way and dropped a bit of paper out into the water. It floated away down the stream and followed the wake of the steamer, which was only a speck in the distance now.

Miss Sylvia sat quite still in the back of the car and watched Patty. Patty did not turn around to talk because she dreaded the look in Miss Cole's eyes, and Miss Cole did not speak because she rather dreaded the reproach in Patty's eyes and voice. In fact, she had almost repented her of her treachery. It was a shabby trick to play the girl to bring her out and cage her in front of a young man whom she evidently admired and would not recognize, to listen to his talking with another girl who all too evidently admired him. Miss Cole was cross with herself and was trying to plan some way to atone. Presently a young man came out from the office, putting on a shabby coat as he came. He had great dark eyes and hair of a Michelangelo drawing, heavy and curling, over his forehead, though clipped close behind as became an American. He came respectfully up to the car, giving a passing admiration to the beautiful girl in the front seat, but speaking to Miss Cole in a soft foreign accent:

"Mr. Hor'-Cor' he say you betta come in office. It too col' out here. He say come inside!" He had wonderful teeth when he smiled and his smile was ravishing and confiding. Patty was interested in watching his face light up.

"Thank you, I'd rather stay in the fresh air!" said Miss Cole crisply.

The young messenger seemed troubled and lingered.

"Yes—nica air—if you got good warm coat! I, myself, feel not cold. But lady sit still! Get cold! Get sick! Mr. Hor'-Cor' he say come in!"

"Well, I'm not coming in!" snapped Miss Cole decidedly. "Who are you? Are you one of the workmen?"

The young man smiled complacently.

"I am Angelo. Yes, I work. Big building back this

one. I work good, hard. I get good wage. I have money in bank. Bime by nexta week I getta marry. My girl over there!" He pointed across the water to the girl. "See! She see me!" He lifted a shabby cap and waved to her. She fluttered a hand and dropped back to her work. "She nica girl. She work, I work. We make good money. We getta marry!"

"H'm! Do you think that's wise till you have enough to keep her so she won't have to work?"

He opened his large eyes wide:

"My girl no work after she my wife. She keep house. She take a boarders, mebbe one, two, five, and we makka more mon'. We be rich some day and have a car ourselve."

He smiled with anticipation, a real dreamer's smile.

"Are you going to live in one of those little houses?" asked Miss Cole curiously. "I don't see how you could keep boarders in one of those, they are so small. Have you bought your house?"

"Oh, na, we go to live with my girl, her people! Her father get leg cut off last month in belt, leth' belt catch. Woof! He go in! No leg any more. He not able to worruk hard any more. We live there and pay money. Yes, we live second house that far row over where that man is walking. Red flower in window. That's how we tell house."

"But, you couldn't all live there! And keep boarders, too!" said Miss Cole aghast. "Why, how many rooms do they have?"

"Four room!" he answered proudly. "One room, me an' my wife." He spoke the word with tenderness, numbering on his fingers. "One room my girl's moth' and fath'. One room kitch' where we all eat, mangé! One room boarders sleep!" he finished triumphantly. "Big room boarders sleep, get eight bed in."

"Mercy!"

Miss Cole's face was a study of horror, and the chauffeur wore a kindly superior smile of amusement, but the young Italian was not noticing. His pleasant smile had turned into a frown of anger as he watched a tall, thick-set man with a black mustache and dashing attire come whistling down the opposite edge of the wharf with his hands in his pockets. He had the air of owning the place and being well pleased with himself. The slim, young, artistic hands of the Italian clinched at his sides, and his jaw set in an ugly line. Miss Cole asked him some more questions and he turned and tried to answer, but it was evident his thoughts were all across the strip of water and his rage was at boiling point.

He watched the heavy-set man stamp up the steps into the office where the girl sat pounding the typewriter.

Patty kept her eyes on the little scene as if it were a moving picture. The girl looked up furtively as the man came in, and then bent closer to her work, turning her shoulder away from the door and appearing not to notice the entrance. The man went over to his desk and took up some papers, but kept turning and looking at the girl, who continued to write rapidly, nervously.

There was a little digression behind her and Patty perceived without turning around that Mr. Horliss-Cole, Marjorie and John Treeves had returned and were standing by the car speaking to Angelo. John Treeves shook hands with the foreigner and spoke to him in his own language, telling him he had passed through Italy just a few months before. Angelo's face brightened for an instant and he tried to respond with his smile, but it was only half-hearted, and his eyes returned their troubled gaze across to the warehouse.

Patty wished the glass room was not so far away. She did not like the attitude of that man over there. He had come over by the girl's desk and was bending over her. Suddenly the girl made a dive under his arm and stood away from him with her back against the wall, her whole attitude one of defiance. There appeared to be no one else but those two in the building. The man reached out his hand as if to grasp the girl's arm.

Angelo quivered and started forward, gripping his hands:

"My God! I kill dat boss some day!" they heard him murmur.

The girl had darted across the wide floor to the foot of an unrailed stair that led straight up from floor to floor. The man sprang after and she hurled herself up the stairs. Their figures showed like tiny silhouettes against the background of the bright morning as they passed in front of the great windows, stair after stair, till they came to the top floor. The slender girl was gaining on the man who labored on behind with great passionate strides. The little group of watchers on the opposite shore were breathless, forgetting one another in the scene before them, it all passed so rapidly. No one had noticed the noon whistle that summoned the men in swarms from the building like black ants streaming away for their dinners. Some lingered about the Big Boss's car watching also. No one had seen Angelo disappear or noticed the circle of ripples on the edge of the water where his lithe body had slipped in. His dark curls were too far under water to attract attention—for Angelo could swim and he had gone to save his girl!

The girl staggered to the top, half a flight above her pursuer, but did not pause even to glance back. She whirled about the top of the stair and flung herself forward toward the great open door at the front, where the iron hook from the block and tackle dangled, swaying lightly just shoulder high. Her pace quickened as she came, her purpose all too plain. With outstretched hands she sprang for the rope, caught it for a second, but could not cling. With a sharp scream of terror it slipped from her fingers, and the ugly hook by some twist of the rope struck her full in the face and knocked her down limp and senseless into the water.

It all happened so quickly, so unexpectedly, that no one had the sense to do anything to stop the tragedy, and only John Treeves seemed alive to the fact that it was not yet over. He dashed his hat and coat from him as he ran and sprang into the water, making splendid strokes toward the spot where the girl had gone down. On the opposite wharf a dark wet figure like a black spider was rapidly climbing up a slippery way, and presently slid around by the back door and entered the building, but no one saw nor cared, for every eye was riveted now on the high open doorway where the girl's pursuer had just staggered panting up and stood looking down in a daze for a moment.

Suddenly, out from the group by the car there hissed a bullet, so close to Patty's ear that she thought at first it had touched her. The next instant the man at the open door threw up his hands and dropped, huddled together on the very edge of the threshold, one arm and a foot dangling over. A great cry went up from the crowd that suddenly surged around everywhere. Many started to run around the end of the inlet which was quite a distance, and one or two jumped into the water. No one seemed to have any definite idea of where the bullet had come from except Patty, who had a distinct remembrance of eyes like Angelo's and a face that was different somehow from the Angelo who had just talked with them and smiled. She did not mention Angelo, however, only saying, "It was a man who stood just here by the machine."

"Oh, it was that dago all right!" said the chauffeur, unbent from his servile silence. "I heard him say he was going to kill him. These foreigners all go armed, and they haven't a bit of sense. Now he'll have to swing for it, and what has he gained?"

"Well, I think he was thoroughly justified!" declared Miss Cole excitedly. "James, I don't see why you don't do something about a state of things like this! You oughtn't to have a man around that needed killing."

"Well, I don't see any sense in Mr. Treeves getting all soaked on a day like this for a silly girl who wanted to commit suicide," pouted Marjorie. "Of course it was perfectly splendid of him. Papa, I don't see why you don't send a boat out after him."

Everything was confusion for a few minutes and nobody listened to anybody else. Mr. Horliss-Cole, his face white and stern, stood on the steps of the main office and gave directions to which nobody paid the slightest heed. Men hurried here and there excitedly, giving other directions, and shouting wild speculative opinions.

The girl had gone down twice before John Treeves reached her side and started back with her to shore.

"Oh, he is bringing her over here!" said Marjorie turning her head away. "How horrid! I hate dead people. Couldn't we drive around the other end of the building?" But nobody paid any attention to her, and John Treeves brought the robes from the car and covered her and Treeves with several others began working over her. A boy started a fire of bits of wood and the smoke of it puffed over across the car and came in their eyes much to Marjorie's discontent. Miss Cole sat up alertly and wanted to get out and go and help, but was restrained:

"For mercy's sake, Aunt Syl, she's only a poor stenographer, don't worry yourself. Let's get out of here as quick as we can. Somebody go tell Mr. Treeves to hurry up. He'll catch his death of cold. He better get into a fur robe and get home as quick as possible."

But John Treeves was not worrying about his health. He had not been through the war for nothing. A little wet and a little cold did not trouble him. He was working with all the skill at his command to bring life back to the pale girl and he paid no attention to the messenger from Marjorie.

Some one had gathered up the man who had been shot and put him on a stretcher. They were taking him to the Immaculate hospital. The report went around that he was not dead, but shot through the head somewhere, probably fatally.

They were bringing Angelo in handcuffs, all dripping, with miserable eyes searching the wharf for his girl. He was shivering but he did not notice it. His heavy hair hung down over his forehead in a great silken wave. They brought him over to where the girl lay and he knelt down all manacled as he was and kissed the hem of her sodden blue serge skirt and wept aloud. He did not realize that they had taken him for a murderer, nor care. He only minded the handcuffs because they held him from his girl.

Mr. Horliss-Cole had finally succeeded in getting in touch with his foreman and giving directions that there seemed some likelihood of being obeyed. He came over to the car now and climbed in, looking white and old, like a child who has broken its doll. This would look bad in the papers. He had always been so proud of the record of his plant. No rows or strikes. No scandals. All praise and pictures of his hospital.

When he found that John Treeves was still working over the girl he climbed out again and went over to him.

"She's alive!" said Treeves lifting a glorified face. "I thought we'd better just put her right in your car and take her to her home. Her people want her."

Horliss-Cole stiffened:

"The hospital is for such cases!" he began in a dignified tone.

319

"Yes, I know," said the young minister half impatiently, "but the brother is here and he is quite set against her going to the hospital, says his mother wants her at home and can take care of her. I think it would be better on the whole. She spoke just now herself and said 'Home.' Now if you will stand aside we'll carry her over to the car. I think we can make her quite comfortable without disturbing your sister—"

Mr. Horliss-Cole stood aside in dismay and watched while the young minister in his clinging wet garments lifted the slender body in his strong arms and bore her swiftly to the car.

Marjorie Horliss-Cole stood back aghast, holding her dress away from the dripping hair of the girl and murmuring quite loud: "Why, the very idea! In *our* car!"

"Now, if you will drive quickly, please," he said to the chauffeur in that tone of command that was usually obeyed. "They said it was the fifth house in the second row, just behind the office buildings."

The chauffeur with an inscrutable look cast a furtive eye at Horliss-Cole and started the car.

John Treeves inclined his head slightly back toward Miss Cole:

"I hope this delay won't inconvenience you, Miss Cole," he said gently. "It seemed to be a matter of life and death to get her quickly to her home. This was the only way."

"Of course!" said Miss Cole with a surprising amount of satisfaction in her tone. Then she took the robe from her lap and wrapped it around the minister's shoulders.

He smiled back:

"Thank you, but don't worry about me. I've been colder and wetter than this many a time in France and it never hurt me a mite."

"H'm!" was all Miss Cole said, but she glanced keenly at Patty. For Patty had turned and taken one of the limp white hands of the stranger girl, and was chafing it softly between her own warm pink palms and then she drew her warm glove on one little limp hand and worked with the other. John Treeves said nothing, but he gave one swift, grateful glance into the girl's eyes and then dropped his glance respectfully. Patty felt as if somehow all the ache and sorrow of their estrangement had somehow been healed in spirit with that glance.

They stopped before one of the tiny gray and white shanties and the old mother with a curious arrangement of tiny plaid shawl upon her head came out to meet them with tears upon her cheeks. Her brother stood holding the door wide open, and two little sisters and a small brother crowded behind their mother's skirt all with a piteous, woebegone expression on their faces.

Treeves was not gone long. He came out with a troubled look in his eyes:

"I'll go back to the place where I left my coat

and hat, and then I'll not trouble you any more," he said with a comprehensive smile that took in Patty's back. She felt it. But when he explained to Mr. Horliss-Cole that he was sorry not to be able to go back with them, but he had promised the mother of the girl to hunt up the young man and take a message to him, that gentleman raised his eyebrows in a way that showed he also was used to being obeyed and said coldly:

"That is quite unnecessary, Mr. Treeves. There are plenty of people here to carry messages, and I scarcely think the fellow deserves any messages. He has made us a great deal of trouble and notoriety unnecessarily."

"I hope you can get him out on bail," said Treeves anxiously. "It seems almost a matter of life and death with the girl. She is calling for him. They are soon to be married."

"That is quite impossible, Mr. Treeves," said Horliss-Cole stiffly, freezingly, in fact. "You must remember he is probably a murderer by this time and must not be allowed to be at large. We should have all our discipline upset and murders in every quarter of the settlement if we allowed him to go free after what he has done."

Patty half opened her mouth with a little quick gasp and turned to speak, then remembered who she was, and thought better of it. If she had aught to say that would have weight this was not the place nor time to say it. She must wait and think.

"Get in, please," said Horliss-Cole commandingly. "It is getting late and I must be at Wall Street before closing time." The tone said that the minister had delayed serious matters for trivial ones, but John Treeves stood back with a quick, graceful movement and bowed:

"I beg your pardon, I won't delay you any longer. I must go back to that cottage again!" and before anyone could say a word he had swung off at his long soldier's stride down the street, shaking back his wet hair and placing his hat on his head.

The back of the chauffeur's neck indicated amusement to Miss Cole's keen eyes that twinkled with sympathy. Mr. Horliss-Cole climbed solemnly, offendedly into his car, and gave the word to go, but Marjorie pouted and rebelled openly:

"I think it is horrid, Papa, to leave him that way all wet. He'll get pneumonia, and then what will his old uncle say? I don't see why you couldn't let that poor man go, Papa. He had nice eyes, and you know if you would order them to let him free they would."

"My dear, we do not let our criminal classes roam at large because they have nice eyes," said her father dryly, "and you do not know what you are talking about. This young foreigner had a grudge against the man he shot and has been heard to threaten to kill him before this. It seems the girl was quite nice looking and the foreman had taken a fancy to her; the Italian was merely jealous."

"Well, he had a right to be!" said his sister. "They were going to be married next week. He told me all about it. He talked very nicely. I was quite interested in him."

"My dear Sylvia," said Horliss-Cole in that condescending tone that often drove his sister to Florida in winter or the mountains in summer. "You really don't know what you are talking about. I have had experience with these foreigners. They are all a bad lot and live like pigs. They can talk, of course. They are temperamental, and know how to work on the sympathies. But you should see how they live. The girl would have been better off in the office making her good pay than married to him to slave her days away keeping house! Now, let us drop this subject. I have been disturbed enough. I do not wish to hear any more about it."

Late that afternoon, in the hour before dinner, when Patty knew that Mr. Horliss-Cole was usually in the library and comparatively unoccupied, she tapped at his door.

"Ah! Miss Fisher?" he said pleasantly as she entered. "You bring a message from my sister?"

"No, sir," answered Patty lifting brave eyes to the cold blue ones. "I came on my own account. I thought I ought to tell you something that perhaps you do not know, about what happened this morning. It may not be of importance, but I didn't feel it right to keep still about it, and I'm not sure anyone else noticed it."

"What is it?" The words were uninviting. Patty could see his annoyance rising.

"Mr. Horliss-Cole, that shot was not fired from the other side of the water, it came from our side, just behind where I was sitting. The man who fired was crouched below the car door on the right, with his foot on the running board, and the bullet hissed so close to my ear that I almost felt it graze the skin. I put my hand up to my ear and saw the man disappearing and hiding the revolver under his sweater. He was a man in a red sweater, with dark hair and big eyes."

"Angelo has big eyes and dark hair," said the gentleman offendingly. "What became of the man you saw?"

"I cannot tell," said Patty anxiously. "I was too excited. I think he rolled under the car and maybe got out at the back. There was such a crowd around just then that it was impossible to see, and it all startled me so that I didn't realize what had happened. Afterward I did not speak because I thought it best to tell you in private."

"That was very wise, Miss Fisher, very wise. You need say no more about the matter to anyone. Just forget it, please. You did quite right to come to me alone with it. That will be all!" And Horliss-Cole turned back to his evening paper and dismissed the matter from his mind.

25

It had been a very annoying week. The foreman at
The Plant had died and the papers were full of it.
There were hints of riot and red terror in every
editorial that appeared on the subject, and it had
kept Horliss-Cole busy to turn the notoriety into
laurels for himself; but he had done it, and the end
of the week found him complacently surveying
the field and finding himself victor at every turn.
There was no longer anything to worry about. The
girl was recovering from her wetting, and going
about her work again with hollow eyes and dark
circles under them. She had been given money
and she would say no more. She didn't dare. Her
father had lost a leg in a leather belt, and had
signed off for a small sum, not knowing any
better, and who was to feed the family if she did
not keep at it? Angelo was safely housed in jail at
a distance where she could not afford to go and
see him. The money that he paid for his board was
sorely missed. There was absolutely nothing else
that Mary della Camera could do but go back to
her work and say nothing. The owner of The Plant
knew that if it became necessary to save talk, he
could even get her to sign a paper for a trifling
sum, saying that the foreman had never bothered
her in any way and that she was not running away

from him, but had determined to end her life because she was so unhappy. She was absolutely in his power, and he was content. He could now turn his mind to things of lesser importance, and among these latter was the young minister.

He had been quite annoyed with him at the beginning of the week, but the young man had not returned until a few minutes ago, and somehow the matter seemed to have cooled down in his mind. Nevertheless he determined to have that talk with him at once as it might have some influence on his sermon the next morning, and also, it might be as well to warn him against any reference to the occurrences at The Plant. It really would be good to get him interested at once in some kind of course of study. It would use up that surplus energy of which he seemed to have such a store, and that kept him doing strange erratic things. What a pity that such a brilliant young man should have such a tendency to meddle in matters that did not concern him. Well, he would have him in with a cup of tea, and give him a few more hints. It was only fair to himself and the congregation on the morrow.

John Treeves said nothing more about The Plant or what had happened on Monday. He discoursed politely about the weather, the state of the country, the likelihood of a change in the policy of the administration at the next election, and the prospect before France and England. Somehow

Horliss-Cole began to find it more and more difficult to get in what he had intended to say. At last he broke in upon a description of the appearance of Germany at the time of the Armistice, and put the matter baldly:

"Mr. Treeves, I have been thinking about a suggestion I would like to make to you. Why wouldn't it be a good thing for you to take a little course of study here in one of our many fine institutions. There's Columbia, there's Union. Now I'd like to see you enter a post-graduate class in something at Union. They have big men there with advanced ideas. You said you had been out of Seminary during the war, and it would help to brush you up. Not that you seemed to need it, of course, only it will be hard for a young minister getting right into the work to keep up with the times without some such plan!"

John Treeves narrowed his eyes and looked at his interlocutor steadily, searchingly, amusedly:

"Yes?" he said at last lightly. "Well, now that is an idea. I shall think about it, of course. And that reminds me, how far is the Library from here? Only a few blocks down the avenue, isn't it? I think I would have time to run down before dinner, would I not? There's a book I very much want to consult before to-morrow, if possible. A few statistics I want to verify. If you'll excuse me I'll go at once." And John Treeves set down his untasted cup of tea and took himself gloriously away from what was meant to be a neat little taste of the Inquisition.

He had spent the first four days of that week in New York gathering up data, much of the time among the men of the Horliss-Cole Plant. He had been by the bedside of the dying man as well as in the neat little home where the girl had been brought from her semi-drowning. Also, he had been much at the jail where the young man Angelo was confined. He had entered into the lives of these people as one who was somehow related to them, and after the first few questionings, suspicious minutes when they stood aloof and eyed him as an intruder, they had opened their hearts and put their trust upon him. It was wonderful how far he had gone into their lives and motives during those four days. Then he had betaken himself back to Maple Brook and walked to his trysting place every day where alone with the sky and his God he communed and asked counsel. No wonder that when he returned there was on his face a look that Moses might have worn when he came down from the Mount. Small wonder that Horliss-Cole had no chance with his platitudes that night.

And Patty, with her new Bible, had spent a wonderful week. She had no excuse to offer that Sunday morning when Miss Cole quietly announced that they would again attend church. She was glad to go.

"I will read the Sermon on the Mount," announced the young preacher, after the choir had subsided from a marvellous rendering of "Unfold ye portals everlasting." Then he proceeded to make the Sermon on the Mount live in new vivid terms before the astonished listeners. The blesseds, read with the term "O the happiness of" substituted, became a different thing. The people who had all their lives thought that pleasure and money and power had been the things to bring happiness, suddenly learned that spirits that were poor, hearts that hungered, lives that were persecuted, meekness, purity, righteousness, were far more things to be desired and sought after. It was startling the way he read it. Each man secretly resolved to go home and read that Sermon on the Mount over again, for it seemed that surely this young upstart of a preacher had put things into it that were not there. "Let your light so shine before men—" began the clear, young voice, and Maxim Petrol began to bask contentedly. Ah, here was familiar ground. Now he could think of that last fat check to the hospital, and the memorial tablet he had put up in the church to the boys who had fallen in the war. But—! What was this? He never knew that it read that way before: "Let your light so shine THAT THEY MAY GLORIFY YOUR *FATHER! NOT YOU.*" No one had spoken those last two words, yet the verse was so read that those words followed, ringing in the ears as clearly as if they had been voiced.

The minister read the first nineteen verses of the chapter, and the service proceeded with music, prayer and collection. At last he stood up to preach:

"I will take my text from the twentieth verse of the Sermon on the Mount," he announced. Maxim Petrol cast a glance of approbation toward Horliss-Cole and settled back comfortably. But Horliss-Cole was wary. This was a slippery young man. After reading like that what might he not do with the good old Sermon on the Mount that had served to curb so many flighty young preachers.

"For I say unto you," thrilled out the words warningly, "that except your righteousness shall *exceed* the righteousness of the scribes and Pharisees, ye shall in *no case* enter into the Kingdom of Heaven!"

Social service! There was plenty of it in that sermon, but it was made most plain that it would not be a passport to the Kingdom of Heaven. Modern efficiency, Americanism, social uplift, all were put under the searchlight of God's eternal test. Such service, well intentioned, efficient and of good results though it might be, was not an atonement for sin, could never take the place of repentance, and remission of sins.

Then the service itself came in for examination.

The young stranger had thoroughly possessed himself of the facts, and he did not hesitate to make them known. He had the statistics at his tongue's end. Did they know how many foreigners came into their city every year and what had become of them? Did they know how many of them had but vague ideas of the way to be saved and were losing what faith they had because of the inconsistent American Christians about them? He made some of the self-satisfied church members very thoughtful as he faced them with their inconsistencies. Then he told the story of a young foreigner who had been three years in jail for buying a stolen watch for five dollars. He took the watch to a jeweler to find out if he had been cheated and was promptly arrested. The man who sold it to him could not be found and he was put in jail. Three years lost out of a young man's life when he had been but five weeks in the new land, and had bright hopes of getting a good job and saving money till he could send for his girl to come over and marry him. And no one in the broad Christian land stepped forward to help him out of his awful situation.

Somehow the congregation got interested in that young man. One or two solid old business men got out their handkerchiefs and wiped their glasses, and stirred uneasily in their pews. Horliss-Cole was most uncomfortable. There had been a case of that sort at The Plant and he had suppressed a small attempt to secure sympathy for the young man.

The minister sketched the possibility of these strangers being tried innocently for murder, and for other crimes of which they were innocent, and he had the colossal nerve to suggest to that noble congregation that it was their privilege—THEIR DUTY—to be friends and brothers to those common foreigners who came across the sea to earn their living! It was not enough that they employed them and paid them a fair wage, not even enough that they built them hospitals where they might be patched up when they lost an arm or a leg doing their work, and sent their children to school and brought them up to take their fathers' places working. Not even enough to amuse them now and then. They should make it their business to see that these men and their children were put in the way of development. That talents they had might be discovered and trained, that their weaknesses, or hindrances might be allowed for, that their desires might be fulfilled. They were children of the same Father. Except your righteousness shall EXCEED—! And most of all they should so represent their Father in Heaven, that these should see and accept Him as their Father.

It was a very trying sermon for some of those stingy rich men and a most enlightening one for some of the rich men who were not stingy. But whichever they were they sat at attention, for no one could be under the sound of that thrilling young voice and not face the facts that were flung at them, facts about disease and crime, housing and jails and hospitals, cases of drunkenness. Facts about churches and what they were *not* doing. Facts about social standards and how they affected the laboring classes. There was not a sentence that did not hold something startling as the speaker neared the close of his remarks and somehow every church member present felt suddenly arraigned before a judgment that was not of earth.

John Treeves had not more than finished pronouncing the solemn benediction before the solid old member who had wiped his glasses so many times was on his feet and half-way up the aisle:

"Young man," said he, grasping the minister's sleeve, "young man, I want you to tell me who that young fellow is that has been in jail three years. I'm going to get out and see what I can do for him personally. PERSONALLY, you understand. He needs his girl to come over right away. Has she stuck to him, do you know? I want to find out all the facts in the case, can you give them to me?"

And while John Treeves was pouring forth the story and giving dates and names for the other man to write in his notebook, Maxim Petrol and Horliss-Cole were standing at the back of the church and shaking their heads solemnly together:

"Of course this can't go on," said Horliss-Cole. I'm greatly disappointed in him. I thought from the way he took my suggestions that he was going to be quite amenable to reason—"

"Well," said Maxim Petrol, "don't be too hard on him all at once. He's original, of course, and that will attract people. I thought that suggestion of yours about a course of study was the best yet. He really has pretty good stuff in him, and being a Treeves—! There's nothing like a good solid institution to tone up a flighty mind. Get him among other students—! Said anything to him about it yet?"

"Yes, I broached the matter, and he said he'd think about it, but he's quite peculiar. One never knows how he is going to take a thing. He almost has the attitude when you admonish him of— well—I could almost say he looks—*amused!*"

Maxim Petrol stared thoughtfully through large, round, shell-rimmed glasses:

"My brother Merriman says he likes to hear him preach because he has a keen sense of humor," he said plaintively. "It may be even that he *is* amused! Yet it scarcely seems the thing in a minister of the Gospel, do you think? Humor and dignity hardly seem to go together."

"It seems to be not quite a fitting combination," said Horliss-Cole annoyedly. It did not amuse him to think he had caused amusement. He had of late years taken himself quite too seriously. "But then everyone knows Merriman is always looking for a joke," he added, taking a grain of comfort.

"Well, it certainly is popular, whatever you call it," continued Maxim Petrol. Do you know what the collection was this morning? More than double any last month or the month before. The people are taking to him. Look at Snuffbox Anderson down there plastering it all over him! And Judge Beech! And did you see the editorial in *The Times* last Monday? It made quite the hit of the Sunday news, that sermon. You didn't like it, but you'll find that kind of stuff takes. It's rot, of course, but people will have it; it's like jazz music and the *Police Gazette.* Just get a man that talks something different from the common run and you catch a crowd and get in the limelight. Not that I like that sort of thing, of course, but I guess we've got to do something if we don't want to dry up and blow away. The old church has been getting behind the times for the last ten years and it's up to the committee to bring about a change. I guess if it's going to please the people and bring in old Treeves's dollars, we'll have to patch him up somehow to suit the more conservative. Try the study course on him and see if it works. I tell you he's got good stuff in him if it were only polished up and modernized a little. It isn't so much *what* you preach, you know, *as the way you get it across,* and that's what he does, gets it across! Now if you can only doctor up his antiquated ideas a little we'll make it a go."

But Horliss-Cole, mindful of the way he had failed Saturday night, took himself to his home in a less self-assured way than was natural. He was by no means certain that he was going to "get it across" with young Treeves.

26

John Treeves took dinner that Sunday with the old gentleman of the fat check book and found much to tell that that worthy soul did not know, both about humanity and also about the Christian religion. But Horliss-Cole sat annoyedly in his stately library and wondered how he was to get opportunity to give a few more broad hints to the young clergyman without sacrificing the whole of his valuable Monday morning.

However, John Treeves walked in upon him about five o'clock Sunday afternoon and sat down affably, opening the interview himself.

"Well, now, Mr. Horliss-Cole, I'm ready to answer your question and I'd like you to do a little favor for me."

"Oh, certainly!" said Horliss-Cole, so relieved that he would have granted him two favors for the moment. "Just take that easy chair by the fire, won't you? And have a cigar. These are my own special brand. Brought them from—"

But John Treeves waved him aside:

"Thank you, no; I never smoke!"

Horliss-Cole still held out the box of large, fat monogrammed cigars, however, with an urgent, indulgent little shake:

"Oh, that's all right, Treeves, we're in the seclusion of my library now, you know, and I don't intend to publish it. Besides, the feeling about the clergy doing such things is largely passing away. In fact, I think it's a good thing. It promotes fellowship among men. You can get nearer to a man over a good cigar than any other way, you know. It's something like the Indian Pipe of Peace—" he finished, vaguely feeling that he was capping a very good climax with a telling illustration.

"Yes?" said John Treeves, dropping into the big chair with a temporary air, as if he had not time to sit back and rest. "Well, I've never found it hard to get near to a man without smoking and I guess I won't try it now, thank you. Somehow it doesn't appeal to me, and I think I'm clearer headed without it. I was going to ask you if you would kindly give me an introduction to your foreman over at The Plant—or whoever has charge of hiring men."

Horliss-Cole reluctantly, offendedly withdrew the cigar box, his face slowly congealing at the request: Was this young upstart going to try and run in some protege? He needn't think he could run The Plant because he was preaching in their church:

"I'm afraid," he said coldly, "that there isn't much chance of getting any new hands in just now; you see, we are turning off men, rather than hiring. This is a slack time and—"

"That's too bad," said John Treeves calmly, "but that is just where you come in, I suspect. You see, I want you to speak the word that will make an opening somewhere. I don't mean that I want a job made out of whole cloth, of course, or that I want any other man put out to serve my purposes, but in such a flourishing plant as I saw the other day you surely must have room for one more good experienced man."

"Who is your man?" asked Horliss-Cole coldly. It did beat everything how this bubble of a young man got up things and insisted upon them when anybody else in the world in his position would be careful how he stepped these first few weeks before the call was assured. The young man did not seem exactly thick skinned either. Horliss-Cole did not understand it. He did not like to admit that he liked the fellow all the better for his independence, even though it angered and baffled him.

"I was speaking of myself," said John Treeves quietly.

"Oh—ho!" laughed Horliss-Cole with a relieved sound in his voice, flicking away the ash from his cigar daintily. "I see. You were joking. Ha! Ha! Quite a compliment to the works I assure you. I appreciate it. I'll have to tell Petrol that. He appreciates a good joke; that is, his brother Merriman does. He's always hunting one. They call him Merry for short on that account, I believe. By the way, Marjorie left a box of chocolates on the table here, perhaps you'll have some of those—" shoving a luxurious box toward him. "Ha, ha! Quite a joke!"

"Not at all!" John Treeves said seriously. "I mean it. I would like to get into the shop for a while and get near to those men. It's just what I've been looking for, a chance for something like that."

Horliss-Cole smiled and narrowed his eyes quizzically:

"Oh, I see! Social service! Of course that might be very interesting to you for a few days, but a thing like that is a bit upsetting to regular work, you know, and the men might resent it."

"You misunderstand me," said Treeves. "I want a regular job with regular wages like the rest, and I want to stick for a year, perhaps, maybe more."

Horliss-Cole smiled once more at his enthusiasm:

"I thought you said it was an 'experienced' man you were offering?"

"I did," said Treeves promptly. "I worked in machine shops for two summers while I was in college. I could run any of those machines and do piece-work in that second building we went through, and I'll warrant that in a week I could work as fast and as well as any man on the floor. I like that sort of thing."

"Well, but," said Horliss-Cole growing more serious since this young man was determined to talk in this impossible way, "do you think that such a position would be compatible with your other work, your—ah—calling?"

"I certainly do!" said Treeves. "You, sir, were suggesting a course of study to me yesterday. Well, this is my reply. I want to do this for at least a year as a study in Humanity. I do not know of any better way to get near to men than to live with them, and work with them and have common interests."

"Those men are scarcely the class of humanity with whom you will be likely to have to do in your life work." Horliss-Cole said it coldly, as if somehow the suggestion had been a personal insult.

"Humanity is the same the world over, no matter in what class it is found," said John Treeves.

"Well, Mr. Treeves, I scarcely think our church would agree to your proposition." Horliss-Cole lighted his cigar once more and gave a puff or two of finality to his speech as he eyed the young man narrowly. He felt much as if he had stepped into a zoo with an escaped lion and been told to put him in a cage again.

"I beg your pardon, Mr. Horliss-Cole," said John Treeves calmly. "But I believe that after next Sunday my connection with that church will be concluded. You said four Sundays in your letter, I believe. I was not expecting to go to work until a week from to-morrow. I can scarcely see what this church would have to do with my affairs after that."

A sort of cold perspiration came out on Horliss-Cole's forehead. What an everlasting pest this young man was, with all his culture and breeding and money. The very idea! What a crazy fool! What on earth should he say next? The committee were hardly ready to show their hands as yet.

"I did not say, Mr. Treeves, that the church would not desire your services after the four weeks were concluded, however," he said impressively, "I think on the whole the committee has been most favorably impressed with you. I should not like you to do anything that would in any way prejudice them against you. For my own part I am very fond of you and would like to see you get a call. It might even come to that, you know, if you play your cards well."

"But I'm not playing cards!" said John Treeves, his whole face breaking into a radiant smile of mischief. "In fact, it would take more than a call from the church to make me even consider such a thing."

"What do you mean?" Horliss-Cole stiffened visibly.

"I mean that I would have to be very sure that God had called me to make me willing to accept a call to a church like that," said Treeves reverently.

"A church like that!" repeated Horliss-Cole haughtily. "Young man, I don't suppose you have been in New York long enough to realize that our church is among the oldest and best established churches in the city; I might say, in the country. It is known from sea to sea. It has been the church home of more than one President of the United States, many senators, and noted men, great financiers, nationally-wide editors and literateurs. Its pulpit has been filled by the greatest orators of their times. Historically you could fill no greater pulpit, young man!"

"But I am not anxious to fill a pulpit historically, Mr. Horliss-Cole. I am not an orator, nor do I feel called to speak to great men. My desire is to get near to the hearts of men and bring them to know Jesus Christ."

Mr. Horliss-Cole looked at the young preacher as if he had suddenly broken out with some very great blasphemy. He was actually embarrassed by the intimate way in which John Treeves spoke of Jesus Christ. It seemed to him a little crude to say the least, and not at all befitting the dignity of a minister of the Gospel. He paused, looking down at the floor offendedly, and while he hesitated for an answer to such purblind folly, John Treeves spoke again:

"Mr. Horliss-Cole, I have fully made up my mind about this, and I would like to settle the matter at once. I am interested in your Plant and feel that I could do good work there, as well as pursue the study I have determined to take up. Are you willing that I should apply for a position in your Plant or must I look elsewhere?"

Mr. Horliss-Cole was sadly put to it for an answer. He certainly did not want the young scion of a great house who had so publicly been associated with the old church to go to work like a common laborer in some other man's plant, for there was no knowing what queer thing he might take it into his wild undisciplined head to do, and no end to the publicity that would be made of it in the newspapers. If the fellow must have his fling in a factory, by all means it was best to keep the matter as quiet as possible. If he let him have some kind of nominal job in The Plant he could control the matter, and arrange things so that he would soon tire of it; also, he could explain it quietly as a little fad of the young man, and it need never come to the ears of the curious public nor even the church as a whole. At any rate he must not antagonize the peppery young man and send him elsewhere until he had had a talk with the rest of the committee.

So, tapping the thick Persian rug nervously with his elegant boot, he lifted his eyebrows long-sufferingly at the young man with a sigh that denoted patience much tried, and replied:

"Oh, of course, if you feel that you must go through this experience I shall be glad to further your investigations in every possible way. I will speak to my foreman this week and see what can be done to give you all opportunity for the study you wish to take up."

It was characteristic of Horliss-Cole that he picked out the only attitude possible to him under the trying circumstances and took his stand as if there had been no other attitude he might have taken. He intended by every word, look and action to impress it upon the young man that this *was* a study in social science, not a taking of a job like a common workman.

John Treeves looked at him a trifle uncertainly:

"You understand, Mr. Horliss-Cole, that I wish to enter as a common workman, plain John Treeves, with no Reverend or any tale of family or friends attached to my name. I want to be one of them and get to know them. I want to try myself out and see if I can live Jesus Christ among them, and bring them to know Him. If I can do that, I shall feel that I have a right to preach. Otherwise I don't think I shall."

"Oh, of course, that shall be as you please," said Horliss-Cole, considering whether it might not after all be kept an entire secret from everyone save the committee. Of course the committee—he would not like to take the responsibility without their backing, for a thing like this was always in danger of coming out sometime, and one must be prepared.

So after the stately Sunday dinner and after Marjorie had gone with the minister to church, he retired to his den and called up Maxim Petrol, who never went out to church at night, though he often frequented the homes of his friends, or some concert hall or popular lecture on Sunday evening. Maxim Petrol was quite ready to spend the evening with his friend, Horliss-Cole, and came tipping daintily in in dove-colored spats half an hour later attended by his younger brother Merriman, a rounder, pleasanter, merrier replica of himself.

"I thought I'd best bring Merry along," he explained. "He's taken a great fancy to that young minister, and as he's on the committee it isn't bad to have three heads instead of two to talk the matter over."

So with the help of a bit of refreshment now and then and a good many gold monogrammed cigars, they talked John Treeves up and down, out and over, and in again to their hearts' content.

"Well, I think you better let him have a try at his socialism," declared Merry Petrol, mixing himself another cocktail cheerily. "It'll make him all the more popular and help to antidote some of his archaic theology. If he gets out among men like that he's sure to be a hero, and nowadays you've got to have something if you want to get a crowd at all. He'll either have to be an ex-ball player, or notoriously broad, so that some people would cry out against him as being unorthodox, or else he'll have to be some kind of a reformer, or he can't make this church go. It's dead and you know it, and it needs something to wake it up. Let him go and work a week, or maybe two—it won't last more than that. No man really likes to work unless he has to; it won't last long, and it'll bring the people in while it does. He'll get off some of his stories. Oh, you needn't wince, Jim, he'll lug in some of your sins, of course, but it'll only show up your virtues all the brighter, and you can't beat this kind of dope for bringing in the people, and getting everybody agog to hear him."

"I should think it ought to be enough that he is a nephew of old Calvin Treeves," said Mr. Horliss-Cole haughtily.

"Well, it isn't," snapped Merry Petrol crisply. "You'll find out we're in a new age. The world is changing and we can't afford to ignore jazz even in the old church. Get me, Jim? He's got lots of pep, that kid has, and that's what we need nowadays."

Five weeks later Merriman Petrol "dropped in" at the Mountain House for a night's rest and a chat with Calvin Treeves on his way to Palm Beach.

Calvin Treeves looked older than when his nephew had visited him, and there was in his eye a kind of frightened backward glance now and then that betokened a constant consciousness of his enemy lurking in the offing. But his voice had the same sporty chirrup and he greeted Merriman with a hearty good fellowship. He was one of the few people with whom he never quarreled and whom he never ordered about.

"Hello, Merry! You here! Now that's the good old sport. Sit down and tell me the news. Hespur get him a drink of something. No, you needn't worry, I won't ask for any. The doctor's forbidden 'em, worse luck, and I'm obeying orders for a day or so till I get on my feet. Had a bad turn yesterday again. Old carcass all worn out. But I'm pretty tough; they can't down me!" He cast the furtive backward glance, and laughed his hollow cackle. "Sit down, sit down. What's the news, Merry, old man! I haven't heard a bit of gossip since I came to this old cat's paradise, because I hate the old cats so."

Merriman sat down and accepted the glass of wine that Hespur proffered:

"Well, the news is that you've got a great little old nephew!" declared Merriman Petrol, draining the last swallow and handing the glass to Hespur, who flushed with pleasure at his words, although his face was perfectly immobile.

"What! What! WHAT! What's this? My nephew! My NEPHEW? How do *you* know I have a nephew?"

"Oh, I know! Don't you think I know what's

going on in this world! Guess I've been listening to him preach the last three or four weeks and he's all there with bells! He's got Horliss-Cole and my revered brother Maxim eating right out of his hand!"

"Horliss-Cole!" The old man's eyes twinkled with triumph.

"Yes, and you ought to see 'em worrying. He's got 'em guessing what he's going to do next and they're so scared he won't accept their old call to the church they don't know what to do."

"He has?" said Calvin Treeves breathlessly. "He HAS! He *HAS?*"

"Oh, yes, and that isn't all, he's got New York by the horns and everybody's crazy about him. You see, when he wouldn't accept the call, Horliss-Cole made him promise he would preach a few more Sundays till they could find some one else. He set it out that the committee didn't want to have any more untried preachers, till they could find one they could recommend, and so finally Treeves said he'd preach if they'd let him alone and let him preach what he really thought. It went hard with 'em to give in to that, but they did it, and so he is pledged to stay awhile, and the people just throng to hear him. They have something about him in the paper almost every day. They call him a 'second Paul.' It seems there was a man in the Bible named Paul. And they can't talk enough about him. He's the sensation of the hour. And the worst of it is he hates it. He told them if they didn't stop writing him up he'd quit. But they can't seem to stop it, and Jim Horliss-Cole and my brother Maxim are going around like a coupla kids driving a too-fast horse and he's getting away with 'em."

The old eyes twinkled and the leathery lips worked nervously, happily.

"Can—does he—what does he preach about, Merry?" he quavered, wetting his dry lips again and again with the tip of his withered old tongue.

"Oh, but that's the best of it all. He lets it out from the shoulders. Gives 'em straight talk about their sins. Oh, he doesn't leave any of them out, stands them all up in front of him every Sunday and shows them how there's no Heaven for them, every last one of them. 'Us,' I should say, for he's had me in, too. Every one recognizes himself, though I doubt if Treeves knows who he's preaching at. It certainly is funny. I laughed till I split the other day watching Horliss-Cole while he was being preached about, old hypocrite that he is, with all his church poses and his benevolences, and his pretenses that he's so much better than the next one. His face was purple with rage, but he had to pretend it was great. And all the time that good old sport of a grouchy sister of his—"

"Sylvia!" There was something strange and reverential in the tone the old man used. Merriman Petrol stopped and stared for a moment.

"Yes, Sylvia, I believe. Well, she was grinning inside. You could see it in the set of her shoulders."

"Does Sylvia go to church?"

"Oh, yes, she comes every Sunday, she and that pretty little quaint thing they call Fisher, some kind of relation that's spending the winter there."

"So they go to church!"

"Why, man, I've been myself! Went first to please Maxim because he was on the committee. Then they put me on and I had to go, and bless my lucky stars if I didn't enjoy it. Some nephew, that is! I don't much blame Marjorie Horliss-Cole for tagging him around. But he's as indifferent as snow in summer. Man! But he's a peach!"

When Merriman Petrol was gone the old man lay silent a long time wetting his lips and picking away nervously at the rug that was over him. He no longer sat in his wheeled chair now, but lay flat on his great deep bed, like an old bird in a too-large nest.

"Hespur!" he said in a weak voice, turning his face toward the dark window where Hespur stood looking out at the stars above the pines. "Hespur, did you ever happen to find a Paul in that Bible?"

"I've seen the name, sir. Yes, sir, come to think I remember passing it, sir. Some letters he wrote I figured, sir. I don't rightly remember who. 'I Paul'—that was like it. I'll take the new Bible that you had sent down from New York, sir, and cipher around in it awhile, sir. There's a thing they call something like a 'Concord' at the back, sir. It'll maybe be having Paul in it. There's notes, sir, that speak how to find it. I sighted a Moses this morning and had a try at him whilst you was napping, sir. It wasn't, so to speak, difficult, sir. I'll maybe find a Paul."

The old man lay and waited eagerly till Hespur had discovered Paul in the concordance, and then listened to passage after passage.

"There seems to be a right smart lot about him, sir. He must have been a rather important character, sir, in them days, sir. It appears to have been an honor to be like him, sir. Now, you take a bit of sleep, sir, and I'll be getting your broth ready, and afterwhiles we have another try at the Book."

And so, with a smile that softened the hard lines in his old face, Calvin Treeves fell asleep for a little.

27

Patty had a whole day to herself for the first time since she came to live with Miss Cole. That good lady was going on a brief visit from morning until evening to an old school friend whom she visited once a year on her birthday. The annual pilgrimage had become something almost sacred since the friend had been bedridden, and looked forward with eagerness always to Sylvia's coming.

"I can't take you with me," explained Miss Sylvia, "because you see she's in reduced circumstances and they haven't room for many people. It would bewilder her and make her feel as if somehow I wasn't as close to her as I used to be if I took some one with me. And she has a little maid servant who will do all for me that is necessary. I shall go and come in the car, and there isn't an earthly bit of use in your being made to take that trip when you might be out somewhere enjoying yourself. You haven't had a day to yourself since you came. Now take it and do for goodness' sake go and buy something frivolous for yourself, or take in a show, or do something nice. You're always penned up with an old woman and it isn't good for a girl. I wish to goodness Marjorie had some sense. You could have real good times together. But she has her head so full of beaus and clothes that there isn't room for much else. There, take that and buy something you'd really like. Spend it *all* and don't think you've got to come and tell me what you did with it, or buy something sensible, or save it. I want you to be *extravagant* for once and act like any girl, and if you don't want to be back till late to-night it will be all right. I can get along without any help for once. I'm feeling quite frisky these days."

She stuffed a roll of bills into Patty's hands and hurried off to her car before Patty could so much as thank her, and when Patty came to count them there was twenty-five dollars, and a scrap of paper on which was scrawled in Miss Cole's odd characters. "Now, mind, you spend it all and don't get anything sensible. I want you to be crazy for once and do as you please."

So Patty went back to her room and sat down and wept a bright little tear, because it had somehow come to her that Miss Sylvia loved her. Underneath all her gruffness she had a heart and she really loved her. Not in all the years had her mother ever done anything like this for her. It wasn't the money nor the amount, it was the wish that she should be a girl and have a good time; the recognition that she had been faithful in her work and deserved something nice. It made a warm, lonely, little feeling around her heart. Oh, if her mother were only like that and she might go home and live like other girls! Oh, if her dear father were only back! How strange it was that she heard nothing from him. By this time surely he must have received her letter, and it would be like him to telegraph or cable at once some little message to let her know she had his trust whatever she was doing and wherever she was. She had been expecting it for a long time and a puzzled, queer, ghastly, little ache was coming now whenever she thought about it.

But this whole long day to herself! What should she do with it? What wild extravagant thing could she think of to do? She might buy some books, although Miss Cole had every book one could think of and then some more. There were one or two necessities of dress she might purchase, but they would scarcely satisfy Miss Cole's idea of extravagance, and she had money enough of her salary to supply all her real needs and lay by some every month. Besides, she had a feeling that this was a sort of a game she was playing with the grim old lady and that it was her turn to move and provide something interesting in the game, something that would be as wild and pleasant to tell as it was to do. So really she wouldn't be doing it all for herself after all, but partly to amuse Miss Cole with the story of it when she got back.

Patty sat down and thought, and the first thing that presented itself as an interesting thing to do was to take a trolley and see if she could find that girl that had almost drowned that day when they were at The Plant. She would take her some flowers. She had wanted to do it last week, but had never had time for so long a trip. Besides, as long as John Treeves was about the house she had kept very close to her own and Miss Cole's rooms lest she meet him. But the young minister had apparently secured some boarding place, for he had not been at the house at all the week before, although he had preached as usual. These Sabbath services were coming to be the bright spots of the week, wherein her old friend came back and talked with her and helped her to know his Friend, God, and to see her own need of a Saviour. So Patty was not worried lest she should meet John Treeves on this expedition.

It did not take her long to dress for the street and she was soon on her way to a nearby florist where she knew she could get almost anything in the way of flowers. She had a royal time choosing them and at last decided for carnations and sweet peas, glowing with color and fragrance and gifted with lasting powers. One great white lily with a golden tongue she had put in the centre, and plenty of asparagus fern for a background. Then with her big box she went happily on her way and after a little enquiry found the right car line to carry her to The Plant.

She felt a little queer going around the place alone after she arrived there, a little as if perhaps she ought not to have come, but she went bravely on, her cheeks rosy with the excitement of the adventure. She came to the big office building where the car had stood. Across the water she could see a figure bending over a typewriter with flying fingers on the keyboard, but she could not be sure it was the same girl. She turned and studied carefully the situation, got her bearings, walked straight to the little house in the long gray row and knocked at the door. There was a murmur inside as of questioning voices, then, when her heart was just beginning to fail her, the door was opened a little way and a woman peered out. She had a worn, haggard face, straggling hair and a faded cotton dress, clean but discouraged looking.

She eyed the stranger dubiously, discontentedly, enviously, but aloof. No one who looked and dressed like that could have part nor lot with her. This girl had come to the wrong place, that was all. In fact, what was she doing at The Plant at all? There was suspicion and distrust written in the woman's eyes.

But Patty smiled.

"Could you tell me, is this where the girl lives who fell in the water about three weeks ago? I do not know her name, but I was in the car that brought her back, and I'm sure this was the house."

The woman rested her hip back against the doorjamb and surveyed her more in detail, shaking her head discouragingly, and saying monotonously: "No unnerstand Ongla."

Patty began again speaking more distinctly:

"Is there a girl here, *Girl,* about as old as I am?" She smiled entrancingly and held up her box. "I've brought her some flowers. See!" and she broke the string and unwrapped the box.

The woman drew back and frowned, with her eyes on the box, but shaking her head:

"No, no buy. No money. No money!"

"Oh!" cried Patty in dismay, shaking her head. "I don't want to sell them. They are a present for your daughter. You got daughter?" she fell into the woman's lingo in her desperation. Oh, if she could but remember a little of her school Italian, a few love songs—that was about all. But just then a big woman in a sloppy calico wrapper, open at the breast and carrying a dirty baby, appeared behind the first one. She had large, dull, black eyes, had long, thick lashes, and wonderful curly black hair, but it was utterly unkempt. Her lips looked sullen and her eyes had a baffled expression: "Yes, she's got a daughter," she answered in gruff English. "What's youse wants of her? She ain't got no money to buy your flowers. What's it fer? The Red Cross? We ain't got no money to pay to nothing any more. Anyhow, the war's over."

"Oh, I don't want to sell the flowers. I brought them to the girl who fell in the river. I wanted to come sooner, but I couldn't. Is she here or has she got well and gone back to work?"

"Yes, she's got well, sorta, and she's gone back to work, only she ain't to work to-day, she's gone to jail to see her young man. He's in jail."

"Oh, did they put him in jail?" said Patty in dismay. "Not the man they called Angelo?"

"Yes. Angelo. Did you know him?"

"Oh, no, I only saw him that day. He talked to the people I was with. But why did they put him in jail? He looked like a nice young man."

" 'Cause they said he shot the boss. They heard him say he would kill him, and so they think he did."

"But he didn't! I'm sure he didn't!" said Patty. "I was in the car when the shot came, and it came from behind somewhere. Isn't there any way to prove that he is innocent?"

"I do no," said the sullen-looking woman apathetically. "They all done all they could. Why don't youse try? That there 'Tree' man tried. He ain't done trying yet. But I don't guess he'll do no good. Mr. Hor'-Cor' he ain't letting him out. He's too stinge, Mr. Hor'-Cor'. You belong to him? Why don't you tell him what you just tole me?"

"No, I don't belong to him," said Patty anxiously, "but I wish I could do something. I certainly will if I find anything in my power. What is the girl's name? Angelo said he was soon going to be married."

"Yes, they was, too, but that's all done now. She's can't marry him to the jail. Her name's Mary. She don't look like herself no more. She was awful good looking, but now she's all gone back. She lost about ten pounds, and she cry all night. She's my sister-in-law. I marry her broth'. I was born in this country, so I speak the English. Mary she speak, too, and she's real smart. She go to school and study and get to be a stenog'pher. She write for the boss. But she was too good looking. The boss he try to go with her and Angelo get mad, and all the time the boss and Angelo they have fight together. Oh, I guess he don't get free. The boss he die and they say Angelo killed him. I guess Angelo get killed. Don't you think? Angelo got no friends to get him out. They have so many laws and we are poor people. Got no money to pay to get him out."

"Oh, I am so sorry!" said Patty, her face quite white and suffering. "Won't you give Mary the flowers and tell her I will try to see if there is anything I can do to help her? I am only a girl and I haven't any friends here, nor anybody that I can ask to help, but—well—you tell her I *love* her—" she smiled brightly, wistfully up at the stolid, wondering woman. Patty opened the box and laid the glory of the flowers in the arms of the older Italian woman, who looked at them in dazed bewilderment as though they were blooms from another world, and then she buried her worn old face in their sweetness and began to cry, murmuring some strange foreign words between her sobs.

"She says to thank you," the younger woman said, preventing the slobbery baby from pouncing upon a great crimson carnation and tearing it into atoms. "She says she ain't never had no flowers like that, and Mary will be glad fer 'em. She says to come again when Mary is home."

And so, with the vision of the weeping mother in the doorway, her arms full of the bright blossoms with the lily in the midst, Patty turned away and went thoughtfully down the clean monotonous way. She was not noticing which way she went nor caring. All the brightness seemed gone from the day since she had heard of this other girl's trouble. And that nice Angelo with the big dreamy eyes, the kind smile, and the reverent way of saying "My girl," "My wife," was in jail! Perhaps going to be hung! How terrible it seemed! How could there be sunshine and joy in a world where a thing like that could happen? She was sure it was unjust, for how could Angelo have shot from the other side of the river when the shot went by her ear? She was sure of that!

Presently she saw that she was coming to a little landing by the river and a boat was on its way over. It was almost to the wharf. It was a large, flat, snubby ferryboat that plied from shore to shore. Why should she not take it and go across? It did not matter much where she went and it would be a trip on the water. She loved the water and the day was bright. If there was nothing interesting over there she could take the next boat back, and on the way she could think what to do with the rest of her day and the rest of her money. She had spent but three dollars so far and she doubted if Miss Cole would be much entertained by the telling of it, it was too painful.

So when the ferryboat arrived, Patty, with a few other passengers, went on board. She stood at the front rail and watched the patches of silver light on the water where the sunshine danced, and wondered why trouble and sin had to be in the world; and why a girl like Mary della Camera had to lose a lover like Angelo when it all seemed so pleasant and hopeful for their future. And it did not seem to be their fault either. Then her mind went back to last Sunday's sermon and she began to wonder about herself and if she could ever find the Friendly Saviour that John Treeves had preached about and claim Him for her own. She was so very lonely and unhappy, poor little soul, out seeking a holiday all by herself on a strange ferryboat!

The boat arrived at a lonely bit of landing and the other passengers hurried away down the road. Patty got off, looked uncertainly around and then decided to walk up the hill in front of her, for it seemed that there would be a wonderful view of the river up there, and it was a sparkling day. She would sit up there and try to think of something else to do. So she climbed the hill, sat down on a fallen log and looked out over the water. It did not occur to her to be afraid, for she could see in every direction a long distance and there seemed nothing but placid country. Patty was not a girl who was afraid of things anyway.

It was like a great painting spread out in front of her, the shimmering water, the busy plowing steamers going this way and that, The Plant across the river lifting tall warehouses and puffing chimneys near the water's edge like dark fringes on a silver gown, the little rows of dismal board houses stretching away in regular aisles, the flat stretching of country beyond, and the trolley line whereon a single car crawled now and then. Far down the river the dim city life lifted vague shapes against a luminous smoky background and seemed a nucleus for noise and bustle. But back here all was quiet and peace. Behind her stretched a light wooded crown of the hill, and wide meadows beyond now covered with brown grass and patches of the last snow huddled in fence corners. It seemed a pleasant, kindly nook wherein no one else had thought to take refuge, and Patty sat still and was glad she had found it. Somehow here for the first time since she had left home there seemed to be room and time to think out her own problems and go back over the last weeks. In the city there was always something ahead to be done, somewhere to go with Miss Cole, something going on in the great house in which her service was required in some way. Now it was writing notes or answering the telephone, now it was painting dainty bits of dinner cards, or arranging flowers from the hothouses, or helping Marjorie to find out what was the matter with a dress that Madame had just sent home, and suggesting how a touch of color, or a different arrangement of drapery would bring about the effect she desired. They had found that in all these things Patty had a knack, a talent. She was artistic in everything she did, and knew exactly how to arrange a room or put on a hat for the best effect that was in it. Mrs. Horliss-Cole had fallen into the habit of saying in any trying situation, "Send for Fisher, she'll know what to suggest. She always does." And she had actually made a proposition to her sister-in-law to take Patty over as her own personal attaché and substitute an older woman for Miss Cole. But Sylvia Cole resented having the bright young girl called "Fisher," and resented the idea of her being anybody's servant in that sense, for she knew that Kate Horliss could never treat a servant as Patty ought to be treated. Moreover she wanted Patty for herself and she put so prompt a veto on the idea that no one ever said any more about it.

But with that city background Patty had little time to think over her own problems, and now under the quiet sky she felt as if she could face them.

There was the matter of the home in the West. How long could she let this go on, her staying away without giving them any clue to her whereabouts? She had hoped that before this she would have had word from her father and be able to judge better what to do. If it had not been for that call from Hal Barron and the detective down in the mountains, she would probably have written to her mother by this time, and explained why she went away, for she was not a girl to harbor insult and injury, and it would have been a very gentle letter, making it quite possible for her mother to accept the situation and let her remain away. But somehow the aspect of a detective, followed so quickly by the visit of Hal Barron, put things in a different light. She felt as if there was something sinister in it, and she could not bear to go back, or to give them a chance to order her back, until her father was surely in this country again. And yet, all the time she was haunted by the fear lest she had after all misjudged them, and there might be some explanation that would at least take the edge from what they had said, and make life more bearable. How gladly would she have suffered punishment for what she had done if she could only have it proved to her that she had misjudged her mother and sister. Then there was another matter which had vaguely troubled her, and that was the old Judge, her father's friend. For some days she had been remembering that her father had charged her not to forget to appear in his office on her twenty-first birthday as he had something of interest to tell her. In her hurry of going away it had completely slipped her mind, and now that she had remembered it she feared that their old friend might think her careless and unappreciative of his interest in her. It never occured to her that the interview could be more than a pleasant birthday conversation, a little loving intercourse to solace her because her father was away, and perhaps he had left a birthday gift for her in his keeping. Well, birthday gifts would keep, of course, and it could all be explained in due time when her father returned, only, perhaps she should have confided in the Judge at such a time as this, and let him help her decide what to do. Perhaps her father would have had her do that. The Judge more than anyone else living was in the confidence of her father, and would know if there was anything strange about her, if she was adopted or anything. And yet, suppose he shouldn't, how dreadful it would be to let the Judge know how her mother and sister had talked! No! Oh, NO! She couldn't have told him. There was no question about it at all.

It never occured to her that she was making great embarrassment for her mother and sister, to explain her absence. She thought that she had been away so much it would be easy to say she was away again. Hal Barron's coming after her could have but one meaning. He had really liked her, and Evelyn's jealousy must have some foundation. Hal Barron had become so detestable in her eyes that she never wanted to see him again. She must stay away until she was sure he was over any such crazy notion, and had gone back to Evelyn. She thought sadly of the future. If Evelyn should marry Hal she would never want to go to see her, or be near her, for she would always remember the awful words she had heard, and always be self-conscious in Hal Barron's presence. If only her father would come back and tell her what to do! She would not mind earning her living, nor being in a house where they did not consider her an equal; if she were sure that she had a right to stay away from home as she was doing without telling anyone where she was. Suddenly her situation seemed to overwhelm her, and she put her head down in her hands and wailed aloud a little cry of heart-brokenness:

"Oh, Daddy, Daddy, Daddy! Where are you? *Why* don't you write to me? Oh—GOD! Where is Daddy—and WHERE are YOU?"

It was the nearest to a prayer she had ever come since the days of "Now I lay me" long ago. All during school God had meant little more to her than Santa Claus or fairies. Church was a ceremony of polite society, a vague placating of a distant peril. But since she had heard John Treeves preach something had stirred within her, some consciousness of a need of her soul, and a great longing and crying out for something bigger and higher than human help could give. The Bible she had bought had been diligently read, although most ignorantly. She had treasured in her memory all that John Treeves had said and she was beginning to grope in a feeble way after the

Light. This stifled cry was the first real appeal to Heaven that her soul had ever made and after it she sat hushed for a long time with her face in her hands and a quieted feeling as if somehow some influence were near to comfort her.

28

For some time she sat there thinking, looking out over the water, trying to find a solution to her difficulties. But at last the chill of the January day began to creep through her whole body, and in sudden alarm she shivered and got up, looking around to see what she should do next. How foolish to have sat here mooning so long! If she should take a cold and be sick it would be horrid, here among strangers. Besides, she was a working woman and had no right to be careless like this.

She cast a glance down to the little empty wharf and out over the water. The low, fat ferryboat was chug-chugging along nearly to the other shore, and it would be sometime before it returned. A survey of the immediate vicinity gave no hint of a nearby trolley line leading cityward. She would have to wait for that boat to come back. There were no houses in sight where she could go and get warm. The only one was so far down the road that she might miss the boat again, so she set out to run up the hill to get up a circulation. In a few minutes she was at the top darting in and out among the little pine trees, her cheeks as rosy as red apples, and her eyes bright with the exercise. After all, it was good to be living, even if one was all alone! And what a beautiful spot this was, with its crown of trees, and its resinous pines scattered here and there among the other bare ones. There were spots of ground pine, and places that looked as if arbutus and wintergreen berries might be found in due season, and there were lovely flat rocks cropping out. She wished she were a little girl to play house there with acorns for dishes, and moss for a carpet. What a wonderful site for a mansion! How strange that some one had not found it out and built there! But then perhaps they would object to being opposite The Plant, although that was far enough away not to be annoying or unsightly.

She walked about on the hilltop until the squatty ferryboat had nosed up to the opposite shore for a while, and then backed lazily and begun its slow crawl back again. Then she walked in a leisurely way down the hill to meet it, idly watching a small boat that had shoved out from the opposite shore and was dancing like a speck in the sunshine on the bright water. She wished she had a boat and might be out there, too.

From the forward deck she watched the little bark dance along a few rods above the course of the ferryboat, and when they passed each other she could see the man who was paddling, his broad shoulders scarcely seeming to move as the long, smooth strokes of his paddle dipped the water. He reminded her of John Treeves, but of course it could not be for how would he be out here? And then he was dressed in workman's clothes. What a foolish notion! But she watched him till the little canoe slid in to the shore just above the landing she had just left, and the man sprang up the bank and climbed to where she had been sitting. He was silhouetted against the sky. The likeness to John Treeves was still marked. But she chided herself for always thinking of John Treeves.

She deliberately walked to the other side of the boat and set her thoughts upon the money Miss Cole had given her. Somehow it must be spent in some unusual way that would please her.

When she reached The Plant and started toward the station where she must take the trolley, the door of the little gray house where she had left the flowers opened and a slight young girl hurried out after her, bearing a long-stemmed carnation in one hand, and holding the blossom close to her lips. She was a pretty girl with wonderful dark eyes and hair like a dusky cloud. But her olive cheeks were pale and thin, and there were dark circles under her eyes, which were heavy with weeping. She wore a shabby little blue serge and her shoes were patched and worn. She hurried up to Patty eagerly:

"Thank you for the flowers," she said shyly. "You were good to come." Her voice was soft and gentle and her speech was not like the other women of her family. She had evidently been to school. Patty could understand how she was able to do typewriting.

"Oh, you have come back!" said Patty turning with interest. "I—I am glad to see you. Have you got all over your wetting?"

"Oh, yes, I am all right," the girl answered indifferently, watching Patty with sad admiration.

"How did you find Angelo?" asked Patty eagerly. "Doesn't he think there is any way for him to get out?"

The girl's eyes instantly filled with tears and she shook her head.

"It costs a great deal of money to do things like that. Even then"—she brushed away the tears—"even then you have to have pull—! If Angelo could get out he might be able to find out who did it. He could get somebody, maybe, to prove him innocent. But"—she made a gesture of helplessness—"it's no use!"

"How much money would it take?" asked Patty thoughtfully.

"Oh, I don't know," said the girl wearily. "A great deal I'm 'fraid. They are hard on people when it's a charge of murder, you know. We have no chance. I work hard every day. I do some typewriting at night. I get a little maybe to pay a

371

lawyer. Not a very good lawyer maybe, but a lawyer, some one to try and help—!" She put out her hands with another despairing gesture.

"Is there no one who will help you? Have you no friends? Is there not some one among your employers who would do something?"

The girl lifted her shoulders slightly, one a trifle higher than the other, lifted her eyebrows, and brought her hands, palm upward, in that indescribable gesture of her people to express incredulity. Her motions were graceful as a feather, her scorn was bitter and resigned:

"People no money! Boss too stingy! Friends— no good when trouble come!" she said, relapsing into common parlance.

"Well, you've got to let me help a little anyway," said Patty with a sudden idea bringing out two ten-dollar bills from the twenty-five Miss Cole had given her. There were still two more dollars left from the sum as the flowers had cost her but three. Perhaps Miss Cole might not like this, but she had distinctly told her to buy what she wanted with the money and she wanted to use it this way more than anything else in the world just now.

The girl stood staring at the money, not offering to take it:

"Oh, you give too much. You are too kind," she murmured.

"Take it please," said Patty, "I have no use for it

now, and I want you to use it to help your Angelo. It will be a little toward paying a lawyer, maybe a better one than you could get without it. I know it isn't much, but if you take it to a lawyer right away perhaps he will begin to work on the case at once. Do you know a good lawyer? They are sometimes not honest. You be sure to get a good one."

"I ask that nice man, Mr. Tree; he offered to help. He brought me home that time when I jump in the water. You know him? He is a good man. He promised to come back."

"Yes, I know," answered Patty quickly, the bright color flying into her cheeks: "yes, you ask him. He will tell you. Now I must go. I hear my trolley coming! Good-bye!" and in a sudden panic she turned and flew toward the trolley station. What if Treeves should come and find her there! She must not risk another minute.

Back in the city she found herself hungry and stopped at a small restaurant she was passing. It was a quiet place and not one of the better class, but it looked clean and there were good things displayed in the windows. Somehow Patty was not in a mood to be finicky that day. She paused a moment childlike to decide which of the dainty pastries she would select for her dessert, and as she turned to go in the door she noticed a woman in a shabby coat trimmed with fur that was matted and worn to the skin in places. Her hat was little more than a shapeless contortion of a bit of black velvet so old that its texture was scarcely recognizable. But it was the woman's eyes, big and hollow and hungry, that attracted her notice. She paused with her hand on the latch and turned back, hesitating. As she did so the woman gave a deep sigh, and the hollows in her cheeks seemed to be drawn deeper. She looked white and ready to faint. In sudden impulse Patty spoke:

"I wonder if you won't come in and eat lunch with me? I'm all alone and would like company."

The woman turned her dull eyes toward the girl:

"Why?" she asked half in contempt.

Now that the words were out Patty was almost frightened at what she had done, but she meant to stick by it.

"Why, just to be friendly. Have you had your lunch yet? I know it's rather late. I stayed out in the country longer than I meant to do."

"No, I ain't had my lunch nor my breakfast nor my dinner last night nor my lunch yesterday, nor my breakfast then either. I don't know when I've had a good square meal, but I'm not the kind you want to invite in there with you, and I ain't a-going."

"Oh, yes, you are," said Patty sweetly. "If you are hungry, so am I, and that's all that matters, isn't it?"

Patty put out a little gloved hand and laid it shyly on the woman's bare, bony hand.

"Come," she pleaded, "we're going to have a nice time together."

"I don't look fit," said the woman looking down shamedly at the shoes that were out at the toes.

"Oh, yes, you do, come!" and Patty drew her inside. "We'll sit down at this little table in the nookery here, and then we'll be more cosy," and she drew her into a high-backed seat beside a little white-covered table and put the menu before her.

"Now, what will you have? Order anything you want. This is my party."

But the woman only sat dully and looked at her.

"Don't you want to choose?" said Patty, drawing the card toward herself. "Well, then I will. Do you like soup first? Oyster soup. How does that sound?"

"Don't!" said the woman sharply. "I ain't had any oyster soup in so long I can't tell when, and if you say it again I'll faint."

Patty smiled and drew a pencil and pad to her, beginning to write rapidly, "oyster soup, roast beef, mashed potato, peas, and beans, apple sauce." Then she shoved it out to the waiter:

"There, I guess that will do to begin on. If we want more we can order it later."

They brought the oysters piping hot at once, and the woman with a kind of dazed wonder upon her ate in silence. It was not until the second course was nearly finished and there was talk of pastry and ice cream that the woman began to look grateful and say a few words about herself:

"I was down and out," she explained. "My husband died ten years ago, and my little girl died, too, and then I had typhoid fever, and when I got up it was a long time before I could get work. There wasn't anybody left much that I cared for, and I just didn't care whether I lived or not. But I had to, you know. You can't just walk out in the river and drown; nobody won't let you. I know, for I tried it more'n onc't. But what's the use? Here I am eating roast beef and enjoying it and knowing I'll be just as hungry again to-morrow and no chance to get any. It's only when you're almost starved or drowned that anybody comes along and stops you. The rest of the time they don't care a hang what becomes of you."

"Oh, but they do," answered Patty pitifully, "only they just don't think."

"Well, what good does that do, I'd like to know? But I don't want to trouble no one. I don't need to live and I don't want to live and I don't see why I should have to."

"Why," said Patty opening her eyes wide and looking thoughtful, "that's just the way I felt once a little while ago. But things all came out right. I guess they will for you, too. There's a person I know would be able to help you, only I don't know how to tell you to find him. I don't know if he will be in New York again. Do you ever go to church?"

"Church!" said the woman with a sneer. "They'd put me out looking like this. What should I go to church for?"

"Well, there's a man preaches in a church here— at least he has several Sundays now. He'll maybe be there again to-morrow. Suppose you go and find out. His name is Treeves, and he knows how to tell discouraged people what to do. Here, I'll write it down for you, and if you go and find him there, just wait after church and tell him how you feel about living. He'll tell you what to do. He is wonderful! He helped me."

"You!" said the woman looking her over, and then "Me!" with contempt. "That's different."

"No, it's not different," said Patty, shaking her head wisely. "We're both souls, and it's our souls that get discouraged, not our clothes, you know. You see this man—well—he KNOWS God!"

The woman looked at her strangely and was silent.

"There's another thing," said Patty, "you must give me your address, and I will tell the woman I am staying with about you. It may be she can find you something to do that will help you not to be so discouraged. I can't invite you to see me because I'm not living in my own home just now and I don't feel free to have guests, but I will write to you and let you know."

The woman wrote at Patty's request her name on

a bit of card that Patty had in her handbag. "Ellen June, General Delivery."

"There! That'll reach me if I ain't succeeded in walking out and drowning or starving to death before you write to me," she said as she pushed it toward the girl.

Patty paid the check at the door and they parted, the woman coming back after a step or two and touching Patty's arm to say "Thank you," and Patty went away wondering whether she would dare tell Miss Cole about her and try to get her some work.

"Well, I've spent the two dollars, very nearly," she laughed to herself, "but just to make it full measure I'll buy some candy with my own money."

So she went into the next big candy shop and bought a big box of the kind of sweets she loved best, the kind she used to buy in school when her allowance had just arrived. Then with it under her arm she sauntered on and on wondering what to do next for an adventure. One more adventure she must have, for she was pretty sure that she hadn't been quite measuring up to Miss Cole's idea of what she ought to do for amusement.

"I may have to take in a moving picture show yet," she laughed to herself as she walked on. She gazed into the shop windows and watched the people she passed, and wandered on, enjoying the freedom to go anywhere or nowhere as the whim took her. She had wandered thus a long way down toward the Battery, and taken a cross-street that brought her near Brooklyn Bridge. She was just a little frightened at the strange foreign faces she met on every hand, and the gibberish she heard talked and began to look around with half-frightened glances and wonder if it would be better to go back the way she came or make a straight line over to the elevated road only two blocks away. She decided for the elevated, for she realized that she was suddenly very tired, and crossing a queer triangular block with high fences, walls, rough-looking people and many heavily laden trucks she saw with relief just ahead of her the rising stairway of the elevated station and hurried toward it.

In the gutter, and over the curb, close under the great rumbling tracks of the elevated, were huddled a number of babies squabbling over a dirty pasteboard box that some one had thrown in the street. They were literally babies, some of them hardly able to toddle, and no older person in sight to be responsible for them. They were dirty and eager and dressed in rags, and their eyes were sharp and cunning, already out for possession in this cold, hard world where they had so recently arrived.

Patty paused and looked at them in wonder and sorrow. Babies! and out on their own that way. One had a great shock of tangled golden curls and eyes as blue as the Irish seas where his parents were born.

Suddenly an inspiration came to Patty. She broke the golden cord that held her bonbons, and opened the box. Before the astonished babies had even noticed her, she had showered upon them each as many wonderful pink and white and chocolate sweets as their dirty little hands could hold.

They looked at her with great round questions in their eyes, and they looked at their hands and then they crammed the candy in their mouths.

Then behold a miracle! For suddenly, from out of the invisible air apparently there appeared more babies, babies toddling, walking, running, babies being carried, all swarming a little throng about Patty holding up their dirty little hands, hungry little mouths, great eager eyes to Patty. And Patty gave and gave and gave until her box was empty, and then wished she had ten pounds more. She laughed and almost cried for still the babies came, like bees to honey. How did they find out?

She tore herself away from their dirty, eager, little grasp and promising to come again, hurried away up the steps:

"And now I must go home!" laughed Patty. "Oh, crazy, crazy Patty! Won't Miss Cole be satisfied with this, I wonder?"

It was all so quiet and different in the great Fifth Avenue mansion that Patty could hardly believe she had been away, hardly believe that anything was but a dream. Miss Cole had not returned yet, but Marjorie was there and bored with herself. She wandered up to her aunt's room, and finding only Patty, sat down for a bit of gossip:

"I'm almost ready to give up," she confided. "I haven't had a letter from Al in weeks, and he seems so far away. It's all like a dream now. Life here is so different. Mother is keen on Dunham Treeves, and he is awfully nice. Next to Al, I like him best of anyone I ever met. Of course he isn't a bit like the young N'yorkers, but perhaps that's what I like about him. Mother calls me perverse, and I suppose I am, but I really couldn't stand a man that couldn't do anything but dance. Of course I like to dance. But just look at the way Dunham Treeves jumped into the water that cold day to save that poor working girl! I admire a man like that. And he'll have stacks and stacks of money. His uncle'll die pretty soon and he'll have all that. I guess there isn't anyone in N'york that has more money than Calvin Treeves. Of course it would be fun to go right into all that. It would be a position worth having. If it weren't for Al—but then he might come back some day and I couldn't help thinking about it. Of course, if I got tired of Dunham Treeves I could always get a divorce and marry Al. And I'd be my own mistress then and nobody could stop me. It might be a way out, you know."

"Oh! MARJORIE!" cried Patty, dropping the magazine she was trying to read and standing up white with horror. "Excuse me, but how perfectly frightful!"

"Well," said Marjorie, looking down half-shamed, "I know—but then everybody is doing it now, and if they WON'T let me have what I want, I must take the best way to get it I can. I would TRY to be happy with Dunham Treeves, of course!"

"Do you want to know what I think?" cried Patty with eyes ablaze. "I think you are not fit for anybody when you talk like that. I used to wonder whether this Al you talk about was fit for you, but now I am wondering whether you are half good enough for him. If you can't stay true to him till he has time to make good and come back, you surely haven't any kind of love for him, I'm sure. And as for the other man, have you no conscience at all? What kind of a life are you cutting out for him? He at least is a good man."

"Yes, and he's fond of me," sighed Marjorie, "but as you say, I ought to be true to Al. That's what I'd like to be, but I sometimes ask myself what use it is. He's there and I'm here, and daddy and mother would have a fit if they knew I was even thinking of him."

"Well," said Patty thoroughly indignant, "you ought to either cast him out of your mind forever or else be true to him, one or the other; I'm sure of that!" and she gathered up her magazine and went to her own room. But instead of reading, she threw herself on the bed and had a good cry. For all of the experiences of the day this last brief interview with Marjorie was by far the most depressing. And the queer thing about it was she couldn't tell just why it was that she felt so terribly about it.

29

From the first Sunday of John Treeves's advent in the New York pulpit there had been a reporter present whom no one had observed. He came early and slipped unobtrusively into the gallery, taking a different seat every Sunday, where he would not be noticed. He was not reporting for any of the city papers, nor yet for the religious weeklies, yet he did his work thoroughly. Not a word, not a syllable, not an inflection escaped him. He was an expert or he could never have caught it all; every rapid fiery sentence, the telling points, the very sound of the voice almost was described. For those were the most unusual demands that had come with his orders. He was to make those sermons live again on paper so that the reader would see and hear almost as well as if present.

Early on Monday morning a thick typed copy of the shorthand notes started through the mail with a special delivery stamp on them to hasten their arrival, and regularly on a Wednesday morning the reporter banked a good fat check in payment thereof.

It was Hespur who received the package and undid it with eager fingers, bringing it to his master to look at and handle while he drew the shade up and arranged the coverlets carefully. Then he took the typewritten sheets and sat down to read. Somewhere Hespur had acquired the ability to read well, or else he was spirit taught, for certainly he read those sermons well, bringing in the footnotes just at the right place, so that old Calvin Treeves should see how his nephew's quiet words had held the fashionable city audience breathless, or had brought the tears to many proud eyes.

The first sermon that he read lifted the old man into the seventh heaven of pride, for he merely listened for the roll of eloquence, the flow of language, the effect upon the hearers. It was *his* nephew speaking to *his* world, and pride soared high, for again he was having his heart's desire. But the second time he made old Hespur read it over the thoughts behind the words began to grip the soul and make him cringe:

"W-w-w-wH-at's that! Hespur, read that line over again!"

"How hardly shall they that have riches enter the Kingdom of Heaven, sir."

The young r-r-r-R-A-S-cal! He has no BUSI-NESS to say that! I'll teach him to libel—!"

"But, sir, excuse me, sir, it's not his own words, I'm sure, sir. Those are the Holy Scriptures, sir, and you mustn't find fault with that."

"The SCRIPT-ure! The DEVIL! It NEVER says that in the Bible! The idea! Poppycock! Well, find it! FIND it, I say!"

"I'll get the Concord, sir, it'll maybe be in it—riches, riches, yes, here it is, sir, just a minute—yes, here it is in—"

"Well, you needn't READ IT again. I don't want to hear it. Anything like that I wouldn't listen to. As if you couldn't go to Heaven because you'd had a little money down here. I DON'T B-E-L-I-E-V-E it, Hespur, do you HEAR?"

"Yes, sir, but that won't change the facts, sir—"

"HESPUR! Do YOU believe I'm going to hell? You do, Hespur. You DO! I never thought you'd go back on me like that." The tears were coursing down.

"Well, sir, I'm not saying just that, sir. It says 'how hardly,' sir. It means it's very unlikely, sir, considering, but not to say impossible, sir. Listen to the balance of the sermon, sir, if I remember rightly there's somewhat more on the subject, sir."

And so they would read and wrangle and soothe and storm, and over again, read and ponder and talk. And when the sermon was conned by heart so that each could take a phrase out of it anywhere and hand it back to the other in argument, they would turn to the Bible and hunt for more on the subject. And sometimes when his master was taking his nap old Hespur would be studying his Bible, trying to find something comforting, and then when the old man would wake up he would produce it.

"I found a nice bit of saying, sir, in the place called John," he would say. "Shall I read it out a bit?"

The old man would growl assent, and Hespur would read:

"Let not your heart be troubled, ye believe in God, believe in Me—"

"But I DON'T believe in God—Hespur! You KNOW I've NEVER believed in God! Blast you, Hespur, now WHAT did you read that to me for— that wasn't for m-ee at all—!" and before the distracted servant knew what was happening the old man was in a tremor of tears. As he grew weaker he seemed unable to control them, and it enraged him to know he was weeping.

"Therey! Therey! Don't take on so, Master! What say we begins right now, sir? It's never too late to mend, as the saying is, sir!"

"But how can we, Hespur, how CAN we?" and the old man pulled himself half up in the bed, grasping at his servant's arm. "Believing is something you've got to do, Hespur, before you *can* do it, you know."

"Oh, no, sir, the young master, sir, said different, sir, in his first sermon, you remember. He said as how believing was an act of the will. It was the assurance, sir, that was to come after, and with that we have nothing to do. You can *decide* to have faith in Him, sir."

The old man was still a long time and then he asked fretfully:

"Well, then, who is this other Person that calls Himself ME? Read it again, Hespur. You *know* I want it read again, why don't you do it?"

And Hespur would read again: " 'Ye believe in God, believe also in ME.' That, sir, I'm very sure, sir, is the Son of God, sir; Him that was Jesus on earth, sir. And listen to this, sir: 'In my Father's house are many mansions—!' "

"Mansions! Mansions! That doesn't sound so bad—!"

" 'I go to prepare a place for you, and if I go and prepare a place for you I will come again and receive you unto myself, that where I am there ye may be also—' "

The old man lay still, thinking:

"Hespur—what would He want with me? I've never had anything to do with Him."

The old servant shook his head and began to turn the leaves rapidly: "I couldn't just rightly say, sir, there's maybe some word on that question, sir—"

"You wouldn't suppose, Hespur, that He could

do it for SPITE? Just want me there to get me in a corner and make me feel uncomfortable?"

"Oh, no, sir, not that, sir. Not at all, sir. Not so I've been always given to understand, sir. Here, now is a bit. I knew I'd come on it. I marked it sometime back: 'For God so loved the world,' mark that, sir, *worrrld,* sir, that leaves out none, sir. God so loved the worrrld, that He gave His only begotten Son that whosoever believeth on Him—"

"There it is again!" snarled the old man, turning his head restlessly from side to side. "Believe, believe, believe, always believe! Well, what if I do?"

"Hath everlasting life, sir. *Hath!* That means now, sir, not wait till you die, sir, but have it now, sir. That means no dying to speak of at all, sir, just a casting away of the flesh, sir, but a living forever, sir, in a new garment, sir."

"HESPUR! DO YOU KNOW what you're *TALKING ABOUT?*"

"Oh, yes, sir. I'm sure, sir. My mother used to talk that way quite often, sir, and my grandmother, sir. I, boylike, didn't take much recognition of it then, sir, but it stuck, sir, and it's all coming back."

"Well, then, you old RASCAL—if you know so blasted much, GET DOWN ON YOUR KNEES AND P-R-A-Y! Do you HEAR? Pray for us BOTH! For I don't want to be without you!"

Hespur got stiffly down beside the bed and

folded his hands, lifting closed eyes toward Heaven:

"Oh, Lord, sir, we Thy humble creatures—!"

"I'm NOT humble," murmured the old man belligerently, "I never was and I WON'T BE!"

"Oh, Lord, excuse me, sir, he doesn't rightly understand that he's in the presence of the great God—!"

"I thought you said He loved me—" whined the sick man.

"Yes, master, He loves you, but you must be humble, sir—" Hespur put a hushing hand on the restless old claw, and spoke in a low tone as if to keep the God of Heaven from hearing how he had to bolster up the old sinner's first prayer. Then he went on in a louder voice: "Oh, Lord, we feel to know we are sinners—!"

The old man uttered a protesting growl but the servant's voice drowned it out, "Yes, sinners, Lord, we find it right hard to own that, but we know it is true. We are some sorry, Lord, but we want to be sorrier yet before we are done. We want to be sorry enough to get you to listen and forgive us, and make us right before God and ready to go home to those mansions. Not that I would presume to ask for a mansion, Lord, only that my old master he's used to me like, and wants me around, and I won't take up much room. I'm handy anywhere, and wouldn't intrude, Oh, Lord, Sir!"

"That's enough! That's enough! Cut out that stuff! Of course He'll let you in Hespur if he lets ME. It's Me that's been wicked all my life. It's me that put my foot on the poor, and crushed out the life from all the pretty things that ever came in my path just to get what I wanted; and even was too stubborn to get the thing I wanted most in my life. Get up, you old rascal, you aren't the sinner. It's ME! Get up and bring me a pen and some paper. I want to write a letter!"

Hespur arose reluctantly and protested:

"Oh, sir, waitey! waitey! Just a day or so till the doctor says you are stronger."

"The doctor's a liar! What difference does it make what he says? You know I won't get any stronger and I know I won't get any stronger and that's all there is to it. GET ME THAT PEN!"

When the letter was finished in a quavering hand, sealed and addressed, he handed it with a weary gesture to Hespur and said in a cross, feeble voice:

"Now, when I'm dead I want you to see that that letter gets to its destination and the white diamond sent with it. BUT *DON'T YOU LOOK AT THE ADDRESS! D'ye HEAR?*"

"Oh, yes; yes, sir, of course, sir. I'll do it, sir. I'll deliver it in person, sir. Don't you worry another bit about it, I'll not forget. Now, that's all right, sir; now you take a little nap."

Old Hespur smoothed the covers and drew down

the shade, brought broth and fed him spoonfuls, then hovered over him, watching his feeble old breath.

But he rallied again as he had rallied many times before, although each time he came up a little more slowly, and not quite so far. His eyes grew to have a hungry, vague look when he awoke from his long drowses, and often they would seem to be searching for something. It was only when Hespur would produce the Bible or one of his nephew's sermons that he seemed satisfied. Now and then a bright little letter came from Patty, like a ray of purest sunshine and it would be read and reread, and kept close to the pillow, where the old hand would now and again grope out and feel of it.

There came a morning when Hespur, watching the old face with anxious eyes, noticing the caressing touch of the letter under his pillow, sat down on his own initiative and wrote a letter:

Dear Miss: *it read,*

Begging your pardon for presuming to address you, I just want to tell you that your old friend Mr. Treeves is not feeling so well, and has not so long to stay. If there might be a way that you could run down for a day and just drop in kind of casual like to see him it certainly would be a heavenly action, for the poor old body gets out of his bed no more, and has no one to cheer him up but me. He dotes greatly on your letters, and it's that pitiful to see him smooth it and touch it when he thinks no one is looking. Of course it's asking a lot, but if you could see your way clear I'd be glad to bear the expenses of the journey out of my savings. And if I am asking too much I ask your pardon, Miss, and God bless you.

Your humble servant,
Hespur Kane.

With a furtive look toward his sleeping master, Hespur tiptoed out of the room and mailed his letter. He would have liked to have written another to the nephew, but did not dare. He had broached the subject of sending for young Treeves one day and it had raised such a rumpus that it took hours to undo the mischief. The old man was determined the nephew should stand by his post. He wanted to hear more sermons, to know he was called to the great church, to read his praises in the newspapers, to be sure he was succeeding. He did not wish him to leave New York until everything was assured, and Hespur began to see that his appearance even most casually, while it might please the old man, would also be likely to upset him greatly.

It was during their reading one day that a new trouble loomed on the horizon for the old man. They had come to the passage: "It is easier for a camel to go through the eye of a needle than a rich man to enter into the Kingdom of Heaven." Hespur was using the new Bible with footnotes that had come only a few days before from a big bookstore in the city. He had seen it advertised and sent for it himself. He took particular pleasure in being able to elucidate a passage of difficult meaning by the aid of the footnotes. Not that he allowed his master to know he was reading footnotes. He usually created the impression that his mother or grandmother had entertained such beliefs, and so explained, the passages carried more weight with the old man. On this particular occasion he would have omitted the verse altogether if he had realized in time what was coming, for he had a vivid memory of the other occasion when the difficulty of a rich man entering heaven had been discussed; but having blurted out the words before he knew, he hurriedly glanced down at the footnote, for the old man had moaned as if in pain, and the tears were coming down his cheeks:

"You know, Mister Treeves, you don't have any occasion to feel troubled about that saying, sir. It's all quite plain—" his eyes were hurrying along the fine print of the footnotes. "It seems—why—now, you know, that needle wasn't a needle at all. That is to say, the needle's eye was a gate, a little gate inside of the great big gate of the city wall, Jerusalem, you know, and it seems, sir, why they say, sir, they always shut that great big gate of the city at sundown every night so no thieves and robbers could get into the city, and then if any travellers came on camels, with big packs on their backs and wanted in, they had to take all the traps off the camel, and lift and hoist him in. The little gate, the needle's eye, that is, was up high from the ground, and they had to lift up the camel's feet one at a time, sir, one at a time, little by little, and push the beast and drag him in, and then the man himself, rich as he was, had to be helped up that way, too. There wasn't room for him to ride in head up with all his baggage hitched on, the way a rich man by rights should go, sir, because the big gate would be shut; but he *Got there,* sir, *HE GOT THERE!* Mind!"

"Hespur!" arraigned the little old sick man. "You're not saying that, you're reading it. Where do you get all that chatter? Let me see the book."

And thereafter he was deeply interested in the footnotes, asking again and again for notes on the passages read, and disappointed as a child if a passage he wanted was not touched upon. One afternoon he suddenly spoke out of what Hespur had supposed was a sound sleep:

"Hespur! You don't suppose the curse will go with the money, do you? You don't suppose if I give my money to my nephew that he will begin to love the money and forget everything else the way I did, do you?"

"Not for a minute, sir! Not for a minute!" cried old Hespur, coming close to the bed. "Remember how I told you about the night on the mountain, sir. He's met with the Lord, sir, and found something better than money can ever give. Besides, sir, don't you remember your own self, sir, begging pardon, sir, how he told you if he had the money he would only use it in his *work?* I think you can trust him to give the money back to God, sir. It's the only place it'll be safe, sir. The only place."

A kind of relief came into the old face, something resembling a calm into the turbulent eyes.

"That's so, Hespur. That's so! Hespur, you're a great comfort!" and the thin old hand stole out and caught Hespur's strong one.

"Therey! Therey! master, sir! You do me great honor to say that, sir! I'll not forget it, sir!"

"But you'll remember the times I've cursed you, too!" wailed the shrill voice. "I've been an ungrateful old sinner—! Hespur, I've made everybody hate me!"

"No, master, no master, not me, sir. You've been a good master to me always, sir. You needn't to mind what you've done to me, sir. It ain't in the account at all. I've just put it all by and took no thought of it. Just you make it right with the Lord, sir; I'll stand by."

"Oh, the Lord! The Lord! He won't take what I've given you! I tell you, Hespur, I've been a great sinner—a very great sinner! I've spoiled more lives, and my own, and I've never stopped to think of the Lord, nor care, and He has been seeing that all these years—"

"But master, master, Mister Treeves, have you forgot, 'The blood of Jesus Christ His Son cleanseth us from all sin.' ALL sin! Have you forgot, sir? 'God so loved the world that He gave His only begotten Son that whosoever believeth HATH everlasting life. God sent not His Son into the world to condemn the world, but that the world through Him might be saved.' And He said, 'If we confess our sin He is faithful and just to forgive us our sin and to cleanse us from all unrighteousness.' Have you forgot, sir, that's in the sermon we got to-day. Cleanse us. Cleanse us from *all!* The blood of Christ cleanses!"

The old man tossed weakly from side to side:

"Yes, but Hespur, that's an awful chance. How can I be sure He'll do it? How can I be sure I've fulfilled the conditions for all that? I'm an awful sinner, and now right at the end when I've had my own way all my life and got mad when I didn't, and cursed and hated and been cruel, how could I take any comfort out of that?"

"He says it. He says if we confess our sins: Sir, Mister Treeves, begging pardon, why don't you confess your sins to Him, sir?"

"Why don't you do it for me, Hespur? Don't you *see* that's what I want?"

"I—I'm not rightly sure that will do, sir, but I'll try, sir, and I'll tell Him you want to say so, too, sir!" and Hespur dropped upon his knees on the floor beside the bed:

"Oh, God!" he cried earnestly, his habitual obsequiousness for once overpowered by his love for his master in this trying strait:

"Oh, God! We have sinned very greatly! We have sinned all our lives! We have done evil in Thy sight. We have not thought about Thee!—We have neglected the Holy Scripture! We have not believed on the Son—!"

"There! THERE! *THERE!*" yelled the old man indignantly. "Stop that! You're praying for yourself! I told you to pray for *me! You* don't need it now. It's *I* that needs it! Pray for me! *ME!* I tell you! Tell Him *I'm* a sinner!"

"He's a sinner, Lord, yes, Lord, He's a sinner, begging his pardon, sir—but so am I a sinner, too!"

"STOP!"

"Lord, he'll have to tell you himself—!" wailed the old servant. "You've promised. You said your Son would take the blame! Just save him, won't you, and take away the fear of going from him! Lord, he'll have to tell You himself. Mister Treeves, master, you'll have to tell Him for yourself. It ain't like it was a message to anybody else, sir. He's the King of Heaven, sir, and you'll have to go yourself."

"What shall I say?" wailed the thin, old frightened voice.

"Say you've sinned, sir."

"Lord, I've sinned!" repeated the old man with anguish like the sobbing of a naughty child.

"Say you're sorry!" commanded Hespur.

"I'm sorry—!"

"Say you're not worthy to be called His child but He's to do with you what He pleases—!"

The old man uttered a shrill scream and clung to the servant's hand:

"No, Hespur! No! NO! Not that Hespur! He promised. He said He would save us all who came to God by Him. You read it just to-day! HESPUR! Oh, God, in the name of Jesus Christ, forgive my sins and make me clean!"

"Amen! Lord, sir! Hear that! You wouldn't go back on Your promises, Lord! You said it! He's believed it! Now save him for Thy mercy's sake!"

The old man slept like a little child that night, and woke with a sweet smile on his face, but Hespur, watching earnestly, could see that he was weaker, and he almost longed for the old anger to break out against him, it was so pitiful to see him meek and gentle this way.

"I feel so—unready—!" the weak voice quavered! "There are things I might have done— Things—but there! I'll have to leave it all! It's like going out to a great dinner without being shaved and dressed! Oh, Hespur! You'll tell the boy sometime, sometime— You'll tell him he's a great deal to undo for me."

"I'll tell him, sir! That I will, sir!" The old servant turned away to hide his emotion.

"You'll take care of him, Hespur, when I'm gone?"

"That I will, sir. I'll do my best, sir."

"He'll mebbe not let you!" sighed old Treeves. "He's headstrong, you know."

"I'll care for him whether he lets me or not," said the servant firmly. "So long as I'm spared I'll look after him, sir. You've fixed it so as I've no need to work for my living any more, sir, and I'll see that he's cared for as well as I can."

It was a cold, gloomy morning when Hespur's letter reached Patty. The day before had been bright, but the memory of it was bitter. Treeves had been at the house from Saturday night and she had seen him go out with Marjorie early in the morning for a walk. They had returned in deep and earnest conversation. It seemed to Patty that she could not stand it to have Marjorie carrying out her avowed purposes that way and John Treeves falling into the trap. It didn't seem like him not to see through a girl like that. And yet, she had to own that Marjorie was very attractive, and most charming when she chose to be. But there was a desolate little ache back in Patty's heart all that day and she found it there yet when she awoke Monday morning. Somehow all the wonderful sermon of the day before had not taken that hurt out of her heart.

When the letter came she read it over twice and then took it to Miss Cole:

"See what came in the mail this morning," she said, holding out the letter. "I wondered if you could tell me of anything I could do to cheer the poor old soul."

Miss Cole's face took on a gray look as she read the letter, and her hand trembled as she handed it back. She sat for several minutes looking unseeingly into space. Patty almost thought she had forgotten to answer, and stood uncertainly wondering whether to go away. But at last Miss Cole spoke:

"Can you get ready to go by the afternoon train?" she said, and her tone was most matter of fact.

"Why!" said Patty looking startled. "You don't mean—that you think I ought to go?"

"Not alone," said Miss Cole. "Of course not. We'll both go! He's an old friend when it comes to that, and when one is dying it's different! Nobody'll think anything of it, for I often run off for a few days, and I go down there frequently. Besides, that Letitia Horliss is coming to visit to-morrow and I can't abide her. She treats me as if I were as old as Methuselah and she had to keep me always in mind of it. Look up trains and see if there's anything sooner that will make connections. I can be ready in two hours if there is. I'll telephone my brother and let Kate know and you can do the rest. You might send Banely to get a trunk together. We won't need but one, because I don't suppose we'll stay forever, and we can send for more things if we do. That's all. I'll ring if I want you, and you let me know as soon as you've made the arrangements."

To Patty the sudden change of program was a relief. It helped to take her out of her own thoughts which were growing decidedly gloomy. She went to work with a will and soon had matters in train for their trip, with parlor car reservations, trunks, tickets and everything arranged. Her own simple preparations required but a few minutes, and at twenty minutes to twelve she and Miss Cole were seated in the limousine on their way to the Pennsylvania Station to answer old Hespur's appeal.

As the Fifth Avenue mansion passed out of her vision she sat up with a little sigh of relief. Perhaps now she would be able to forget some of the things that were always hurting her, and some of the problems that perplexed her night and day.

30

"It is growing very dark in the room, Hespur; dark and cold. Why don't you light the fire?"

"Yes, sir, yes, sir; I will, sir!" Hespur, with tears on his sad, old face and a troubled look at the clock, gave a stir to the already bright fire and turned back.

"It's a dark day, Hespur, a dark, dark day."

"Yes, sir, it is that, sir, but it'll soon be that bright, sir! You'll see, sir! Now, shall I read a bit?"

He glanced at the clock again. It was almost time for the doctor's train. He touched lightly the cold hand of the old man and tucked it under the blanket. He wiped the perspiration from the waxen brow.

"Yes, read—read about the blood—" whispered the old man, nestling among his pillows, and groping under the blankets with his chilly hands:

"The blood of Jesus Christ His Son cleanseth us from all sin—" repeated Hespur, kneeling beside the bed and watching the growing pallor of the waxen face. "As far as the East is from the West, so far hath He removed our transgressions from us—" Hespur had learned the lesson well in the weeks in which he had been studying the Bible, but farther back than that it was ingrained into his soul, in the old country when he was a little fellow

402

by his old grandmother's knee at the fireside. He had wandered long and far from that teaching but it all came back to him now, as the Word that is writ in the heart will always do, and he did not have to stumble and hesitate for the words now when the need was great and his soul was wrung for the old child who was passing into the shadow so rapidly.

"There is one—about the lamb in the valley—" murmured the withered lips.

"Yea, though I walk through the valley of the shadow I will fear no evil, for Thou art with me—" repeated Hespur, and a smile of peace came over the old man's face.

"Be not afraid, neither be thou dismayed, for the Lord thy God is with thee, whithersoever thou goest," went on the old servant, searching about for the words the old man had liked oftenest to hear. "Fear thou not for I have redeemed thee, I have called thee by thy name, thou art Mine!"

On and on, from promise to promise, went the faithful servant, watching the face that had grown dear to him through the long, hard years of his service, dear because it was so pitiful in its self-made loneliness. Hespur did not hear the soft tap at the door, nor its opening. He did not know that anyone had entered until suddenly the old eyes on the bed opened and looked up into Patty's sweet pitiful face, and a smile broke out over Calvin Treeves's face, a smile like a passing ray of light on a swift, hurrying cloud. Then his eyes searched farther, and his face lit up with a most wondrous light, for the instant glorifying the haggard and spent clay into the semblance of Calvin Treeves as he used to be before the devil of Greed and Power took utter possession of his soul.

"Sylvia!" he said, and his trembling hands went out eagerly for hers. "Sylvia! *You've come at last!*"

Sylvia Cole knelt beside the bed, took his cold hand in both her own, and stooping, kissed him on his stiffening lips.

A soft murmur of content came from the old man, and his eyelids fell shut. Patty crept close and took his other hand in hers, and Hespur stood back with bowed head waiting as was his place, now that the others more fitted had come to do his master honor. The doctor had come silently in, laid a practised hand on the feeble wrist, and stood back in the attitude of waiting also.

"Hespur! The blood! Say the blood!"

"The blood of Jesus Christ His Son cleanseth us from all sin," repeated Hespur obediently.

"Sylvia!" the old eyes opened again and sought her face. "You know about the blood?"

"Yes, Calvin, I know," she said in a clear, steady voice. "Yes, it's all right."

"He—He's—forgiven me!" he trembled out. "I've been a great sinner but Christ has forgiven—Syl-via—can—*you*—forgive—me—too?"

"Yes, Calvin. I forgive you!" Sylvia kissed him once more, and he seemed to be content. They thought he was gone, but after a long silence he murmured:

"I—will—fear—no—evil—for—Thou—art—with—me—!" The voice trailed off again, then rose clearer, triumphantly. "HE'S HERE! Hespur, HE'S HERE! Don't forget to come, too!"

"I'll not, sir! I'll be there, sir!" choked Hespur gallantly, and turned to the window to hide his sobs.

The doctor drew the ladies away, and shut the door, and old Hespur was left to do the last service for his old master. Calvin Treeves had passed to meet his God!

Two hours later Hespur knocked at the door of Miss Cole's room and handed her a letter and a little white box. Then to Patty, who had opened the door, he gave another box.

"And this, Miss, he wanted you to have. Only last night he had me get it out and mark it for you with his love, and I was to do it up to-day and send it on to you."

When Patty opened the box she found the ring with the blue diamond. But when she went to Miss Cole to ask what she ought to do about it she found her sitting by the window weeping over a great blazing white diamond on her finger, and an open letter in her lap. Patty gently closed the door and stole away.

John Treeves had been working in The Plant for nearly eight weeks and was already counted an expert in the work he had chosen. He was still preaching in the New York church. "Supplying the pulpit," he called it, till they could get hold of a man they would be willing to call, for he had steadily refused to listen to their arguments, and they had settled down to wait for a time, hoping to make him see the light after he had tasted a little of the weariness of toil and lost some of his high spirits; for there was no denying the fact that they wanted to find no other man in his place as long as they could possibly keep him. Also some of the committee had an eye to that hundred thousand dollars.

He was intensely interested in the work he was doing and the people he was among. He had taken board in one of the little gray houses where the husband and father had been recently killed in one of the machines, and where the young son, barely seventeen, was the only wage earner left for a family of seven. The woman was exceptionally clean and careful and Treeves had a little white-washed room to himself, furnished with a canvas cot, a chair, a wooden table and his trunk. He had some army blankets to supplement the scanty bed clothes, and he felt entirely comfortable. He was doing just what he wanted to do, get close to the people. He wore the same kind of coarse, cheap clothes that they wore, and ate at the oilcloth-covered table in their kitchen the same kind of food they ate. They thought him one of themselves. His genial smile and kindly ways won their hearts and his broad shoulders and strength won their respect. Also, although he had shown himself a skillful and rapid worker he never was averse to helping one of them, and never showed any desire to show up better than anyone else in the eyes of the foreman, which won their admiration. He was so unassuming that as yet they had not even been curious about him, for although his speech was different from theirs, he had plenty of army slang, and democratic ways, and those who earn their living and grow dog-weary with the struggle against hunger and poverty are not curious concerning those who drop down among them and toil as they do, falling in with their conditions and habits. He was clean, very clean, that was the only thing they noticed strongly, and many of them were that.

Already he had made many friends and comrades among the workers; already there were overburdened women who had come to look upon him as a sort of angel of mercy; at night gathering their little children around him and playing games and telling stories. A little sick child in the community would rather have "Tree" as they took to calling him, to hold him and pet him than his own mother, and many an aching back and arms that were heavy with carrying a sick baby were relieved for a blessed hour when John Treeves had finished his work and eaten his supper and was ready to give himself to the people.

In one of the side streets of lower New York, in a quiet boarding house, he had a room where he kept his Sunday clothes, his books and his writing desk. Here on Saturday nights he would betake himself, going in at dusk with his rough, cheap suit he had worn from The Plant, a shoddy overcoat with collar turned up and an old cap drawn over his eyes, and coming out the next morning fine and comely in the garments that befitted his station. As yet the reporters had not got onto his trail, and he came and went in peace. They had besieged him on Sunday for interviews, and he had smilingly told them a few brief facts, stating that he was away all the week, only coming to New York for the Sabbath, and that his home was in Maple Brook. The few that had persevered far enough to take a trip to Maple Brook had got very little satisfaction out of it; Mrs. Burnside, telling them that "he came and went now and again, and you never could tell when he'd be there and when not. Mostly he was writing or reading or walking up the mountain when he did come." Those who had ventured went back with a constructed story about his love of nature, and his habits of study, but no one had as yet found out the truth. Horliss-Cole had managed to conceal it from all but two of the committee so far that he had allowed the minister to work in his plant.

The morning after the death of Calvin Treeves his nephew was almost late at the works. He had been sitting up all night with a sick boy whose mother was worn out, and he looked worn and tired himself. Little lines that took away the boyish look were beginning to show themselves around his eyes since he came to live at The Plant, for life, as not even the war had shown it, had been passing like a panorama before his eyes, and he was meeting great problems every day. The burden of sin and poverty had been laid upon his shoulders, and he was wondering how he could lift more of it from others not so able to bear it.

He went quietly to his machine, greeting the men about him with a smile. He had a pleasant word for everyone, but he was not talkative that morning as he went about putting his machine in order for the day.

"Well, I guess, Buddie, you wisht your name was anything but John this morning, don'cha?"

"How's that?" asked John Treeves pleasantly, always ready to enter into conversation, even if it were but a joke on himself.

"Ain't you seen the papers yet this morning?" asked the other wonderingly. For Treeves had distinguished himself by being one of the few men who took the morning paper and read it on the way down to the shop.

"Why, no," he said, "I stayed all night with Johnny Fusco and didn't get back to my room. What's the news?"

"Only another millionaire croaked, that's all," said the workman cheerily, clinking his oilcan into a slot, and mopping it off with a big, dirty rag. "Oh, man! If all that money could just be divided between us hard-working men there'd be some justice in things! If I had my way every rich man would have to leave his property to the state at his death, and the state would divide it up. No one gets any of it that has over a certain income, big enough to live comfortably on. Then things would keep evening themselves up all the time, see?"

"Why, yes, I see that some men could be lazy all their lives and still have enough to live on while the rest of us would have to work all the harder to make up for them, and not get any more for it. You wouldn't get very far on that plan."

"Well, there's something wrong somewhere," said the man looking puzzled. His philosophy couldn't carry him far into the subject because all he said was repeated from what he had heard in labor agitation meetings and books on socialism, and even those were a little mixed. But he went on: "Now take it here. This man's left his millions; I don't know how many of them there is, more'n anybody else in New York has, I guess; anyhow, it's a lot, and he's left 'em all to his nephew, some little runt of a sissy, or some big fat slob that will

410

lie back and roll around in luxury while WE WORK for him! I say that's unfair! Now, if it could be left to a man like you, why it would be different! You would know what to do with it, but these here lazy millionaires that hez to hev their beefsteak cut up fer 'em every morning before they can eat it. It gives me a pain in the neck. I say it ain't fair. I says to Billy, I sez: 'Oh, boy! Wish I was that Dunham Treeves feller this morning; wouldn't I make the cash fly!'"

"Dunham Treeves!" said Treeves looking up with a sudden start.

"Yes, that's the young feller's name what's got all that money, millions and millions. Same name as yours; ain't that funny? That's why I said I guessed you wisht your name was anything but John. Call me anything. Call me Dunham, so it's Treeves. Ha! Ha!"

John Treeves had been through too many experiences not to have learned a good control of his face. It served him well now, for after the first quick flicker of his eyelashes his face became unreadable, and he turned away to polish up a spot on his machine, saying only:

"Well, that is curious, isn't it?" But his hand shook as he started his machine on its daily clatter, and he pushed the pieces of metal through mechanically with his thoughts far away.

After a few minutes' rapid work he suddenly stopped his machine and went in search of the

411

foreman, explaining that he had been up all night and would like to get off for a little while.

"He's all in," explained his neighbor workman. "I seen he looked white when he come in this morning. He didn't make as much fuss as I thought he would about that young millionaire feller havin' the same name as him. I thought it was real curious."

John Treeves hurried out to find a morning paper and saw the flaring headlines. "CALVIN TREEVES, The MULTIMILLIONAIRE, dies of heart failure in the South. His nephew, the famous young preacher of this city, inherits the entire fortune which it is supposed will prove to be much larger than is known." There followed a sketch of Calvin Treeves's life and attainments, the number of clubs he belonged to and the town and country houses owned by him. The account stated that the death occured quietly with Mr. Treeves's faithful old man-servant, who had attended upon him for thirty-five years, as his only companion.

John Treeves stood as if stunned. A great reproach came to him that he had not tried to do more for his uncle while he was alive, and regret that he had never made the slightest attempt to bring him to the knowledge of his Christ. All his life he had harbored a feeling almost amounting to hatred toward the man who might have been so much to his mother and had not been. Until his vision upon the mountain, he had openly acknowledged this attitude, and rather been proud of it than otherwise, but since his new faith in Christ and the love that had come into his heart for all the world, he discovered that this feeling had changed and melted into one of deep pity. He had been planning to run down again soon and see the old man and try to bring a little cheer into his life. He had been deeply touched by his uncle's seeming to care about him. It somehow seemed to wipe out the past; and now he was surprised to find that he had a feeling of being alone in the world, all close of kin gone!

Of the matter of the fortune he thought little. It was a mistake of course. His uncle had distinctly said he would not leave him the inheritance if he did not give up his plans and come to live with him, and he had positively declined. There could be nothing in it of course. In fact, he had so little care about it that he promptly forgot it until later, when he heard the men at The Plant talking about it and wishing it had been left to them.

As soon as John Treeves had finished reading the account in the paper he went to the telephone office and called up Hespur on long distance. He had no very definite idea or plan save to express his sympathy and to ask if there was anything he could do.

Old Hespur greeted him with relief: "Is that you, Mr. Treeves? Oh, *well, then!* We've been telegraphing hither and yon to find you. Yes, sir, we're bringing the body home to New York, sir, the old residence on the Avenue, sir. It was his wish, sir, that you should have the service; just a short one, sir. Mostly Bible and praying, sir, if you don't mind the mention. He called me three weeks ago, one day, and he says, 'Hespur, if I should ever die,' just casual like, sir. He says, 'Hespur, I'd like you to see that there isn't any lauding and praising and talking about me. Just let me slip out quiet like,' he says, 'with a bit of prayer and a verse,' he says, 'and I'd like my nephew to say them. I've been an old sinner, and he knows it,' he says, begging his pardon, sir, 'but I'd like him to say all there is to say, and I'll not have a mummery,' just like that he says it! Begging your pardon, sir, for suggesting, but I thought you'd like to know."

"Yes, Hespur, I'm glad to know," said John Treeves in a husky voice deeply touched by the old servant's words. "I wish I had known he was going. I would have liked to see him again. I think I was too hard on him."

"Not a bit of it, sir! He said so himself, sir! And he wouldn't have it that I should tell you. He wanted you to stick by in New York. He's been reading of your sermons, sir, and he's well pleased. But I'll tell you all that when I see you."

"Do you wish me to come down at once, Hespur?"

"No, Mr. Treeves, begging your pardon, now that we've found you I think we will start immediately. We've wired and made all arrangements. The doctor was his friend and knew all about his wishes. He'll come with me, sir. If you could just see to things at that end. You'll find all our telegrams at the Treeves office in the city. And you might meet us as near as Philadelphia if that won't be too much trouble, sir. There's scarcely time to come down and go back. Thank you kindly, Mr. Treeves, and I'll turn everything over to you when we get there, and I hope as how you'll approve."

John Treeves called up the Treeves lawyer in the city, discovered that the arrangements for the funeral were completed, learned the hour of the service, and a few other details that were necessary, and then went back to his work. The other men looked up surprised when he returned to his machine. Somehow they had not expected him, and his white, grave face made them suddenly sorry for him:

"You hadn't oughta set up two nights running, Tree!" said Billy passing that way to get a drink of water. " 'Taint right to get no sleep at all. Man can't stand that and work. You'd oughta lay off to-day."

Treeves smiled wanely:

"I had some sleep last evening, Billy; I'll be all right." He was touched at the sympathy the men displayed because they thought he was not well. It made his heart glad to think that he had won them that far. Then he sighed to think how much there was to do yet for them ere he could hope to have the hold on them by which he might lead them to his Saviour.

John Treeves finished out his day's work, for he did not wish the men to suspect that he was in any way connected with the dead millionaire, or all he had accomplished during the weeks of his life among them might be swept away. They would be as aloof as if he lived in a separate star and look on him at once with suspicion if they thought he belonged to the moneyed class, even by so slight a connection as a disowned nephew.

But he explained to his foreman that he must be away at a funeral of a near relative, and quietly slipped away at dusk, after having assured himself that Johnny Fusco was out of danger and on the mend.

All the way up from Philadelphia where John Treeves boarded the private car which was carrying the old man's body in state, Treeves sat with the old servant listening to the account of the last few weeks of his uncle's life. His heart grew humble and shamed as he learned how the Lord had used his own sermons to bring conviction and salvation to the old sinner's soul. Often the tears flowed unchecked as Hespur told the story in simple, plain words, leaving nothing out. Hespur was eloquent because he loved the old man and he wanted the nephew to understand.

He had told parts of the story once before to Miss Sylvia Cole, at her own request, because he believed his master would want her to know, and because he believed she had a right to know. She had listened in quiet grief to the end and then had thanked him. And he had turned with gentle dignity prepared to put the interview so far from his mind that it would be sealed henceforth even from his own thoughts; but she had spoken again:

"Hespur, what are you going to do now? I mean—afterward."

He turned and answered gravely:

"I shall look after the young master now, Miss Cole."

"Of course!" she said thoughtfully. "I had forgotten. I was going to say if you had nowhere else that I—but it is better so."

Hespur looked at her with a wonderful deference in his true eyes:

"My lady!" he said with a low bow of acknowledgement. "*My lady,* I thank you! If it ever came to that I should be glad, too. But at present there is the young master, and I promised Mister Treeves, my lady, that I would stay by him and look after him."

"Yes, that is right, Hespur. You are a good man, Hespur. I feel as if you were—my FRIEND!" And Miss Sylvia Cole got up from her chair, came across to where he stood, and took that old servant's hand in a warm grasp of perfect equality.

After the funeral John Treeves and old Hespur were asked to return to the big, dark library and listen to the reading of the will. As the nearest relative, the only one present, John Treeves, went of course, but he went with little interest, expecting to listen to a long list of hospitals, libraries and colleges to whom bequests were to be made. He had already decided that if his uncle had relented so far as to leave him a small sum he would devote it to helping make the lives of his fellow-workmen brighter and better. He had not yet anything but vague ideas, but if it should prove to be a few hundred, or even a thousand or two, there were a number of things that were terribly needed. If he only could buy outright a few houses and fix them up! But of course that was impossible. It was Horliss-Cole's plant, and he was only a workman. He must do his work quietly. There would be little lame Jose who needed an operation, and the two children of Fortunato who needed glasses, and the old woman, Congetta, who ought to have special treatment for the asthma. Oh, well, he could use a lot of money of course if he had it. How grand, for instance, it would be if he could build a big board structure in which he could hold meetings! He had broached the subject of church services in the amusement hall to Horliss-Cole, but he had not thought well of it. He said the people had their own churches and he should not care to interfere with their religion. He calmly ignored the fact that The Plant was several miles from any kind of a church, and the people neither owned cars nor had the carfare to go to New York for service. Treeves's heart ached for an opportunity to tell these people the Gospel story. As it was, he could only live it quietly day by day and trust to chance opportunities to speak to souls and tell stories to the children.

When the will was read, leaving practically all of the vast fortune whose sum total was so great that it was fairly incomprehensible in everyday terms, to "my beloved nephew, J. Dunham Treeves, without hindrance or conditions," John Treeves sat dumb, staring, unable to realize what had taken place. With the exception of a few paltry legacies to distant relatives and old servants, the estate went intact. The money he had declined, run away from, and scorned, and had come down upon him in spite of himself!

At first he was almost inclined to think there must be something wrong, and this was a will made before his uncle had talked with him. But when he found that it was made only three weeks before, and after he had read the letter which Calvin Treeves had written to be given him after the reading of the will, he began to understand.

The letter was short, written by the old man himself, and quite characteristic. It ran:

Dear Nephew:

Well, you've beaten me out! You've had your way and I like you all the better for it! You wouldn't be bought, and you showed me my money wasn't worth anything, so here it is! Do what you want with it, only don't ever let it get between you and God or love. I'm an old reprobate. I've told God about it, and if all you preach is true I guess He's forgiven me and going to give me another deal somehow. If I get in over there I'm going to hunt up that mother of yours right away and apologize on my knees to her. She's a winner, and I'm an old fool and a sinner. If the blood of Jesus Christ you talk about can save me, it can save anyone in the world. You tell 'em so from me if you find a chance, and maybe that'll help to make up for some of the harm I've done. You didn't want the money so maybe that'll keep away the curse that goes with it. And I want you to know I'm proud of you boy; and your preaching has brought me to trust in the blood of Jesus Christ to save my fool soul!

Your mistaken old uncle who loves you,
Calvin Treeves.

John Treeves looked up from the letter and met the lawyer's obsequious glance, looked around the luxuriously furnished library of the stately old mansion where his own father had been born, and realized that it was all his, and then bowed his head in his hands.

He would not stay there that night. He said he must think. He promised to meet old Hespur there the first of the following week. So he went out into the crisp evening air of the city, and walked away from his ancient mansion, and took the trolley to the works. That night he slept on the little hard cot in Congetta's wee white-washed room, took his breakfast on the oilcloth-covered table with the clean little children, Filicie and Rosina and Salvator and Dominico and Jose; went down the little aisle of a sidewalk to the shop, where he took his place as usual at his machine, spoke to Billy and John and Nick; laughed with the men as if nothing had happened.

The reporters besieged the old house and tormented the life out of Hespur, who met them all with the cool reply that his younger master was out of town for a few days and it was uncertain when he would return. But Hespur knew more than he told them, more even than the most of the committee of the old New York church where John Treeves preached, for he had gathered up his hat and overcoat from a handy closet near the door, and quietly followed his young master at safe distance out into the night. As it was not the first time that he had shadowed him, he had no trouble in keeping him in sight, and he came back later, having waited outside the little gray and white shanty until every light went out, and he was assured that the inmates were asleep, and having possessed himself of a list of those inmates by a careful questioning of a little boy in the street who accepted certain coins greedily in exchange for his information. Hespur was no fool. He put two and two together, and held his peace. He believed in the younger master. Also, he believed in his Christ.

He busied himself in setting the house to rights with the help of the servants who took care of it usually, and making it as it should be for the reception of the new master, but as he did it he questioned whether after all it was not a superfluous task. He doubted if that democratic young man would ever live and move and have his being among those costly surroundings. He had to admit that he would have enjoyed laying out fine raiment and serving him in lordly halls, but if his master saw things otherwise he was ready even to follow him down to that little gray and white shanty at the works and serve him there with thrilling hands. Was he not his master? Did he not love him well? Was he in turn not serving the same Christ to whom the old servant had but recently dedicated himself?

Hespur went to church that Sunday and heard his young master preach, sitting in a quiet corner under the gallery looking as much a gentleman as any whom he had ever served. Sunday night John Treeves came back to the ancestral house.

He had spent the week working in the shop, living with his fellow-workmen, and thinking. He had taken the noon train on Saturday out to Maple Brook and without stopping to accept Mrs. Burnside's hospitality, much to that good woman's distress, he had walked down the hard frozen road, across the bridge, and climbed the mountain to his trysting place. It was a long walk for a short stay, for it was very cold. But the stars were bright, and the midnight train must be caught back to the city. John Treeves felt he could not decide what to do next without getting to this quiet place where he could almost feel God standing close beside him, where the presence of the Christ seemed to illumine the dark, and bring light to his soul and understanding to his mind. There was no other place in the world as still and alone-with-God as this where his mother had been with him, and where he had first found Jesus.

When he went back on the late train his face looked rested and quiet and the great purpose that had been forming in his soul seemed crystalized in his eyes. He knew now what he was going to do.

Sunday night he and Hespur sat up late, and Hespur was telling him much about the old master, and about the effect of his own sermons on him.

"And now, Mr. Treeves, master"—he looked at the young man with the utmost devotion—"I'm ready at your command. I promised the old master that I would stick to you and care for you as I've cared for him and I mean to keep my word."

Treeves smiled a kindly appreciative smile:

"That's good of you, Hespur, I'm sure," he said, "but you see that's not necessary at all. I've never had a valet or a servant of any kind in my life and I wouldn't know what to do with one."

"That's all right, Mister Treeves, master, but there's plenty of things I can find to do to make it easier for you, and I'm quite used not to having to be told. I've served in the Treeves family for nigh on to forty years, take it all in all, and I'm not thinking to stop now. I come straight to Mr. Treeves's when I first come to this country. I was first footman, then butler, and then he took me for his personal."

"Yes, I know, Hespur, it's a long service and I'm sorry to break it up, but you see I'm not like my uncle. I wasn't brought up to this kind of life and I wouldn't be able to stay here." He looked around on the costly trappings everywhere. "It is quite too grand for me. I don't know just that I'd want to sell the house, perhaps not. I haven't made any plans yet. I think I'd keep it though for the present at least. You see my father was born here. I should want to get to know and love the place for his sake."

Hespur's eyes softened.

"I remember your father quite well, sir. He favored you a great deal in his looks, sir, that firm set to his shoulders, too, but your eyes, I've heard say they were your mother's."

"Yes," said Treeves gently, "they said my eyes were like hers. But she had wonderful eyes!" He was thinking now.

Hespur's attitude said, "And so have you," but his lips moved only to say "I'm at your service, master, however that may be."

Treeves looked troubled.

"Look here, Hespur, I'm really sorry to spoil your plans, but indeed I can't take you. Perhaps we could arrange to let you stay here for a while, and of course I'll see that you don't suffer financially—"

"It's not necessary, sir, the old master he saw to that, sir. I've a stipend twice as large as need be for the rest of my natural life. I ask no wages from you ever. I only ask to stay and care for you, sir."

"Indeed, Hespur, this is devotion and I appreciate it, but—well—you don't understand, of course. I'm not just a regular minister. I don't intend to stay in that big, wealthy church. It isn't my work at all. I amuse them and I antagonize them, but I'm not doing them a bit of good. I've got to get next to real men who are working and doing things. I've taken service under the heavenly Master, Hespur. You said you'd read some of my sermons, then perhaps you know what I've said there about it. I am trying to serve Christ and I feel He wants me to get down among the poor and needy and lead them to Him if I can. I live in a very plain way right among the working people, Hespur; there's no place there for a servant."

"Oh, I know, master, sir, I know," said Hespur quietly. "I've seen the wee shanty where you sleep at night, and the starved little children that huddle around the table there at your meals. I know you're working in a factory at a machine. I know, and I'm not afraid. For, Mr. Treeves, master, sir, I've taken service under the same Jesus Christ, sir, and I'm ready to go with you into any little shanty you want, sir, only so I can stay and take care of *you,* sir."

The look on John Treeves's face changed into a glorified one. He sprang to his feet and put out both hands, grasping the other man's firmly, heartily:

"Then we're brothers, Hespur, aren't we? Come on where you will. We belong together from now on, I guess. I hope you won't be worried at me. I'm afraid I'm quite different from what you'll think I ought to be."

"I'll not worry, sir. I promised the old master I'd stick, and if you wouldn't *let* me, why then I'd stick anyway, and I'm quite proud to be your serving man, sir."

"But you must remember, Hespur, no servant about it. You are my brother, remember!"

"Have it the way you like, sir, I'm taking care of you; that's all that matters to me, sir!"

John Treeves stuck to his job at The Plant until closing hours day after day, and the men he worked with saw no change in him. But as soon as dusk came on he hurried into his street clothes and took his way to the city. He had transferred his belongings now for convenience from the cheap little boarding house to the big mansion uptown, but he kept his room in the boarding house and went there always to make himself more presentable for his evening's work, for he did not care to have the limelight on his life just now, and wanted to do everything possible to prevent talk, even among the few servants he had retained in his own house.

And on that very first Monday evening after his talk with Hespur he went to work on the plans that had come to him for his work, while he walked under the stars that night on the mountain at Maple Brook and talked with God about his fortune.

Before the end of the week he had bought a large section of land on the opposite shore from The Plant, covering several thousand acres of meadow and wooded land, and including the little hill overlooking the river, where Patty had sat on that day when she had gone by herself for a holiday. By Saturday evening, also, he had found the great man who was great enough to be small enough to understand what he wanted. Together they sat over pencils and papers, evening after evening, talking and planning and drawing and erasing and drawing again. Also, in the after-noons, as soon as Treeves was free from the shop he would shove out from the shore a little old canoe he had purchased from another workman and paddle across the river to meet the great man over on Patty's hillside. Then the two would wander over the meadows, and through the woodland, and stop, point, measure, pace it off, drive little stakes, and wander on to do the same thing over again.

There was no danger of anyone interrupting them, for the little village for whose convenience the ferry went across had straggled farther down the river and no one had come up over the brow of the hill to build. The land had belonged to a large estate, the owners of which would not divide. So there was nothing to invade or annoy and no one to spy on their plans.

One of John Treeves's stipulations had been that whatever was done should be done quickly, because he believed that now was the time to do a thing, not to-morrow or next year. And because there was no lack of money to back his enterprise, and because the times were hard and men were eager for work, prices being so high and people being afraid to buy or build or indeed do anything that they could help doing, the keeping of this stipulation was altogether possible.

In the second week a small army of men arrived with picks and shovels, and the plans laid out by the little stakes and cords became a reality in neatly dug squares and trenches. Stone began to arrive in big automobile trucks from a quarry that had been discovered not many miles away, and to enter the new tract from above and beyond the hill, quite out of sight of the little village, and also hidden from the sight of The Plant across the river by a thickly wooded road which ran on the top of the bluff for some miles along the bank.

The first work was done at the far edge of the new land, quite back from the river, and the men were brought in the morning and carried away at night by large truck loads so that none of the people in the settlement at The Plant ever saw or heard or guessed what was going on. That, too, was a part of the plan of John Treeves, who had worked it all out in detail as he ran his sheets of metal into his machine and turned out good work, and much of it, day after day.

It is surprising how much can be done when there are workers enough, and money enough, and above all, will enough. In a very short time there had come a great change over the tract of land that

John Treeves had purchased. It had been bought under the name of his lawyers, and the Treeves name did not appear in public at all, so that no one in that region had the slightest idea what was going on, or who was at the bottom of it. The people of The Plant knew that John Treeves often went out in a canoe on the river after his work was done, and they marvelled that he cared to exercise so hard after a long day's work, but they went no further in their curiosity about him.

And then one day the army of workers broke through the sheltering screen of evergreens and came out to dig in full sight of the opposite bank. They looked like myriads of ants crawling over the bluff from the wharf by The Plant, but no one noticed for several days. Then some one asked if they were fixing an auto road over on the opposite shore, and some one else said he heard the sound of sawing and hammering and wondered if they were thinking of putting up another manufactory opposite. Perhaps it would be in their same line and then Horliss-Cole would be mad. He wanted the whole shore to himself. Another idle speculator in gossip declared he had heard that a rich man was building himself a home; and so the matter passed for some time and no one took the trouble to go over and see. Strangers passing on long-distance automobile journeys, slowed up and wondered at the clusters of beautiful little stone structures that were rising and wondered what the great cellar in the center was for, and the other one farther off to the right, and those two other large ones. Perhaps it was a hotel with private cottages attached. How charming! They must look it up when they returned, might be a pleasant place to spend the summer sometime when they couldn't get away from the city far! But no one from the region close around came to investigate until the preliminary work was all done.

There was one especial little bungalow, just in the edge of the woods, with a glimpse out one way toward the river and over the little hill, and with a glance out the other toward the large structure that was slowly rising stone by stone over in the very center of the big hill that sloped gently down to the river in front. This bungalow seemed to suddenly spring into full-fledged houseship in a night, and one morning men from The Plant looked over as usual, and looked again, and then squinted their eyes, and looked a third time. Was that a house over there! A house! It must be the sunlight on the water creating a mirage. No, it was a little stone house with porches and a wide chimney on the outside running all the way up. There were hemlocks about it and it somehow had the air of always having been there. It was not large nor grand, but pretty and cosy. Oh, so cosy! A perfect dream of a little home where one might be happy! Men pointed it out to one another and couldn't understand it, and wished they had time to go over and investigate. It couldn't be that that house had been there all winter and they not have seen it. It wasn't possible it was one of those patent hang-me-up houses. It looked substantial and as if it belonged there. It was built of solid masonry.

It was this special house that Hespur came over every day or two in the car to watch, and advise about. He made them put the butler's pantry in just the right spot, and planned all the closets and windows with a view to comfort and ease, and he watched the fireplace with a jealous care. And once as he stood with his hands behind his back musing over the mullion window that was being set in the stone in the peak of the roof, he murmured softly to himself:

"Oh, I wonder if the old master can see it. I wonder now! What a comfort he would a-took with it setting in front of that fire, now wouldn't he, poor dear!"

And evening after evening as John Treeves and the great man who was helping him in this wonderful operation worked away on the wide mahogany desk with their great sheets of drawings and plans, Hespur would stand behind Treeves's chair and watch and listen and assent. Now and then Treeves would ask his advice, and Hespur's eyes would shine and he would always answer with alert readiness to suggest, yet never for a moment lost his sense of their relation as master and servant. Nevertheless, underneath his dignity, old Hespur was never forgetting that night when John Treeves took him by the hand, and called him "brother."

31

"You never told me," said Miss Cole thoughtfully one morning about two weeks after Calvin Treeves's funeral, "what you did with the rest of your twenty-five dollars. You surely couldn't have spent it *all* on a dinner for that woman and flowers for the Italian girl. Of course, if it's private I don't mind, only if it isn't it would be interesting to know."

Patty smiled and looked worried.

"I didn't tell you because I was afraid you might perhaps not agree with me about it."

"What's that to do with it? I told you to spend it the way you wanted to, didn't I? Well, I meant it. Out with it!"

Patty laughed.

"Well, you'll think it was throwing it away, but I gave it to Mary della Camera to make a nucleus for a fund for getting her Angelo out of jail. She said if he could get out on bail he might be able to get some proof that would clear him. I knew twenty dollars wouldn't go far, but I thought it might start some lawyer till he got interested, and maybe some one else would help them out if they had a start."

Miss Cole's eyes were on her thoughtfully.

"Well, you seem to have done a good many things for other people out of that twenty-five dollars. But I'm sure I don't see where your holiday came in. However, it was a great thing to do, I should think. Why didn't you tell me sooner and let me help? Suppose you go over and find out how they are coming on and see if they need more. If they do, I'll send my check."

"Oh, Miss Cole, that would be beautiful! But— but I think maybe I ought to tell you that I don't think your brother would approve. I've been some troubled about it ever since lest maybe I ought not to have done it, living in his house this way. It wasn't well—quite loyal to the family, but I somehow had to do it."

"Nonsense, why shouldn't my brother approve?"

Patty told her how she had gone to him about the shooting and he had told her to keep still about it.

Miss Cole sniffed.

"H'm! Well, I don't always approve of *him* by any means. Bring me my check book. Now, get your hat and be ready to go. It's a bright spring day and you need a change. If that's your idea of a holiday, have another."

So Patty fluttered off quite happily. It was exciting to be the bearer of such a substantial check as Miss Cole had made out, and her eyes shone bright as two stars as she took the trolley for The Plant.

It was a great welcome she received at the little gray shanty, and the family gathered around and touched her shyly, her beautiful dress, her coat, the bit of fur she wore around her neck. They looked at her hat and the little jewel that fastened the lace just below her white throat, and they looked at her lovely face. They said brokenly, "You nica lady!" And when Mary della Camera came from her office work at lunch time her eyes shone gloriously, and her pale cheeks grew the faintest rose underneath the clear olive. The eyes grew sad again almost immediately, however.

"I thank you. But I'm afraid it is no use. There are too many against it. Too many!" she sighed. "That Ivan. He hates him! He wanted to go around with me, but I wouldn't. I go with Angelo only, and he hates him! He would kill him if he got the chance. I don't like that Ivan! He is sly! He pretends to be a friend, but I think he is an enemy!"

They carried Patty around from house to house, showing her off, and she took the little babies in her arms and played with them, and found out all about the mother's troubles. They took her to Congetta's, to the house where Treeves boarded, and Patty had no idea that upstairs, treasured away in the bottom of his trunk, lay a snapshot of herself taken five years before with two long braids down her back and a big white hat tilted back on her head. If she had known that at this hour John Treeves usually entered that little gray door and sat down at that oilcloth-covered table for his dinner, she would have flown on swift wings away from the place and never gone back. But happily for her John Treeves had been suddenly called across the river in his little canoe to see about some point of question on the buildings, and had gone without his lunch that day and missed the sweetest sight he ever saw. Patty went happily on her angel way, promising a dolly here, a ball there, a strip of flannel for the old woman with the asthma and a pink bonnet for a new baby. It was all a joyous time to Patty and she stayed so long going from house to house and putting down in her memorandum what she had promised so that she wouldn't forget, that she quite forgot there would be no time to go across to her bluff again and watch the boats go down the river awhile. So she had to hurry away. But she left a trail of sunshine in her wake, and they called her the pretty lady with the smiling face. John Treeves heard of her, and wondered. Tried to connect her with some one in the city church, wondered if after all Marjorie Horliss-Cole had forgotten herself long enough to accept his suggestion of doing something for some one else, and then forgot it again in his multiplicity of cares.

436

But Patty went again many times with little gifts, some of them from Miss Cole, who was deeply interested in every detail of the visits, and one day she went to see Mary about something Miss Cole had suggested in Angelo's behalf, and finding her still at work doing extra time at the office, she determined to take the ferry trip once more while she waited and discover whether there were violets on that bluff across the river.

She stood watching the water wash in silvery laps away from the side of the old boat, and it was not until they were half-way across that she raised her eyes to the opposite bank and discovered the little stone house peeping out between the hemlocks.

"Why!" she said to herself. "I never saw that house before! How strange! Have I made a mistake and taken the wrong boat, or has the course of this ferry line been changed?"

But, no, she could see the very log on which she had sat, now as she looked to the little bluff. How strange!

She got off the boat at the landing and danced up the hill on eager feet, standing shyly off by her log to look at the house, and discovering to her surprise that it was a new house, quite new, not yet finished. The workmen seemed to be still in it, fixing the window sashes. As she drew nearer, curious to see what it was like on closer acquaintance, she saw that there were other houses beyond, many of them, dropped here and there among the trees quite carelessly and naturally, as if they grew there and belonged. It was like a fairy tale, finding the empty meadow and woodside where she had wandered but six short months before all trimmed out with pleasant dwellings this way.

There were walks laid out, too, and in some places men were spreading cement upon them, and setting out hedges, and shrubs of various kinds. Vines were growing here and there by porches, young vines apparently just planted. She turned to look another way and there before her rose a winding path of broad, low steps as wide as a city sidewalk, leading up in a great easy curve to a wonderful building on the very top of the hill, in the midst of the whole settlement. And now she saw that this was really the heart of the whole beautiful scheme, for each house, however it was set and wherever it was, faced toward this central building, half hidden from her eager gaze by the tall trees that were just putting out rich draperies of green. She turned into the winding stair and exclaimed in delight. At either side were broad stone railings or walls and men were working away at the front upper surfaces cutting letters in clear relief a sentence to a level, and sometimes one on the front of the stair rises. The first great curve of the railing swept around before her as she stepped up and the words that faced her, fully completed were "I was glad when they said unto me, Let us go up to the house of the Lord."

"Oh!" said Patty. "How wonderful! How beautiful! Who could have thought of it!" And then a memory came to her that brought a dreamy look to her eyes, that summer long ago and an afternoon on the vine-clad porch, an old engraving and a talk they had. The picture was of a temple set on a height, and children winding up a broad stair, singing as they went, and underneath the words: "I was glad when they said unto me, let us go up to the house of the Lord. My feet shall stand in the holy place." How odd that this should be the same words! The talk had started when she had said that she hated to go to the school church it was so dull and uninteresting, and Mrs. Treeves had showed her this old picture and told her it had always been a kind of symbol of what she thought the Lord wanted His service to be to those who loved Him, happiness, and joy and willingness to serve.

Patty went on up the broad stairs finding new verses at every turn.

"Come now, and let us reason together, saith the Lord. Though your sins be as scarlet they shall be as white as snow, and though they be red like crimson they shall be as wool. The blood of Jesus Christ His Son cleanseth us from all sin. The wages of sin is death, but the gift of God is eternal life through Jesus Christ our Lord."

"Come unto me all ye that labor and are heavy

laden, and I will give you rest. Take my yoke upon you and learn of me for I am meek and lowly of heart and ye shall find rest unto your souls for my yoke is easy and my burden is light."

They wound along the staircase on either side. Such beautiful stone letters, wrought with vines and flowers now and then, a single thought on each level. Now it was salvation from sin, now it was rest to the soul, now it was hope and joy and peace to be obtained. Always in tiny letters below there were the references, and Patty stopped several times to note them down in her little book that she carried in her handbag, they were such wonderful words that she wanted to find them again. Then at the last turn she came out from behind dense growths of laurel and hemlock and pine, grouped like a portal, and there before her stood the church, a temple if there ever was one built upon earth, reminding one of the rare old cathedrals of the old world, yet with an air all its own that brought memories of the pattern given in the Mount. There was a great bell tower in which even then workmen were busy placing a chime of wonderful bells, and more stone cutters were chiselling away at the work about the entrance.

"Jesus Christ the Chief Corner Stone."

"The stone which the builders rejected, the same is become the Head of the corner."

That was what she saw on the great corner stone.

And there were other verses chiseled here and there, standing out at you from the lily work on the pillars. Only lilies at first they seemed, and suddenly some word of God would stand clear to the eye, some startling promise. Oh, it was marvellous! What a brain and heart to have thought it out in these finest details!

And then, as she stepped up to the wide doorway, there stood Hespur, looking down at a bit of mosaic flooring that had just been finished into which had been wrought the words in little gold cubes of stone, "I had rather be a doorkeeper in the house of my God, than to dwell in the tents of wickedness."

There was deep feeling in the old eyes of the serving man as he looked up and saw her, and quite as if it were a natural thing to meet her there, he said in a husky voice, pointing to the words:

"I'm thinking, Miss, that'll maybe be my job some day, and I'd like it rarely well, I would!"

Her face kindled understandingly.

"It would be great, wouldn't it?" she responded eagerly. "What is this place, Hespur? Who built it? I just wandered into it. Is it private property?"

"Oh, why didn't he bring you here, Miss? It belongs to the young master. He's building it, Miss, for his people. The people over there at The Plant where he works. But you mustn't tell anybody. Not a soul, you know. He's keeping it for a surprise. When it's done he's going to bring them over a few families at a time and rent them these little houses at cost, very low, Miss, less than cost, perhaps. He's not going to make any money on them, you know. And they're wonderful little houses, so cosy, so handsome, all different, fireplaces, little windows, bathrooms, quaint corners and seats and settles. Miss, you should go through them. He'll take you through, of course. But the people are not to know he's doing it. They will think some rich man has made the place. For he is just to be their fellow-workman, the man they know and love. He's figuring to preach to them here of a Sunday, but week days, they'll work together just the same, and he'll be one of them. That's his little house down there by the bluff overlooking the river. He'll live there, and I'm to keep house for him, and whatsoever sick or poor body he picks up to nurse for a while. We're going to move over next week. Down there is a school for the children, and over there is the hall where they'll have lectures and concerts and a band, and a place for the growners to study some, too, and over there that big pool; that's the swimming pool and gymnasium. Oh, it's going to be a fine little town some day. It's gladsome, it is, and I'm waiting to see their faces when they first give it a look over. He's not got a name for it yet. He's figuring on that now."

"It ought to be called Joyville!" cried Patty, eagerly looking around with a swelling heart and eyes that were starry with the wonder of it all. So this was what he was doing with his money! She might have known!

"That's the very thing, Miss! You'll have to tell him, Miss. He's about here somewhere. He'll be here presently. He went in the church with the architect, something about the verses on the altar. He'll be out and take you around. There's a lot more to see. The workmen's houses have every convenience, even to machines for working that run by electricity. You see he's figuring to make life a little easier for the women folks so they will have more time to bring up the children in the right way, and there's to be Mother's classes to teach them how. I hear all the talk and it's wonderful, Miss. Step this way and we'll find the master!"

But Patty was looking at her wrist watch in a great hurry.

"I'm sorry," she said with very red cheeks, "but I must fly. I mustn't miss my boat. Miss Cole is expecting me. Another time, perhaps. It's been beautiful and wonderful—but I MUST go!" and Patty turned and fairly flew down the long, low staircase and down the hill to the boat landing, looking all the time furtively back, fearful lest she was being pursued.

But somehow the name of Joyville got fastened to the new village.

32

The next morning Patty was sitting by the window with the morning papers around her, waiting for Miss Cole to be ready to have the news read to her. Miss Cole loved to hear Patty read, and they often talked over events together and had a pleasant time of it. But this morning just as Miss Cole seated herself in her willow chair, and drew her shawl around her shoulders to keep off the draught from the open window, Patty suddenly dropped the paper she had been glancing over and stood up. Her face was very white and her lips were trembling:

"Miss Cole," she said in a voice that she was evidently having hard work to control, "could you excuse me a little while? I—I don't feel very well. I would—like to go to my room!"

"Why, of course, child!" said Miss Cole looking up anxiously. Patty was never ill. This was a new development. "Isn't there something I can do for you? Some medicine? Shan't I call the doctor?"

"Oh, no," said Patty, who was already almost out of the door. "I'll be—all—right—in a few—minutes!" There was a catch in her voice at the end that sounded almost like a sob. Miss Cole got up and looked down the hall after her, watched until Patty entered her own door, then she turned back puzzled and picked up the paper Patty had been reading, scanning the page where it had dropped. All at once understanding came to her. Down in the lower corner of the last column she found a little item.

"Daniel P. Merrill, the great western financier, has been lost at sea on his way home from a business trip to South America, where it is rumored he has been investigating silver mines. He leaves a wife and two daughters. The steamer went down off the coast of Brazil and all on board were lost. No trace has as yet been found of the body and it is not expected that it will be recovered."

"H'm!" said Miss Cole thoughtfully. Then she went and locked her door and sat down at the telephone table, calling up Western Union. She sent a telegram to her cousin in the West:

"Find out immediately all you can about Daniel P. Merrill's movements and his family, financially and otherwise, especially the present whereabouts and a description of the daughter Patty. Wire me as soon as possible."

Then she sat down to wait. Meantime Patty in her room was weeping her heart out.

Later in the day the answer arrived.

"Person in question lost at sea on way home from business trip to South America. Widow handsome, disagreeable, stylish and selfish. Daughter Evelyn more so. Daughter Patricia absent for some time. Can't get explanation of whereabouts. Family seem eager to conceal it. Financial affairs very much involved on account of death of father."

"H'm!" said Miss Cole aloud to herself. "I know a lot more, don't I?"

But Patty had cried out the storm of sorrow in her heart and got control of herself. She had knelt beside her bed and cried with her whole heart to the Helper John Treeves had been preaching about:

"Oh, Jesus Christ, this is Patty. I'm all alone now, daddy's gone. Won't you help me to bear it? Won't you help me to know what to do? Help me now, because there is no one else to care."

Then Patty got up and washed her face, drank the tea that the maid brought to the door with a message from Miss Cole asking how she was feeling, and bravely erased the traces of her recent tear storm. Then with a white face and dark circles under her sad eyes she went back to Miss Cole and asked if she might read to her now.

"Well, no, not now," said that good woman eying Patty keenly. "I don't think you are fit. You need petting up. You found some bad news in the paper this morning, didn't you?"

Patty started and looked troubled.

"Yes"—she hesitated—"the death of—a—friend."

"I'm very sorry—dear child!" said Miss Cole in a most unusually tender tone that almost brought the tears again to Patty's eyes. "I won't harrow you by talking about it. Would you like to go away anywhere for a while or make any change in your plans? You know I can arrange things to suit your convenience."

"Oh, no, thank you!" said Patty. "There's nothing I can do. I've decided it's best for me to stay right here."

For Patty had been thinking it over and it seemed that she must keep entirely out of the way. The words that Evelyn had spoken about money led her to believe that there must have been financial reverses about which her father had not told her. Very likely he had gone to South America to try and save his fortune, and now that he was dead there would be less money than ever. She would not go back to complicate matters. Let Evelyn and her mother have what there was, she could earn her living.

Miss Cole watched the white face doubtfully and wished she knew what to do. She was pretty sure that life was not made any easier for the girl by the fact that John Treeves was often at the house to see Marjorie. What a fool a man could be sometimes! She had no patience whatever with him. She had almost a notion to call him into counsel and find out what he knew about Patty Merrill, only it didn't seem quite square to do that, and Miss Cole was always a good sport and tried to play fair.

That very afternoon John Treeves had left the house in Marjorie's company and Patty had watched them go up the avenue, having caught a glimpse from the hall window as she passed. It was not easy to put it out of her mind. She began to wonder if her prayer had really been heard. It seemed as if everything that she had ever cared for was taken away from her. Probably John Treeves was taking Marjorie to see his wonderful village, and she turned away and sighed. Then the memory of her great loss would roll over her overwhelmingly and she would draw a deep trembling sigh.

Those sighs were the only outward sign that she was suffering and they almost drove Miss Cole distracted. She spent her whole thoughts trying to find something with which to cheer Patty, and as soon as she left the room on an errand she sent off another telegram to her cousin:

"Spare no expense in finding out if the father is really dead. Send some one down there if necessary. Cable for evidences. Say nothing to the family."

Meantime Treeves and Marjorie walked up to the Park and sat down behind a screen of spring shrubs all in bloom:

"Now, Miss Marjorie," said Treeves, "I've had a letter. I didn't want to tell you at the house because some one might come in while we were talking and it might be misunderstood. You see, I don't believe in anything underhanded, and your father is my friend. But I promised you I would find out if that young man was worthy of your interest and I've kept my promise. I have to tell you that he's all and more than you said. I've made a thorough investigation. I've seen his mother, and his home, and I've had letters from two old school friends of mine and an army friend who are all located in the Philippines. They all speak of him in the highest terms. They say he's clean and fine and brainy and courageous. They say nothing daunts him, and everybody likes him, and best of all he's being true to you. He's not running around with other girls, nor travelling with the natives. He's told them all he's engaged and coming home to be married some day when he's made his fortune. In fact, they said so many things in his favor that I began to wonder whether you were worth having all that much manliness wasted on you. You'll excuse me, I promised to be frank. Maybe you'll think I'm brutal, but I'm interested in that chap out there as well as you and I'd like to see you make good, too."

"You certainly aren't very complimentary," said Marjorie, making a wry face, "but I'm not in love with you, so go on. You've been awfully good to me anyway. I guess I can stand it. Probably it's all true. I'm beginning to see I've a good many faults."

"Well, now, you're talking," said Treeves hopefully. "And to tell you the truth it was your telling me the other day that you had decided to try my way and give yourself to Christ, that made me feel I would tell you all this. That and your going over to the works so often and being kind to those people. When I heard how they called you the lady of the smiling face, I concluded you were beginning to forget your selfishness and think of other people. The fact is, I couldn't stand seeing a nice, clean, fine, unselfish chap like this Winters tied up for life to a lazy society woman who never cared a rap for anything but her own pleasure."

Marjorie flashed him a curious look of mingled amusement and anger. "You certainly are frank," she said, "but you've made one mistake. I've never been over to the works. I hate the place. I've never taken the trouble. I wouldn't know how to go about it. I guess maybe I am selfish."

"You've never been? Well, who the dickens is it then? I made sure it was you. But you'll get there now you've given yourself to Him. You can't help it. It goes with the giving of yourself. Good works are no good as a means to get to Heaven, but they are the result of your love for Christ. You can't help loving and helping others when you love Him."

His voice had that reverent gentleness that made Marjorie look at him with awe.

"But I have something more to tell you. I wrote

to the man himself, and I mean to let you see the letter. Your parents didn't want you to correspond with him, but I think you have a right to know the result of my investigations." He opened the letter and read:

My dear Mr. Treeves:

I want to thank you for taking an interest in my affairs and for your kindness to Miss Horliss-Cole, for I know you have been kind to bring about even this much communication between us when we are separated in this unpleasant way.

In answer to your questions I want you to know that I am making good out here as fast and as well as I can, and I am enclosing some letters from my employers to prove that I am not speaking on my own authority. I realize that I did a very audacious thing to fall in love with a girl of such wealth and social position as Marjorie, but we love each other and I am going to make good for her sake. I don't believe in asking her to marry me until I have enough to keep her in comfort and some luxury such as she is used to, but I do intend to accomplish that as quickly as I can and prove to her father that I am fully able to provide for and take care of her. I think she loves me enough to give up the wealth for my sake, but she is very young and I won't let her do anything like that. I mean to make her father see that I am good enough for her. *I MEAN TO BE GOOD ENOUGH.*

Thank you for letting me know that she is well and still remembers, and if you get a chance and think it is all right, give her my great love and tell her I'm doing my best.

Yours sincerely,
Allen Winters

Marjorie sat quite still and listened to the letter, her eyes glowing with a deep fire of joy. Then she answered quietly:

"Thank you. That will keep me for a long time. I'll be true. I haven't always been as true as he thought I was. I got discouraged and blue and selfish, I know, and was ready to cut into almost anything to have a good time and forget, but it's different now. I'm going to get ready to be a woman. I think God is going to help me, too, and I thank you for all you have done. I shall be of age in six months, and I shall have some money of my own left me by my Grandfather Horliss. I'm going to wait until I'm of age, and then I'm going to tell father that I still love Allen. If he isn't willing I should stay at home then and write to Allen, I can go away somewhere and take care of myself. But I'm not going to do anything wild, you needn't be afraid. I'm going to stop being a fool, and learn to live and be happy on a little money, so that Allen won't have to stay away any longer to get rich for me. I'd rather have him poor than to be so long apart."

"I like the way you talk," said Treeves. "You're a good sport. Now, if you'll excuse me for not walking home with you, I'll go to a business appointment I have. I'm already late. And here's this letter if you care to have it. I've already answered it, and I'll add a line to him about this interview if you wish."

He handed her the letter and bowed and left her. She wandered happily about the Park for a while with the precious letter and then walked quietly home by herself with a smile on her face. But Patty didn't happen to see that. She only saw the remnant of the smile an hour later when they happened to meet in the hall, and she thought sorrowfully that she knew what made it.

33

There had been a growing unrest at The Plant ever since the murder, and as the day drew near for the trial of Angelo, and it began to be almost certain that he would be convicted of the murder, the feeling of indignation swept over the little community like a wave that could not be controlled. Treeves began to feel it in the air. He heard it constantly in the fiery talk that went on about him in the shop, and in the hot arguments that raged in the evenings when the neighbors dropped in on one another and discussed the matter. In all this talk Treeves kept silent, although it was known that he was working with all his might to help Angelo; still they had no faith that he could do anything. What was he but a poor working man like themselves? "Tree" he was to them all now, nothing more. They did not know that he was the popular preacher in a big New York church, nor yet that he was the owner of a fortune large enough to buy out many times the whole Plant. They would have opened their eyes wide with incredulous scorn if anybody had told them that the new buildings across the river about which they were now beginning to have great curiosity were owned and built by his design. He was just their fellow-workman, in sympathy with them, indeed, and believing he was going to be able to help Angelo, but powerless, they thought.

There was a man, Ivan, a low-browed foreigner of a mongrel type with hot, red, hurrying eyes and a tongue that flashed forth venom. He was a skillful workman in some special line, and there was none like him when he worked, but he was a dangerous man, and in league, Treeves believed, with some outside order of anarchists or something of the sort. He had watched him much lately and two or three times had been on the point of warning Horliss-Cole about him. Then had desisted, for the man was less dangerous here where he could be watched, than discharged where he could work his will against them without being observed.

It was three days before Angelo's trial, and it was early evening. Patty was alone in the great house except for the servants. The family had gone out to a dinner given by a relative. Even Miss Cole had felt it incumbent upon her to accept, though she grumbled a good deal about it all the time she was getting ready.

Patty was always restless when she was alone without duties. Then most of all she missed her father. Also, she was worried about Angelo. She had not heard how things were progressing in a long time. Since she had learned from Hespur that Treeves worked at The Plant she had been afraid to go over there lest she might meet him, but she had written to Mary della Camera asking how things were progressing and if there was anything she could do. As yet no reply had come.

Patty was just preparing to sit down to her solitary dinner served to-night in her own room, when the maid came up to say that there was a boy down at the servants' entrance who insisted on seeing her. Patty hurried down and found Mary's small brother Dominic, a boy of twelve, with eyes like great black pansies fringed with black curling lashes. He might have been the model for one of Raphael's cherubs, so soulful was his glance. He spoke English well:

"My sister send me. She said you would know what to do," he said in a low tone, looking around furtively to see if anyone was listening.

Patty drew him into a little storeroom where they could talk undisturbed.

"There has been awful things going on," he said, looking at her eagerly. "The men are mad. They are going to do things to-night. They are going to mebbe blow up the Works to-night. They are going across the river and put bombs under the new town over there. Joyville, they call it Joyville—" Patty caught her breath. "It will be *Hellville* by morning if something doesn't stop 'em. Nobody can stop 'em but Tree and we can't find Tree!"

"But why do they want to do a thing like that?" asked Patty, her eyes wide with horror.

" 'Cause they hate Mr. Hor'-Cor'! They say he make 'em work, work, and little pay. Poor houses and big rent. Houses leak, and he won't mend 'em. He makes *us* mend 'em."

"But the village, the new houses and the church—! Why should they hurt that?"

"They say he build it for his bosses. He build nice houses for them and let the laborers live in old houses—!"

"But that isn't so. Mr. Horliss-Cole has nothing to do with the new settlement across the river. I know, for I happen to know the owner. He is a good man!"

"You couldn't make them believe that. Nobody couldn't make 'em believe nothing but Tree. They think Hor'-Cor' is going to get Angelo hung and they're mad and they'll kill him if they could find him! Nobody can't stop 'em but Tree, and we can't find him. He's gone somewheres else to live and nobody don't know where he's at."

"Oh," said Patty with her hands clasped together, "I know—at least I think I do."

The boy gripped her hand eagerly, "Come get your hat. We go!"

"Oh," said Patty, "I couldn't go to-night, but I can tell you where the house is. You know that first house up on the bluff across the river? The one you see from your front porch?"

Dominic nodded: "Suppose he not there?"

"Oh, but Hespur would be—I'm sure—you could tell Hespur."

"No!" said the boy decidedly. "I tell no one but you and Tree."

"Perhaps I ought to tell Mr. Horliss-Cole and have him send the police!"

The boy's face darkened.

"You go back on us, too! You turn yella!" There came an old man's look on his set young jaw. A look of utter hopelessness, and tragedy, yes, and a desire for vengeance, too. "You tell on us, and get the police and Angelo get hanged. Mr. Hor'-Cor' get more mad and turn us all out. We *all* die!"

"Oh," said Patty putting her hands over her eyes, "don't! Of course I wouldn't do that! I was only trying to think what to do! Of course he mustn't know it. Mr. Treeves is the one. He will know what to do. I will go with you and find him. Wait for me here a minute. I will get my coat and hat and go with you."

"I am going out for a little while. You need not keep my dinner for me," said Patty putting in her head at the pantry door, and then she flew up the stairs to her room. She was down in a moment more, and they were out in the street together. It seemed somehow a relief. The lighted streets, the people hurrying home to their dinners, the quiet stars above: it seemed to give her steadiness. Nothing so dreadful as blowing up The Plant and the wonderful village—Joyville, Joyville! He had named it that! Nothing like what Dominic had been telling could happen in a world where things went by law and order. It seemed absurd almost to think it could. Then she looked at the set face of the boy by her side and hurried on.

They took the trolley to The Plant. It was a full three-quarters of an hour before they reached there, and then the ferryboat had just gone as they arrived at the landing. The tail lights blinked leeringly at them as they looked across the water as if the boat, too, were in league with the devil against righteousness and peace and—Joyville!

They waited quietly, not talking, for Patty did not care to be seen out there alone with a mere boy at night, although it was early yet, and Dominic hovered in the shadow of an old shed and peered out at any approaching figure. He seemed anxious and alert, like a man who had much responsibility.

When they were on board the ferry Patty began to realize what she was doing. After keeping out of John Treeves's way for all these months she was going deliberately into his presence! But then it could not be helped. Dominic might not have found him, and HE MUST BE FOUND! She set her lips in a firm little line and began to try to plan. Up there on the bluff a friendly light twinkled out over the water. Some one was there all right. He was likely having his supper. She would tell Dominic to go in and she would remain outside in the shadow. If he was there she would tell Dominic to keep still about her being there at all. He could take Mr. Treeves over at once. They would likely go in the canoe and wait for the next boat, and she would follow later on the boat and slip around by a back way to the trolley and go home. She was glad she had remembered to bring her veil. Of course it was thin, but it would help a little to conceal her identity. She loosened the folds and arranged it in full drapery about her face.

Silently the girl and boy climbed the hill, and Dominic knocked at the door, while Patty stood in the shadows of the laurel bushes. The boy had not questioned her directions:

But instead of Hespur's tall form standing in the lighted doorway when it was opened, there stood a little lame boy whom Patty had never seen before, and Dominic did not seem to know:

"No, he ain't here!" answered the boy promptly. "Neither of 'em ain't here! Mr. Hespur he's gone to town fer something Mr. Treeves wanted at the big house, and Mr. Treeves he's gone out in the woods about a mile. Somebody come along a little while ago, some young man, and said there was a fellow named Angelo had broke jail and got away and he was up here back a piece laying in a barn dying of a shot he got while he made his getaway. They said he wanted to make a confession and they wanted Mr. Treeves to come and hear it. Something about a murder."

"It's a lie!" murmured Dominic under his breath, drawing his old cap down over his young-old face. "It's a LIE! Angelo never broke jail! Angelo knows better'n that, and Angelo ain't got no confession to make, 'cause he never murdered that man! It's a lie and somebody's doing dirty work. I better go get help!" and Dominic turned and fled down the bluff toward the shore.

"Dominic! Wait!" called Patty stepping out of the shadow in a panic; but Dominic was out of sight and in a moment more she could hear the splash of a paddle. He had wrenched the lock of Treeves's canoe and was going back across the river as fast as he could go.

Then Patty turned back to the boy.

"Which way did you say Mr. Treeves had gone?" she questioned.

"Straight up that road to the road gate, and then back along the Pike. He said it was about a mile. The man that told him said it was an old red barn back in the meadow behind the second farm house."

"Did you know the man who brought the message?" asked Patty.

"No, I don't know nobody round this dump. I live in the city. Mr. Treeves just brought me out here 'cause I been in the horspital havin' an operation and the doctor said I needed country air. I'll be glad to get back to town, I will; nothin' to see out here but water and boats. Gee! I'm sick of it. Mr. Treeves is all right, of course, and Mr. Hespur he ain't so bad, but I wantta get back."

But Patty had not stayed to hear it all. She was walking rapidly out the newly paved road toward the gate of Joyville and in a moment more she turned into the Pike. The stars were out in thick spring clusters, and a faint little thread of a moon hung near the tops of the trees. It was not so dark when one got started and the road was straight and wide and empty. She was not much afraid. She kept telling herself that it was early yet, and no one knew she was coming, so why should she be afraid? Perhaps an automobile would come along in a minute and she could ask the people to take her a little way. They would think she was going to one of the farm houses.

But no friendly car came, and she sped on her way. It seemed miles before she reached the first farm house and there was only a dim light in what must be the kitchen window. The second farm house was nowhere in sight. She flew on feeling as if she were leaving the last hope behind. It seemed an endless way before a dark house appeared, stark on the horizon where a luminous spot from the river managed to glimpse between the trees. Yes, there was the barn, and a faint light flickered, more like a glow than a light. Now and then it wavered as if the wind moved it and Patty hurried on until she reached the door, then paused an instant to quiet her pounding heart. It was almost more than she could do to speak, and her voice sounded like a sob of joy as she said:

"John! John Treeves, is that you?"

"Patty!"

He rose from a stooping position over a pallet of hay on the floor where a dark form lay huddled, and came to meet her. The flickering candle stuck on an old tin can sent shadows over his face, but there was joy and wonder in his eyes and voice as he came to meet her with out-stretched arms.

"Patty! Little Pard! How did you come here?"

He took both her hands in his and let his eyes devour her and for a moment she stood so, looking in his face speechless because her breath was gone. The fright, the unusual responsibility, the long, hard walk, the terror of the darkness and loneliness all seemed to drop from her at sight of him. She felt weak and tired and wanted to drop down and be comforted. But instead she remembered what had brought her here, and began to gasp it out even before she had regained her breath.

"You must go," she pleaded, "you must go and stop them! They are planning terrible things to-night and no one else can do any good!"

But he paid no heed to her words, only looked in her eyes and said with conviction, "Patty, it has been *you* all the time. I knew it! You have been hiding from me. Patty, why did you do it?"

"Oh!" said Patty laughing and crying together. "Never mind now, I can't stop to explain. You must go back at once to the men. They are going to blow up The Plant, and the new village, and perhaps shoot Mr. Horliss-Cole and then nothing we can do will save Angelo from being hanged!"

"Patty! How should you know about all this?"

"Dominic told me! He came to the house for me, and I came out here to help him find you, but when he heard you were here he shouted something about 'dirty work' and somebody being a liar, and rushed off. I think he took your boat and went back to get help. You must go quick! You really must. He thought they were planning to do something very soon! He said nobody but 'Tree' could stop it!"

"Patty! You are the lady of the smiling face!"

"But never mind now," said Patty. "Go quick!" and she began to pull him toward the door.

John Treeves stopped her.

"Patty, I can't leave. Look at there!" pointing to the unconscious figure on the straw. "That man is dying. He is Angelo's good-for-nothing brother. I think he knows something about the murder that may set Angelo free. He sent for me to take a confession, and when I got here he was unconscious. He roused once and said enough to make me sure he knows something. I've sent for a doctor, but I must stay and get it all if he should rouse again."

Patty considered.

"I will stay!" she said quietly. "I can take his confession and write it down even if I am not you, but I cannot quiet those men who are bent on destruction. You will have to go."

Treeves looked troubled.

"I can't leave you here alone with a dying man, Patty! I think Dominic is unduly alarmed. All was quiet when I left. Besides, Dominic was wrong about thinking there was 'dirty work,' as he called it. This man might easily have been mistaken for Angelo. I think the messenger was genuine."

Patty looked troubled. Angelo had succeeded in fixing upon her mind the necessity for Treeves's immediate presence at The Plant. She could not get away from it.

"You must go!" she said firmly. "I am not afraid to stay. You can send Hespur or somebody when you have time, but I am going to stay now. Don't you remember how you used to call me Little Pard? Well, I'm that now and this is my job. Go, quickly!"

"You—Darling!" he said, and turned and went swiftly, calling back, "I'll send Hespur at once. It won't be long."

He was gone and she was alone in the great barn with the dying man. She gave a shiver and looked around her. She had been very brave before him, but she was deathly afraid now and trembling in every nerve. Then she bethought her of her new-found trust, and dropping on one knee on the dusty floor, she whispered:

"Dear Christ, this is Patty again. Won't you please stay with me and take care of me? And, oh, don't let anything happen to John—for Jesus' sake!"

Then she got up, and taking the candle went over to the huddled figure in the corner. Holding the candle high, she examined his dark, sodden face carefully, wondering what kind of a man he was, and whether she could hope to rouse him and get a confession from him before he went entirely from this earth and took his knowledge with him.

She noticed the features so like to Angelo's as she remembered them, and the dark curling hair, like baby lamb furs, so black and silky. And then to her great fright the long lashes on the sunken cheeks suddenly lifted and looked at her, looked long, and twinkled with a certain cunning, reminding her of something—what was it, cunning,—stealth— something dreadful? Ah! The murder. Those were the eyes that had looked out from behind the car that day, and slipped away before anyone could see. That was the man who had crouched below the running board.

She stopped to think a minute, standing breathless with the candle still held high. The lashes had closed again and the man was still as wax. He did not even seem to be breathing. She had a feeling that he was just crouching to spring upon her. Her every breath seemed a prayer. "Help me! Help me!"

Suddenly a great calm came upon her and she knew what she was going to do. Kneeling softly beside the man, she spoke in a gentle voice:

"I am Mr. Treeves's friend. They sent for him to help Angelo out of trouble. He asked me to stay here and take care of you till he could get back. Is there anything I can do for you?"

The big eyes slowly opened again, this time without the cunning in them, and searched her face, then seeming satisfied the man murmured: "Water!"

She looked around and found a tin can half filled with water, and putting it to his lips, lifted his head and supported it till he could drink. He fell back almost exhausted with the effort and for a moment she thought he was gone. Then he opened his eyes again:

"Write this down!"

He spoke better English than Angelo. Perhaps he had been in this country longer. She searched hurriedly in her bag for her pen and a bit of paper.

"Angelo did not kill that boss!"

She wrote with hurried fingers while the man watched her:

"I kill that boss!"

She wrote again:

"I hate that boss. He go after my girl, too, five years ago."

She continued to write:

"Angelo did not kill anything! I kill! Angelo a good man. That's all. I sign my name."

She finished the writing and put the paper before him against her pocketbook and steadied the pen in his hand, lifting his head while he slowly, painfully scrawled out his name "Nicolo."

When it was finished he dropped back heavily. Then with an effort he groped in the bosom of his flannel shirt and pulled at something. She tried to help him, thinking he wanted more air, and loosed the button, but he drew forth a small revolver.

"There!" he gasped his breath going fast. "I do it with that!—Take it to prove—!"

Still kneeling and holding the ugly little weapon in her hand she heard a sound outside. A car! They were coming for her! Or perhaps it was the doctor. She sprang to her feet and stood watching the door, the revolver still in her hand, half hidden in the folds of her dark skirt. The man at her feet had fallen back again and had not heard. He was beyond all human hearing ever again. But Patty stood and waited.

The car stopped and the door was suddenly flung open wide with an oath, and a gruff, "Come on now, you rich man's son, masquerading as a laborer! We'll teach you to pry around into honest men's business so you can get us all into jail on some pretext or other! Come on, we got you good and fast!"

Patty stood still, her eyes large with horror, and watched them as they came in, three big, rough men with evil faces. It seemed to her as all the evil forces of the earth and hell had united to draw her down to earth. Her face grew white and her heart stood still; with what consciousness she had she cried in her soul: "Oh, God, Help Patty! Oh, God, Help now!" Then she slowly lifted the revolver in her trembling hand and pointed it at the foremost man, who suddenly stopped and fell back astonished!

"What the devil! Where's Treeves! Who's the girl?"

But Patty had never shot a revolver in her life, and her hand trembled violently. She had no idea whether the thing was loaded or not, and she did not know how to pull the trigger, but she knew that she was going to try if the man took another step nearer her.

The men drew together for a moment and took stock of her in the wavering darkness, and stealthy hands went slyly to their hips. They were three against one, and good shots at that. But who was this girl? If they hurt her what would be the consequences? They were not ready just at present to clear out. They had other fat in the fire.

"Mr. Treeves left me here to take care of this sick man for a few minutes while he went for help. He will be back right away," she said bravely in a clear voice. "I think I hear him coming now!" and in her heart she cried, "Oh, God, bring some one quick! Bring some one quick!"

The men were breathless for an instant listening, then the foremost cursed out: "Oh—none of that bunk. You're here to get that man's confession. Well, did you get it? Yes, I see you did by the look in your eye. Well, hand it over here and we'll let you go. Come, we haven't any time to waste. We've got to get out of here. Hand that over and we'll leave you alone."

"They are coming!" said Patty sweetly, with a look like summer clouds with glory on them. "They are coming! Hespur! John! Come quickly!"

And actually out of the night there came the sound of a rushing car and voices. Several voices, and one crying, "This way! This way! Don't you see the light?" It was Treeves's voice! He had come back to get her!

The men looked at one another and cursed in low, quick tones, then as one man sprang back through the door and scattered into the night, leaving their car in the bushes, where they had driven it. Into the open door they had left came John Treeves, anxious, eager, holding a flashlight above his head. Came straight to Patty and took her into his arms:

"You poor little girl!" he whispered, and then he set her free and turned about to the others who had entered. Hespur was there first with a white anxious face, and three tall policemen behind.

470

The sight of their brass buttons brought Patty to her senses:

"There are three men outside. Get them quick!" she shouted. "They were threatening me. They came to carry Mr. Treeves away!"

The policeman made a dash into the bushes, blew a blast on a shrill whistle, and soon the whole region roundabout seemed to be alive with men.

"Dominic started something when he went back," smiled Treeves as Patty lifted wondering eyes. "He told them some one was out here trying to murder me, and that the lady with the smiling face had come out alone to rescue me. They all left their plots and came hot foot, and I met them on the way. Nothing would do but they must come back with me. Hespur brought the police-men. He belongs to the dispensation of law and order. When he got back to the lame kid and found you had been there and gone off alone in the dark, he 'phoned the police station and almost demanded the state militia to come out after you."

A little later when the body of the dead man had been carried away in the car that the three men had left, John Treeves and Hespur took Patty back to the little stone house on the bluff for supper, and then Treeves took her home. Word had just come that the three men had been caught, and were being taken to the lockup for

471

the night, and Patty rested back in the car beside Treeves feeling that the awful crisis was about over.

"Patty," said Treeves as the car flew along under the stars, "do you know that when your mother died—"

"But my mother isn't dead, John—" said Patty startled.

"I mean your own mother, little Pard! When your own mother died, your father wanted my mother to take you and bring you up as her little girl."

"Oh!" said Patty.

"Mother couldn't do it because my father was at the point of death and she had to give every minute to him. But afterward, when he was gone, and she would have taken you, your father had married again, and your new mother had insisted that you should never know that you were not her own child!"

"Oh!" said Patty. "Oh!" in a relieved tone. "Then that makes it all plain! Oh, if I had only told you before I might have understood."

They had so many things to talk about. Patty had to tell him all about it then, how she had overheard her mother and sister talking and how she had come away, and found something to do. And how they had somehow traced her to the mountain house; and how she had been afraid to recognize him because her father would not want her mother

472

to be disgraced. The story seemed so much shorter now than when she was living it.

They were still sitting in the little reception room near the library talking when Miss Cole came home ahead of the others who had gone on to some other function, and she paused astonished, then came grimly in and greeted Treeves as though he had been a constant caller on Patty.

"We may as well tell Miss Cole now, Patty," said Treeves with a glorified look at the girl. "Miss Cole, I want you to know that I have just asked Patricia Merrill to be my wife and she has said yes, and we want your blessing. You needn't feel that it is a sudden thing, for we've been in love with each other since we were children, I think, only I somehow lost her and she wouldn't be found—!"

Then they all talked at once and Miss Cole found herself with Patty in her arms, talking as fast as any of them.

"There's only one thing," said Patty wistfully after it was all told, "if Daddy only knew! I'm sure he'd be glad how it's turned out, but if he only knew!"

"Perhaps he does!" said Treeves gently, looking at Patty with an adoring smile.

"No, I don't think he does yet," said Miss Cole grimly with a twinkle behind her eye, "but he stands a pretty good chance of knowing pretty soon. I may as well tell you that I've been raking

South America with telegrams for some time and I have pretty convincing proof that Daniel. P. Merrill isn't drowned at all. He was booked on that ship that went down, but he didn't get to the shipping point in time to go, so he is safe, and he's on his way home now. I had a telegram to that effect last night. As no one knew where his daughter Patricia was, naturally she didn't get any word."

Patty gave a little scream of joy and smothered Miss Cole with kisses. "Oh, Daddy! Daddy!" she cried. "Can anything be more wonderful! And here I thought I had lost everything out of my world!"

"But I can tell you, Miss Patty Merrill," went on Miss Cole, "you had better get ready and take the first train for the West to-morrow morning, for there's a terrible to-do about you out there. It seems you own the house that your stepmother and sister are living in at present. The property was your maternal grandfather's legacy to you and everything was so tied up about it that the poor selfish ladies couldn't get a mere pittance to live on till you were there to sign the papers. They couldn't prove that you were dead, though they had almost reached the point of trying to, and so they have been dependent on charity. You left the old family lawyer, your guardian, in a terrible fix, too, when you cut and run. You'd better get back and fix things up. Your stepmother has been almost turned out of the house."

"Oh!" said Patty wonderingly. "How strangely everything is turning out! But I don't care for the old house, or property or anything now. I'll give it all to them. What do I want of it? John and I are going to live in JOYVILLE!" and a beautiful light broke out on her face, and was reflected in Treeves's face.

It was after Miss Cole had left them and they were saying good-night that Patty voiced a misgiving:

"I'm—not good enough for you, John," she whispered. "You're so wonderful! I never really prayed till a little while ago—but—" and she whispered very softly, "I've given myself to *Him* and I think He's taken me."

"That is better than being good, darling," he said as he kissed her reverently. "None of us are good. It is Christ living in us that makes us anything at all."

A few minutes later Patty knelt beside her white bed and prayed:

"Dear Christ, this is Patty again, and I guess it will always be now, because I am yours. I knew you wanted me, and accepted me to-night because you heard my prayer and saved me in that awful time—and saved John, too—so now I'm yours for whatever you want. Oh, Christ, you've been so good! I love you!"

She knelt there in the moonlight a little while

and let Him bless her, and then she crept into her bed and slept.

No haunting shadows of the evening's horror came to trouble her rest, for she was dreaming of Joyville.

About the Author

Grace Livingston Hill is well known as one of the most prolific writers of romantic fiction. Her personal life was fraught with joys and sorrows not unlike those experienced by many of her fictional heroines.

Born in Wellsville, New York, Grace nearly died during the first hours of life. But her loving parents and friends turned to God in prayer. She survived miraculously, thus her thankful father named her Grace.

Grace was always close to her father, a Presbyterian minister, and her mother, a published writer. It was from them that she learned the art of storytelling. When Grace was twelve, a close aunt surprised her with a hardbound, illustrated copy of one of Grace's stories. This was the beginning of Grace's journey into being a published author.

In 1892 Grace married Fred Hill, a young minister, and they soon had two lovely young daughters. Then came 1901, a difficult year for Grace—the year when, within months of each other, both her father and husband died. Suddenly Grace had to find a new place to live (her home was owned by the church where her husband had been pastor). It was a struggle for Grace to raise her young daughters alone, but through everything she kept writing. In 1902 she produced *The Angel of His Presence*, *The Story of a Whim*, and *An Unwilling Guest*. In 1903 her two books *According to the Pattern* and *Because of Stephen* were published.

It wasn't long before Grace was a well-known author, but she wanted to go beyond just entertaining her readers. She soon included the message of God's salvation through Jesus Christ in each of her books. For Grace, the most important thing she did was not write books but share the message of salvation, a message she felt God wanted her to share through the abilities he had given her.

In all, Grace Livingston Hill wrote more than one hundred books, all of which have sold thousands of copies and have touched the lives of readers around the world with their message of "enduring love" and the true way to lasting happiness: a relationship with God through his Son, Jesus Christ.

In an interview shortly before her death, Grace's devotion to her Lord still shone clear. She commented that whatever she had accomplished had been God's doing. She was only his servant, one who had tried to follow his teaching in all her thoughts and writing.

Center Point Large Print
600 Brooks Road / PO Box 1
Thorndike, ME 04986-0001 USA

(207) 568-3717

US & Canada:
1 800 929-9108
www.centerpointlargeprint.com